F(

Never before in the history of p~~rofession~~ been put on trial for murder. As would be expected, this sensational event drew the attention of all media entities in the country. Add to that the fact that a superstar was the accused, the story went worldwide. The fact that he played for New York Giants roiled up the most vocal fans in the sports world in Brooklyn and Queens. The fact that he was a native-born Texan accused of killing one of the most powerful men in the area, slowed Texas shaves and haircuts to a near standstill as barber's normal hand gestures became violent jerks of anger. Worse yet, the presence of a fairy princess movie star in the mix bought the attention of everyone else.

All humans start to learn right from wrong fresh from their cradle days. Their first experienced punishment is a gentle correction by a parent, usually their mother, and they begin to be taught right from wrong. They will live the rest of their lives under societal behavior rules established by others; rules that are constantly being changed and refined. The intended meanings of these rules and laws are interpreted differently by those who apply corrective action and punishment. There is no such thing as "equal justice for all." This does not keep us from developing the philosophy that violators of the law are the "bad guys" and the rest of us are the "good guys," even though we begin to violate the rules at very young ages when we disobey our parents. Far too many of us cross over that very fuzzy line that makes us a criminal. Criminals come from all walks of life, rich and poor, well-educated or not, stupid or not, large in size or small, with all hues of skin color. All criminal activity is not detected, and many criminals are never brought to justice. Even a small percentage of innocent people are charged with a crime, and unfortunately, some are convicted.

Trials by a jury are reserved, usually, for the most serious crimes. The jury pool consists of people who have learned right from wrong from a wide range of disciplines and social environments. Legal scholars tell us that the average defendant brought before them, under guard, sometimes shackled and in prisoners uniform and thoroughly investigated by the "good guys" is considered guilty as opposed to "innocent until proven guilty." The whole legal world knows that the burden of proof rests on the shoulders of the defense attorneys to prove innocence. Those attorneys, when armed with the facts, almost always begin seeking a plea bargain, which is where most cases end up.

At the other end of the spectrum, the scales of justice are sometimes tipped the other way, in favor of the defendant. Seldom, if ever, does a juror want to believe that an idol or a superstar or any famous person could be guilty of a serious crime and most certainly of cold-blooded murder. In these cases, the state has a nearly impossible task. "Innocent until proven guilty" then prevails.

There are cases when the scales balance out. They are sometimes referred to as "celebrity on celebrity crimes." The accused defendant and the victim[s] each have their worshipers in the jury pool. This book is about a "celebrity on celebrity" case. It brings with it all the spotlight that the press and gossip can possibly bring. National television was to have cameras inside the courtroom for the first time. Large numbers of reporters and their supporting staffs along with curious onlookers would gather in droves. Sides were drawn and wagers were made throughout the western world. It was watched with particular interest in the legal world. It would stimulate the desire of several of the greatest defense lawyers to search for a piece of the action, and professional witnesses hurried to get their resumes in to both sides.

Stakes are high when a home-grown NFL superstar quarterback is facing a death sentence for the murders of the most powerful man in west Texas and his bodyguard. High stakes bring on high costs to those who can afford them, and they bring in the support of other influential politicians and wealthy people who attempt to influence the action. In this case, some surprises would come from the most unlikely places.

Power bases for men in early Texas and the West were established mainly by Spanish land grants and the subsequent transfer of these grants by the revolutionary Texas government after the war with Mexico. Unfortunately for women, they gained power only when they fell heir to land or by gaining control of their men. Land ownership was true power until oil – black gold – was discovered under some of that land. Then revenues from that oil produced the first walking, talking billionaires. Equally important, the liquidity of this wealth allowed for personal fortunes to grow at a more rapid pace, and the sizes of individual power bases swelled along with it. Powerful family dynasties were formed during this period. The Parker dynasty was one of these. Human nature and personal egos, being what they are, led some of the heirs to this power to do great things for humanity. Others let personal greed take control of their lives. They learned that "Big Money Talks and Murder Walks

CHAPTER ONE

Trial of the Century

Minnie Mae Joiner stood up in the packed Ector County, Texas, courtroom and shouted with all the gusto that the lungs of a five foot, one inch and 105-pound, 74-year-old woman could muster in the vernacular of a west Texas cowhand, "Judge, that boy is my grandson and his name ain't Tripp or Jimmy and it ain't J.J., its Jimmy Jack Joiner, by dang, I'll not stand by and let him be called anything but that. His mamma named him Jimmy Jack, and that's what he'll be called."

Judge Abraham "Abe" Sullivan was brought out of retirement for this high-profile trial. He was a surprise choice by the prosecution and defense. He was considered to be somewhat of a maverick, a self-described second coming of Judge Roy Bean. Now he was shaken from his near dozing condition by this outburst and began pounding his gavel and shouting for Minnie to be quiet, sit down or be removed from the courtroom. In spite of all the noise, most everyone in the room heard every word of Minnie's shouted demand. Some laughed, some were shocked and some sat up at attention after nodding off from boredom brought on by listening to prosecutor Walter Warren live up to his nickname of "Windy" Warren delivering his opening statement, which had droned on for an hour and 20 minutes. This was, by far, the biggest stage that he had ever performed on and he had every intention of taking advantage of this once-in-a-lifetime opportunity. Millions would be watching, for the first time in Texas courtroom history, on delayed television broadcasts. "Who knows," he thought, "this just might propel me into the governor's office come election time."

Minnie shouted back at the judge. "Don't bother to throw me out, 'cause I'm leavin'. I can't stand the railroadin' job that you're allowing Windy to put on my boy." By then, a bailiff had a strong grip on her arm, but Minnie Mae loosened his fingers effortlessly, with hand strength that is a gift from years of milking cows, chopping wood and pulling calves at birth. Her little bowed legs carried her well ahead of her entourage of family and friends composed of Tripp's estranged but still wedded wife, Patricia, and her parents, Coach Sam Carr and Mrs. Eldred, and Tripp's agent, Sammy Cane, as they exited the building and passed through the media throng and spectators assembled on the lawn and sidewalks. A gaggle of reporters attached themselves to the tail end of the little parade as Hal Hall, Tripp's friend from the defense team, ran past and took the position as escort, as per Tripp's instructions. The little group was quickly escorted across the street past the small businesses that fronted the courthouse on the town square. Past Massey Hardware, Bob's Grill, Argenta Drug and around the corner to the defense headquarters in the law offices of Clarkson, Graddy and Jones, as they stayed one step ahead of the curious media and hurried inside. No one in this group wanted to allow Minnie an opportunity to give the reporters a piece of her mind.

This murder case had been making headlines since the arrest of home-grown superstar National Football League quarterback Jimmy Jack Joiner months before, and now with the trial at hand, the circus had come to town. The event was the biggest Texas murder story since the assassination in Dallas of President John Kennedy. Media representatives from all over the world were present, sent by their executive bosses with orders to drain every drop of news from the story and broadcast it all over the world. Camera crews were present and the news anchors from two of the three major nightly news networks were doing their broadcasts from the courthouse lawn each day. Don Lawler, CBS news anchor, and his crew were the first to arrive and secured the choice location on which to set up. Two cameras were aimed towards the front of the old historic courthouse and a third was hand held for scanning the crowd and seeking out local places and things of interest. Lawler, a native Texan now based in New York, was more attentive to detail and more assertive to his director as the broadcast piece script was being developed. His instructions to the makeup artist were more critical. He seemed to be more worried about the natural dark circles under his eyes than usual. It was noted by the crew that he was more nervous than ever before. This was his first big assignment in his home state since he had become the Big Kahuna in the Big Apple. This was also becoming his biggest stage performance to date, in spite of his interviews of presidents and world leaders and the personal danger of reporting in war zones.

As events played out inside, Lawler tuned up his rich baritone voice much like an opera singer would, humming a few notes of a recognizable Broadway musical in order to establish the key in which to speak his first word. Then he began to speak, unaware of the drama of the trial and unaware of the ejection of Minnie Mae Joiner. "You see behind me this beautiful and historic old courthouse, with a history of many famous murder trials. Immediately to my left is the spot where temporary

2

gallows were erected and on which a hanging took place as a result of guilty verdicts rendered just inside those doors. There will be no gallows this time, regardless of the verdict, but one of the greatest sports kings of our generation, NFL quarterback Jimmy Jack Joiner faces a possible death sentence for the murder of billionaire oil baron and political machine king Horace "Judge" Parker. Tripp Joiner is also on trial for killing John Malham, Judge Parker's bodyguard and sheriff's deputy who purportedly died defending Parker.

"Joiner is well defended by a legal team led by the famous defense lawyer Herman Sherman, known to all as "Mule Sherman." His team includes Will Clarkson, considered the best in west Texas. This made-in-Hollywood fairytale is being recorded for CBS television marking this date as the first time in history that television cameras have been allowed to film a trial in a Texas courtroom. Key excerpts of the trial will be broadcast throughout the entire trial, and each day's proceedings will be will broadcast in their entirety after the late evening news.

"The famous actress Vita Vorhees, granddaughter of Judge Parker and former childhood sweetheart and ex-fiancée of Tripp Joiner, will be one of the many famous people expected to be in daily attendance and possibly called as a witness. Prosecution spokesmen will say that they will prove that these were revenge killings for the--uh---um------cut."

Lawler noticed the eyes of his crew members and onlookers being diverted away from him and towards a commotion at the courthouse doors. He stopped talking and took in the scene just as Minnie Mae pranced down the sidewalk towards the street. Questions were flying around without answers and someone shouted that the old lady leading the pack was the grandmother of the defendant, Tripp Joiner. The little broadcast crew huddled up in order to rethink strategy. Should they try for an interview with her or perhaps try to find out what happened inside? There was plenty of time before the evening news was to go on the air. Lawler came back on camera to add. "What just happened in the courtroom is not clear to us at this moment, but I am sure that we have it all recorded with our inside cameras and will show it to you later, so stay tuned to this channel for this history-making event."

Back inside, Judge Sullivan had sent the jury out and was having a bench conference with the lawyers. "At this juncture, I am sure that I will not hear the word 'mistrial' mentioned, so let's hear what both sides have to

3

say. Windy, you go first." Windy was livid. In his mind, he had been flying high on the big stage and was rudely interrupted.

"Your honor, the state was badly harmed by this event, which was probably staged by the defense in order to weaken my opening. I think they should be reprimanded, and I think that you should repair the damage with the jury." The judge replied by asking defense counsel Herman Sherman to respond.

"Well," said Sherman, "To be honest with you, I hated to see the incident occur and I can assure you that we had nothing to do with it. In fact, the state was stumbling all over the place and weakening its own opening by repeating the same points over and over again. Mrs. Joiner was right in her statement that the state had called the defendant by at least three names. If Mr. Warren had been observing the jurors closely, he could have seen the pain and boredom on their faces. I would like to proceed from right where we were. He was helping our case. As for a statement to the jury, I would like to think that you would let both sides approve it ahead of time."

Judge Sullivan's eyebrows shot up. "I will *not* ask for prior approval. I have handled hundreds of cases in my time. And besides, I am not called Honest Abe for nothing." He tried to inject a little humor, but no one laughed. "I will use the standard disregard language and apology line and nothing more. State can continue after the jury is called back, but I do hope that you are about finished."

As they left the bench, Sherman whispered to Warren, "If you ever accuse me again of dirty tricks, we will settle the issue outside the courtroom after the trial." Warren said nothing but whirled around to determine if the judge had overheard the threat. He clearly had heard but he responded by extending his arm and hand with palm up, indicating that he would hear no more on this subject. Warren returned to his table with a reddened face and took a drink of water as he chatted with his team and gathered his notes, waiting for the jury to be recalled.

This lull in proceedings had given Tripp an opportunity to look around the room, yearning to make eye contact with some friendly faces. He was shocked and dismayed to find very few. Instead, most would look away to avoid eye contact. What was it? What did it mean? Then he knew. It felt like a knee to the groin. He thought, "They think that I am *guilty*! But

4

why? They have heard none of my side of the story. All the prosecution has done is make promises about the evidence that they intend to present. True, the promise to put an eyewitness to the shootings on the stand sounded ominous, but fair-minded people should not jump to judgment so fast."

A depression funk began to creep over him as he understood what was happening. His day began with excitement and bright anticipation of getting out of the confines of the little cell. He needed air and to be in the presence of friends and football fans. He had experienced nothing but adoration and hero worship since his glory days in high school. There were more NY Giants football jerseys sold with his #6 than any other sold in the country for the past four years. He gave his time and money to many charities. His mind could not comprehend this perceived cruelty. Lunchtime finally came and went, but he was not able to choke down a bite of food. The defense opening consumed a good part of the afternoon, doing little to boost his spirits before early adjournment. The presentation of evidence would start fresh tomorrow at 9am sharp.

Another surprise awaited Tripp as the door slammed behind him in his little eight-foot-by-ten-foot cell. A strange feeling of security came over him. "Unbelievable!! This place actually feels good to me." He made a vow to force himself to eat whatever meal disguised as food was brought to him as he lay back on his iron cot. "One way to shut out the current events of my life might be to relive every moment of it as it happened prior to the date that hell began."

The evening television replay, as expected, was watched by countless millions, as legal railbirds gathered to gossip, to speculate and to wager on the outcome. The cameras had been mounted such that no juror was seen through either lens. Much was said about the large number of people seated at the defense table compared to that of the prosecution. Local experts wondered how the defendant was able to convince Sherman and Clarkson, introduced as co-counselors, to work together. Surely there must be some friction between such giant egos. There was a man and wife team of psychologists seated next to Hal Hall, identified as a defense clerk and friend of the defendant. A defense paralegal, Deb Beaton, completed the team of six, doubling the number for the prosecution. District Attorney Warren was joined only by his chief assistant and a paralegal. Some knew the background of Hall, a lifelong friend of Jimmie Jack Joiner. He was an orphan and shoeshine boy

5

turned practicing barber. "What was he doing there?"

This hodgepodge appeared to be a formula for disaster. They could be right, but there was also serious friction on the prosecution side. The DA had denied his assistant's request to share stage time before the national TV audience. They also disagreed about a key decision, whether or not to open their case with the testimony of their eyewitness to the murders.

CHAPTER TWO

Family Owned and Operated

Football buffs will tell you that for decades, a disproportionate number of National Football League quarterbacks, beginning with Sammy Baugh, came out of Texas high schools. Just about any old Texas cowhand can give an explanation quoted directly from the barbershop bible – chapter and verse. "It be in they {sic} blood. Most baby boys born in west Texas be born with large, strong hands coming from their forefathers wrestling steers, roping calves and milking cows. They can grip a football like no other." Texans pay no attention to similar claims made by fans in other parts of the country.

Jimmy Jack Joiner was born at home on the Double Bar 6 ranch in Ector County, Texas, to Colton Roy Joiner and his wife, Karin Ines Mueller Joiner, the trophy wife who Colton had brought home with him from his U.S. Army tour in Mannheim, Germany. The 6, as the ranch was known to locals, was one of hundreds of the so-called family owned and operated ranches in west Texas. The end of the Texas War of Independence and the creation of the nation of Texas caused mass migration of settlers from the east and eventually allowed for development of so many of these ranches. These family members are quick to tell you that the true meaning of "family owned" is that every family member was required to work from sun-up to sundown, six days a week, every week, regardless of weather. Chores were assigned to the very young and the very old.

The day Jimmy Jack was born, Karin insisted on finishing her daily chores and waited too long to start to the hospital. When she and Colton saw they could not make it in time, they returned home to give birth to their baby boy. Colton liked to brag that he personally delivered the little son he was so proud of. He soon was eager to show off Jimmy Jack to the world, much in the way he put his pretty wife on display at every opportunity. They never missed a dance or a rodeo. He even started to attend church again. And he put his own skills on display at rodeos, where he performed as a skilled roper and cutting horse rider. His father, Sam Houston "Dub" Joiner, had taught him well.

Tradition had it that neighbors from far and wide would come to see the new baby, doing their part to predict the future of the newborn.

"He is going to be long and lanky like his father and his grandfather."

"Look at the size of those hands; he's going to make a good cow hand."

"With those long legs, he'll sit a cutting horse real good."

"He will have a rope in his hands by the time he is three."

Not a single person mentioned the word "football" or "quarterback." The ever-efficient Karin fed her guests well but moved them out quickly. After all, she had chores to do. She had brought the traditional German work ethic with her, fitting right in with the lifestyle of a west Texas ranch wife and mother.

The pleasant details of Jimmy Jack's early childhood and events prior to his birth were recalled over time, usually in stories told sitting around the old natural stone fireplace. The fact that he was orphaned at age two along with the details of the tragic accident were not revealed to him until he was five years old. After hearing things from other children in Sunday school, he began asking Minnie Mae questions.

A fiery head-on crash of the family pick-up truck with a gasoline hauler had killed his parents as all were returning from a rodeo in Mesquite, Texas. Miraculously, the boy was thrown clear at impact and wound up sitting in a ditch with only a knot on his head, scratches and bruises. Minnie Mae explained in her story to him, "You were a miracle baby. God must have something special in mind for you." She repeated this line many times over the years, until he finally asked her what that meant.

After some thought, she replied, "It means that you are going to be famous for doing good deeds. You may be a big evangelist or scientist or a doctor or maybe even governor of Texas."

Jimmy Jack responded, "I only want to be a good calf and steer roper like Paw Paw Dub, and maybe a good rancher too." She pointed out the pictures that been on display all his life, and he just now began to understand the pictures of the small boy sitting on a man's shoulders, and the same boy sitting on a woman's lap, and the three of them mounted on a horse, with the small boy holding on the saddle horn with his first pair

8

of real cowboy boots prominently displayed.

More photos emerged from the cedar chest, laid out on the dining room table for Jimmy Jack's exploration and enjoyment. A whole new world had opened up. It was better than Santa Claus at Christmas. A zillion questions poured out right up to and then past bedtime. There was not much sleep for Jimmy Jack that night as he tried, to no avail, to remember his parents. The photo gazing began again next day, and a make-believe memory started to develop as he daydreamed about hearing their voices and doing things together. This daydreaming never ceased. Even into adulthood, he sometimes heard their voices and saw them in his dreams.

Now deep into his new world, with his appetite whetted, he began going back again and again to the old antique chest for more photos. He came across an album with strange writing on the margins and on both sides of the photos. One picture was clearly that of his mother, younger and thinner and with other children. This discovery obviously begged for answers. Minnie Mae explained that the writing was in German and the people were his mother's family back in Germany. The old couple were his other grandparents. The questions as to why he had never known or seen his other grandparents would be answered later. Minnie Mae was not prepared to tell the whole story about his grandfather disowning his mother, Karin, when she married an American soldier and why he hated Americans, and that he probably would never meet any of these people. Enough was enough for now.

Exploring the cedar treasure chest triggered Jimmy Jack's curiosity in another way. How were photos made? The old Kodak was brought out, and Jimmy Jack earned his first lesson in its use. Much to the consternation of the grandparents, this interest lasted up to and into this first day of school. He shot a full roll of film on that first day, before the camera was confiscated by the first-grade teacher, Miss Dollarhyde. She gave strict instructions that it was to be picked up at the end of the day and never to be seen again.

The first day of school is a major milestone in every child's life. Excitement exceeds all expectations, as kids arrive from all directions and in all sizes, shapes, colors and clothes. It doesn't take long for every self-respecting west Texas boy to earn a nickname. Even some girls get nicknames, mostly unwanted and assigned by boys. Jimmy Jack got his in the first hour of class.

Miss Dollarhyde began with the same instructions and expectations for discipline, safety and so forth that she had used for 31 years. She then called each student in alphabetical order to come forth and write his or her name on the blackboard. This was her way of giving the first test. Most could do it, but some could not. She helped these few get through it and then printed each name clearly above the student's own writing.

One little boy, a bit on the chubby side and with vivid red hair, carried on a continuous commentary throughout the entire process, in spite of being scolded repeatedly. He was warned that he must speak only after first raising his hand and being given permission. He spent most of the day with his hand raised. This young man was Hal Hall, who would later become Jimmy Jack's lifelong friend and attorney in the fight for his life.

Miss Dollarhyde carefully printed JIMMY JACK JOINER in capital letters above his written signature, and Hal blurted out, "Hey, I really like that! JJJ, Triple J; that's what I'm going to call you, and everyone else will too."

Hal was immediately scolded for his habit of speaking too loudly and out of turn, a habit that would never be broken in spite the threat of harsher discipline. The teacher's threat was for real. But as it turned out, Harold Hall was right. Triple J was shortened to Tripp and it stuck forever. Tripp then dubbed Hal Little Red, and that name stuck for three years until Tripp helped him change it to Hal. Yet some of the older boys and total strangers would call him Red for the rest of his life.

Sending a child off to school for the first time does not affect the starting time in the day of a ranch mother. She always rises well before daylight to start her chores. Outdoor chores begin at "first light" after a hearty breakfast. This coincided nicely with the arrival of the school bus, which was, remarkably, almost always on time. The Double Bar 6 ranch was near the outer boundary of the bus route, which meant Tripp could take a seat near the front of the bus and be first off at the schoolhouse stop. He learned, soon enough, to try for a seat near the back of the bus on the ride home, because that was where the "action" was.

No boy wanted to be kissed goodbye in the bus doorway by his mother, grandmother or by anyone else for that matter. On the day of his first school bus ride, Jimmy Jack bolted away and jumped on the bus as Minnie Mae leaned down to hug and kiss him. Thereafter he made it clear that he would walk out to meet the bus by himself, but he did look back to see his grandmother standing on the front porch. He did not see Paw Paw peering around the corner of the barn with tears in his eyes.

Ranch children are taught independence in dealing with their personal needs at a very early age. This frees up time for busy parents and starts them on their way to being responsible for a small share of duty in running a family operated business. Easy chores are assigned initially, increased in scope and difficulty as the child matures. The gift of a horse is a ranch child's milestone, signifying trust in their ability to care for it. Children often begin choosing names long before the horse is presented. Most of these young riders are allowed to compete in local rodeo events as soon as they reach the eligible age.

Paw Paw Dub was a roper of some renown and often performed rope tricks to the delight of any onlookers. It seemed only natural that in his play sessions with toddler Jimmy Jack, he began to teach simple roping techniques. Roping tricks soon followed. He made his grandson a small rope and constructed a roping dummy complete with genuine cow horns. Unfortunately, young Jimmy Jack spent more time roping furniture than he did roping the dummy. After he broke a lamp in Minnie Mae's parlor, the rope was never seen indoors again.

Now, with the rope on the back porch, the young wannabe calf steer roper made a habit of picking it up every time he exited the back door. He would make a loop and attempt to catch anything in sight. Dogs, cats and chickens were the usual targets. They soon learned to flee on sight of the wannabe. Cats were almost impossible to lasso, but he would occasionally make a catch, and a God-awful noise and fight would erupt, bringing all hands running. He learned to spin a large ground loop and jump into the center of it, then twirl it over his head and make a cast. This habit continued until he was grown. Jimmy Jack Joiner had dreams of performing rope tricks at the biggest rodeos in the world.

CHAPTER THREE

A Princess Comes to Town

Now, as he continued to rot in his jail cell, Tripp thought back on his life, zeroing in on the fourth grade. "Big year, yeah, real big, both good and bad," he surmised and grimaced. That was the year he punched his ticket to heaven, as he won his first barrel race, roped his first calf in competition, was taught to use firearms, killed his first deer and was introduced to the game of football. These were the positives. Then came the negatives. Evita Sue Vorhees came to his school and Hal Hall, his closest friend, just up and disappeared.

Minnie Mae and young Jimmy Jack never missed church at First Baptist. She sang in the choir and sat in her assigned seat in the alto section, and he sat in his assigned seat in the second row, center section. The assignment allowed Minnie Mae to prevent his misbehaving.

Paw Paw Dub most always drove them but seldom came in. Instead, he joined up with the regular coffee drinkers who always met at Bob's Grill on the town square. Since the establishment was closed on Sundays, Bob Brooks let the little group in the back door and joined them in the consumption of free coffee. Someone usually brought donuts for the second breakfast of the day. In bygone days, he had attended every service, but unable to go the full hour without a smoke, he would slip away from his back-row seat and go outside to smoke a cigarette.

Minnie Mae caught on real fast to his lie about having to use the restroom and would scold him about it after the service. Now, a man can only stand so much scolding over a simple thing like skipping out for a smoke, so he started the coffee thing. Might as well be scolded for something worthwhile. Little Jimmy Jack, once aware of the total picture, interjected himself into one scolding session by asking a simple question. "Paw Paw, why do you dress up in a suit and tie just to go drink coffee at Bob's?" His grandmother then added him to the scolding session.

Paw Paw looked at him, winked and said with a smile, "I believe you have just pushed one of grandmother's sore spots." Conversation was over without the answer to his question.

Pastor Harvey Eldred was a hell fire and damnation type of preacher. When the congregation left the service after one of his sermons, they were filled with the determination to kick Satan out of their lives and serve the Lord in a more meaningful way.

From where 10-year-old Jimmy Jack sat, it appeared that the preacher was always looking at him and directing some of what he said only to him. At the altar calls after every sermon, he would feel a tugging in his heart urging him to step forward and take the pastor's hand. One day he did just that. He made a "profession of faith" and asked for baptism and membership into the church. With no nay votes from the congregation, he was voted in.

A feeling of happiness and bliss came over him and he wondered if this might be the fulfillment of Minnie Mae's prophecy that he was a miracle baby. God had something special in mind for his life. Still beaming, as members lined up congratulate him in church custom, he saw his grandmother join him, but there was no grandfather in sight. After a momentary pain of disappointment passed, the joy returned.

A large number of attendees always fled for the exits after the benediction without standing in line to greet new members. Junior Dancey was one of those hurriedly departing, fingering his Zippo cigarette lighter with one hand and his cigarette pack with his other. Wife and son were trailing when his son, Tommy Ray, tugged at his father's arm and asked if he could join the line. Junior asked why.

"Because Jimmy Jack is in my class and he is a friend of mine."

Junior moved on but looked back and hesitated as the boy standing in front of the pulpit came into view. "That boy can't be your age. He is a foot taller than you."

"Yes, he is," Tommy Ray replied. "He is not only the tallest kid in school, but he can outrun anybody."

Junior and Tommy joined the end of the line to congratulate Jimmy Jack. Junior got a quick bio on him from his son and was prepared to expose this oversized kid to his first of many future football recruitment pitches as they took their turn to greet.

"This is my friend, Tripp, Dad, and this is my dad, Mr. Dancey." Tommy made the correct introduction.

Mr. Dancey followed. "Congratulations, Jimmy, welcome to full membership, I have been seeing you sitting on the second row now for a very long time, and I know your grandparents very well, and as a matter of fact, I knew your parents." Then he got right into the real purpose of his being in line. "By the way, I understand that you are not into sports right now."

Jimmy Jack was a bit taken aback. "Well, I guess that's so, but I am into rodeo big time. And according to my grandmother, I am into too many things."

Junior replied, "Young man, you have football written all over you. I coach the Massey Hardware Lobos in the PeeWee league. We were league champions last year and each team player has a trophy to prove it. Don't we, Tommy?" Tommy affirmed with a nod as Junior continued.

"We are having our meeting of player prospects and coaches next Saturday at the high school football field and would very much like for you to come out and check us out. I can tell you right now that we would like to have you as a Lobo. Talk to your grandparents and ask if I might give them a call and talk about it. Here, take my business card with my office phone and my home number on it. Please give me a call and let me know when I can visit with them."

Minnie Mae, standing in front of Tripp having her own conversation, heard only the few of Junior's words. She saw Tripp take the card and immediately thought that something was being offered for sale. She swelled up like a toad as she curtly remarked, "This is the end of the line. We must be going on home now." Tripp heard her mumble, "I can't believe he would have the nerve to be selling you a Bible or something. What was he pushing?"

"Football," he answered.

It took a phone call and a face-to-face meeting with Minnie Mae and Dub before permission was granted for Tripp to attend this first PeeWee football league meeting, but it was absolutely clear that permission was granted for this one time only. And Junior must provide transportation to and from.

The business card displayed Junior's given name, James Dancey, sole owner of Dancey Insurance Agency. Minnie Mae glanced at the card again as Junior and Tommy arrived early to pick up Tripp for the meeting. Junior purposely had not mentioned that this was to be for newcomer tryouts, and he was pleased to see that Tripp showed up wearing boots instead of sneakers. He wanted to keep his talent for speed to himself, and he had other plans to keep him "under wraps," so to speak.

Being somewhat shy, Tripp offered up very little conversation on the ride to town. Most of the banter was between the two boys, but Junior joined in some.

"Hey, Tripp, you ever heard of sandbagging?"

"Sure. That's when you shore up the levees during floods."

"No, I'm talking about a coach's word. We sometimes find kids that we want on our teams and ask them to not go all out in the tryouts so that the other coaches will not try so hard to get them on their teams. Fair enough, right? We work hard to find good players and should be able to keep them. All coaches do this, so that makes it okay. Plus, we have a draft after the tryout."

"But, Mr. Dancey, you didn't tell us that this was a tryout. And what do you mean by draft?"

"It means that we get to pick our players by drawing a number from a hat. If you get number one, you choose first, then second picks and so on. I might draw number one, but my chances are slim since there are six teams drawing. If we have enough players and sponsors, we might be able to add another team to the league.

"Mr. Dancey, I don't know what you mean by not trying hard. That would be dishonest, wouldn't it?"

Dancey thought for a second and replied, "Not the way I mean it, but forget what I said. Just be yourself and do what the coaches ask." His

15

mind was already working a on a new plan. He realized that Tripp's size alone would make him a high draft pick. He continued, "I may need some extra help getting the team to and from practice and helping out with drills and stuff. Dads do this all the time. I'm sure Paw Paw Dub would help me out with this every now and then, so I'm adding him to our helpers list. Will that be OK?"

Dancey had just negated the need for sandbagging. The rules allow for a player to be placed automatically on a team without going through the daft, if a parent or legal guardian is the coach or one of three assistant coaches on that team. Paw Paw would now be an assistant coach without his knowledge. Massey Hardware had their new star player.

Everything went as planned. On the way home, the trio happily laid out a strategy for obtaining final approval from Minnie Mae for Tripp to play the whole season.

After minor protest, Minnie Mae caved, but with the understanding that there would be no more rodeos until football season was over, and also with the imperative that no ranch chores could be neglected. On hearing her verdict, Junior and Tommy let out loud whoops, but Tripp smiled and said nothing. He was going to miss entering the Midland rodeo coming up next month. He had his horse Dollar tuned up and running nearly a half second faster around the barrels than ever before. His rodeo skills just might get him in the money. No one could possibly know that this was the launch of a football career to span more than 22 years, one that would bring fame and fortune.

Tommy began to fit nicely into the playground routines of Tripp and Little Red, as the duo became a gang of three. Little Red promptly named them The Three Musketeers and conspired to use the strength of this powerful little group as a way to shed the Little Red moniker. His popularity, or his notoriety as some saw it, had grown as word spread of his special library and the study of law. In addition, he was already helping tutor slow-learning students in higher grades. Time had come for Little Red to be called Hal.

He stood before a gathering of students outside at recess to make this announcement. A threat of a "knuckle sandwich" awaited non-compliers, and Tripp and Tommy each quietly doubled up one fist as planned. This childish little show of force did the trick. No one ever uttered "Little

Red" within ear shot of The Three Musketeers again.

****

A golden carriage pulled up to the steps of the South Elementary School front door in Odessa, Texas. The carriage doors opened to allow the princess to step out on the sidewalk, and the driver motioned for her to proceed up the steps. The staff was prepared for her arrival.

A visit the day before from her mother, Lilia Parker Vorhees, daughter of the famous Judge Parker, included an inspection of the school. After declaring it suitable, she arranged for the transfer of her daughter, Lavita Jane Vorhees, from a private girl's school in Dallas.

The doors of the golden carriage did not swing open but raised straight up. The carriage was in fact a Lamborghini. An Italian sports car rarely heard of in the US, much less ever seen in person. The timed spectacular arrival was meant to be witnessed by as many pupils and staff as possible. The timing was perfect. A large number of people stopped to gawk, point and speculate as to what was going on.

The driver was the aforementioned Mrs. Vorhees. It soon became clear that this show was much more about her than her daughter. She was dressed in her finest expensive clothes, opulence dripping off of her in the form of enough diamonds to choke an alligator. She was a handsome woman, with light blond hair and Nordic facial features.

Lilia struck a pose and looked around for the media and the photographers. There were none. This came as a great shock to her. After all, there had been a news release the day before from Parker Enterprises that she, Lilia Parker Vorhees, had been named head of all of the Parker charities. A leak to the favored television station hinted about her appearance at the school. She had rehearsed answers to anticipated questions about her visit to the school as well as her new job. She had visited the school the day before and had spoken at great length about who she was and what she was prepared to do to improve the school with the fund that her father, Judge Parker, had gifted.

"You will have a blank check when it comes to buildings and equipment. Nothing is too good for my daughter and her little classmates. Just say when, and I will send an expert to assist you." This boasting might or might not have bought her celebrity in Dallas, but it went over like a cow chip in a punch bowl to this proud and dedicated west Texas school principal and the teachers with her.

The fourth grade Parker princess, embarrassed by her mother's actions, raced inside taking two steps at a time. Once inside, she was properly introduced to her teacher and her classmates. All were just faces to her, but she noticed Tripp because he was taller than the rest and smiled as she spoke to him.

One girl approached her. "My name is GiGi Smurl, and I am so pleased to meet you, and I will be happy to show you the ropes."

Lavita recognized real sincerity in her eyes. "Thank you very much. I would like to sit with you in the cafeteria this first day, if you don't mind."

"Oh, I would just love that. We can walk down together."

Over lunch, they discovered that they shared several "likes" and "dislikes." An immediate fondness for each other took hold. They discovered that both had been tiara toddlers. Beauty pageants, at the insistence of their mothers, had continued to this day. These two girls, like thousands of others, were being pushed straight to the Miss America Pageant or to Hollywood as mothers were living out their own fantasies. The odds of being struck by lightning were lower, but everyone had fun along the way. Something about wearing make-up at age three made little girls feel grown up and beautiful.

Now, as a nine year old, GiGi had a pretty face, with perfect skin, brown eyes and dark brown hair. Her legs were a bit short for her long torso. Lavita ["Call me Vita"] had brilliant and piercing blue eyes, almost white hair in pigtails and a face covered with freckles and high cheek bones and her legs were long and straight. She had the rudiments of a classic beauty. Only their mothers could see 10 years down the road when total beauty would manifest itself.

More and more of their free time was spent together. They shared homework and honed their pageantry walking and posing. Performing with a book on one's head to improve posture meant that a book was always present. While performing, the other hand raised a pretend microphone to her mouth as she narrated the action to the pretend audience. GiGi was better at this than was Vita. In fact, she began carrying the pretend microphone with her everywhere she went, much to the amusement of the other students. This became her comic modus operandi. Until the day all joy left her life after witnessing murder.

CHAPTER FOUR

Lawyers Sometime Arrive in Boxes

In the third month into the first-grade school year, Miss Opal Dollarhyde threw in the towel. She was giving up on young Hal Hall. She had tried every method ever learned in her long teaching career to corral this uncontrollable little genius. To make matters worse, bullies soon made Hal their favorite target.

Being a red haired, crew cut, pudgy little runt was obviously not his fault, but it did figure into the blame equation. Little Red, as he was now called by all the boys, discovered that staying near Jimmy Jack Joiner as much as possible kept the bullies at bay. He stuck like glue to the much larger boy for protection. He reminded Joiner of a lost doggie that he sometimes cared for as a part of his daily chores. But this doggie was smarter than his protector. The lifetime bond of friendship had begun, although neither of them knew it.

A conference with parents was the next most logical step for Miss Dollarhyde, but Hal had no parents with whom to consult. Miss Gertrude Calhoun was presumed to be his legal guardian, but the enrollment forms left out the word legal. "Probably not a problem," thought the teacher, and she proceeded without consulting her principal.

She had worked with Miss Calhoun for nine years prior to her retirement. In fact, their classrooms were next door to each other, and they ate lunch together most every day. Their personalities were as different as day is to night, but they shared the bond of spinsterhood. Neither had ever married for the same reasons. The two, both shy and unattractive, brought very few boys around to meet the parents, and none had ever passed muster. They both loved children and made excellent teachers. They both rued that they had none of their own. Miss Dollarhyde dominated their lunchtime conversations with gossip, but Miss Calhoun talked only about the children. Neither had much of a social life outside of their respective churches, where Gertrude was in charge of the baby nursery, a tenure of more than 40 years. She cared for each baby as her very own. Opal attended all church services and attended a movie once a week. She was self-conscious about her skinny frame, but her tight pocketbook kept her from gaining weight.

The two met for a dinner date while a friend looked after Hal. After exchanging pleasantries, Opal Dollarhyde jumped right in. "You know, I've never known the complete story of how Hal came to live with you. I believe that his mother is the daughter of your sister in Louisiana. Is that right? And you've been keeping him since he was a small baby?"

Gertrude hesitated a beat. "Well, I've never told anyone the complete story before. I suppose I was somewhat embarrassed, and in the beginning, I expected his mother to return for him at any moment. Then as time went on, like about a year or so, I had lost complete contact and became so attached to the baby that I began to hope they never came for him. Hal had become the child I had always dreamed of having.

"Then, I started to fear the government would come. I never legally adopted him, you know. I still have that fear, but I don't believe that his mother will ever return. If she does show up and try to take him from me, I *will* go to court. I'll fight her to the end."

Opal interrupted. "What kind of mother would do this to a baby?"

"I like to think she was under the spell of her male companion and on drugs to boot." Gertrude continued, "He was calling all the shots and she cow-tailed to him at every turn. I can't understand why. He was a good-for-nothin' Hadocol salesman from Baton Rouge and had met her when she was a stripper and pole dancer in New Orleans. She lost her job when she became pregnant, and I suppose, looking for help from someone other than her family, found this guy. She wasn't sure who the father was, so he was of no help."

"They took off for Las Vegas, where he intended to set up a Hadocol distributor. She was to return to stripping as soon as the baby was old enough. In the meantime, she would help him set up the Hadocol demo circuses." Gertrude described the cold January night when the pair, Huck Miller and little Louise Hall, arrived unannounced with a broken car heater, a slipping transmission and a trunk full of Hadocol.

"I heard a loud knock on the door and opened it to see a weird little man wearing checkered pants, two-toned shoes and a bowler hat." Gertrude could still feel the startled jolt at the sight. "I stepped back and could see the tiny girl holding a cardboard box and a cheap suitcase. Another box was beside her on the floor. I began to recognize my niece. I had not seen her since she was a small child."

Gertrude explained that as they moved inside, a weak cry came from the box. "I thought it must be a cat, but Louise pulled a little baby from the boxful of clothes and blankets."

With all of their travel money, and then some, used up on auto repairs, what began as an overnight stay lasted for weeks. Huck tried to find temporary work, with no success.

"I kept the baby while Louise waited tables. That didn't bring in much, so I made them a pretty substantial loan, with a promise they would be on their way. They stayed around while Huck negotiated with Dudley Leblanc, the inventor of Hadocol.

"Then one morning, I woke up to find them gone. I was left with the baby and a note saying they would return in two weeks to pick him up. That is the last that I ever saw of them. A post card arrived in about a week saying the return had been delayed indefinitely because Huck was in jail. No other information. No return address, no phone number, no nothing."

Gertrude recalled that after a while, she contacted her family in Louisiana, but they knew nothing. A month or so later, her sister called to say that Louise had gone to California with a friend and that she would contact Gertrude later. "There has been nothing since. I hope there never will be. I pray to this day that no one will ever come to take my baby away. My pastor says that is a major sin, but I don't care. Am I just awful?"

Opal was awestruck by this incredible story. "Honey, I think you have been an angel of God. I could not have done what you did. Now, let's get down to business and solve Hal's problem. I have tried everything. I've been giving him advanced work, against school rules. This week I gave him a fourth-grade math book, and he informed me that he is past that at home. I brought him some advanced Texas history books and he seemed to enjoy those. Have you come up with anything?"

"As a matter of fact, I have." Gertrude explained, "He likes history and

22

loves my father's old case law history books on judgements rendered by the courts. Each is identified by number and date which also intrigues him. He reads a lot at home. As a matter of fact, he reads most all the time, except for watching a few TV shows I'll allow."

She reached into her bag and pulled out a folder as she continued talking. "I prepared this as an option. It calls for us to gather up all the books on case law that we can get loaned to the school. They'll be returned and replaced as needed. This is beyond me to pull off. It's going to have to be a school project and is probably against somebody's rules somewhere. What do you think?"

"We might be able to get the support of Mrs. Jones, my principal," replied Opal.

"She is young and progressive. She just might take the risk."

Days later, Mrs. Jones disappointed both women by denying the request. But she did promote Hal to the third grade. While the move did help to increase Hal's interest in school, it exposed him to more intense bullying. The already small boy was now dwarfed by the size of his classmates. Now even more dependent on Tripp Joiner for protection, his shield was now in another class.

Eventually, Gertrude resorted to home schooling. Hal lost much more of the needed contact with other children. He sought out every opportunity to go fishing with Tripp and to hang out at every athletic practice that was within walking distance but made no attempt to join a team of any kind. He began to take on more chores around the house, so it came as no surprise when he picked up a broom at the barbershop and swept up the cut hair around the chair.

"He is learning to take charge," thought Gertrude. No one suspected that Hal had just started a career at Mac's Barber Shop, one that would take him to meet his destiny and fame.

Soon, Hal was sweeping around all the chairs and began to receive tips from Mac and others. This drove him to ask for more chores. He worked himself into a part-time job cleaning the toilet and the entire shop for a regular piecework salary.

Hal liked having his own income. It gave him a feeling of independence now that he fully understood what being an orphan really meant. He often went to the bank with Gertrude, and she eventually encouraged him to open his own savings account. The shoeshine stand located on the sidewalk in front of the bank fascinated him.

An old Hispanic man, with snow white hair, ran his shoe business with a flair. He knew all the fancy shoeshine moves that ended with a loud pop with the shine rag. He sang songs in Spanish while people waited in line. Pocket change and one dollar bills half-filled a two-gallon glass jar at his feet.

Hal was soon asking the old man more questions than the old man wanted to be bothered with, but he answered every one. He learned all about the polishes and the rags. He learned why the shine man spat on every shoe. "It gives a spit shine." He learned that the money in the jar was "seed." A plan began forming in his mind. Hal's favorite seat in the barbershop was an antique shoeshine chair sitting in Mac's corner. He took his plan to Mac.

"I will set up a shoeshine business and give a free shoeshine with every haircut. I will set up a seed jar and work just for tips. Can you beat that, Mr. Mac? You furnish the polish and the rags. I promise you this will double your haircut business!"

Mac had serious doubts, but Hal's enthusiasm was irresistible. "We'll give it a try, but don't be too disappointed if it fails. You can forget about doubling my business, but if you are satisfied with your tips, we will keep it going."

Hal was in business the very next day. He showed up with a large stack of advertising fliers, which he posted around all of downtown. Two large law firms nearby made natural targets for the ads. One day in the not-so-distant future, Hal would be matching up customers with legal questions with his law firm customers. Meanwhile, Mac found that he did, in fact, have less time between customers needing haircuts.

With Hal spending more and more time at the shop, so did Gertrude. She had begun introducing him as her son; thus, the assumption that she had adopted Hal. The barbershop joke became that the avowed spinster must be shopping for a date. Maybe she was.

24

As the shop was closing one evening, she invited Mac to bingo night, which included a low budget dinner at the senior citizen center. Overhearing the invitation, Hal began nodding his head "yes" vigorously. Mac and his deceased wife had loved playing bingo and had often attended this same event many years before. He was reluctant to be seen in public with Gertrude, but he reluctantly accepted.

Mac and Gertrude arrived early, and she led him to her accustomed seat. They each purchased the limit of five bingo cards. Mac was pleasantly surprised to find faces he recognized from his old playing days. He was beginning to enjoy himself when Gertrude blurted out for all to hear, "Folks, let me introduce my date. This is Mac, and I have informed him that this date will *not* be followed with romance, should he happen to have that on his mind, because I am a virgin and I shall forever remain one." This brought some laughs, her own being the loudest.

"Are you bragging or complaining, Gertrude?" asked a lady at the next table. This brought the biggest laugh.

Mac jumped in. "That sure takes a load off my mind." The party was on.

Hal, Gertrude and Mac became a regular threesome. Gertrude began preparing a meal or two per week for Mac, and she put out a spread like none Hal had ever seen before, except when the preacher was invited to dinner.

With Mac hanging out there several times a week playing board games and working crossword puzzles, Hal began to fantasize about Gertrude and Mac getting married. Then he would have a real home with parents like all the other kids.

But after several months of bliss, tragedy struck. Gertrude was running late for bingo. When she met Mac there, she complained of indigestion and skipped the meal of fried chicken and mashed potatoes. Her favorite. She was winning nothing at bingo, not telling jokes or laughing at Mac's. She was not even bragging about something new that little Hal had done. Something was clearly wrong. The night ended when she grabbed her chest and fell unconscious over the table.

An ambulance arrived, and Mac went after Hal, who was spending the night at a friend's. Once in the waiting room, they were informed that she was still alive but gravely ill. Brother Jobe arrived soon after and led a prayer. The doctor came out again and said something to the two men out of hearing range of Hal, or so they thought. He heard the words "will not make it through the night."

Pastor Jobe made a phone call then took Hal by the arm and told him a snack was waiting for them at his home. They were to go there and spend the night. Mac would stay with Gertrude. Hal begged to stay. He knew Gertrude was dying, and they were shielding him from the death watch. He wanted to stay with Mac, who had become like a father to him. Hal thought about running, but the preacher had a strong grip on his arm and led him out to the car and pushed him in.

Snacks were on the table when they arrived. The entire family of six kids and wife quickly seated themselves. The preacher blessed the food and offered a long prayer for Gertrude then gave everyone a chance to pray. Hal did not pray, nor did he eat. The food was gone in seconds. Hal could not resist the stare of the girl across the table, who grinned like a Cheshire cat. The atmosphere was eerie, almost spooky. He hated this place.

Mrs. Jobe tossed Hal a pair of undersized pajamas and assigned him to a bed to be shared with a younger son. He kept his street clothes next to his bed and pretended to fall to sleep. He wanted no small talk with his bed mate or with the two other boys in the bed across the room.

Earlier, Hal had examined the bathroom window to secure his escape route. Within two hours, he was on the ground running across town towards home. He reached there completely out of breath, crawled under the house, and came up into the master bedroom closet through a hinged door. Only then did his thoughts return to Gertrude.

Tears flowed as he prayed a simple prayer. "Dear Jesus. Please keep Miss Gertrude from dying. I need her very much. She is like a mother to me. If you need her more than I do, to take care of all the little babies in Heaven, then you take her. But please tell Mac to take care of me. Amen."

Hal felt a little better now and began thinking clearly. He would need to stay where he was, in the closet next to the escape hole in case anyone came looking for him. He was certain that someone would be searching for him as soon as he was discovered missing from the Jobe home.

He had guessed right. Mac entered the front door very early in the morning and walked through the house calling his name. "Gertrude is dead and if you are hiding, you must come out."

Hal had the urge to answer but decided to stick to his plan. He wanted no part of any funeral. He had seen plenty of dead bodies on television and in movies. They all had eyes staring in space. Blood would be all over the place. Some even had worms eating on them. He always closed his eyes, and his friends made fun of him, calling him chicken. No, he was never going to look at a dead body, not even Miss Gertrude's. There was plenty of food in this house. He was going to hide out here until all this was over. Simple logic told him that if he called the barbershop in a bit, they would call off the search without him talking to Mac.

When the sound of Mac's footsteps assured Hal that the coast was clear, he dialed the number. Lou, the second chair barber, answered.

"This is Hal. Will you give a message to Mr. Mac? Tell him that I did not like staying at the preacher's house and that I will be staying with friends for the next several days. I will be back to work after the funeral, so don't give my job away. Thanks, Mr. Lou." He hung up before Lou could respond.

Hal's plans quickly went awry when Gertrude's family arrived for the funeral. They poured into the house, depositing suitcases in all the bedrooms except Hal's. Gertrude's sister, Agnes, was in charge of making room assignments. Then her focus was on locating little Hal and bringing him home. One phone call led to another and to another. She was not satisfied with Mac's explanation that he was safe with a friend. No Hal turned up. She called the police and they began to aid in the search.

It was clear to Hal that he would have to find another place to stay. He toughed it out one more night, sleeping on the ground under the house while developing a new plan. Come morning, he would slip out to the bank, pull money from his savings account and hail a cab to the Double Bar 6 ranch to stay with Tripp. They had several empty beds in the bunk house.

Things started well. He made to the bank. There he ran into trouble. It seems that the bank had no procedure for children to withdraw money from their accounts without a parent or guardian. Hal was not about to take no for an answer. His loud complaints alerted a manager, who began asking questions. Hal refused to give answers. A passerby recognized Hal from the barbershop. The whole story was out. Hal bolted from the bank and ran straight to the barbershop.

He sat down in the shoeshine chair while he caught his breath. Seeing only Lou and a silver-haired customer, he blurted out, "Where is Mac? I've got to hide at Tripp's house. They are after me. They are making me go look at Miss Gertrude and then they are taking me to Louisiana and I ain't going."

Lou replied. "Mac is at the funeral, where you belong. Calm down and get ahold of yourself. Why did you not go to the funeral?"

"Cause I don't want to look at no dead body, especially not Miss Gertrude's."

"Let me take you to the cemetery for the burial ceremony," Lou offered. "You can catch up with Mac there. That will make him very happy."

"No! No! Miss Gertrude's sister will catch me there and take me to Louisiana! I ain't goin', and you can't make me!" With that, Hal ran into the restroom and locked the door. He remained there for what seemed like hours. Because it was. Finally, Mac returned and lured Hal out.

"I have an idea." Mac handed the phone to Hal. "You call Agnes. She'll be back at your house by now. Apologize for your bad manners. Then tell her that you are safe with a friend and will be returning home soon. Then hang up the phone. She'll be obligated to notify the police, and they'll probably call off their search. You can go home with me tonight, and we'll sort out all this mess tomorrow."

Hal did as he was told. On hearing his voice, Agnes immediately started to scold him, even while he apologized. She was still talking as he hung up the phone. But she did call the police, and they, in turn, called Mac. They asked that he do his best to locate Hal so that temporary custody could be scheduled. Mac said he felt sure that he would be able to locate the boy and produce him at a hearing. All seemed well ... until a deputy sheriff walked into the barbershop. He was a regular shoeshine customer and friend to Hal. Those in the shop relaxed a bit.

Deputy John Malham had received the alert of a runaway missing child. He was just checking on his friend.

CHAPTER FIVE

₁wo Gun' Comes to the Rescue

ᴢeputy Sheriff John Malham, bodyguard for Ector County Judge Horace Parker, was the first law enforcement officer to take advantage of free shoeshines offered at Mac's Barber Shop. Many more followed suit. Most west Texas officers wore boots. They tried never to be caught with an unshined boot, lest he be scolded by a superior officer.

The first time Deputy Malham sat down in the chair, he asked one question. "Free, huh?"

As he pointed to the sign, Hal replied. "Yes, sir," and that was it. No other words were needed.

The deputy never removed his dark sunglasses or hat during the 10-minute process. Hal was totally intimidated by his demeanor and appearance. He had never before seen anyone wearing two pistols. Maybe in western movies, but never in real life.

Hal made no attempt to start a friendly conversation but kept a smiley face according to the protocol drilled into him by Mac. He tapped under the toe of one boot, the sign that he was finished, and Malham stepped out of the chair, dropped a quarter in the tip jar and walked out the door without a word. His departure set off the usual stream of barbershop gossip and stories about his powerful boss and the Parker family. He was called Two Gun because he was a crack shot with either hand. Rumor had it that he had killed several criminals.

Two Gun became regular as clockwork. Hal unlocked the secret to conversation by commenting on his beautiful pearl-handled guns, asking if he might hold one in his very own hands. Two Gun responded by unloading one of them, looking through the barrel as a double check then handing it to Hal, grip end first.

Hal stuck it in his belt, backed away a few paces and began practicing his quick draw ala Gene Autry. Everyone enjoyed a good laugh including Two Gun, who had a reputation of never smiling at anything.

30

As time went on, the conversations grew longer, and the tips grew bigger. All their conversations included some gun talk, and Hal learned that the pearl-handled pistol came from his idolization of General George Patton of World War II fame. Their conversations often lasted past shoeshine time.

Soon Hal got up the nerve to ask Two Gun to shift his hair cut business to Mac's Barber Shop. He did, and everyone was able, for the first time, to see him without his hat and dark glasses. This took away his aura of meanness and mystery. He seemed to open up, even to other customers, but he never said a word about his boss, the judge.

He and Hal eventually became close enough to compare their lives as orphans, or almost orphans. When Gertrude died, he was greatly concerned about Hal's future. He hated to see this little genius entrepreneur and future lawyer end up in an orphanage, unable to develop his potential without his law library. A hearing on temporary custody would answer a lot of his questions. His money was on Mac being the winner, at least for now.

The hearing was scheduled for 9:00 the following day in Juvenile Court. Mac hired a lawyer to plead their case. Three other cases were scheduled for the same time, and Judge Geraldine Foster held all the case folders in a stack on her desk. She called the cases as they came off the top.

As bad luck would have it, Harold Hall came up last. By that time, Judge Foster's demeanor had changed from sweet and smiley to sour and scowling. She was working into the lunch hour now but wanted to finish before breaking for lunch.

After their lawyer's opening statement, each petitioning entity were asked to testify. Pastor and Mrs. Jobe, Dub and Minnie Joiner; Junior and Sue Dancey and Mac Reed all stood as separate requesters of temporary custody. She quickly announced her decision.

"Since this young man has a tendency to flee household living accommodations, I am going to send him to an orphanage of my choosing for three weeks and initiate a search for his birth parents. At that time, we will make a permanent custody decision. My office has a working agreement with Saint Joseph's Children's Ranch near Midland. They have a tremendous record of safety and security. I am assigning the

Texas Juvenile Justice Department to take him into custody and transport him at the close of this hearing. We will allow you to go pack one medium suitcase and bring it back here after lunch. My suggestion is that you go to the orphanage, meet the people there and make for a smooth transition. You will receive a packet that will provide you with the rules for visitation and so forth. My clerk will provide you with directions to the orphanage. This hearing is adjourned. The rest of us will take a two-hour lunch break."

Everyone stayed with Hal, who was fighting back tears but trying to look brave. A man and women dressed in casual street-clothes showed their badges and introduced themselves to Hal and the others, offering kind assurance. They would go with Hal to pack the bag. Goodbyes were said all around and Hal was taken away.

Only Junior Dancey noticed that Hal had asked to look at his copy of the map to the orphanage and had not returned it. Junior knew why he wanted the map. The little red headed devil was already planning his escape and where to run and hide. Junior shared these thoughts with no one, not even his own wife.

Junior's suspicions proved to be right, but it took Hal longer than Junior expected. He would have wagered it would happen in four or five days, but Hal ran away on the eighth night.

He had traded chores with a quickly cultivated new friend whose job was to secure equipment in the outdoor storage building at the end of each day. He climbed the brick fence behind the building just after dark. The weather was cold and windy, and he was clad in a light jacket with a baseball cap on his head. The cap hid his bright red hair.

The orphanage was located just off Highway 191 on the outskirts of Midland. Hal headed straight for the highway then turned right, towards a truck stop he had seen. The plan was to get a ride from there to Odessa. He would watch the trucks that were entering from the east and would be leaving to the west. Logic told him that if they took on a full tank of fuel, they would not be stopping again anywhere nearby and would continue on past Odessa. Highway 191 passed through downtown, and the driver would certainly have to stop at one of the many intersections.

Once at the truckstop, Hal began looking for a truck that offered a decent hiding place. He did not want to hide by hanging under the trailer support structure. He could attempt to crawl into a sleeper while the driver was eating. But there were plenty of cattle haulers on the road, and that would be his first choice.

Hal got lucky, and after about an hour of waiting, a dually pickup truck pulled up to the fuel pump. It was towing a large cattle trailer with a gooseneck hitch. Perfect! The trailer was empty. Perfect! The driver was alone. Perfect!

He slipped into the trailer when the driver went in to pay his tab. He was lying down in the front of the compartment. He felt relieved when the man, clearly a rancher, started the engine. But the rig did not turn towards the highway. Instead, he pulled into the parking lot, parked beside other rigs and went back inside the diner door. He stayed for a full course meal.

Hal was beginning to shiver from the cold breeze and was a bit nauseated by the strong odor of fresh cow manure. He began to have second thoughts about his choice of rides. Just then, the driver exited the diner and approached the rig. Hal flattened out on the floor but was prepared to flee if discovered. Luck was still with him.

The truck pulled out onto the highway, headed towards Odessa. With a sigh of relief, Hal relaxed a bit and began to plan his next move. What if they hit all green lights in downtown Odessa and were not forced to stop? Easy! He would simply hang his upper body over the side and shout, surely being seen in the rear-view mirror. The driver would most certainly stop and out the back he would go. His nearest haven would be the barbershop, within easy running distance. Plan on!

As hoped, they caught a red light at the second main intersection. Hal was over the rear gate in a flash. He never stopped running until he reached the front door of the barbershop. There was practically no traffic in the middle of the night. As expected, the door was locked.

His plan was to break in through the small restroom window, but it was too high above the ground for his reach. He turned his attention to the alley behind the store and started looking for a ladder or an empty trash can or any object he could use for a climbing aid, but he found nothing after several city blocks of searching.

Hal needed shelter but had nowhere to go. He knew that he was a wanted person now and must remain out of sight. His only choice was to enter the crawl space beneath the porch and wait for Mac to open the shop for business. He would persuade Mac to take him out to the Joiner ranch, where there were countless hiding places. He could stay there until everything returned to normal, then he could move in with Mac and resume his shoeshine business.

Once again, he began to gather his thoughts. He knew that he was first missed at the orphanage bed check at 10 pm. By now, a search of property buildings and grounds would have been conducted by staff and maybe even some of the older boys. The local police would have been notified. An alert would have gone out on all patrol radios, and the standard search procedures for runaway orphans would have taken place. This was not an unusual occurrence, and since he knew of no orphan who had ever been lost, police acted without excessive urgency. Hal had learned from the older residents that relatives would be the first contacted and those on his visitors list would be next. He figured that Mac and others would be contacted about mid-morning. By then, he would be hidden on the Joiner ranch.

The plan was working, but Mac was still hours away and the cold was getting to him. Wind was howling between the porch planks, producing weird noises. The stench of cow manure on his clothes was overwhelming. For the first time, Hal was truly frightened. He pulled his legs up against his shivering body, his knees under his chin, and cried for his mama. The mother he had never known.

Finally, Mac arrived on schedule and had his key in the door when he was startled by the presence of Hal. The whimpering little boy grabbed him by the leg and said, "I'm cold. I'm real cold."

Mac removed his coat, wrapping it around the boy's body. "My goodness. Where did you come from? How did you get here? Let's get you inside and warmed up.

"Go into the restroom and wash up with hot water. Take off your shirt. There is an old hunting coat of mine hanging in the storeroom. Put that on. I'll turn on the restroom heater. You stay there while I go to the cafe to get you some hot breakfast. Lou will be here at any minute and I will be right back. We have some serious talking to do."

With that, Mac headed out the door as Lou was coming in. Although Mac was back in about 20 minutes, it seemed an eternity to the hungry Hal.

He wasted no time pleading his case. "Mr. Mac, you gotta get me out of here quick. They are after me. You need to take me to the ranch so that I can hide. Tripp will hide me there while this all blows over. Then I can live with you and get back to work. We can...."

Mac cut him off. "We need to go to my house so that you can get a proper bath. The remainder of your clothes and other possessions are there now. We will sit down there and make immediate plans for your future."

"I have plans. I need to hide in a big hurry."

"Don't worry. You will be safe there. Now, no more talk from you until you finish your breakfast." Mac fended off questions from the curious Lou and others now in the barbershop. Then they were out the door.

As they arrived in the driveway, Hal finished his story about the escape. Mac marveled, "How could he pull off such a feat?"

After a fast shower, Hal sat down in a chair. Mac pulled up another directly facing him, looking him squarely in the eyes. This little red headed monster had better understand everything that was about to be drilled into his brain.

"I need for you to hear me out and then you can have your turn to speak. I am the closest thing to a father you have right now, so this gives me the right and the duty to act like one. You are dealing with a very tough period in your life right now. Fortunately, you are one tough little character.

"You can win without hiding, but you need my help and that is all that I am offering. You are exceptionally intelligent. Miss Gertrude cultivated your brain such that you could get your high school diploma and start college correspondence classes right now, if the schools would only let you. You own your own business and are earning your own income. Miss Gertrude willed to you funds for a complete college education plus a weekly allowance. You are financially secure and you have many powerful friends. Some are law enforcement, some are lawyers, some are ranchers, some doctors, some ministers. You already like law books, which is an amazing jump on a future law career. You have …"

Hal could not hold it any longer. "I don't want to be no lawyer. I want to be a barber. Lawyers fight for a living. People pay them to fight. I hate fighting, I have been running from fights all my life. I am too small to fight. I do not want to be no lawyer!"

"Calm down! It is my time to talk. Remember? You are, like it or not, still a child and you have plenty of time left to choose a livelihood. Everyone experiences tough times in their lives when their toughness is severely tested. Our next hearing with the juvenile judge comes up in a few days, and we must be fully prepared for it. We are lawyered up for court, and we have started a signature petition at the shop, asking for your assignment to a guardianship living arrangement.

"Four families have applied to become your guardian. These include me, the Joiners, the Danceys and the Jobes. In that order of priority, if that's ok with you."

Hal had moved himself to the front edge of his seat and could hold back no longer. "No, no, not the Jobes. I need my own bed. I have had my own bed all of my life, and the Jobes have no spare bed and they have a weird girl there who never stops staring at me and smiles all the time. It gave me nightmares. Please, not the Jobes. I need to hide at the Joiners until the hearing, and then I can live with you. I need to go back to work."

"You are not fully understanding what I am trying to drill into that thick little head of yours," Mac warned. "That will not work. It will be just another example of your running away from authority, another strike against you. You must be standing before the judge with a record of squeaky clean behavior in these last few days before we make our case for custody. You must be someone who will abide by the rules and conditions she assigns. No, young man. Here is what we are going to do.

"We are going to leave right now, before they come here looking for you, and go check you in to the detention center. You are going to prove to the world just how tough you are, something that you, I and your friends know. You are going to show them exactly what a model resident looks like. You are going to say yes sir, no sir, and thank you to every instruction."

With that, Mac handed Hal his coat and his bag and out the door they went without another word. He kept positive words flowing during the drive to the center. "People are signing the petition, even as we speak, and we are particularly interested in signatures of your many law enforcement customers. Lawyer signatures are important, too, and we will have many of those. We will overwhelm them with sheer numbers and we also have some VIP witnesses lined up for the hearing."

Hal said nothing until they entered the front door. "Ask them to lock me in a cell by myself."

Deputy Sheriff Malham had picked up the alert of the runaway as it was spread to Ector county law enforcement authorities and had begun his own search. He ended it quickly when the alert was downgraded to "Captured. Held at the Ector County Juvenile Detention Center."

Next afternoon, he drove the sheriff's car to the edge of the barbershop parking lot, as far from the building as possible. He stuck his head inside the front door, got Mac's attention and motioned for him to come outside.

Mac followed Two Gun to the car. There, he joined Judge Parker, the Big Man himself, in the backseat. Two Gun remained outside, perched on a front fender. Naturally, every curious eye in the shop was glued to the car, but no one could see who was inside through the shaded windows. A few minutes later, Mac exited from the rear door and came inside. The car drove off.

He answered the barrage of questions with simply, "I will fill you in later." When the questions began again, Mac responded, "What car? What meeting? There was no meeting. Let this be loud and clear. *Nothing happened!*"

That evening, as promised, a little red headed boy appeared at Mac Reed's home and burst in with a smile on his face. Hal ran straight into Mac's arms and gave him a big hug that lasted until Mac forcibly broke loose. "They told me that I am free. Am I really free, Mr. Mac? Can I live with you now? Can I have my own room?"

"Yes Harold, you are free, but you must never talk about this. If you do, everything might possibly be undone. Do you understand me?"

"Yes, I know how to keep a secret."

But secrets fall victim to the barbershop grapevine. The old timers labeled the story as just another example of west Texas frontier justice, the good guys rescuing a small child from the hostiles. Somehow, all the records were wiped clean.

It would be years before Hal would learn the whole story. He couldn't understand why Two Gun never again entered the barbershop. He missed his friend. "He promised to take me to the shooting range and teach me how to fire his pistols, left-handed first and then right-handed. He said that you must always take on the hard part of a task first and that way you will always find it easy to finish. He taught me that, Mr. Mac, and I will never forget it. I will probably never learn how to slap leather like Quick Draw McGraw unless another Two Gun comes in for a shoeshine." He looked around for a laugh at his attempt at a joke.

It would also be many years later, when Tripp Joiner is charged with the murder of Judge Horace Parker and Two Gun Malham, that Hal Hall would have to deal with the bitter irony of his best friend, the closest thing to a brother that he had ever had, facing a possible death sentence for killing his childhood rescuers. The only thing that kept him sane was convincing himself that Tripp is innocent, and of this, he had no doubt.

CHAPTER SIX

What is Football, Anyway?

Youth football is played over all of Texas under the control and guidance of many organizations with different names and different rules. Pee Wee, Pop Warner and YMCA are just a few. Tripp's Pee Wee teams for fourth, fifth and sixth graders had a fall league for tackle football and a spring league for flag football. He was recruited into the 10 team fall league. Tackle football, being the roughest, drew more players, more teams and more sponsors, and of course, more spectators. Games were played on Saturday mornings at two locations. Rule books were strict on ages and required birth certificates. Many had weight limits, but Odessa did not. There were no kickoffs, punts or extra-point kicks. Instead, the ball was placed on the receiving team's 20-yard line, the intent to punt was stated, and the ball was placed 30 yards down field. Extra points were awarded by giving one point for a successful run attempt and two points for a successful pass attempt. In other words, the foot was taken out of football.

Minnie Mae attended every game, with Paw Paw Dub attending as many as he could. After all, Saturday mornings had always been shopping days in town for ranchers. Minnie Mae had never seen a football game in her life, not even on television, so she had many questions for anyone unlucky enough to be sitting around her. She had seen most of her second game when she asked loudly more than once, "What is football anyway? I ain't seen a ball kicked yet." This brought derisive haw-haws all around, but Minnie Mae was not the least bit embarrassed. Junior Dancey's wife witnessed this and left her friends to sit with Minnie Mae. She remained her rules coach for the remainder of the season.

Most of the players played both offense and defense. Tripp dominated on both sides of the ball and led the team to a one-loss season. He was voted MVP by the coaches and set tongues wagging about next season's needed rule changes. This came mostly from the losing coaches, but some sponsors were also talking to the rules committee.

The hubbub got worse the following year when Tripp made a tackle that broke a youngster's collarbone. The opposing coach for the next scheduled game announced that he would forfeit the game unless Tripp was held out on defense. Coach Dancey refused and the game was forfeited.

The ruckus grew rapidly so that the league president called an open meeting for all interested parties. Order was maintained only by considerable effort of the coaches. The vast majority were of the opinion that Jimmy Jack Joiner was causing enough havoc to destroy the game of Odessa Pee Wee football, and something had to be done.

Changes in the rules seemed to be the only option, so the rules were changed. These changes were made effective before the next games would be played. They were clearly designed to make Jimmy Jack ineffective. A weight limit was placed on a ball carrier. His weight exceeded the limit by 10 pounds, which meant that he could pass the ball only and not run with it, if he continued to play. Since their offense featured 90 percent runs by Tripp, someone else would play. The rule was also made that anyone exceeding the weight limit would be allowed to play on the line of scrimmage only and could not block or tackle down field or outside of three yards from his position. These rule changes were voted on and passed by vote of the coaches and sponsors.

This move made sports page headlines in several local media outlets and became known as the Jimmy Joiner rule. Obviously, the actions did not sit well with many, especially those involved with the Massey Hardware team. Minnie Mae Joiner knew practically nothing about football, but she understood what just happened to her boy. She pulled him from the team.

Tripp pitched a rattlesnake fit and refused to eat or do his chores for a few days, until Paw Paw brought home a cutting horse that Tripp had always wanted. This gave him another rodeo event to focus on and something to take his mind off football. He stayed out of football until the eighth grade, his second year in junior high school. He had joined the basketball team the year before and discovered that he was pretty good at that sport as well. The comradeship of sports and the urging of coaches lured the oversized boy into basketball and back into football the following year, where he again excelled and attracted the attention of the high school coaches.

His name was brought up to Coach Carr in a high school strategy

40

planning session by offensive coach Mutt Stephens. "Have you been reading about this Joiner kid? He's the one who made headlines when the Pee Wee league changed their rules, and now he's burning up junior high. Coach, you are always telling us to give you one more freak and you will give us another championship. Well, I believe we have a freak of nature right here in our own backyard. The booster club will not have to recruit his father. He lives in our district."

The word "freak" was never used outside of tight coaching circles for obvious reasons. No parent would ever stand for their son being called a "freak," even though this was a positive term for a very rare, exceptional player. A "phenom," as the media might say. A player coveted by all coaches and sometimes encouraged to transfer to other school districts through enticement of job offers to parents. No coach participates in these enticements, but avid booster club members have been suspected of this activity. The winning tradition was so strong under Coach Carr that many player's parents took jobs in the school district and transferred their little all-stars into the program. There are so few true freaks that this is mostly a dream, but coaches are always dreaming.

The head coach responded to Mutt, "Well, we will see what we will see in a couple of years. Now let's set about creating a few freaks with this year's squad."

A plaque on the wall directly behind and above Coach Sam Carr's desk read, "Capture the mind and the body will follow." In his mind, this tidbit of philosophy contained the secret weapon for a high school coach to be successful, and he had used it on every boy who came to play football for him.

Coach Carr felt a tingle pass through his body as the excitement of starting a new year of football built. He felt in his bones this would be a good year, maybe a championship year. Didn't he always feel this way?

Even through the gust of hot August air outside, he could almost imagine the looming nip of fall air. No doubt, this was his favorite time, even better than the end of the season when holding a trophy and listening to praises. This season of dormant Friday night lights was the best. Folks said Coach Carr was born to be a coach. They were right.

CHAPTER SEVEN

Numbnuts

Sam Arthur Carr was born in Arkansas to a cotton farmer father and a schoolteacher mother. He was a highly competitive, undersized overachiever who competed with his older brother in everything. He once got out of bed in the middle of the night to pick cotton so he could win the prize for most cotton picked that day.

His grades and football skills earned him a scholarship to the U.S. Naval Academy, where he played quarterback in an option offense. After graduation, he began his naval career in pilot training.

After receiving his wings, he was sent directly to Vietnam to serve aboard the USS Constellation and to fly the F-4 Phantom aircraft. He flew only four missions before being shot down over Hanoi by a SAM missile and taken prisoner.

Sam was confined in the infamous Hanoi Hilton prison with other captured American fliers. All were subjected to brutal interrogations and tortured to give up military information and to make anti-American statements. Most eventually gave in, but a very few held out and never broke.

A fellow prisoner wrote a passage in his book about one of those few. "Lieutenant Sam Carr was too stubborn to be a prisoner of war. This should have and almost did kill him. He should have signed a statement like the rest of us."

According to his mother, Sam inherited his stubbornness from his father. In prison, when the first beatings and rope bindings started along with efforts to brainwash him into making anti-American statements, Sam decided to brainwash himself. First, he convinced himself that he could withstand the torture. Then, he made himself believe that he could feel no pain at all.

He tried laughing as they beat him, but this brought a beating into unconsciousness that almost killed him. There was no more laughing after that, but his contempt was obvious. Somehow, he convinced himself that pain was mental, not physical. If he could shut the thought of pain from his mind, he could withstand it at all costs. He gave it a name – numbnuts.

The young soldier filled his idle time with football thoughts. He started planning to be a football coach after escaping from his hellhole. He created new offensive and defensive plays with assignments for each player beyond any seen before. He spent much time on a plan to teach numbnuts to his future players.

Eventually, a prisoner exchange allowed his permanently damaged body to be loaded on to a cot and flown to freedom. The lifetime souvenirs of a limp and a crooked elbow were never discussed. Players and fans assumed these were the result of old football injuries.

Today, he was about to start the embedment procedure with the incoming class of players. He had spoken the same words for years, and he knew everything by memory. This welcome had become a ritual and pure drama. There was no doubt in his mind that it was his destiny to be a molder of men, beginning with the capture of the minds of boys, his boys. There were 19 in the new group, with all but three being locals, and the rest, transfers from out of town.

Assistant coaches introduced themselves and took care of preliminaries. The attentive but somewhat apprehensive group awaited the entrance of the head coach, the legendary Sam Carr. Every move he made and everything he said for the next several minutes was designed to "capture the mind."

Coach entered from the door directly behind them, opposite the door from which the other coaches had entered. This was intentional, of course, so as to silently be standing before them, almost before being noticed. He stood motionless except for his eyes, which moved from player to player and established eye contact with each. He stared each one down until they blinked or looked away. He then moved on to the next.

This was his method of establishing dominance from the start. The players were impressed by what they saw but the coach was not. There was not enough beef, he thought. Coach was dressed in typical white athletic shorts, black shoes with no socks and a sweatshirt with "Panthers" across the front. A whistle hung around his neck. His tree trunk legs – football legs – signified a fullback or guard instead of the option quarterback he had been. A burr haircut topped off his look.

He paused for a few seconds and then began to growl in his best Bear Bryant voice. "I am Sam Carr. You may call me Coach or Coach Carr."

He paused again for several seconds in order to set the mood and then began his indoctrination.

"In the days of the Roman Empire, a game was played with much more violence than our football. In fact, the game was played for life or death. Gladiators fought wild animals and each other. Often, the loser was killed. Emperor Vitellius came to power at the apex of popularity of a gladiator named Attilus, who was one of the few who were not slaves. Attilus had reached rock star status and had lived to hear his name spoken everywhere. This troubled the emperor to think that a gladiator was more loved than he. His wife disliked this very much herself and began to urge him to correct the situation by pitting him against lions and the most feared gladiators. He killed them all.

"Then one day a brilliant idea came to Emperor Vitellius. He would have Attilus fight five other gladiators on the same day. His opponents would be selected from the very best of the Roman Empire, and if he survived the first four bouts, he would then face the next best in all the land. This type of match had never been organized. Vitellius would gain popularity through the great excitement and fervor created. So the match was began to a record crowd. Leaders from other lands came from far away to witness this spectacle. Anyone who was anyone paid huge ticket prices in order to be in the Roman coliseum.

"Since he was not a slave, Attilus could not be forced to fight, but if he refused, he would be branded a coward and his career would be over. Pride overcame common sense and he stepped forward to die, or so he thought.

"Attilus dispensed with the first, second and third opponents fairly easily, although things got progressively more difficult. He began to struggle

44

with number four and was severely wounded, but somehow survived. "Number five entered the arena overconfident as he saw the condition of his opponent. He began to toy with Attilus in order to prolong the fight and to enjoy the cheering crowd. He glanced at the Emperor to witness his cheer and smiling face. This fateful glance cost him his life as the blade pierced his throat. But at this same moment, Attilus also collapsed to the ground, bleeding profusely. He could see the sand turning crimson as it soaked up his blood. The crowd, thinking that he, too, was dead, began to moan, then go silent, then cheer as he slowly came to life. The roar of crowd noise was heard miles away as the victor was carried around the circle. Now even the Emperor began to cheer, lest the people turn on him.

"Attilus had a secret weapon with him that day. He was able to drain every ounce of strength from his muscles and he was able to block out the pain of injuries and the pain of fatigue. Our winning record here at this school has made the public and our opponents wonder if we might have a secret weapon. Let me tell you something. *We do*!

"Gentlemen, this is your first day of learning to use this secret weapon. All I need is your mind, and your body will follow. If you honor this request, you will play for this team. If you do not, you will always be a bench warmer.

"This weapon has a name. Everything of value has a name. Our weapon is called 'numbnuts.'" As expected, this brought grunted giggles from the players, but Coach Carr pretended not to notice.

The coach moved to the blackboard, reaching for a piece of chalk as he beckoned the lad nearest to him to step forward. He asked him his name.

"My name is Raeburn Roberts."

Coach Carr then raised his hand with chalk between his fingers to near the top of the blackboard and appeared to be drawing a short horizontal line, but he lifted the chalk slightly so that it left no mark.

He then asked, "Raeburn, do you see this line? It represents your ultimate potential."

Raeburn hesitated because he could see no line. He tentatively answered,

"No, sir, I don't see no line."

"You don't, eh?"

"No, sir."

"That, son, is because there is no line. It's invisible, because no football player knows what or where his full potential is. You must keep reaching for that invisible line. Every day in practice, your main goal is to get better. Your coaches will teach you how to keep track of your progress. You *will* progress daily towards that line. That's numbnuts.

"No one else, to my knowledge, in high school football does this like we do. We do a number of other things differently. Maybe this has something to do with our winning more than anyone else. We grade everyone's performance in games and provide you with a method of grading yourself in practice.

"Our practice scrimmages are set up differently so every player on the field gets to participate every day. We also do a jersey presentation ceremony for you and your family. This will take place next Saturday. A duplicate game jersey will be presented to you as you say the short pledge to your school and teammates. That is provided for you in your packet along with your play book. We expect that you will start the learning process today."

"I'm ex-military. I believe in discipline and repetitive drilling. You will run plays over and over again until you get them right. Our coaches practice the policy of tough love. We may embrace you and congratulate you on one play and kick your little gimlet ass on the next. The good Lord has located your ass at the right kicking level for this very purpose, and we won't let Him down.

"Our jobs, yours and mine, are to win football games. But we have another chore even more important. We're building character.

"Every teammate is your brother and will be treated like one. No name calling of any kind will be heard coming from your mouth, even in the heat of anger during a fight. You will say ma'am and sir to your teachers and your coaches.

"You will not smoke tobacco or drink alcohol. A good number of you have the imprint of a round can showing in the back pockets of your jeans right now. The use of smokeless tobacco will be frowned upon but not punished. I will leave that issue like this. When you start to notice that the wearing of your game jersey has brought considerably more attention from a pretty girl, look at her and imagine what she might look like with stained teeth and tobacco juice running from the corner of her mouth.

"This town loves Friday night football and they will put you on a pedestal. Wear your jersey to school and wherever you wish. It is a status symbol. You will stand out as if in a spotlight. Some say that I encourage this practice in order to keep an eye on you. Not so. The public will do that for me. Honor this spotlight by building your character."

Coach Carr could see in the boys' eyes that he had hooked them. "My next topic is both a character issue and a conditioning issue. I'll conclude my remarks for today with this topic so my words are fresh on your minds as we exit through that door to the practice field. Here's my opinion about football players and sex.

"This is not about safe sex; this is about no sex. If I thought that I could get by with it, I would lock all of you in a chastity belt and hide the key until football season is over, but I don't believe I would be an effective coach from a jail cell. The strongest urge a man has is the desire to survive – to breathe, to eat and to drink. The second most powerful urge is to have sex.

"The peak of a man's sex drive comes at the early age of 19. If you go from zero to peak in just a few teenage years, then there must be a tornado raging in you right now. I know; I've been there. I'm not naive to think that I can whip a tornado, so I'm not about to try. I'll just leave you with this story.

"The best wide receiver who ever played for me made first team all-state as a junior. College scouts from all the major programs were on him day and night trying to get his commitment to their schools. He could have played anywhere he wanted and probably could have made the starting line-up in his freshman year.

"I became close to this young man because he needed special attention.

47

He had a tough home life. His mother was a single mom trying to support four children on her pay as a waitress. He had an older brother in prison, and was more or less, being raised by an older sister in a high crime neighborhood.

"At my wife's encouragement, he spent a lot of time at our home. Our young daughters loved him like a brother they never had. Guess what. He fell in love with a pretty little girl and quit coming around.

"He showed up at fall practice 30 pounds under weight and looking like that he been run over by a truck. He was pale and with no energy. Even though he passed his mandatory physical exam, I took him back for more tests, but nothing showed up.

"I took this mystery home with me and told my wife about it. She knew right away what his problem was. She said he was girl whipped. I knew right then she was dead on.

"He was like a son to me so I felt I could come directly to the point and ask the blunt question. He immediately agreed. After we discussed the situation, he agreed to spend less time with his girlfriend, but he failed to do so. His performance his senior year was very much subpar, and his attitude was worse. His grades fell, and the scouts vanished.

"By season's end, only one scholarship offer remained. It was from a no-name junior college in Oklahoma. He never enrolled there because he had to marry his knocked-up girlfriend. This boy took a laborer's job in the oil patch and settled down in a rent house to start a baby factory. The last I saw of him, he was working a second job as a weekend security guard at the mall in order to help support his large family."

Coach Carr hesitated a moment, then walked to the door, leaving his message hanging in the air.

One by one, as instructed, the players walked by him to exit the building. He shook their hand and got the name of each one. As he did, his piercing eyes penetrated through the brain, the entire body and all the way to the soles of their feet. Sam Carr had mastered the art of using only his eyes to make a statement and ask a question at the same time. He asked only one question aloud. "Are you ready to pay the price?" Each answered a resounding "Yes sir!"

Every player left the room feeling in his heart that he had sworn an oath, and as each exited the building, his body language said to all who might see, "Move over, little boys! The big boys are coming to play some football!"

Coach Carr followed the group out to the field to join the other coaches. His mind drifted back to the handshake with his quarterback freak. He was thinking, "This is the first true freak quarterback who has come through this school during my career." He reflected on Tripp's physical tools, starting with his hands with long fingers and a strong grip. "If I had hands like those," he thought, "I could have been a passing quarterback instead of having to run the option most of the time."

Tripp's hands were lined with callouses and his arms gently rippled with muscle, one sign of a true cowhand. Coach found himself visualizing the grip on the ball and the throwing motion of his arm, wondering if he would have to change either of these. Does he grip the ball across the laces or with his fingertips on the seams? His hands are large enough to grip and throw without thinking about the seams.

Later, as Coach Carr discussed the young player with one of his coaches, he admitted, "What we don't know, and will not know until he sees considerable action, is whether he will make the rapid enough decisions necessary to find an open receiver or to know whether and when to throw the ball away. Will he force the ball to an unopen receiver too often?"

Some passers with great arms and confidence do this. Few quarterbacks without quick minds become great players, but many quarterbacks with great minds and lesser physical tools have become professional hall-of-famers. Joe Montana was an example.

Coach wondered, "Will I be so lucky that my guy will have both? If so, we can start to dream about another state championship."

He struggled to force himself out of this daydream world and back to reality, suppressing a smile as he arrived in the midst of the coaches and the gathered squad.

Tripp Joiner's first high school football practice had officially started.

CHAPTER EIGHT

Running of the Bulls

No one remembers for certain who and when the tradition was started by a senior football captain, inviting all senior lettermen to an after-season outing. But all remember who started the running of the bulls.

Larry "Bull" Turpin was the undisputed alpha male co-captain of a Panther team that had just finished an 11 and 2 season when he decided to change the routine of a fishing trip or a lavish dinner party and plan something more exciting. Fresh on his mind was a television piece about the running of the bulls in San Fermi Pamplona, Spain. He was inspired by the excitement, the thrill of danger and the tie to his nickname of Bull.

This prompted him to plan a trip to the bull ring in Juarez, Mexico, and to create his own version of the run. Attendance for the trip would, of course, be mandatory.

The plan called for the leader to wait for a bull to enter the ring then leap in, with everyone following suit. They would make a complete circle around the ring and exit the other side, then flee to their vehicles and make their escape to a safe rendezvous. On the arrival at the rendezvous, Bull promised to have a special treat waiting. No one argued with Bull about any part of the plan after this 270-pound giant of a man threatened a broken nose and twisted balls for failure to comply.

The victory surprise would be a visit to Boys Town. Most Texas men and teenage boys had heard of Boys Town but none in this group had ever been there. The destination was actually not a single place; every Mexican border crossing town had one. In fact, the name Boys Town was not a name at all, but slang for the location of the designated bordello zone.

By law, bordello zones featured houses kept together, usually at the edge of town, so the government could maintain tight control of this heavily taxed tourist industry. Strict health inspections were routine so as to

50

prevent the spread of venereal diseases, which would naturally destroy the industry.

The number of houses permitted varied from town to town, as did the sizes and opulence. The nicest houses charged the highest fees and so on down the scale.

In Boys Town, there was no shortage of beautiful girls at any time of day or night. A steady stream of applicants came to these bordellos, with the pipelines fed mostly by peasant farm families and the poorest inner-city people. It was common for fathers to wish for a beautiful daughter to become a house madam. Most girls jumped at the chance to escape from dirt poor poverty to a rich and glamorous lifestyle. Enough money was earned to enable their families an escape from poverty as well.

Bull had done his homework. He knew that he may have to select the smallest and most run-down house in the area in an attempt to hold down prices. He planned to be in front of the house of pleasure when he announced the surprise. He had prepared and practiced his speech. "We are here so that all you virgins can lose your cherries, so follow me for the greatest thrill of your lives."

He was advised to negotiate a price of $15 each. They would draw numbers as a method of selecting the pecking order. Of course, Bull would go first. The time limit was 20 minutes per, but many would probably finish with time to spare. In addition, no one would card them for a Mexican beer afterward. Anyone who had as much as a single hair above his upper lip was deemed legal.

The senior players gathered outside to start the long trip to their first pit stop. Bull warned that no mention of Boys Town would be allowed, not in a hundred years. He mentioned again the broken nose and twisted balls that awaited any rat fink. Now he had added sign language with the words, touching his nose and twisting one fist in the other. Later, this gesture would take on a name of its own – the sign of the rat.

Over the years, veterans of the run grew into a loose-knit fraternity, and guidelines were passed from one senior captain to the next. One such guideline was the escape plan, in case a runner was captured leaving the ring. Since they had agreed to stick together, come hell or high water, all would surrender with the captured one and gather around the security

51

police captors. They would flatter the one in charge by asking for the captain of the group, who would probably be no more than a sergeant.

Standard procedure for Mexican policemen dealing with an incident like this is to advise the offender of the grave seriousness of the crime and tell them that they are going straight to jail as handcuffs are applied.

The polite question is then to ask, "Captain, is there anything that we can do to avoid being taken to jail?"

Bribery is technically illegal, of course, but a way of life in Mexico and practiced openly at every level with almost any government employee. The secret is to use diplomacy, always deal with cash and never show the cash until a deal has been struck.

The guidelines explained that once the first question has been asked, the captain will probably say that he might be able to accept the fine on the spot and show you the courtesy of paying the fine for you. Then you ask the amount of the fine and he will give you a number. You then express doubts about coming up with that large amount of cash and attempt to negotiate a lesser sum. If the captain does not volunteer a solution, ask him if there may be a way for him to appear in court and pay the fine for you. You become a naive tourist asking a stupid question and nothing more.

"Whatever you do, never strike or fight with a policeman," warned one team leader to another. They have a way of locking tourists up in squalid jail cells for extended periods without a way to contact a lawyer."

The team co-captain or designated spokesman would do all the talking for the group while inside the country except when each person did his own negotiation with the whores in Boys Town. None of the planning between one senior co-captain and the next was ever put to pen and paper. This was one reason the veil of silence was never penetrated in any serious way. Rumors floated around once in a while, but these were quickly denied and shoved back into the closet. Another rule was that when brothers met accidentally or as planned, the sign of the rat was exchanged as a greeting. Over time, the twisting of fists was used only to designate an obvious serious warning; generally, the simple touching of the nose was used. It was almost a military salute. Those around town who saw the gesture of nose touching had no idea what it meant.

52

Co-captain Tommy Ray Dancey started plans for his run with the bulls by collecting ticket money from each player. Although required, this confirmed their attendance.

He asked for Tripp's money with inflection in his voice that Tripp read as "Are you going?"

Tripp replied as he shelled out his money, "Of course I'm going. Why do you ask?"

Tommy snarled back, "Because you are, as the old folks say, tied at the hips with Lavita."
Tripp ignored him. "Let me know if you have any slackers."

"I may have one," replied Tommy. "Twobirds is saying that his mother is refusing to give him permission. She said she had a dream in which her son would be in great danger."

"Yeah, the Indians are always having dreams of one kind or the other. That's their nature."

"Well," continued Tommy. "Twobirds says that his mother's dreams always come true. He'll just have to tough it out and go without her permission."

The expedition left on schedule. Tommy Ray drove one car, Tripp another and Milky Dean the third.

Frank Chavez was the spokesman because of his fluency in Spanish. Although most all west Texans could converse somewhat, they couldn't hide their Texas accent.

At the well-planned time and on his signal, Tommy led the charge over the wall and around the ring, with Milky bringing up the rear. Things went smoothly until the exit from the bull ring, when Milky decided to hesitate atop the wall, take a few bows and shout, "Ole!" as he did his best matador's pose.

As he hurried to catch up with the others, he collided with a beer vendor, and both went sprawling across the concrete, surrounded by beer bottles and broken glass.

Someone yelled, "Cerveza gratis!" and the scramble was on.

Before a scratched and bleeding Milky could regain his feet, a burly member of la policia was firmly affixed atop his back with a choke hold around his neck.

Tommy took a quick head count at the exit gate and discovered Milky was missing. He halted the brave matadors and led reluctant chickens back to join their missing comrade and share his fate, whatever it was.

Chavez had been rehearsing his role, never dreaming that the worst would actually happen. But he was ready. "Move aside," he told his men. "Let me speak to the Captain."

Everything went according to the book, except Chavez ad-libbed by conjuring up some real tears and added a note of plea to his words. Tommy whispered, "He is going to blow it."

A capture had not happened in the past four years. Twobird's warning now seemed ominous. But the well-rehearsed bribe went down as planned, and the little group proceeded to Boys Town with considerably less money in their pockets. One of the cheaper houses was now their only option.

They entered the parlor and bar, trying to look like seasoned veterans without success. The madam recognized them as first timers, and immediately made them comfortable. She saw to it that their orders for Corona beer were taken and then explained the rules.

Fortunately for them, business was slow and a good selection of girls was available. Tripp picked last and followed his choice to a small room up rickety stairs. He moved fast to pay the negotiated price while explaining to the 30-something, slightly plump lady that he was paying for 20 minutes of conversation only.

The girl agreed in broken English, "I get one like you every year or two. You want your friends to think you are going along with the rest, but do not want to."

Tripp responded, "I have pledged myself to be faithful to the girl I will someday marry, and I intend to keep my word. Can you understand that?

If you don't mind, let's finish this in silence."

She played along by doing her nails as she sat nude in a chair beside the bed. Tripp tried not to watch but was intrigued by her skill in dealing with two-inch nails. If temptation arose, he did not admit it.

CHAPTER NINE

A Cowboy Can't Sip 'Til There's Hair on His Lip

Pansy was her name and Mac Reed was her game. Hal didn't remember her last name nor did he wish to. This woman was squeezing him out of his space, and he resented it.

Mac had met her at the bingo hall one night when she seated herself, without invitation, at the table with Mac's regular group. She plopped down in the chair that had remained vacant since Gertrude's passing. She was a four-year divorcee who started to play group bingo in order to meet more people and take away her loneliness, or so she said. No one doubted that her words were partially true. They were interpreted by most at the table to mean, "I am shopping for a husband."

She was very attractive and considerably younger than Mac, who was a bit flattered by her attention to him. It did not take long for her to wheedle a dinner invitation. Mac brought her by his house for an introduction to Hal.

Their relationship grew to the point that she seemed to be present with Mac most all the time, or so it seemed to Hal. One by one, his freedoms were taken away.

The first to go was his practice of running around the house clad only in his underwear. He was to always greet her politely then to keep out of sight the rest of her stay unless a meal was involved. "Whatever you do. Do not belch, fart or pick your nose in her presence." chided Mac. "You will always behave like a perfect gentleman, as you do around our barbershop customers."

Next to go were his and Mac's off days, Sunday and Monday trips for fishing, camping, hunting, hiking, ball games and about everything else that a father and son would do together. In three years' time, Mac had truly become the father that Hal never had.

56

Pansy began to take more interest in Hal and made a habit of asking more and more questions about his early childhood. These questions were painful to him and he refused to be drawn into long conversations. She once asked him if he would like to have a new mother in his life, and he immediately fled from the room. There was now no doubt about her intentions. She was going to marry Mac. A catastrophic change was about to come down and Hal had nowhere to turn for a solution. Mac had warned him about future periods of trials and hard times, but in his mind, Mac would always be there for support. In this case, it may not be possible.

He turned to Tripp and Tommy, more to vent than to seek a solution. He was already bombarding them with questions about his body changes and they assured him these were signs that he "was turning into a man." Both were ahead of him in this stage of life. They each had a girlfriend and kept him briefed, but he wasn't prepared for the strength of the sudden urge to be around girls his age. Yet there were none in his life to mix with. He wanted to hold a hand and maybe even kiss one.

Tripp and Tommy had female schoolmates, but Hal had been home schooled. Young girls never came into the barbershop. He was not a regular churchgoer, so church socials were out. There was an older girl waiting tables at the White Eagle café, and he felt drawn to spending more time near her. The very odor of her body, tobacco breath included, excited him and frightened him at the same time. "Weird," he thought, but it mattered not because she wouldn't give him the time of day. He found himself watching the cheerleaders instead of the ballplayers. He wanted to have a girlfriend like his friends but had no place to meet one. He was working on a plan to have a party of some kind, which would require Mac's assistance. Now this problem with Pansy had taken top priority and finding a girlfriend would have to wait. Just another headache for now.

Hal began to grow more nostalgic about the great times Mac had brought his way. He had taken him on his first airplane ride. They had enjoyed every entertainment park and all major historic sites in Texas. They attended lots of local sporting events, even junior high football and basketball games. He now sat alone at many of these. It just wasn't the same when there was no one to high-five or to moan with about a bad call. He was almost in tears when the good memories surfaced. Other than Gertrude, Mac was the best thing that ever happened to him, and he

57

was about to lose Mac to Pansy.

Except for dealing with the new problem of body changes, Hal was living a near perfect life. Mac had pushed him to take his GED and then to take the ACT examination for college entry, which he almost aced. This brought many letters from prestigious universities. Hal chose to load himself up with correspondence courses, a decision that produced a workload keeping him adequately occupied. With the barbershop closed on Mondays, he spent those days at the local barber college working towards his barber's license. He was still reluctant to get serious about a career in law.

Hal also took on responsibility for two new black lab puppies, litter mates he had named Jet and Blackie. It mattered not that Mac had named them Mutt and Jeff. The pups didn't seem to be affected in the least bit by being called by two names. Their complete care came from Hal and they slept beside his bed.

There was absolutely no way that the old feeling to flee from trouble would ever enter Hal's mind. He intended to stay and fight. He would find a way to learn to live with the changes that Pansy would bring, and bring them she did.

She arrived one evening with a box containing selective cooking utensils and announced, "Prepare yourselves for some good old-fashioned Texas high plains dining." Thus began wonderful meals almost daily, but they came with a price. Hal and Mac suffered through endless Pansy-dominated stories about her life growing up on a ranch on the high plains. Some were, no doubt, directed to Hal.

One "auk" work chore story after another came out of her mouth. They were "auk" stories because she held her hand to her throat in a choking motion as she told them.

"The dirty work would gag you. Especially cleaning the outhouses. The youngest children did the dirty work at home and the youngest cowboy in the range camp had to keep the campfire burning through the nights."

Hal reminded Pansy that he himself started each workday with "auk" jobs, including cleaning toilets at the barbershop. But the point wasn't to prove himself. He took all this to mean that Pansy had no plans to take over the dirty work when she moved in, and he was sure now, more than ever, that she was planning to make her move soon.

A case of wine with two goblets appeared on the kitchen counter one day. "A glass of red wine each day makes a man vibrant and a woman smile. We will make a habit of having a glass with dinner." Pansy threw a glance at Hal. "In a few years, you can join us.

"The wine is Weidekehr Pink Catalba from Altus, Arkansas. My favorite. I order it by the case."

Hal noticed that the wine was not red at all. It was light pink. He decided to not ask the obvious question. It looked like sweet soda pop, and he knew right then that sooner or later, he was going to have his first taste of alcohol. The temptation began when he first noted Mac keeping a half pint of gin, which he took by the tablespoon for sore throat. Hal had never yet yielded to the temptation. He was always allowed to leave the table before wine was poured. Pansy would toss a little reminder in now and then that Hal was not to touch the wine. "As they say on the high plains. A cowboy can't sip 'til there's hair on his lip."

The temptation grew until he could resist no longer. One evening after dinner, he found himself in the kitchen alone. Hal took a sip straight from the bottle and almost gagged. He was expecting a cola soda pop taste but instead got a strong "whang." One sip was enough to satisfy his curiosity.

Mac stopped on the way home from work one day in front of a clothing store and told Hal, "Go inside and pick out a suit and tie. We're going to have a wedding next Sunday and you're going to be my best man."

There it was. The dreaded announcement. His life was changing once again. Being the best man took some of the sting out of the announcement. Yet another sign that he was, indeed, growing into manhood. But it still hurt. Into the store he went. With Mac's help, he picked out a suit, shirt, bow tie and new pair of shoes.

As expected, Pansy soon arrived at the house and insisted that Hal try on his purchases for her inspection. To their surprise, she approved.

Wedding plans hastily came together, and decorating began for the backyard ceremony and reception. Wedding invitations were limited to close friends and relatives, but the list grew daily during the last days before the wedding. Mac and Hal erected a tent and wrapped up all their other assigned duties just on time. Hal marveled at the amount of food and bottles of champagne delivered for one little wedding. Pansy was determined that this event would be much bigger and better than her first wedding. Hal decided right then that he was going to try a taste of champagne. Surely, it would be better than plain Arkansas wine. He would just wait for the perfect opportunity.

The wedding went on without a hitch. Pansy was stunning in a new blue dress she had purchased from JC Penny and new hair-do from Jo-La-Ru. The happy couple waved goodbye to their guests and left for their honeymoon in Mexico. Although Hal was designated cleanup duties, a few of the more sober guests stayed behind to help. Hal made certain that all remaining food and beverage was left behind. He was planning to have his own coming into manhood party. As the last guest departed, his party began. He turned a champagne bottle around and around, examining the label.

Next, Hal showed proper manners, pouring his first taste into a wine glass. Once again, he was shocked by the taste. Surely there was a good reason why so many people drink this stuff. He forced the first glass down and then a second before he felt something happening. His mind started to float. He discovered what "high" meant in the drinker's vocabulary. Hal wanted to fly higher and he did. He realized that he was feeling guilty. And he looked around to see if anyone was watching him get drunk. Getting drunk was precisely what he intended to do, without knowing or caring what the consequences would be. He had heard of hangovers but was willing to pay the price.

Now far down the road to inebriation, Hal's little party turned into a pity party. His thoughts drifted to the sad turn of events in his life and certain changes after the honeymoon. Tears welled up in his eyes as he thought about Gertrude's death. He began saying aloud, "I must be getting pretty drunk, Gertrude, and I'm sorry. We never talked about this did we? Guess I was too young when you died to talk about adult stuff. Bet you didn't know that I'm a young man now and I'm looking for a girlfriend. I will try to pick one that you will approve of, but the pickings are pretty slim. There are plenty of girls in school, but you made me so smart that I skipped school. Tripp and Tommy are helping me find one, but I don't believe that they are trying very hard. I need you so much. Mac is good to me, but he just got married and now he has Pansy."

Hal poured another full glass and continued his one-way conversation with Gertrude. "You would be proud of me. I'm not going to run this time. I'm going to be a man and stick it out. When I find a girlfriend, things will be much easier. I am ashamed to admit that I have quit going to church lately, but I'm thinking of starting back. I might be able to meet the right girl there. I'm thinking, maybe, that God is punishing me for not coming to your funeral, even though I knew that you were already in heaven and not in that casket. I know God is mad at me for dropping out of church." Now Hal was drinking straight from the bottle as he moved from the chair to a seat on the floor.

Suddenly he froze. He thought he heard a male voice. "Mac, is that you? Who is here? I said, who is in this house? Oh no. It is God who has come for me!" Hal began to weep until he passed out. Six hours later he stirred immediately grabbed his head, realizing the full meaning of "hangover." The headache took hours and several aspirins to remedy. He raised his hand high in the air and swore an oath to never touch alcohol again.

After a week, Mac and Pansy returned. Hal tried to avoid them as much as possible. All the touching and kissing and Pansy sitting in Mac's lap was too much. Pansy had packed the house with her furnishings, transferring much of Mac's to the garage while making plans for a garage sale. Everything that belonged to Hal was squeezed into his bedroom and bathroom. He buried himself deeper into his studies and started to focus on a serious strategy for meeting a girlfriend. The cafe waitress was the only prospect at the moment, so he started there.

Her name was Mille Myers. She was 26 years old, already a two-time divorcee. She shared a three-room apartment with two other women. One was also a divorcee who worked with her in the cafe. The other was a man-hating spinster.

Their apartment was near the café, located above a corner drugstore. The three spent their off hours together; no man was ever seen with them. Since Mille had never given Hal the time of day, he knew that smart strategy was required. He started with the premise that "Money talks and BS walks."

Mac had taught Hal that the correct amount for a tip was 10 percent of the tab including taxes, so he started to dine there more often, always ask for her table and tipping her 20 percent. Bingo! It worked.

Mille began having friendly conversations with him, asking his life's story and telling him hers. Hal was pushing for more than conversation. One day the chance came. She reached and felt his hair and asked, "Is this color real? I've never seen hair this bright red before."

Hal felt a bolt of lightning pass from the top of his head, through his groin and to his toes. He reached and felt her hair, making some flattering comment as he felt a second bolt. Now he was getting somewhere.

Mille jerked her hand back as he reached for it. It had taken weeks to get this far and he was not ready to give up. "Girl, you must've thought I had a snake in my hand."

"No, I know men pretty good. I can see where this is headed. You were about to ask me for a date, and I can't do that."

"Why not?"

"Because you're a minor, and I'm too old for you."

"No, you're not."

"Don't you know that it's illegal for adults to date minors?"

"I won't tell anyone."

"I want to be your friend, but I can't date you."

"Would you date me if I weren't a minor?"

"Why, of course." With that said, she turned away and broke his heart, but he never forgot that promise.

He was back the next day with his 20 percent tip and many questions. He even asked Mille's help in finding a girlfriend. The only option that seemed to have a chance, she thought, was the church option. "Where do you go to church? How about going to some socials for kids your age. Every church has those. I met boys there."

"I don't like my church."

"Why not?"

"The preacher frightens me?"

"Why?"

"Because he always looks at me and tells me that I'm going to hell."

"You've gotta be kidding me. He tells that to everyone until they join the church. Here you are pretending to be a man asking a grown woman for a date and using that for an excuse to skip church. As a friend, I'm telling you to go to that church or one of a hundred others, sit on the back row or somewhere in the center of people your age, ask about the next church social and be there.

"If the first time doesn't work, try again and again until it does. Keep coming in here with a progress report. And by the way, cut my tip back to 10 percent. Save the rest for your girl." She surprised Hal with a quick kiss on the cheek then sent him on his way, even while another bolt of lightning made him dizzy.

Hal soon took her advice and church services led to his first church social. He couldn't wait to tap a pretty girl on the shoulder. He paid the price for his impatience. He saw a girl about the right height and with a pretty mane of hair falling over her back. He steeled his nerves then approached. Tap, tap. The girl turned to meet him. It was the preacher's daughter, with the smile still glued to her face.

CHAPTER TEN

Bent Penny: Torcido Monedar

A new customer seeking a shave, trim and a shoeshine changed Hal's destiny once again.

An impressive looking Hispanic man entered the front door just after Mac flipped over the closed sign to display open. "I am a stranger to these parts, and I need some fast service in order to be on time for an appointment. Can you take me right away?"

Mac responded, "You are in luck, stranger. You are first in line. Have a seat in my chair."

Hal noticed this tall, aristocratic man's old-style Mexican rancher's clothing with silver-toed boots. He smelled like money to Hal, which probably meant a large tip was coming. Hal always made certain the tip jar was properly placed and seeded with paper money.

Mac asked the standard barbershop question, "What brings you to town? My name is Mac Reed."

"My name is Martinez. I am a rancher from down south of here."

"Oh yes. I've heard of you. You have a big spread down on the river."

"I hope what you have heard is good news. My family has been there since long before Texas existed."

Mac repeated his question, "What brings you to town?"

"Actually, I am here to see a lawyer located in the building up the street. The government just notified me that they are going to reroute the river by cutting across a bend on my property to shorten it for navigational purposes as a part the big project just approved by Congress. I am opposed because it would cut me off from horseback access to over 2,000 hectares of prime grazing land. I believe that there is more to it than that. Informants tell me that they know that I have, in the past, provided aid to illegals. I am opposed to illegal immigration, but once they are here, how can you not care for cold and hungry children? Some arrive seriously ill and need medical help immediately. Some of the women are pregnant."

Hal silently took this all in. He quietly went back into his room and returned before the haircut was completed. He held a neatly folded note. "Good morning, señor. My name is Hal. I hope your day turns out well."

Martinez replied, "I believe it could, but this would not be the first lawyer with whom I have consulted and be given little hope."

After the cut, Hal performed a quick shine, which Martinez rewarded with a nice tip.

"Good luck," Mac offered as he rose from the chair.

Hal followed him to the door and handed him the note. "This might help your lawyer." The note listed a case file of an identical case, in which the court ruled in favor of the landowner. Hal couldn't resist putting his case law knowledge to good use.

The rancher crossed the street to the law office, reading the note. He returned about two hours later, stuck his head in the shop door and gave Hal a thumbs up.

Hal had no way of knowing that he had just taken his first step as a lawyer, or that it would carry him in a direction he would not have wanted.

A few weeks later, a young man climbed into his stand for a shine. He spoke in heavily accented English. "Good morning, sir. My name is Jorge. Are you Hal?"

"Yes, how is your day going?"

Jorge replied, "Señor Martinez sends his best wishes." He hesitated then asked, "Do you speak Spanish? My English very bad."

"Yes. Some."

In Spanish, Jorge explained that he was looking for free or inexpensive services for people who had no proof of citizenship. He made no mention that he was one such person, but Hal gathered as much. Señor Martinez had told Jorge that he felt Hal could be trusted to a limited degree, but he was proceeding very cautiously.

Hal answered agreeably, "I don't have such a list, but give me a few days and I'll see what I can do. Perhaps I can give you some legal direction for free. Let me see what I can come up with. Come back in a few days."

"I have a new job, but Saturday is my off day. I will come back then."

Jorge did that and received a list, along with a promise from Hal that he would update the list occasionally.

Hal didn't discuss the source of his information, a lawyer who was a regular shoeshine customer of his and had been dealing with illegals for years. A man of Hispanic decent, he was willing and able to help with the list.

As Jorge returned from time to time, he began to trust Hal more fully. He began to share bits of information about an organization by the name of Torcido Monedar, an enemy and deterrent to the Mexican drug cartels. The English translation, Bent Penny, was their code name, and actual penny coins were folded in the center and used as a calling card to signify their membership.

The group was originally formed in Houston in response to drug cartels who were targeting illegal immigrants as fertile recruiting ground for their runners, peddlers, soldiers and prostitutes. The cartels satisfied basic needs of immigrants as a means of filling their recruit pool. The strongest lure was fake identity papers, which allowed them to get driver's licenses.

Bent Penny offered no fake identity papers, but it did provide many legitimate services and even set up an undercover bank to make loans. They recruited help from people like Hal and Señor Martinez, who joined other wealthy patrons with funding of charity. Job opportunities with safe employers were shared. In time, Bent Penny organized additional chapters, whose members volunteered long hours to the cause. Jorge Via was president of his local chapter.

Hal was amazed at his discovery. Fighting cartels seemed worthy but quite dangerous. One night, after months of sharing names of support to Jorge, he and two other men came to Hal's home. They handed him a bent penny. Hal agreed to swear an oath of secrecy, and they inducted him into Torcido Monedar.

Years later, that penny would come to serve him well.

CHAPTER ELEVEN

Lefty Ropes the Princess

Every Texas school child is taught at a very early age that without Texans on horses, the United States would be a much different place. Our diets would consist mostly of sheep and goat products instead of beef. Our vast plains would be managed by herders instead of cowboys. Early means of transportation would have been nonexistent until steam engines were invented, allowing riverboats and trains to be powered over narrow corridors.

Owning or being around horses as a way of life created a culture that outsiders can hardly understand. They know that horseracing is the "sport of kings" and that polo is the "sport of the rich," and they see horses with mounted police or horses performing in a circus, but none of this translates into a culture akin to a religious cult. Ranch children participate in organized rodeo events starting as young as four. Rodeo competitions filled their needs for outdoor sports long before baseball, football, track or basketball.

Bronc busting, born out of the necessity for taming horses to work cattle, became a commercial enterprise when someone noticed that a bucking horse always draws a crowd. Why not charge admission to the spectacle? Other rodeo events such as calf roping, steer wrestling, and a crowd favorite, bull riding were added. Barrel racing for girls made rodeo a family sport, adding to its popularity. Old timers swear, "Once horse blood runs in your veins, it never goes away." This may explain why wealth or celebrity have never seemed to keep people out of the saddle.

This was certainly true for football great Jimmie Jack Joiner and movie star Lavita Sue Vorhees. But the famous Judge Horace Parker, one of the most powerful men in local history, seldom mounted a horse after he went off to college. Instead, his inheritance of oil-rich land and multiple related corporations propelled him into a long tenure as county judge.

Judge Parker owned race horses, but his personal attention to rodeo horses changed when his granddaughter began to compete in barrel racing events. He sought out the best horses and trainers to ensure that his "little princess" would always be successful to the maximum of her ability. Soon after the girl and her mother came to live with him, he introduced Lavita to horse society with the gift of a little filly. She witnessed the birth of the filly and began spending all possible time in the barn and corral. Riding lessons became a top priority followed by the desire to compete. She was forever hooked. Horse blood had seeped into her veins.

Jimmy Jack Joiner began riding alone at the age of three and entered his first rodeo at four. He was a contestant in the gentler mutton busting (sheep riding) competition. As they say on the plains, "He, too, was born with the blood in his veins and a rope in his hands."

At that time, Tripp had no other ambition than to be a cowhand and a rancher. He became a regular winner right away and often daydreamed about becoming another Marlboro Man, whose picture he saw on billboards everywhere.

The path to becoming a famous Marlboro Man seemed elusive. He needed to ask someone for guidance, but who? The answer came when he heard Paw Paw say to Minnie Mae sarcastically, "If you ever need a smart-ass answer to a question on any subject, just ask Rod."

Jimmy Jack went to Rod Rodriquez, ranch foreman, that very day and asked him if he knew anything about becoming a Marlboro Man. He replied, "Not much, but I do know one test you must pass. You have to roll a cigarette and light it with a match using only one hand, so the other hand is free to hold your horse reins. Let me show you how it's done."

Rod pulled his Bull Durham tobacco sack and cigarette papers from his shirt pocket, rolled a cigarette and finished the job by swiping the match tip on his pants leg. He then gave Jimmy Jack his "makings" and walked off, literally leaving him holding the bag with an unsolved mystery on his hands. Why would Marlboro Man be required to hand roll a cigarette when he smoked factory-made Marlboros?

Rodeo youngsters, wannabe cowboys and cowgirls, like all other children of their ages, get creative while standing around idle between events. They find games to play. A rope is always handy so there are many rope games known to all. Jump rope has many versions and is played by girls and boys alike. Jump the loop is a favorite if a good twirler is available.

Jimmy Jack was an expert with the twirling loop. He could throw a large loop with a consistent circle, and jumpers would jump in and out of the loop while the twirler stood inside. Lavita Vorhees and GiGi Smurl, classmates of Jimmy Jack, could always be found playing rope games with him. They always drew a crowd because they could jump with three inside the loop at the same time.

Judge Parker, observing their frivolity one day, remarked loudly that he disapproved of anyone throwing a rope around his little granddaughter.

His daughter, Lilia, spoke up. "Let it be, it's only a game."

The judge snarled, "That cowboy is left-handed and left-handed ropers are bad luck. A leftie broke the neck of one of my most valuable quarter horse yearling prospects."

Just then, Jimmy Jack lassoed the two girls and pulled them tightly to him and they all collapsed to the ground with loud laughter.

Judge marched straight to the office of the event director, who assured him that the young man would be instructed to stop this dangerous roping practice. But nothing was said about keeping the youngsters apart. They were schoolmates, after all, and continued to hang out together, eating. teasing and enjoying the other's company for many years. In their teenage years, touching, handholding, hugging and then kissing naturally followed.

By then, Jimmy Jack was known simply as Tripp. He asked Lavita for a first formal date at age 14, and she immediately accepted. Tripp had begun driving ranch vehicles at a very early age, typical of most all ranch kids. He was now driving a pickup truck to school.

One day, he drove Lavita home from school. Thus began the process of dating, first gaining her mother's permission for tightly controlled togetherness and a sit-down meeting with Judge Parker. He laid out the rules with a stern lecture to Tripp.

Soon Tripp and Lavita were "going steady." The new couple began to spend every possible waking hour together that was not allocated to school activities, chores and rodeos. Over time, family members began to talk about eventual marriage.

Their friendship then courtship eventually led to a formal engagement announcement. Judge Parker began to refer to Tripp as "son," and he attended all his football games and rodeo events.

Lavita entered the Miss Texas beauty pageant, finishing first runner-up. Seeing a future in her beauty, Judge Parker insisted on getting her an agent. He fronted a small production company, landing her a small acting part in a movie. Combined with Tripp's fame as a football star, the couple became famous to Texas hero worshipers. Media began to chatter about this Hollywood princess and prince.

But one day, the headlines instead featured their broken marriage engagement. Both parties released their versions of events, but truth be known, Tripp broke it in a bitter jealous rage after finding her with another man at the Parker mansion.

Heartbroken, Lavita made several attempts to repair the damage. When Tripp refused, her despair turned to scorn. She considered the event an insult to the Parker princess. Revenge by a scorned woman became the name of the game. Ultimately, the game became the great tragedy, including the loss of several lives.

CHAPTER TWELVE

From Heaven to Hell via The Hilton

Tripp Joiner obviously had no trouble finding women to date after his disengagement from Lavita Vorhees. His meeting and marriage to Patricia Dollar had no fairytale aspect to it, but it produced true love and bliss, which resulted very quickly in the birth of a baby daughter. Mary Mae, named for Patricia's mother and Tripp's grandmother. Tripp's love for this child was true worship.

When an important bit of good news comes your way, it has a way of making the day seem brighter. Colors seem more vivid. Jokes are funnier, and somehow, present company seems to be more interesting and entertaining. That was the aura surrounding Tripp when he returned from New York.

Tripp had gone up the day before for an examination of his healing shoulder. According to his surgeon, he was ahead of schedule in his therapy. In a few weeks, he would be allowed to soft toss a football. He could almost smell the grass on the N.Y. Giants practice field.

He was flying as a guest of Melvin Pilkington, principal owner and president of the Giants. He was his boss's boss, and they were traveling in style in his personal jet. Just the two of them with the pilots in the eight-seater.

"Just call me Mel" was on his way to a west coast business meeting and had offered Tripp this first-class taxi service. Mel was proud of his plane, with less than a hundred hours on its new engines. He took 20 minutes to show Tripp around the entire plane, from the cockpit to the baggage compartment, and of course, to the fully stocked bar and small kitchen. The fridge was loaded with fine meats, veggies and fruit. Tripp had flown in private planes on many occasions, but this had to be the finest.

Mel was in the midst of a new mega bucks spending spree and was in the mood to share some details with Tripp. He was about to learn, ready or not, the Pilkington version of how to run an NFL franchise. The conversation drifted into players' salaries and their relative value to the team, which made Tripp uncomfortable, but he took the opportunity to ask about trade rumors that were floating around about his favorite receiver and road roomie, Zip Devereaux.

Mel's assurance that the rumors were unfounded and that they were surely started by the many inquiries about his possible availability returned Tripp to his good feeling aura. The two-hour conversation ended, and Mel changed seats to begin nursing a gin and tonic. Tripp chose a bottle of mountain valley water and began to get a little antsy as his thoughts again turned to his girls, Patricia and Mary Mae.

Tripp could visualize them as if they were sitting next to him. It was hard to examine the image of his little daughter without noticing her little natural curls. She was the only member of the family with natural curls. Another one of life's mysteries, I suppose. My, how he loved those girls and his grandmother, Minnie Mae. He couldn't wait to see them. He felt the urge to tell the pilots, Matt and Zack to put the petal to the metal. At that moment, a voice came over the speaker from one of them saying that he was going to briefly change course so that all could have a glimpse of a gorgeous sunset. An unusual move perhaps, but Mel came alive and the two of them took in the beautiful sight, a fitting end to daylight on Tripp's special day.

They planned to land at Midland International Airport, where his wife and daughter would be waiting. Then off to Cattleman's Steakhouse for dinner and a little celebration of good news about his rehab and return to play. Mary Mae had her sixth birthday coming up in a few days and was anxious to share her party details with her daddy. She was proud of these, her first self-made plans (made with the help of her mother, of course) and she was ready for some serious bragging.

The plan was delayed a bit when the boss wanted to reacquaint himself with Pat and to meet Mary Mae for the first time. He walked with Tripp to the visitors lounge while the plane was taking on fuel. His delightful personality charmed the girls and he surprised Mary Mae with a birthday present. He had done his homework well. A little charm bracelet loaded with tiny footballs danced on her tiny wrist and brought plenty of giggles and a polite thank you. Shortly, they said their goodbyes then off to the restaurant with plenty of time for Mary Mae's bragging about all of her details.

They arrived without reservations, but this was not a problem. The hotel maître d' recognized Tripp immediately and gave them a choice table. One of the perks of being famous.

The celebration began with two glasses of wine and one lemonade before the special hors d'oeuvre, salad and Texas T-bones. Mary Mae, like most little ranch girls learn to eat steak at a very young age and could somehow put it all away. Constant chatter about the coming birthday party only added to the love and joy felt at table number six. In fact, happiness was overflowing all over the place and Tripp expressed his by drawing a little smiley face on his napkin and pushing it to Patricia.

She smiled, winked and touched the bridge of her nose. She had just given the sign of the rat, the secret Panther senior class football sign that meant, "I read you."

This must have been an accidental touching of the nose, he thought, since he had never told her about the Running of the Bulls and the secret sign. Plus, this had been a signal used by him and Lavita Vorhees, one that he had no intention of sharing with Patricia. So he mouthed, "What?" and spread his hands in the "I don't understand" gesture.

She responded simply, "Later."

Thankfully, Mary Mae fell asleep early on in the 20-mile drive home. Patricia Joiner snuggled up close to Jimmy Jack Joiner on the front seat as they each, in their own way, silently expressed pleasure in going home together again.

Once there, Tripp did not ask about the sign, but Pat had to tell her story. "You haven't asked about the nose touching thing, I was feeling upbeat and was having a little fun with you when I gave you the sign. Buddy Handley brought his injured dog in today and told me about playing high school football with you and asked if you were still using the sign of the rat. When I asked what he was talking about, he explained that it was a secret sign of a secret fraternity that meant, 'I read you, do you read me?' Or something close to that. It was a form of a greeting."

Tripp grunted, "That was an old high school thing and I don't use it anymore." That was the end of that. Or so he thought.

Tripp had some catching up to do with ranch business after being gone for several days. His grandfather backed him up as a part of their seasonal agreement. Tripp ran the ranch in the football off-season and Paw Paw ran things, all be it reluctantly, during the season.

He was so busy that birthday morning slipped up on him, but Mary Mae was not about to let him forget. She came slithering into bed between her soundly sleeping parents well before sunup with a shouted wakeup call and a loud reminder that this was *the* day. Most of the day revolved around the birthday party, which was declared a roaring success by all. Mary Mae declared that her favorite gift from her father was the jumping rope that he had dyed Red Raider red with the handles painted N.Y. Giant blue. She insisted that a hook used to hang it be installed just below his hanging lasso, and below that, she placed her red tap dance shoes. Tripp wondered how a few hours spent with 11 small children could be more tiring than a Giants football game.

Mary Mae wore herself out jumping on her new rope while wearing her red tap shoes, and she was in bed soon after dark. She had even composed a tune to accompany the jumping and tapping, "Tap-tap-tap to the river and back. Tap-tap-tap to the ocean and back. Hop-hop-hop to China and back. Skip-skip-skip to the river and back," fine tuning over and over and over until she fell sound asleep. Patricia commented that Mary Mae must have plans to become a singer and dancer someday. Tripp was sitting at his desk doing paperwork when Patricia sat down on his lap. This more often than not was a sign that she wanted to have a serious conversation, and he greeted her with, "What?"

She responded, "What makes you think I want something?" Before he could answer, she continued. "Being with these children today made me tingle, I guess is the word. It reminded me of the promise we made to have our second baby about five years after the first. It has now been more than six years."

Tripp started to speak but she pressed her finger over his lips as a signal to let her continue, and she went on with her speech. "My practice at the vet clinic is now established well enough and since I have become a junior partner, I will be able to take some time off when the baby comes. We both agree that too much difference in ages between siblings is not a good thing. Maybe we will get a son to follow in your footsteps or maybe we get another daughter to follow in mine. It doesn't matter, but I want to start some plans now if you agree.

"The baby should come in your off-season, so we must start our plans ASAP. We have so much to be thankful for now. We are set financially, and you will be retiring in a few years to be here to help raise the kids. You are an almost perfect husband married to a perfect wife – how can you not agree to my proposal?"

Tripp's eyes asked if Pat was finished; he saw her approval to speak. "First let me correct something. You are an almost perfect wife married to a perfect husband. Now explain to me what these so-called plans include. You knew before you asked that my answer would be yes, yes, yes. I want a son this time and we must do everything to make that happen. I have heard that there are things doctors can do to affect the sex assignment of an embryo. Check into this. That is all I'm asking you to do. But while you're at it, there are old wives' tales about going on a high protein diet. Oh, and research the methods used by the Cherokee Indians. There is something about having the squaw perform a ceremonial nude dance on a night of a full moon," he said with a smile.

Not quite sure how much of this was said in jest, Patricia cut him off. "Your chances are fifty-fifty, and don't expect me to start practicing voodoo magic. If we don't get a son this time, we'll try again. I will dance nude for you sometime, but it will not have any effect on the outcome. It might, however, speed up the conception date."

A promise made was a promise kept and planning would begin next day. First it was time to get some sleep after a very tiring day. They went to bed without knowing that there would soon indeed be a new addition to their family. But not a new baby. An adoption of sorts. An adoption without papers.

Zip Devereaux made a habit of calling often to inquire about the healing progress of Tripp's left arm. On this particular morning, the call came early. Zip was Tripp's best friend in professional football and was an all-pro wide receiver with tremendous talent. Unfortunately, his football talent did not carry over in his ability to carry on a pleasant conversation on any topic but football. Phone conversations with him never included an exchange of pleasantries, not even a good morning. He just started talking as if you had been standing next to him for an hour. This call was no exception.

He pleaded, "Give me the doc's report. Did he release you to begin throwing the ball? I plan to be out there soon, and I can run a few short routes and catch a few tosses if you're up to it."

Tripp began the update. "I can't start throwing yet but the doc says I am ahead of schedule with the conditioning program. There is no static pain and none with throwing motion movement, so I am pleased but a bit antsy. Now tell me why you really called."

"I jumped the gun a little bit there. I need a favor, a real big favor. It has to do with my baby sister, Debi. The one you've always called your adopted daughter, remember? The one who spent most of three summers staying with you on the ranch and who fell in love with the horse world. The same one who talked her father into buying her a horse and kept it stabled in New Orleans at outrageous costs but soon gave it up for a teenage boy."

Zip was rambling on in order to drive home his point. He was good at that and Tripp knew to wait him out.

"She has dropped out of Tulane where she had a free ride in music so that she can devote all her time singing with a band. She does have a great voice and a promising future, according to the critics. She's earning pretty good money and is getting a little out of control for a 19-year-old, but that's not the real problem. The real problem is drugs. I have been around them enough to know that they all do drugs except for Debi.

"It's just a matter of time until she will be hooked, too. I have come up with a plan to get her out of that mess. She just had a nasty split with her boyfriend, so now's a good time to get her out of town. I with the help of others have her convinced that the fastest way to the top for a singer is in country and western. Now here comes the favor."

Tripp could already smell it. Zip went on, "If you could get her an audition with your buddy who owns that big country and western honkytonk just south of town, I know he'll hire her. Unknown to her, I'll pick up part or all of her salary for a while in order to make it all happen. That will be a deal he can't turn down. Once he sees what she will do for his gate, he'll offer to give my money back.

She'll need her car so I will drive her out and pray that it makes it that far. If you will let her bunk at the ranch until she can find a place in town, I would appreciate it. But here comes the hard part. I need you to look out for her while she's there. She will, sooner or later, meet a nice boyfriend who will take you off the hook."

Tripp took this all in as the story unfolded. Ultimately, he consented. "If this is something that you and your family are really sure about, I'll help. But don't forget, I'm out of town a lot and I'll be gone for half a year at a time for football. And so will you."

They agreed to a deal. Tripp shared the plan with Pat, the audition was scheduled. Tripp never divulged that he had loaned down payment money to his old friend Tommy Dancey for the purchase of the Spurs Up club. This in itself was a guarantee to an audition.

Tripp and Zip sat with Tommy during the audition, which included three songs – two New Orleans torch ballads and a classic Patsy Cline song written by Willie Nelson called *Crazy*. Debi accompanied herself on piano and the little group was surprised to see that all club employees within earshot had gathered around to listen. A prolonged ovation erupted when Debi Devereaux finished *Crazy*. Tommy asked for her agent and when she pointed to Zip, they were ushered into Tommy's office to agree on terms. Little did he know but Tommy had just made himself one great deal, and Debi had just signed her death warrant.

Minnie Mae prepared a "welcome home" meal for Debi, who immediately began to recall many fond memories of her summer visits at the ranch and her immersion into the horse world. She shared some of these stories with the little group. She told how Minnie Mae had almost given up teaching her how to milk a cow only to assign her the chore of milking one cow per day. There were laughs all around.

Minnie Mae waited for her chance to be nosy, asking Debi for details of her new job. She blurted out, "You do know that we Baptists don't believe in singing in honky-tonks. People go there just to dance and get drunk. I wish you would come and go to church with us. You could join our choir and do plenty of solo work there.

Paw Paw Joiner, sensing Debi's embarrassment, jumped in with his favorite uncouth and off-color Baptist joke. "Do you know why Baptists don't have sex standing up? …So people don't think they are dancing."

No one laughed or even smiled but Paw Paw. He surely must have felt the dagger of dirty looks from all others present, and he for certain felt the kick in the shin from Minnie Mae. It was a good time to heed Tripp's suggestion and head to the parlor for homemade chocolate pie, Minnie Mae's specialty.

After the little reception, Debi met up with Rod Rodriquez, ranch foreman and the man that taught her how to ride. She asked for a tour of the stables and to be reacquainted with her favorite mare, Pamper. Rod volunteered to saddle the horse.

Off they went, at a walk at first as she adjusted to the western saddle again, then at an easy gallop. Pamper could run all day at this easy pace and Debi tired before the mare did. A slow walk back to the stables included a nice chat with Rod as he bragged on the natural way she "sat" a horse. She momentarily daydreamed about entering a barrel event again. She quickly snapped back to reality as she refocused on her upcoming club debut. She also knew that because of her work schedule and conflicting sleeping hours, she needed to find a place of her own. An apartment in town would do fine. She would ask Patricia to help her with that.

Debi was there to learn to be a country and western singer and to punch her ticket for Nashville, but it was her different sound and style from New Orleans that started to draw record crowds. The local media began to spread the word far and wide. She was able to sprinkle in a few country songs, but it was evident that the people came to hear the new stuff. She wore evening gowns instead of boots. This choice accentuated her soft beauty and made the ranch hands and oil field workers want to stand and listen, much to the consternation of their dance partners.

She soon became a part of the "in" crowd and became a prime invitee to all the big parties and charity events. Within a few months, she was the most talked about celebrity in the area. This inevitably attracted the attention of Vita Vorhees, who was a bit jealous about the new kid on the block stealing her thunder with the press and the public.

Vita decided to search Debi out at the next big party, forcing an introduction in order to become better acquainted and invite her over for tea. Debi was flattered by the invitation and readily accepted. After all, she had never before met a movie star, let alone been invited to visit one at home.

Meanwhile, Vita came out to catch a performance at the club with GiGi Smurl and their husbands. The group was utterly astounded with the talented young lady. This raised her jealousy several notches as she noticed that for the first time in her memory, all eyes were on the singer and not on her. GiGi could tell that a scheduled visit to her shrink would come none too soon for Vita.

The little tea party with Lavita and GiGi went well for Debi, but it seemed to be over much too soon. Debi left feeling excited and upbeat, believing the feeling was shared by all. Wrong!

Debi was barely out the door when Vita turned to GiGi and said, "Were you listening to her? All she wanted to talk about was Tripp Joiner. It was Tripp this and Tripp that. Tripp, Tripp, Tripp. She has a definite crush on him and if she is not sleeping with him now, she soon will be. That little Cajun winch is too big for her britches and needs to find some other town to sing her little sexy songs. Don't you agree?"

GiGi answered, "She has a crush, alright, but I think it's more of a big brother crush and not romantic at all."

She could see that Vita was headed into one of her dark moods and needed to be headed off. There was no other person in the world who could openly criticize and chastise Vita Vorhees to her face but GiGi Smurl, and she was about to enter her "scold" mode.

GiGi had developed her own abstract way of doing this back in their child days of practicing poses for beauty contests. She would hold an invisible microphone to her mouth and speak as the voice of the announcer. Now, with mike in hand, she began to speak, "What we have here, ladies and gentlemen, is a failure to communicate and a failure to understand present circumstances. The lady does not understand that the rooster has flown the coop. What the lady needs to do is to take her narcissist butt down to her shrink's couch now before she does something really stupid."

Vita interrupted, "Shut up and I mean *now*! I will not listen to any more of your crap today. This is serious business."

80

"Ouch," responded GiGi. "The lady is trying to make me feel like I am no longer her best and only friend who is always around to keep her out of trouble."

"GiGi don't forget for a moment that you are my paid secretary. And I might add, very well paid."

"Sounds like I've been demoted again, huh?"

"Why don't you go home early today? I have some planning to do."

GiGi obeyed her wishes and left for the day, knowing that Vita probably needed her now more than she had in a long time. She expected to get a call later in the day, but none came.

Little Mary Mae was growing too big, she said, to sit in her daddy's lap much anymore but she still pestered him to take her to Hal's Barber Shop, where Hal had converted an old shoeshine chair into a throne for the little princess. Her special tiara stayed with the chair, untouched by man or beast between visits. She loved Hal like a favorite uncle, and it wasn't just because of the chair. He could make her laugh like no other person could and she knew that a special candy treat would always be hidden well enough to require a "treasure hunt." If her visits stretched out more than a week or two, Mary Mae would point out to Tripp that he was in need of a haircut and would conspire with her mother for confirmation. The result was that he was never late for hair cutting time.

It has been written that when good times seem to go on forever, look closely around you because trouble will surely be on its way. Tripp was not looking or expecting trouble, but it came anyhow, and it came as *hell on earth*. It came, would you believe it, in the form of a beautiful woman, and that woman was Vita Vorhees. She had developed her all-inclusive plan. She would prove to Tripp that she could have him anytime she wanted. She would get her final revenge for Tripp's break-off of their engagement by ruining his marriage to Patricia. And she would force Debi Devereaux to leave town.

The first opportunity to start the ball rolling would come in two weeks. The fundraising committee for the Professional Rodeo Cowboys Association was meeting in the hometown of two of its strongest fundraisers to start plans for the next event for down and out rodeo performers. Tripp and Vita had their invitations as usual. Tripp never missed a meeting, but Vita never attended one and she had no intentions of attending this particular one. She would, as always, participate in the event once plans became final. She had other plans that would take her to the Hilton hotel location of the meeting.

Tripp went by the barbershop for a trim, then on to his meeting. He arrived 25 minutes early for the social hour. Always early and never late was his motto.

A smiling bellman with a fresh $100 bill in his pocket and an envelope in his hand hurried to greet him in the lobby. The typewritten note said, "Come by room 423 before going to the meeting room. I want to bounce a controversial idea off you before I bring it up to the committee." It was signed B.J. "That would be Chairman Bill Jones," thought Tripp. After tipping the surprised bellman, he was off to the fourth floor.

On the door, just under 423, was another note directing him to come in and join "them" on the balcony. Tripp knocked twice as he entered the door, which was held open by the thickness of a notebook. He picked up the book and announced his arrival as the door closed behind him.

A familiar aroma of perfume entered his brain at the same instant as he caught sight of a nude woman. There stood Vita Vorhees in all her glory, positioning herself between him and the door. He grabbed her arm as he spoke. "What in the hell are you doing?"

She answered, "What does it look like to you? You have seen me like this more times than you can count. Take your hand off my arm or I'll scream." He loosened his grip and began an attempt to talk his way out of the situation. She instead grew close and put her arms around him. He pushed her away and made another attempt to leave, but she blocked his escape.

More talk, more perfume aroma, more arms on his neck, more fixation on those gorgeous eyes, more scrambling of his brain that caused him to weaken and he knew it. He didn't notice that he was slowly being led to the bed until he felt himself being pulled down on top of the familiar gorgeous body. Old times were back, and old habits took over.

Each knew by instinct what the next moves would be. They were lost in pleasure and stayed there until they both collapsed with exhaustion. Neither one spoke a word. Tripp rolled out of bed, hurriedly dressed and headed for the door. Vita called out his name.

He turned and heard her say, "You still belong to me and I can have you anytime I want you." With this, she touched the bridge of her nose with her finger, the sign of the rat.

Tripp slammed the door as he left, but for just an instant a thrill lingered. He had just been seduced by a woman who could have chosen, at this stage of her life, to have just about any man in the world.

Tripp's mind was back in the real world before he reached the elevator. He knew he was in deep doo doo and needed time to think. He said aloud, "Stupid, stupid, stupid." He loved his wife more than anything else in the world. He would give up his own life in order to save hers and they both knew it.

He hesitated at the elevator then decided to go on to the PRCA meeting. He disembarked the elevator at the mezzanine level, found the meeting room, picked up a bottle of water as he passed by the food spread and started to make the handshake round. He sat down as he began to fake interest in the proceedings and noticed people around staring at him as his empty stomach growled. He took advantage of the break to cram down some food as he isolated himself, praying for a miracle solution to his problem. All he got was "Stupid, stupid, stupid!" He could still not think clearly. He would call Hal Hall as soon as the meeting ended.

Hal took his call and Tripp said only that he was not feeling well and would be coming by in a few minutes. Other than looking pale, Hal could see no other signs of illness. He heard the story and decided that he, not Tripp, needed a shot of whiskey.

Knowing that Tripp didn't drink whiskey, he produced an Alka-Seltzer, which Tripp guzzled down with, "This fool stunt may drive me to drink but it hasn't yet."

"You need to buy some time to think," Hal suggested. "You need to fake sickness and sleep apart from your wife tonight. You need to take a shower before you even go home, because Patricia will immediately pick up the scent of the other woman on your skin."

"Where did you learn that piece of crap?"

"In my barbershop of course. We learn everything about everything there. Besides, I can smell her perfume from here."

Tripp took the shower and left with the understanding that Hal would call ahead with the prearranged story. The story was that Tripp had come by not feeling well, took some medicine and headed home. It was probably nothing contagious, but, as a precaution Pat should have another bed ready for him and let him sleep in the next day. Patricia bought the story and followed the game plan exactly. The bed was ready, she took his temperature and tucked him in. Tripp had bought himself another thinking day.

Meanwhile, Lavita had dressed slowly. Something unexpected was troubling her, and she did not like it. A sleeping giant had been awakened. Wonderful memories of the many years of true love for Tripp, from childhood to engagement, flooded her mind. A happy smile was on her face, and tears filled her eyes. She admitted to herself that she still loved him. "How can this be?" she asked herself. "I hate him, and I love my husband."

Tripp had been barely out of sight when Vita called GiGi to update her on her plans. Part one had been successfully accomplished and part two must proceed immediately, with GiGi's help. All she was being asked to do was to make a few selected phone calls in order to spread the rumor about the Hilton tryst. The rumor must reach Patricia Joiner within 24 hours, before Tripp could create an alibi and practice his lie. GiGi must first call her mother, knowing that she would then immediately start a series of calls to every member of her bridge club, in particular Madge Magroot. Madge was the key messenger in the rumor chain because she was a friend of an employee of Patricia's vet clinic. This should be enough to do the job, but a backup phone call was ready if needed.

GiGi did her part and reported back after things were all in motion. "Thanks, darling. Action is about to take place. Goodbye Patricia."

"There is something else and I am a bit reluctant to share it with anyone, but here it comes. This little revenge party sort of backfired on me. I know now that I must have Tripp back in my life on a permanent basis. He's now hooked for an occasional roll in the hay, but I need more than that. I still love him."

"Oh, *no*," moaned GiGi.

"I know now that is possible to love two men at the same time," Vita replied.

"When did you become a Mormon man?" GiGi replied sarcastically.

Vita ended the conversation saying, "I am holding up three fingers and telling you to read between the lines."

It took two days for the rumor to reach Patricia and a showdown with Tripp came very soon after. He was considering several options as to which lie he would tell if, in fact, the rumor reached Patricia. He was, of course, hoping against hope that it did not, but by now, he had concluded that the main thrust of Vita's actions was to get full, overdue revenge by attempting to ruin his marriage.

Lie option number one was to say that nothing occurred. This whole absurd tale was a false rumor deliberately spread in order to do him harm by a vengeful woman.

Option number two would be that, yes, he had been lured into the room, but he had walked away from it. He would then have to come up with a reason for not telling Patricia sooner if he had been totally innocent.

Option number three would be to confess the truth and fall on the mercy of a wife who loved him very much and who still knew, he hoped, that he loved her. He chose option number one.

Patricia did hear about the rumor at work and was not overly upset at the moment. There had been untrue scandal sheet rumors published about her famous husband in the past and all had been false. However, she could not push this one out of her mind because this was about his former fiancée who lived in the same town and thrived in the same horse culture as Tripp. She needed assurance from her husband and knew that a good hug and kiss would go along with it. That would feel really good about now.
She left work early and drove home with only the slightest bit of apprehension. She was not really worried just yet, but she should have

been. Tripp was surprised by her sudden entrance to his home office. This alone was almost enough to let his guilt show. Patricia picked up on it and moved right into the rumor.

Little Jimmy Jack Joiner had never ever been a good liar and swift punishment from his grandmother had always followed each attempt. Patricia was not far into the rumor story and did not need to finish before she knew that he was guilty. Tripp had always, without exception, looked directly into her eyes when either was addressing the other. This was one thing that she liked about him from the moment they met, but now he was not able to maintain eye contact. *Guilty*!

Patricia finished the story and waited for his response, but before he finished his denial, she burst into tears and left for their bedroom. He followed. The yelling and screaming started there. Minnie Mae grabbed up little Mary Mae, who had started to cry, and whisked her out of hearing range.

Patricia started to pack a bag but changed her mind when Tripp offered to move into the bunkhouse until some better arrangements could be agreed on. She did make it very clear that she was inclined to immediately file for divorce. Part two of Vita's plan was working perfectly. Part three was proving to be more difficult. It was going to require some help from her Hollywood agent and Judge Parker.

Less than a week later, Vita was venting to GiGi. GiGi had heard enough of it for one day, but she kept her mouth shut. In fact, she had about all she could stand from the paranoid egotistic woman, period. It was beginning to cause trouble at home with her husband and they had just quarreled about it this very morning.

When Vita traveled, which was often, she was required to travel with her, and this produced 24/7 workdays. Now at home, Vita was taking up more and more of her off time with long phone conversations and senseless requests. Vita was complaining that the gossip grapevine had reported that Patricia Joiner had hired a lawyer but had not yet filed for divorce. Part two of her plan would not be complete without a complete split in Tripp's marriage. She might be experiencing a morbid sense of pleasure and a feel of victory had she known of the turmoil going on in the Joiner household.

The tears of little Mary Mae caused Patricia to hesitate in going the immediate divorce route. She needed more time to think. Mary Mae cried herself to sleep every night, begging for her daddy, and many times Patricia shed tears with her on the same pillow.

Minnie Mae was working hard to save the marriage. She brokered an agreement in which Patricia and her daughter would remain in the ranch house so as to not move Mary Mae from her stable environment and where she received her day care from Minnie Mae. For now, there would be no visual or verbal contact between the two feuding spouses. Tripp moved a double wide onto the grounds behind the main barn and out of sight of the house, to be used as office space and living quarters. He would also be available for Mary Mae on a daily basis.

Tripp was running the ranch in a hostile environment because all ranch residents and employees took Patricia's side. It was tough to take, and Tripp offered to turn all duties back to Paw Paw, but he was turned down. He had no intentions, however, of moving away from his daughter, hoping that eventually things could be patched up. Minnie Mae reported that Patricia said if his tryst had been with any other woman besides his ex-fiancée and longtime lover, she might be willing to make an attempt to forgive him. For some reason, this news gave Tripp a small feeling of hope.

Minnie Mae also offered to set up counseling sessions with their church pastor or another professional. Tripp agreed but Patricia said no. The ordeal was taking a heavy toll on his health and he was sleeping very little. Recurring nightmares all ended with his daughter begging him to come back home. When with her, he had no answer for her questions and no real answer to her pleas. He was eating poorly and losing weight. His personality had changed. He was harsh and demanding with the Rod and the ranch hands. Rod was having a hard time keeping some from quitting. Hell was getting hotter.

Lavita was now fussing with GiGi about the time it was taking for execution of part three of the plan. Debi Devereaux had to go. The plan was perfect. There was absolutely no way that it could fail.

The ultimate bait was Hollywood. All mankind knows that every little girl grows up dreaming to be a Hollywood star, do they not? This little singer would be no exception to that. All the right people and resources were in place. Her agent, Trace Axelrod, would be in town on business, hear about the hot new singing sensation and catch her act at the Spurs Up then introduce himself. He would drop the names of a few of his clients, including Vita Vorhees, and ask one question. "Have you ever considered doing gigs in Hollywood and maybe even working in the movies? Let me leave my card with you as you think things over."

Trace would send a contract to Vita, who would personally take the good news to Debi. This move was going to cost a pretty substantial chunk of change but would be chicken feed to Judge Parker. He just had to be persuaded first.

Something like this had never been a problem before, when his little princess crawled up into his lap and pursed her pretty little lips with, "Pretty please?" He was already committed to bankroll her next movie and it was scripted to contain band music. Debi had the looks and the voice to enhance the movie, not harm it.

It was a perfect plan, but now Trace was dragging his feet. He had never dealt with a situation quite like this before and the contract was most troublesome. It must contain a year's worth of gigs and substantially more salary and living expenses. His budget requirements, and he knew that Judge Parker would demand a fixed budget, had to include "palm greasing" money for some club owners. His word and recordings from his client would not be enough to satisfy most. He had no idea what figure to pencil in for this estimate. He had bought the way in for more than one client but not one as green as this one.

Lavita solved the problem by offering to use her own money for any budget overruns. But Trace was still not moving fast enough. He had his lawyer assessing his liability exposure. He was definitely going to need more insurance coverage. Lavita continued to vent to GiGi. She would still have to deal with the task of selling Debi on the idea once everything was in place.

CHAPTER THIRTEEN

You Just Punched Your Ticket

Debi Devereaux no longer returned the calls from Vita Vorhees. The enemy of Tripp Joiner was also her enemy, Hollywood star and all. With GiGi Smurl in tow, Vita was headed for Debi's apartment parking lot in her baby blue convertible. Debi would be met as she returned from the last Sunday morning Mass, the attendance of which she never missed. Everything was now in place to execute the third part of the plan. All Debi needed to do was to accept her trip to Hollywood. This should be a no-brainer.

The timing was perfect, but Vita's friendly smile and greeting met with a cold stare and a weak, "Hi." Vita held up a brown envelope and with forced excitement in her voice gave her the good news. "Trace Axelrod sent this draft of a wonderful contract for you to approve. This is your ticket to Hollywood, little darling. Jump in the car with us and let me fill you in with some details."

Debi was momentarily speechless, but the lure was too strong. She moved into the back seat and Vita joined her there with GiGi behind the wheel. "We're headed for the drive-in at McDonald's. Join us for a snack as we chat and take a short drive."

This got a reluctant nod from Debi and off they went with Vita spelling out some of the main details. "One year of guaranteed gigs, a song in an upcoming movie and all at a doubled salary." She opened the contract and spelled out more detail.

Debi remained dumbfounded and silent. She suddenly needed help with none in sight.

"All we need is for you to fill in the date and sign. I know you'll need some time to review the contract with your advisers, but time is short."

Debi found her voice. "You do know that my parents will have to sign this with me and they're in New Orleans."

"Why?"

"Because I am only 19 years old."
"Oh."

"I want my brother to be involved too."

"Oh." This was not going well for Vita. After a moment of silence, she added, "This deal is not going to last long. Trace needs someone right now or he will lose the gigs. You review it, sign it and we will overnight it to your parents for their signature."

"*No*, I can't do that, I won't do that. I need some time. I have a commitment here at the Spurs Up and some personal obligations to fill. I've signed a lease on my apartment. This is a bit overwhelming."

"You have nothing here that money won't buy you out of, and Trace is prepared for all of that." Vita was now into her selling mode and was riding hard on the Hollywood dream and Debi's once-in-a-lifetime opportunity. They were approaching the turn-off to a familiar teenager hangout, and Vita directed GiGi to turn and park at the Lover's Leap county park. She was determined to get a commitment, a "Yes," and was beginning to become sufficiently irritated enough to make a threat.

GiGi sensed this and tried to head her off. She joined in with her own sales pitch as Debi began showing signs of irritation and asked to be taken home. Things started to get really ugly when Vita blurted out, "Now listen, sister, a great deal of money has been invested in this and it has been for your own good. Now I can't force you to become a Hollywood star, but I can damn well make you sorry if you don't. I can make your little job at that second-rate club disappear instantly and I can prevent you from getting another, so get ready to pack your little cardboard suitcase and get on the first bus for New Orleans or some other podunk city. There is not enough room in west Texas for the two of us, and who do you think is going to be left?"

Now Cajun fire was coming out of both ears as Debi shouted, "Now the truth is out. You are jealous, and it's clear to me now that your hatred of Tripp Joiner has something to do with this. Lady, you are one sick puppy!"

90

With this, Vita slapped Debi hard on the cheek. She took a fist to the mouth in return. Cajun girls raised with three brothers learned to fight like boys, with their fists. GiGi started to enter the back seat with a natural impulse to defend Vita, and Debi knew it was time to exit over the trunk of the open convertible. Vita grabbed her by both legs, intending to stop the escape, but Debi managed to get one foot against Vita's face and push with all her might. Vita was forced backwards and down into the floorboard and Debi made good her exit over the back of the car.

Vita came out of the car with blood flowing from her mouth, screaming profanities and showing her notorious bad temper. "I'm going to kill you!" GiGi grabbed her by the arm, trying to hold her back. Debi thought about her purse and lost shoe but saw no way to get them now.

Debi was unsure where to run and glanced towards the FM road more than a hundred yards away. Seeing this, Vita positioned herself in a blocking maneuver and forced the pursuit down a trail which led towards the overlook of the canyon with a high cliff overhang then down to the canyon floor. Down into the canyon Debi went, wearing her best Sunday dress and only one slipper. Her two pursuers followed in jeans and boots. Debi's bare foot was already bruised and painful, but she was well ahead of Vita, with GiGi trailing. She hesitated when she reached the end of the trail, not knowing which way to turn. She turned left up the canyon and was facing a very dark cloud with lighting in the distance. This added to her fear, but she continued on and managed to stay ahead of the two women trying to run in high heeled cowboy boots.

Tripp had been working alone this Sunday, it being the hand's day off. Minnie Mae, Paw Paw and Mary Mae had gone to regular church services, but Patricia had stayed home. She had avoided going out in public since the split except for work at the clinic. Tripp's newest venture was an experiment with the development of a herd of Santa Gertrudis cattle. The calves could be marketed as breeding stock instead of table food and brought more than triple the price.

This was a small herd of valuable cows with half grown calves that required daily inspection and feeding. This herd was kept in what had been known for generations as the "bull pasture," on leased land located about four miles east of the Double Bar Six. The only source of water was a single well pumped by a windmill. There was no barn or covered

91

shelter but antiquated cattle working pens had been there for over a hundred years. Tripp was there with his horse and feed sacks in his truck. While riding through the herd, he discovered a cow with an injured leg, which required a close examination.

He drove her and her calf into the working pen squeeze chute to have a look. He found a deep cut with inflammation and signs of infection. Tripp injected an antibiotic and decided to take her into town to his vet. He managed to squeeze the cow and calf into one side of the trailer and his horse into the other. The calf followed his mother into the trailer without a problem but began to act up soon as the horse was loaded. His Brahma blood, inherent in the Santa Gertrudis breed, explained his bad behavior and dislike of being trapped next to a horse. This resulted in the constant movement of all three trailer occupants and caused the trailer to be unstable as Tripp towed it down the FM blacktop road. He used a slower towing speed, a concern given the forecast of a coming storm. Tripp was trying to beat the weather.

Rod was on the other end of the two-way ranch radio mike. With a phone in his other hand, he was trying to work out arrangements with the vet on a Sunday afternoon. Rod confirmed that everything was set, so Tripp turned his attention to his favorite station, playing country music with breaks for weather reports. George Strait belted out a sad lost love song and Tripp's thoughts went immediately back to his wife and daughter. He found himself avoiding listening to music more and more. He could not stop the tears from forming in his eyes. Natural instinct caused him to glance from side to side as if someone might notice. "Big boys don't cry in this family." Paw Paw's words came back to him from his sixth birthday when the gift of a pony did not materialize, and he had never forgotten those words. Now it was happening far too often. He didn't bother to wipe them away.

The diesel engine in the Dodge dually began a loud clatter as it pulled the hill approaching the canyon. He would, momentarily, be coming abreast of the turnoff to Lover's Leap county park, the tailgate party hangout for every teenager raised in this part of the county for the past 50 years. He instinctively glanced down the lane towards the parking lot and was surprised to see a blue convertible parked there. There was only one car like that in the whole county. It had to be Vita Vorhees' baby blue Mercedes with the paint job customized to match her eye color. "Surely not," he thought. "What could it possibly be doing there?"

Tripp hesitated a moment and moved on. He wanted to keep as far away from that woman as he possibly could. The highway turned right as it followed the bend of the canyon. He rounded the curve and his curiosity caused him to look down the canyon. A bright blue object on the canyon floor caught his eye. He stopped his truck and took his binoculars off the window gun rack for a closer look and recognized Debi limping badly along the canyon trail.

Shock, anger and a wave of fear passed through his brain simultaneously as he saw Lavita and GiGi running down the trail towards her. It was apparent that she was running from the other two. It was also extremely odd that she was wearing a dress. His apprehension grew as he jumped back into his truck, made a U-turn and sped back to the park, jumped out of his truck and headed for the trail off the cliff down to the canyon floor.

The storm was drawing closer. A flash of lightening and a loud clap of thunder stopped the girls in their tracks. Vita Vorhees had very little to fear in her life, but she was terrified of thunder and lightning. She shouted, "Let's get out of here," and started running back in the direction of the trail up the canyon and to her car.

GiGi was right behind Vita until she heard Debi crying out to her for help. She had collapsed as she started back to the main trail and sat on a large rock. GiGi went to her aid and Vita returned as they were examining Debi's injured foot. Vita's closeness made Debi nervous. The anger in her eyes was still apparent and Vita began to curse her again.

Debi blurted out, "Keep that crazy bitch away from me." Many people suspected that Lavita Vorhees was slightly insane and a few, like her psychiatrist and GiGi Smurl, knew that it was a no doubter, but no one ever dared to use the word "crazy" in her presence. It was like throwing dynamite into a campfire. The explosion was immediate and gigantic. Lavita pounced on the sitting Debi and knocked her off the backside of her seat and onto the rocks behind. Her own entire body weight was on top as Debi's head split open as it landed on a large rock. Then she slammed the head of the unconscious Debi against the rock four more times in rapid succession. Blood went everywhere. This caused Lavita to recoil and moan, "Oh God, what have I done? I didn't mean to do it! It was an accident. I didn't mean to do it! GiGi help me!"

Tripp had begun to shout as soon as he got far enough down the canyon wall to see what was happening, but no one seemed to notice. He has witnessed everything. He arrived still shouting "Stop!" as GiGi pulled the crying woman off Debi to the ground. He took charge and started barking orders as he pulled his shirt off and cut the sleeves off with his pocketknife. He folded one sleeve into a compress bandage and wrapped the other around her head. This held the bandage tight enough to suppress some of the bleeding.

"Get up the hill to my truck and get on my radio and call for help. It's tuned to the ranch house and all my vehicles. Tell whoever answers to get on the phone and start an ambulance this way. The radio is mounted under the dash and has an on/off button and another on the mike. Turn it on and press the mike button and start talking.

"I will bring Debi up and put her in your car. You head towards town with your blinker lights on and pull over when you see the ambulance. GiGi, you drive, and Vita, you hold her head up. Do you understand?" He was talking more to GiGi because Vita was standing like a frozen ghost and was still crying. She would be useless. He would be behind them in his truck but because of the loaded trailer, he would be much slower. "You won't need my truck keys."

GiGi grabbed Vita by the arm and started the climb out. Tripp hoisted Debi's unconscious body onto his shoulder and followed. Tripp had to halt the arduous climb twice as he caught his breath and changed shoulders. His surgically repaired left shoulder began to ache immediately but there was no time to worry about it now. He made it to the top without collapsing, only to discover that the car was gone. The girls had abandoned him. He knew beyond reason that they had not called for help. He laid Debi gingerly on the truck seat and dried her face with a towel from his emergency kit then started for town as he worked the radio. Rod answered immediately and started calling for help on the phone. They kept the radio connection open so Tripp could follow the developments.

His lights and blinkers were on and there was no problem connecting with the ambulance. The transfer was made a mile or two from the city limits, and Tripp followed to the hospital. He stayed on the radio and instructed Rod to meet him and exchange vehicles so he could take the injured cow on to the vet.

Debi was taken into the trauma center at Ector County Hospital. The irony of wheeling Debi through the doors with a sign above that read Horace Parker Trauma Center went unnoticed to the first responders. This center, the best of its kind in west Texas, was one of many examples of the Parker philanthropic activities and buildings named for the grandfather of the creator of this tragedy.

As expected, there was no sign of Vita's car or its occupants. The girls had abandoned Debi for good. This decision was made by Vita when they reached the top of the climb from the canyon out of breath, but she had regained her composure. She had convinced herself that it all had been a terrible accident. She ran to her car with the convertible top down saying, "My poor car; it's probably totaled." She opened the door and water poured out.

Meanwhile GiGi was getting into Tripp's truck. Vita ran to her and stopped her from using the radio. "Don't turn on the radio, we're leaving here. We were never here. Don't you understand? Do what I say and come on."

GiGi started to protest but to no avail. She was pulled into the car; the top went up and Vita grabbed Debi's purse from the back seat and tossed it into Tripp's truck. She failed to notice the slipper down on the floorboard. She burned rubber as she pulled out of the parking lot and again as she hit the highway.

GiGi was still arguing. "That girl is probably going to die, and that makes you a murderer. You just punched your ticket to hell and to prison for the both of us."

"Just shut up. I told you we were never there."

"How are you going to prove that? There is one big famous male witness back there who hates us both."

"Judge will handle him for us. He has always said that every man can be bought if you're willing to meet his price. Don't think for one moment that he is going to allow his darling little princess movie star granddaughter to go to prison."

"But Tripp Joiner is no ordinary poor man. He is a wealthy man in his

95

own right. He's too rich and famous to be bought."

"There are ways to substitute force for money. It's called coercion and my grandfather knows how to play that game very well."

"Well, I'm done with the whole business. I'm getting off this train. You can take this job and shove it. As of this second I no longer work for you."

"Okay, quit if you want but you'll play your part in my game until the heat blows over, or you will witness the full power of the Parker family. I can promise you that, and you can consider this a threat. Look at me now."

GiGi did. She saw something in her eyes that she had never seen before. She was seeing what Debi saw. She was looking at an angel of death. She changed her mind. She would follow orders as long as necessary.

Tripp rushed into the ER waiting room and to the attendant's desk to inquire about Debi. It took some persuasion to convince the young lady that he was someone eligible to know, even though he was not a relative. He was standing there in wet and bloody clothes with sawed-off shirt sleeves and bloodshot eyes.

The ER doc, having been alerted by the ambulance driver, came looking for him as he was talking to the attendant. Debi was still unconscious but alive and was now being prepared for surgery. The doctor would not tell him more but said that right now he needed a statement from Tripp and asked him to accompany him to his office. There was a city policeman present who had followed the ambulance in. He was also asking for information. Rod had just arrived to get the keys to Tripp's truck. He had brought Tripp a change of clothes. The attendant came to the office with the insistent Rod right behind her.

The two men sat taking notes as Tripp spelled out all the details, including the names of Vita Vorhees and GiGi Smurl. It was clear that both men recognized the name of Vita Vorhees. They were already in awe with dealing with Tripp Joiner and now were looking at each other as they heard Vita's name.

The police officer stood up, excused himself and went to call his immediate superior officer. He was dealing with something too hot for him to handle and needed help. He was told to stop his report and wait until his superior officer arrived, which he happily did. His Odessa Police Department lieutenant arrived shortly and took control of the document and made a phone call.

The doc had continued his questioning as a number of hospital staff began to gather outside the office, including the hospital administrator on duty. The lieutenant patiently waited for the injury inquiry to finish, then he finished the police report, instructing Tripp not leave the building. He also determined that the extremely high profile nature of this case, given that he was dealing with the granddaughter of the notorious Judge Parker, warranted contacting his chief of police, He, in turn, called for the county sheriff, district attorney and FBI station chief to meet and determine how this investigation should proceed.

Meanwhile, Tripp returned to the waiting room and was seeking change for a twenty. He needed coins for the pay phone. Debi's family must be notified. He was asking everyone, but no one in particular, and didn't get a response to his pleas.

The hospital administrator overheard Tripp's frantic attempt to find change and offered to let him use his office phone. Tripp reached his good friend Zip Devereaux first and broke the bad news to him along with all the details. Zip was devastated and irate with Tripp. However, his anger was understandable to Tripp who had promised to take care of his 'Baby Sister' and had failed. How could he say he's sorry and have it mean anything?

Tripp then called the ranch and was told that Minnie Mae and Paw Paw were on their way. Zip called back to say that the family would be flying in next day. Tripp returned to the waiting room to await the arrival of his family members and further instructions from the police.

The Parker machine was already at work as the midnight oil was burning. When Vita and GiGi reached town, they went straight to the Parker mansion, where they found Lilia Vorhees in bed with her half empty quart of Jose Quervo tequila. Judge Parker and Two Gun Malham were playing gin-rummy with a bottle of Jack Daniels' Black Label whiskey within arm's length. Both were well down the road to happy land and into some serious gambling but not too drunk to understand the gravity of the situation. Vita had no problem selling the idea that it would be best if their presence in the canyon had never occurred.

He called for a council meeting at the mansion. Within an hour, the husbands of the two women and the machine's dirty deeds team were exchanging ideas in the parlor. The women and husbands stayed out of it as they witnessed the pros at work. The preferable option for most was to make it an accidental fall from the cliff top. Similar accidental deaths by falling had occurred before in the very same location. The presence of Tripp Joiner would be explained by his notice of Vita's car as he drove by and he stopped to investigate. He came upon the accident and decided to use it as an act of revenge for what Vita had done to him. An attempt should be made to bribe him or coerce him into changing his testimony, but if that failed, then they would fall back to the first option.

Others agreed with Vita and argued for the disappearing act. Her presence there would surely damage her acting career. This option must be executed immediately if it had chance of working. One member of the group asked if GiGi would buy off on a plan that she and Debi had been there alone sightseeing when Debi fell. She would be paid a very large sum of money if she agreed. She and her husband both spoke up and killed that proposal in its tracks. It was decided that the fabricated story would be that the women had been in Mexico at the Parker villa at Puerto Vallarta for two days and would remain there for another week. They were there on business and some time in the sun. An invisible trail must be provided for getting them there and a fake visible timeline trail created for their departure date from home.

The clandestine trip to Puerto Vallarta would take them by small plane, a Cessna 180, from the oil field inspection crew, to a small strip near Falcon Lake near the Parker fishing cabin, then across the lake by boat to a meeting with a Mexican contact, then on to Puerto Vallarta from Aeropuerto Internacional Quetzalcoatl in a PEMEX jet. The Mexican contact would be Jorge Gusman, an exec with PEMEX, the government-owned oil company.

Jorge was the judge's eyes and ears in Mexico and had been on his payroll for several years. His company had been a major customer of the Parker oil field equipment production company, and the judge found him to be the perfect contact. He had been hired legally because the Mexican government allowed their underpaid executive employees to hold second

98

outside jobs as consultants. He, like the matriarch of the Parker dynasty, had come from an aristocratic Mexican family. He was educated at Texas A&M and traveled extensively in the U.S. He had visited the Parker home on several occasions. Jorge had known Vita for several years but had not seen her since she became famous.

The judge had flown in and out of Mexico to meetings without going through customs, flying directly to Mexico City. Jorge had the clout to hide the trail and to establish fake early departure and arrival times to Puerto Vallarta. It would take a while longer to create the phony departure trip, so the girls were sent on their way before daylight and arrived at the destination before dark, where they made their presence known immediately. All of this was the easy part. They still needed to buy off Tripp to keep him from testifying before a grand jury. This would be much harder to do. As they would learn, it would be impossible.

Debi Devereaux died two days later without regaining consciousness. Her parents, sister and brothers, Zip and Dirk, were at her bedside. Tripp and his family were in the waiting room. In addition to having to deal with the pain of a dying family member they were frustrated with the lack of information coming from the police. Other suspicions began to creep in when they were told that the accused women had an alibi. They claimed to have been out of the country when the event occurred.

Dirk began to have doubts about Tripp's story and confronted him about it. "It sounds strange to me and just a little bit too coincidental that you just happened to be driving by at the exact moment that this all came down, and you just happened to look down that canyon and see three women more than a quarter mile away."

Tripp seized his arm and said, "I don't know where you're going with this, but it will cease right now! I should have told Debi to stay away from that crazy woman and I should have been looking after her more closely."

Zip pulled Dirk away to keep things from getting out of hand and the family departed with the chaplain for consolation and prayers and to grieve in private.

This new accusation, added to his own feeling of guilt and a grieving heart, was getting to Tripp. He was supposed to be a tough football player. Coach Carr had installed numbnuts into his brain, but he needed something more. Maybe prayer was what he needed.

He walked outside towards his truck and tried to start a prayer but could not find the words. He was supposed to be a born-again Christian, yet he could not pray. Something was bad wrong with him or with God. He knew that Minnie Mae would be praying.

"That's it," he said. "She will be praying so I don't need to." He just punted the ball. "God, I need to get away from here. See, that is a prayer. No, it was not, it was cursing. Thou shall not use the name of thy Lord and God in vain."

His mind was scrambled with conflicting thoughts. He was now next to his truck and he climbed in and started the motor. He must be cracking up, he thought. "They say that a mind sometimes just snaps. Who are they? What people? I need to know who they are. I need to talk to them or to somebody."

Tripp was trying to numb his brain as he raced towards home. He suddenly found himself in the tack room reaching for a bridle. His horse, Duke, came running to him as he reached the corral, expecting the usual treat. He hooked up the bridle and left the gate open as he rode bareback down his favorite path to the river.

Without the usual warmup, Duke was spurred into full gallop down the path that he knew so well. Tripp had his eyes closed and his arms spread wide as he startled Duke with a long scream. "AAAAAAH!"

Duke did not flinch as he ran wide open to the river. Tripp let the longtime feeling from childhood of comfort on horseback seep into his brain. He trusted his horse, as always. His brain began to clear. He opened his eyes. They were nearing the river. Duke was taking him to his favorite spot on earth. They had been there together many times before as he sat under the elm tree and sorted things out. He rolled off the horse and lay on his back. Then he prayed.

CHAPTER FOURTEEN

I Am a Cop, Not a Politician

"**E**xtraordinary events call for unprecedented action." Francis Hedgecock was the compromise choice to head the investigation of the Debi Devereaux death. "Call me Frank, or Bud," he said as he took the very slim file from the hands of the chief of police.

Hedgecock was considered by law enforcement pros to be the best homicide and cold case detective in the area. He had been with the Midland County Sheriff's Office for nine years, after being forced to resign from the Boston PD. He had become addicted to gambling on the horses and was frequently seen in the company of a man convicted of race fixing.

Frank was a man with a brilliant mind and an Ivy League degree. Unfortunately, his appearance did not match his pedigree. To say that he stood out in a crowd would be a gross understatement. He was 50 pounds overweight, wore frightful clothing with no socks and was never clean shaven. His bald pate and ever-present cigar finished off his cartoon-like character. Conversation with any Texan quickly identified him as a "damn Yankee" with a northeastern accent.

The Daily Racing Form was his Bible, always in his possession. Frank was a borderline alcoholic, with the gambling habit still controlling his life. He used the "cinch" technique for betting on horses and won consistently, but in turn, he then lost most of winnings betting on pro sports. His bookie made money on him by passing on his horse bets to Las Vegas and keeping his bets on pro sports.

Frank lived alone in the cheapest three-room apartment in town. The only visitors allowed were his partner and a middle-aged prostitute, who also cleaned his bathroom and kitchen and changed his bed sheets once a week. The mystery of the day would always be how he got hired in Midland. Only one person knew the answer. It came as a favor from his boss, who had fought with him in combat.

His horse bets required endless hours of study, with his face constantly buried in the Daily Racing Form. He never changed his routine. He bet only one very carefully selected horse on any given day. He would bet everything he had in hand on the horse to show only, never to win. His goal was to average a 10 percent profit. His logic was that a 10 percent per day profit on his investment was far better than bank interest. Unfortunately, betting on pro sports didn't come with a condensed handicap method.

Bud Hedgecock became a legend for his ability to obtain confessions from his perps after all others had given up. He would isolate himself with the accused and with no cameras or voice recorder present and come out of the meeting with a signed confession. This happened so often that word spread that he was using torture, physical abuse or coercion to get results. The truth was that he had two secret weapons.

One was that he was a walking, talking and breathing lie detector machine. If he could make the accused look him in the eye, he could read a lie. Only hardened criminals and the very meek could beat his machine.

Second, if the accused had a family, he would convince him that he would be a protector of their family members, especially children, while he was in prison – but only if he confessed. These were not idle promises. He had helped many family members find financial aid, jobs and education. This instinct was developed in him when he was a small boy. His father, a plumber's helper, did time for the death of a man in a barroom fight. His neighbor, a Boston policeman, aided his family in many ways and became a surrogate father to him, carrying him hunting and fishing with his own sons. He practiced baseball with Bud and taught him how to throw a curve ball. Most important, he helped his father find a job after coming home from prison. Bud became a boy scout and took the oath seriously, promising himself that when his chances came, he would emulate Mr. Miller. This method of "coercion" was never revealed to his partners or superiors, but the criminal element of local society had heard the rumors.

The newest and greenest detectives became Bud's partners because he preferred it that way. He was not impolite but considered them to be little more than drivers for him. He answered all their questions but most of their on-the-job training came from observation.

His current partner, Burt Silver, was the son of a Cherokee Indian and his Hispanic wife. Burt, known as Tonto, was a green detective but an experienced Midland cop, and a very fine one at that. He was sharp, both in dress and in brain power, and was fearless. His shooting range numbers were much better than Bud's, but he resisted the temptation to rub it in. His professionalism was evident from the get-go but he neither expected nor received a compliment from Bud. He quietly followed the lead from his superior officer and avoided too much conversation.

Tonto was curious, though, about the constant horse race handicapping of his partner. He found himself questioning the ever-present copies of The Daily Racing Form and listings of race entries. He was not a gambler but knew that Bud was. He received an abbreviated lesson on how to handicap a race, but that it was out of curiosity only. He had no desire to violate policy by betting on a horse. He had coffee with Bud every morning and waited for him to don his clothes. He never failed to toss Bud the deodorant bottle and a breath mint as he dressed. Bud preferred using perfume instead of bathing to kill his body odor. His peers avoided personal contact with him but always asked permission to read a copy of his solved case file when it had been submitted to the DA for prosecution.

The two detectives were working a cold case when given the case. Crime scene teams were dispatched to the canyon early on, but all knew that a continued downpour of rain here and upstream had flooded the entire canyon floor and had probably played havoc with any evidence in the parking lot. Bud was irate and raising cane because no search warrant had been issued for the two women or their vehicle. Someone in high places was holding it up. Politics were clearly at play, so the two detectives set out without waiting for a warrant in search of Vita Vorhees and GiGi Smurl.

They started at their individual residences. No one answered the door at either place. Soon after they left the Smurl residence, a radio call came in. What the hell were they doing? They had been observed at both places and a call had come in from the one and only Judge Parker to the sheriff and to the county judge with a vigorous complaint. Both women were out of town, he insisted. More politics. It would get worse.

Two days later, the search warrant was still on hold given that evidence had been obtained verifying the location of the women in Mexico. The

FBI had requested the CIA to use its assets in Mexico to attempt to locate the women. They were successful but had avoided contact. No attempt was made to locate Vita's convertible. By now it had been scrubbed clean and dried out.

Debi's death triggered an autopsy and a reclassification of the case to possible homicide. Bud and Tonto had been to the crime scene twice. The second visit included Tripp for a reenactment, but they learned little.

Bud made plans to attend the autopsy. He always wanted to personally see the nature and extent of the injuries. He never stuck around to watch the opening of the body. He would read the details in the coroner's report. He was debating options for interviewing the girls in Puerto Vallarta, but decided to wait on the report, considering the promised arrival of the girls back home in a few days.

No detective liked any type of interference in his investigation, and Bud hated it with a passion, especially if the interference was politically motivated. He was now on the verge of exploding. The sheriff was politely suggesting that Jimmy Jack Joiner be completely eliminated as a suspect before pressure was directed on Vita Vorhees. The governor even had his nose in it and so did the mayor. No one wanted to see a rush to judgment against the local movie star or for that matter, the superstar quarterback.

The autopsy report came out with some curious wording. "The cause of death is determined to be by blunt force trauma to the head by impact with a hard rock surface. The means of force application is not determined but is not inconsistent with a possible fall from considerable height." This news spread like wildfire, and after being washed through the media editorials and gossip grapevines, gave hope to most everyone that their heroes were safe from blame.

Two of the people who did not share in the euphoria were Bud Hedgecock and Tonto Silver. Veins stood out in his neck as the irate Bud shouted to Tonto, "They have bought the box and fixed the race."

Tonto asked, "What the heck are you talking about? What do you mean, 'bought the box?'"

Bud replied, "Don't you understand anything about horse racing? Have you never heard how races are fixed? Crooked trainers dope horses to make them run faster. They can also make them run slower by tanking them up with water right before a race or by restricting the horse's ability to breathe by stuffing gauze up a nostril. Ages ago, the industry stopped doping by testing urine from every winning horse immediately after a race. The crooks beat the system nowadays by bribing the urine tester. He swaps urine samples from another horse and all is covered up. This is called buying the box. They might also force a good horse to run slow for a while in order to build up the betting odds, then let him win. They lay their bets off away from the track in bookie parlors and such so as to not drive track odds down. This is a rare event, of course. For the most part racing is honest. Otherwise, I couldn't be making a living betting on horses."

"I did not hear you say that," said Tonto. "Now explain more about the report."

It was evident that the Parker camp was hedging their bet on the Mexican alibi story in case some evidence turned up that put some of that story in question. A witness might break down or another might turn up who claimed to have seen Vita or GiGi in town on the day of the killing. They could fall back on the theory of accidental death. This might also have a secondary benefit. It might be used to provide an easier way to bribe Tripp. All he had to say was that it was an accident, and everyone would be clean. After all, most of the public wanted it to be an accident. The pros in the "dirty business" squad had now managed to muddy up the water, making Bud's and Tonto's job more difficult.

The girls made it back to town and an interview with Vita was scheduled. GiGi was a basket case, which made it easy to keep her out of reach. She was now in psychiatric care and temporarily locked away in an undisclosed clinic.

Bud rushed to get what he could get from Vita. He knew that she would be lawyered up with the best in town and would not be allowed to say much. He would get to GiGi in time and expected to learn more then.

He was right. He got nothing from Vita. She did not show up for the scheduled interview. Two lawyers were there to inform him that she was under her doctor's care for exhaustion and would be available in a few days. He was given a written report of the bare essentials of her trip. He detected a partially hidden story of the existence of a shack-up connection between the two women and two very famous Mexican men who were connected to the movie industry. This smoke screen was implied to be the reason to conceal facts. "These details and the witnesses' names are irrelevant and none of your business. Until you can prove that they are, they will not be disclosed." The lawyer spoke like one who thinks he is dealing from a winning hand or running a brazen bluff.

Bud responded, "Please don't let the witnesses die or disappear, because I will find them sooner or later."

Bud was still unable to obtain a search warrant. He wanted to have a look at Vita's car, even though he knew that it had been scrubbed by now. He was familiar with most of the "car scrubbers" or professional detail services in town. Tonto found Vita's detailer at his third stop and learned an interesting detail. Vita sent her car in on an irregular basis but at least once a month. The car was a four-wheel trash bin. It was evident that she never violated any "Don't Mess with Texas" litter laws, because once litter entered the car, it never left until removed by the detailer.

Curiously, it had been scrubbed before it was brought in by Vita's husband, Tony Bender. He had pointed to the sign on the wall that said, "We detail every inch of your vehicle," with a nod of acknowledgment before he left.

Bud and Tonto were brainstorming strategy. "Let's go fishing, Tonto. Let's plant a little bait." Tonto's visit to the detailer had given Bud a thought. "Let's start putting a little pressure on the Parker camp."

"I thought we were holding off with the pressure until we had cleared Tripp."

"In my own mind, I have cleared him. Let's spread it all out. Let's assume for a moment that he is guilty of something. In our interview, he passed my lie detector test, but let's look at simple logic. Technically, he could have made the timeline work. He possibly had enough time, barely, to pick Debi up after church. We know she went to church. Then he went out and picked up his injured cow with her calf and stopped by Lover's Leap for some reason. Was he there sightseeing with a sick cow in the trailer? Was he trying to put the make on her? Did he decide to kill her or

106

let her fall off the cliff, go down into the canyon, rescue her, bandage her up with his own shirt and carry her to the hospital while she was still alive so that she could possibly tell the whole story?

"You can eliminate murder right away as a possibility because a killer almost never has enough remorse to try to save his victim so that victim can send him to prison.

"Next, she was wearing the same dress as she wore to church. She would have changed to jeans had she known that she was going out to a ranch with a man and his horse, or she would have gotten there in another vehicle and he just happened to find her there alone.

"Next, we know that he had been on the radio. His ranch foreman made several calls trying to find a vet to meet Tripp ASAP to deal with the cow. Let's see, what else do we have? Oh yeah, he made up this elaborate story in order to get even with this gorgeous movie star for seducing him. Come on! This doesn't even qualify for fairytale fodder. If you agree with me, hear my little plan."

Tonto wasn't sure he wanted to hear it, but he had no choice but to listen.

"I want to run an ad in the paper with a picture of the shoe that matches the missing shoe," Bud explained. We'll add some garbage about how important this shoe is to our investigation and we'll offer a reward to the one who brings it in. Now you and I both believe that the shoe probably washed downstream in the flooded canyon, but we are not really needing the shoe. We are trying to get someone in our suspect's group to bite and ask about or go searching not knowing if it might contain evidence of not. Should it happen to turn up, it will be interesting and maybe important where it was found."

As they discussed the plan, someone else was smelling a dirty story. Faye Enderling was the youngest and newest domestic staff member in the Vita Vorhees/Tony Bender home. The showplace mansion was built more as a status symbol than as living quarters. Tour guides brought busloads of tourists to gawk daily at the residence of the famous movie star.

The staff consisted of three maids, cook, gardener/driver and butler who supervised them all. He did the hiring and firing but followed cookie cutter guidelines set down by Judge Parker. Thorough vetting by

107

professional employment agencies was required. Only Catholics need apply.

The Parker family had always believed that Catholics were more honest than the rest of civilization. They, as with many of the super-rich, had a paranoia about petty theft by employees. The vetting process with Faye turned up a perfect employee by their standards.

Faye was born into a Texas hill country ranch family and grew up wanting to follow into the footsteps of her hero, Mother Teresa. She spent several months in a convent with intentions to become a nun before changing her mind. She was a frail, shy and homely little thing when she went to work as a maid. She, like all domestic staff members, was required to sign a contract, mostly for secrecy and non-disclosure purposes. It came straight out of Hollywood. It was the star's means of preventing scandalous stories from being published in the tabloids. The paparazzi must be held at bay. Faye considered her signature on the piece of paper to be akin to an oath.

On the night of the injuries to Debi Devereaux, Faye was rousted out by the butler, handed a hair dryer and instructed to dry out the interior of the blue convertible. She was irritated by this assignment but set out to complete the dirty task without complaint. After all, it would not be as bad as her daily chore of cleaning all the toilets.

She had second thoughts about which was worse when she opened the door to Vita's trash bin. She removed all the obvious trash and dumped it in its proper place. She then placed all the personal property items into a black trash bag and placed the bag on a garage shelf. It contained a hairbrush, a pair of designer's sunglasses, a discarded make-up kit, a tube of lipstick, a hair clasp, a ball cap and a girl's slipper. The drying out process took hours, but she got some pleasure in awakening her boss for approval. She ignored his displeasure.

"You should have waited until morning to wake me."

She replied, "It *is* morning!" and went off to bed.

The servants were called together for a briefing. They were told that Ms. Vorhees was in Mexico for a week or two and that she was the subject of some wild accusations. They were reminded that they were, as always, forbidden to answer questions from anyone. Not to worry. No one was allowed into the house to ask questions.

A few weeks later, the police ad seeking information about a pictured shoe and with a promise of reward appeared in the local newspaper. An alarm went off in Faye's brain and a shiver went down her spine. She recognized the shoe and slipped unnoticed into the garage. The undisturbed bag was on the shelf. Sure enough, the slipper was a dead match. Now that she was holding it, it felt like a hot potato. "What do I do now?" she asked herself as she placed it back into the bag and returned it to the shelf.

Faye knew something was going on and it smelled rotten, but she was not able to connect the dots. Her curiosity was overwhelming, but secrecy was the name of the game in this house and too many questions could cost her her job.

Her conscious was killing her. She had to do the right thing but what would that be? She wondered what Mother Teresa would do. She tried praying about it and an answer came back clear and simple. Mother Teresa would return all property to the proper owners. She took the bag contents and shoe to Marcy, Vita's personal maid and said, "These were in the garage."

Marcy returned the items to their proper places. The cap went back in a box with several others and everything else went into cabinet drawers. Faye discretely packaged the shoe and addressed it according to the newspaper ad instructions, added far more than enough postage stamps and dropped it in a postal pick-up box downtown.

Bud Hedgecock was obviously excited when he opened the package but was surprised that no one was seeking the reward. To him, this meant that someone was afraid to step forward. To carry the logic one step farther, this person could very well be afraid of the Parker family.

Tonto considered this logic to be a stretch but agreed with its potential value if they could determine where it was found. They both considered that the discovery of this new piece of evidence sufficient cause to make another plea to the DA to take the case to a grand jury. They went knocking on his door. They had long since begun to bypass their superiors and were dealing with District Attorney Walter Warren directly.

Walter found time for them right away but announced that he had to be in court in two hours for a minor bond hearing. "Windy, you promised to take another look at going to the grand jury if we brought in another piece of evidence. Now we have it. We have the missing shoe, and someone other than Tripp Joiner carried it from the scene. I need your help with a search warrant, and I need to question Vita Vorhees and GiGi Smurl and everyone else in the Parker clan right now."

Windy began a mini lecture, "Now, men, we are political animals whether we like it or not. Professional politicians run this country whether you like that or not. The higher their political office, the greater their influence. Every powerful politician who has a stake in this game is trying to exercise his or her influence. I, too, am an elected official responsible to the voters of this county.

"This may be the most important and closely scrutinized case ever to hit west Texas. I don't have to point out to you that we have two public heroes and one of the most powerful men in the country involved in one way or another. I, nor anyone else, is going to make the mistake of moving too fast.

"You have not been able to break the iron clad alibis of your suspects and there is some question now about whether it may have been an accident. Do you understand where I'm coming from here?"

Bud responded, "Hundreds of cases have been taken to grand juries, search warrants issued and arrest warrants made based on eyewitness testimony of a credible witness. Tripp Joiner is a credible witness. His family are pillars of our community. I have looked him in the eyes. He is telling the truth. I'm sure that he will agree to take a polygraph. So far, this has been a one-sided investigation. I need more access to the suspects and their alibi witnesses. I am a cop, not a politician!" With that, he and Tonto exited the building.

Less than 24 hours later, Bud got word that the Parker camp was offering up one of their alibi witnesses, a Mexican national by the name of Jorge Gusman. He was amenable to an interview in his office in Mexico City within a week. Arrangements were made and Bud was on his way in three days.

He took a cab to his hotel, ate a snack then studied his notes until midnight, though he knew the details by heart. He was up early and at the impressive PEMEX complex 20 minutes ahead of schedule. Ushered into a meeting room, he found himself outnumbered four to one.

Gusman seated himself between two lawyers and next to an interpreter. After introductions, he explained that he would be speaking through the interpreter, because although his English was decent, he wanted to make certain that every word was clearly understood by both parties.

Bud had expected this. This was clearly orchestrated by his lawyers. Bud would lose his advantage of reading eyes and facial expressions and other direct reactions to unexpected questions. Gusman would have more time to think while waiting for the interpretation. Bud understood simplistic parts of the Spanish language if spoken slowly enough but it was of little help here.

Gusman explained his business relationship with Judge Parker and the Parker family. He was also a fishing and hunting partner of the judge and Two Gun Malham. They fished for large-mouth bass on Falcon Lake as well as other lakes in Mexico in the Parker's Ranger bass boat. They also hunted white wing doves on both sides of the Falcon Lake near the Parker cabin in the U.S. and near his lake home on the Mexican side. They preferred dove hunting in Mexico because there were more doves in the Mexican corn fields than in the American maize fields.

The evident strategy was to overwhelm Bud with meaningless details, but Bud made no effort to slow down the drivel. Gusman rambled on and on as if to delay the questioning. He finally began to disclose details of his part in the alibi.

At the urging of a friend, whose name he would not reveal, he agreed to arrange an introduction to Vita Vorhees. This friend was a famous Mexican movie star with a worldwide reputation as a Latin lover. He wanted to become personally acquainted and to make a movie with her. Gusman sold Vita on the idea and she came to the Parker cabin on Falcon Lake with her constant companion, GiGi Smurl.

He explained that the party of four spent more than a half day boating and partying in his powerboat. At the end of the day, they traveled via plane to Puerto Vallarta from Nuevo Laredo, where the party continued on for two more days. At that time, his friend left for California and he to

111

Mexico City.

Gusman was very clear and sure about the dates but refused to provide more details. Not only would he not give up the friend's name but refused to answer questions about the plane's ownership or description, and Bud still had no clue about other corroborating witnesses on the key first day of the meeting.

The Parker camp had thrown him another whitewashed bone but maybe he had opened a small crack. When enough small cracks are opened, a large one develops, large enough to break the case wide open. What he needed urgently was a face-to-face meeting with Vita Vorhees in order to use his lie detecting eyes to sort out the truth from her famous blue eyes. She was nowhere to be found for the moment, but Bud could be patient. Politics had slowed him down but not stopped him.

CHAPTER FIFTEEN

An Unexpected Bonus

"**H**ey, Tripp. How are you doing? This is Mule Sherman from Houston. Do you remember me?"

"Yeah. Sure. Of course. It's been a while. How are you?"

"I'm doing great; I'm just looking for a way to get my $40 back from our little golf bets at the celebrity golf get-together after the Texas Hall of Fame dinner. Remember?"

"Yeah, sure, Mule. I should have raised the stakes on you when I saw you walk on the first tee wearing western boots."

"What you didn't know, old boy, was those were special golf shoes designed to look like boots. I got the idea many years ago from seeing a pair on Roy Rogers at the Crosby Pro Am. I'll have you to know I was playing to a three handicap when I was your age, and my money was not so easily taken in those days."

Mule got down to serious business. "Listen, here's what I really called about. I've been reading about the huge mess you seem to be in with the unfortunate death of that young singer, and I'm calling to offer my help."

"Well, I appreciate that, but as you would expect, I've consulted with my family lawyer and have an appointment with the N.Y. Giants law firm. I've made no choices yet, but I'm sure I'll get the legal help I need."

"Yes, of course, but I am talking about help on top of that.

"I'll explain, but first, since this is not yet a lawyer/client relationship, I need to ask you a question. The snoop who wrote the tabloid article quotes the ER people as having said that your hospital report mentioned two other women, one being Judge Parker's granddaughter, were present at the scene. All the main media headlines and stories seem to follow that same line. Is that true? Just say yes or no."

"I will answer that with a yes but won't answer any more questions right now."

"Good, then I'll go on. I have a serious bone to pick with Judge Parker and his political machine since he sabotaged my campaign for governor when I ran against him. It took months and a lot of money to finally fix the blame. If you recall the media story, I had just defended a high-profile Wall Street broker on trial for Ponzi scam and gotten him acquitted. According to the story, my huge fee was being paid, in part and with his help, by insider trading. I was leading in the polls prior to this and judge was running third. Of course, neither of us won and the rest is history.

"I want to get even with that bastard but there's more to this mess that you may or may not know. You are dealing with a ruthless political machine here, one that will stop at nothing to get what they want. Someone from the scene is going to be blamed for this death, and it ain't going to be a member of the Parker family. Word on the street is that the DA is being pressured to call a grand jury in order to indict *you* for murder. You need a very good criminal defense attorney. Immediately.

"Now, I'm prepared to be your lawyer on a pro bono basis except for expenses. To be perfectly honest with you, I need a high-profile case right now, and this case is about to become as high as they come. We can win this case, and my financial rewards will come from added business that a victory will bring. And rest assured, we *will* win."

Mule continued to describe his deal. "If you take me on, we will make a temporary verbal agreement for now that you can cancel later, if you wish, after you talk to your camp. This will allow the rest of this conversation to be confidential under lawyer/client protection laws. If you agree to this, we can go forward with the full account of the events and then my opinion. What do you think?"

Tripp answered, "I'll give you all the details and I'd like to hear your comments but that's all I want for now. If we continue later, we'll set up a joint meeting with my family lawyer and the Giants legal firm. Ok?"

"Yeah, fine, Tripp, but what I wanted to say first is that you are dealing with an organization that is drunk on power and will stop at nothing to get what they want. Mr. Parker will not let his movie star granddaughter's

114

career be destroyed by a grand jury witness, even if he happens to be a famous NFL quarterback and local hero. The pressure will come in many forms and if you don't cave in, your life itself could be in serious danger. Don't be caught off guard just because you were nearly a member of the Parker family. Now send me the complete details and we'll move on from there."

Long after the call, Tripp's head continued to spin as he analyzed what had just happened. The most famous trial lawyer in America had offered to join his case pro bono. Of course, his name had entered his mind from the beginning. He was a fellow Texan who grew up in Ft. Worth and played football at the University of Houston. He had earned his reputation as "lawyer of the stars" by defending and winning murder cases for high profile defendants such as movie stars and the super-rich and famous. He could rightfully claim that he had never lost a capital murder case. A few of his cases had ended in hung juries and had eventually been pled down to lesser charges, but it was true. He had never lost a murder case.

Tripp's only previous face-to-face association with Mule was a brief golf fundraiser in which they played a few holes together and shared the same table assignment at the banquet. But Tripp had known his reputation for years, as had most every other news watcher in the country.

Mule's peers marveled at his phenomenal courtroom success rate, and many were determined to follow suit, so they analyzed everything about him. His standard costume, a buckskin coat with tasseled sleeves, shoestring western tie, cowboy hat, oversized belt buckle and silver toed boots, were an easy call. He wanted to draw everlasting attention to himself, to be the center of attention in the courtroom. He would pull attention away from his client and keep the jury focused on his every word. He was intelligent and always well prepared but there had to be something more. Maybe it was just luck, or could it be "magic" of some sort? Truth is, there was magic, but the others never discovered it.

Herman Sherman's magic began just as with practically every toddler ever born. It began with an adult performing a hidden coin trick and shouting, "Magic!" as the coin miraculously appeared. Magic was introduced into that child's vocabulary and would forever remain. More tricks were learned, but his Grandfather Miller taught a special brand of magic. One that he was expert in by years of practice.

He began to teach the little boy how to read the minds of people by studying their body language, facial expressions and the answers to leading questions. His grandfather gathered up every piece ever printed on the subject and placed the details in Herman's hands. He absorbed every word like a sponge. Without knowing it, a magic tool was planted that would eventually give lawyer Sherman an "edge."

Herman was the only grandchild to his maternal grandfather, a widower who devoted most of his spare time to entertaining little Herman. He was determined to educate him in his field of medicine and turn his practice over to him when the time came. He was a practicing psychiatrist with an office in downtown Ft. Worth. Over time, he was hired by many lawyers as an expert witness in trials mostly involving cases involving clients pleading innocence by reason of insanity. He was also used frequently in jury selection procedures. This sideline practice would eventually come into play as he attempted to influence the future of the youngster.

Herman was born with natural athletic ability. He was large for his age and had oversized hands. Yet he could run with the fastest kids in the neighborhood. If a ball of any shape or size was included in a game, he was there competing and loving every minute of it. It was natural for him to constantly look for a move that gave him an advantage or "edge" over his opponent.

This strategy was naturally reinforced by every coach in every sport that he participated in. Winning meant everything. When team sports came along, long hours of practice came with it. Grandfather Miller often took him to practices and later to games. When winning games started to be a natural expectation, superstition forced him to begin to wear the same shirt to every game. This continued even after the tattered rag had to be worn out of sight.

Around the time of high school graduation, Mule Sherman found himself deeply in love with a cheerleader whom he had met in his drama class and who had shared the lead in a school play. She was only a junior with no college plans when Mule went off to the University of Houston on a football scholarship. He intended follow his grandfather's footsteps by getting a psychiatry degree, and Mule's sweetheart planned to follow him to Houston a year later and to pursue a law degree.

Once together again, long range plans for marriage began to form. The little sweetheart began to push Mule towards a change in his major to match hers. Her dream was for the two of them to join in a private little romantic law practice back home in Ft. Worth where after a few years, he could have a great future in politics. "You have already gotten me in the governor's office, and I haven't even graduated from college yet," he joked.

"No. President of the U.S.A." They were curled up on a Galveston beach talking about their future together.

"No thanks. I'll stick with my childhood dream."

But once again, the art of female persuasion raised its powerful wand, and only two months later, Mule had changed his mind and his major. He had no way of knowing at the time, of course, that this little dimpled brunette had provided him with a path to a riches and fame.

Mule's college football career ended with a few pro teams nibbling about, but one more look at his crooked nose in the mirror and a twinge of pain from his ruined left knee stopped his temptation. Brains prevailed over brawn and he accepted a full scholarship to Stanford School of Law. He arrived on campus in style, driving a new Oldsmobile convertible, a graduation gift from his family, and wearing an engraved locket from his sweetheart that read, "My heart is yours forever."

Unfortunately, after a year apart, she began dating someone else and later married one of his old football teammates. He then proclaimed himself to be a "confirmed lifetime bachelor playing the field." His nickname "Mule" bothered him little when the attraction of his Olds and pocket full of money supplied by his grandfather kept female companions lined up.

Graduation with honors earned him a good selection of job offers. Mule took a position with a prestigious L.A. firm. Although initially a boring career with few opportunities to perform in the courtroom, he finally got a huge break.

A case came to the firm representing an aging, has been movie actor who was charged with killing his fourth wife and her current lover. This case was a surefire loser and none of the senior attorneys wanted to touch it, so it was dumped on Mule's desk. He gladly took it with the large payday that it brought. He set out determined to win it, and did just that, with a plea of innocence by reason of insanity. His psychiatric magic had given him the "edge."

Mule's stardom skyrocketed him to the top of the case load. His winning record continued, and his fame spread nationwide. His case load spread with it. He traveled a lot because his rich and famous clients were being tried near where the crimes were committed. His handpicked team traveled with him from city to city and set up shop in the offices of a local attorney who would be added for his or her local knowledge. Others, such as local private investigators, were added as needed. The core team became family and were on call 24 hours a day. Only the very wealthy could afford this team.

After several years of fame and fortune, Mule began to feel the itch of running for political office, just as his high school sweetheart had dreamed. By then, he had split his ties with the original firm and opened his own office. He moved it to Houston, where he was a folk hero, for the sole purpose of eventually running for governor of Texas and he began to build a political base. He married a young paralegal nearly half his age and built a large home where they started to plan for a family.

After three short years, he did run for governor in a five-man field and was soundly defeated by the antics of Judge Horace Parker. This race left him not only financially weak but also the sworn enemy of Judge Parker and his entire family. But his star with the rich and famous did not dim.

Now Tripp saw that start shining on his case. A few days after their first conversation, Mule followed up. "If I may, let me make a suggestion. Give me a few more of key details of the incident now and I'll get the complete report given to the police by you and the others present. Let's see if we can't put a great team together."

Tripp was still uncertain. "The Giants organization is standing behind me and brought up the name of Will Clarkson. Do you know him?"

"Yes. He's considered to be the best around with cross examination of prosecution witnesses. He usually demands the role of chief counsel, so he may not want to work for me. And he will surely not be working pro bono."

"I'll get back to you."

CHAPTER SIXTEEN

As Big as Footballs

Bud and Tonto snooped around Falcon Lake doing boring grunt work as they looked for anything that might verify or disprove the alibi story. They found no records of fuel purchase or other service for the boat, even though one particular marina attendant had serviced the boat on several occasions in the past. Bud hoped to find mention of engine use according to recorded hour meter readings, but none existed. Yet one interesting fact did turn up.

Marina sales were down considerably on the crucial day of the alleged boating party due to bad weather and poor boating conditions. There had been no mention of this in the interview with Jorge Gusman. This was no major breakthrough, but it was another indication that they were on the right track. Their second visit to Nuevo Laredo had still not produced a list of departing private planes. Mexican requirements for keeping that type of information did not equal U.S. FAA standards.

The Parker informant in the sheriff's office passed along daily information and when the judge received this update, he was not unduly alarmed, but Lavita Vorhees was. She was becoming more nervous by the day as these little nails continued to hammer into her perceived coffin. The missing shoe discovery was particularly disturbing to her if not to the team hired to protect her.

She had been told to stay away from GiGi but disobeyed and went to visit her at a psycho ward. She found her sane but freaked out about going to jail for something that Lavita had done and that she had try to stop. Sooner or later she and Lavita would be interrogated, and Lavita was not sure that GiGi could maintain the alibi. She told no one, especially Judge Parker or her mother that she was scheming again. She had manipulated Tripp Joiner before, and she just might be able to do it again. It was worth a try. She knew Tripp's daily ranch routine and made her plans to catch him alone.

All the distractions of the past several weeks had thrown Tripp behind in

119 of the past several weeks had thrown Tripp behind in

119

his Double-Bar-Six ranch work. He was back to his routine of climbing out of bed at five, showering and shaving then having toast, nuked bacon and coffee for breakfast before meeting with Rod Rodriquez, ranch foreman. Rod always arrived at seven and let himself in through the unlocked door of the double wide.

Tripp had his face buried in the planning notes when he heard a vehicle door slam and the front door open. A glance at his watch told him that Rod was an hour early. "Strange," he thought as he heard the footsteps halt behind him. "Grab a cup if it's perked and grab a chair."

"Good morning, darling." The voice blew him out of his boots. He turned before he had completely overcome the shock to find Vita Vorhees standing with a big smile on her beautiful face.

"You have bigger balls than footballs!" he shouted.

"The word is boobs not balls. I think you meant to say you have boobs as big as footballs, "she responded facetiously. "Have you forgotten so soon? I bet you haven't had a woman since you tried to drive me through the mattress at the Hilton hotel."

"Get out! Get out, now!" he shouted. "You are not welcome here. Get out now." He rose from his chair, grabbed her by the arm and the back of her belt, lifted her so that her feet had no traction on the floor and ushered her towards the door.

"You have been indicted for murder," she shouted. This stopped him in his tracks.

"That is an old rumor planted by your people trying to coerce and frighten me."

"No, it just happened yesterday. I got it from a good source. Let me explain."

"Tell your story and get the hell out of here."

"OK, but I have some good news. I have brought you some legal defense money. I scrounged up almost 50 thousand dollars. Most of it came out of mother's safe and she doesn't know it yet. I can get my hands on another 50."

"I can handle my own legal expenses. This is clearly some sort of a bribe attempt and I am not buying."

"No, wait. Let me finish. I didn't mean to kill Debi. It was an accident. We were fighting. She could just as easily have killed me. It was not murder and it can never be proved in court even if gets that far. GiGi and I picked her up that day to present her a trip to Hollywood – every girl's dream. I had the contract in my hand and showed it to her. She was excited but said she couldn't sign, that she was underage. She would need her parent's signature, and besides, she had a signed contract where she was now working.

"I explained that all of that could be worked out, that she should sign it and then take to her parents. She was making up all kinds of excuses and I began to lose my temper and she slapped my face and started the fight. We fought on the parking lot and she took off down into the canyon and there we fought some more. GiGi was trying to break it up but that little hot-blooded Cajun wouldn't stop. She spat in my face and cursed me over and over.

"We were headed out to the car ahead of the storm when it all started over again. You saw only the very end of it but is was an accident and I will swear in the name of Christ Jesus that it was."

"I saw it and it was no accident. How can you call the continued banging of her head on a rock an accident?"

"Let me finish." She was now about to get into the real meat of her scheme. "If you don't want the money, give it all to her family. I can start a fund and raise at least a million dollars. Maybe more. The autopsy report shows that it could have been an accident. All our fans want it to be an accident. All the politicians, even the governor, want it to be an accident. All you have to do is to change your story to say that you came up on the scene because you were flagged down on the highway by GiGi and you came down into the canyon where I was rendering aid and then you carried her to the hospital. We were all soaking wet and all messed up mentally, so you sent us home. Nothing can be done to bring that girl back, but something can be done to make life a little easier for her family. What do you say? Will you do this for them, for you and your

121

family and for me for old times' sake? Don't forget your football career. This may end it. Take the deal!

"There is one other thing for you to worry about. I fear for your safety. You are in danger. The judge will never let you testify before a grand jury. He will stop you one way or another. Think about your baby daughter. What will she do without a father?"

"Stop it! Now, Vita, that is a threat on my life and I now know that this all came from the judge and not from your evil little mind. My answer is *no*. Now goodbye." He pushed her out the door as he added, "Tell the judge to come after me if he's brave enough and I will enjoy tying a can to his lard ass as I send him back where he came from."

"Don't you know that he will send Two Gun or someone else? He will not come himself." She gave him the sign of the bull as the door slammed behind her.

Rod drove up as Vita was leaving. He came in the door saying, "I saw your little sweet thing leave this briefcase on your doorstep. I thought that you had finally learned your lesson about dealing with her."

"It isn't what you think. The judge just sent over 50 grand in bribe money with a promise of 50 more."

"Then you need to report it to the police right now."

"I don't think so. She is calling it defense money assistance and is claiming that it came from her and her mother's personal funds. I need to think about it for a sec but I am inclined to go shove it up the judge's ass. I would get a great deal of pleasure out of that. Dump the money out and count it. I need a witness to this whatever I do."

Rod counted the money. "49,400 dollars. The judge is a little short."

This made Tripp count it himself and he paused. If it had come from the judge, it would have been exactly $50,000. But he continued. "I want some pictures of this. I need a shot of us with the money and I need to document the date. Grab yesterday's newspaper off the couch and we will include it in the shot."

After taking the photos, Tripp said, "I want you to go with me to the judge's office. He will be there at nine o'clock sharp if he is in town today. Either way we will leave it on his desk. I will tell the detectives about this later and show them the photos. We have plenty of time to finish up business here, finish our breakfast and make it on time."

"I believe you are making a mistake with this move. The cops will need the real money, not photos, for evidence. There may be fingerprints and other evidence and don't forget about Two Gun. You can't go in there threatening the judge. That ape might just shoot you."

"I'm going and you are going with me. You will wait in the office door and do nothing but watch."

They arrived a few minutes after nine and Tripp pushed past the protesting receptionist. Rod waited in the doorway. The judge was behind his desk and Two Gun was sitting on the couch with a cup of coffee in his hand. Tripp took long strides across the office with a smile on his face and said, "Good morning, Judge. I am returning something that belongs to you."

"Thanks but no thanks."

Tripp plopped the case on the desk and promptly left, with Rod trailing behind. No words came from the mouths of the judge or of Two Gun, but the receptionist was still protesting.

"So much for shoving anything up anywhere," sighed Rod.

"Now that was a stupid move. That boy has always been impulsive, easily provoked and prone to make stupid mistakes." Judge opened the bag and examined the money.

"First of all, this is not my money. I think that I know where it probably came from. Another stupid move and from my own granddaughter at that."

Two Gun spoke up, "It would have been a really, really stupid move if he had made any kind of threatening move towards you. I would have put a bullet between his eyes and that would have solved our problem once and for all."

"Now that would have been the worst move of all. I am talking about shooting him in front of a witness."

"Are you saying that I can shoot him so long that there are no witnesses?"

"No, I'm saying that if he becomes provoked enough to attack you, an officer of the law, then you can legally use your weapon to defend yourself. Do you understand what I am telling you?"

"Yes, I understand exactly what you just told me." A final solution had just been designed.

Tripp was in no mood to carry on a conversation with Rod on the return to the ranch. He could not shake thoughts of the deal Vita was offering. Maybe he should call Zip Devereaux and brief him. A million dollar offer to the family might should be mentioned. If he changed his story, it would make him a perjurer but that would be small potatoes in the equation. He probably would not be prosecuted anyway. The politicians and their ilk would want to protect the image of the local hero. If the Devereauxs involved their lawyer in this, and they most certainly would, the amount that the Parker camp might be willing to settle for could be in the millions of dollars. Knowing Vita, she was already looking for a way to approach the Devereaux family. Maybe he had been a little hasty. He decided to call Zip.

Zip did not like the idea. He, as did Tripp, wanted to send Vita Vorhees and GiGi Smurl to prison. He believed that his parents would agree with him. His brother would probably vote yes if he thought that he would get a share of the payoff. His family was not in desperate need of money. Just the opposite. His father's chain of pawn shops were thriving, and he, himself would be joining the business when his pro football career was over. However, he ultimately agreed to take the offer to his father.

His father's response was quick and emphatic. "No! No way!" He wanted punishment for his daughter's killers and was shocked that anyone would consider otherwise. No one could know that the fate of Jimmy Jack Joiner had just been sealed.

CHAPTER SEVENTEEN

This is My Angel

The idea to eliminate Tripp Joiner as a threat to the imprisonment of Lavita Vorhees by killing him sounded good at the time. But now, as Two Gun began his planning, doubts began to pile up in his mind. His target would not be an easy mark. Sure, Two Gun was a skilled marksman with either hand and always had his two Glocks holstered on his belt. And true, Tripp was never armed in public. His only firearm was his 30/30 saddle gun mounted in his truck's window rack and probably not loaded. But Tripp was a large man in superb physical condition and conditioned beyond football playing shape by his life as a rodeo steer wrestler and roper. He was intelligent and fearless and much quicker on his feet than was Two Gun.

On the other hand, Two Gun was a weightlifter and 30 pounds heavier. "Why worry?" he thought. "This killing is never going past the shooting with my pistols anyhow."

Tripp must be lured to a time and place of Two Gun's choosing and without the presence of witnesses. Tripp would be attacking an officer of the law who has a right -- no, a duty -- to defend himself and prevent the deranged man from harming innocent people. It must all be executed to perfection because the investigation would be intense and performed by the FBI. The shooting of a super celebrity by the bodyguard of one of the most powerful men in the world, one who carries a grudge against the victim, would garner scrutiny by every imaginable source.

Tripp must be irate and reckless when he arrives. The best way to make this happen was to frighten his wife, Two Gun thought, and that would be easy to do. She would be easy to find at work, and he had the advantage of approaching her in a marked law enforcement vehicle with "Sheriff" printed on the doors and with a siren and blue lights in good working order.

Deputy Malham spent long minutes working out the details with numerous options for changes in circumstances. The first move would be to deliver a friendly message.

Patricia Joiner walked to her car after a trying day at work and noticed the police car parked next to hers with the driver door adjacent to her door. She recognized Two Gun's smirk and immediately smelled trouble but did not panic or show fear. Instead she took an aggressive approach, with a sarcastic, "What are you doing here? Shouldn't you be protecting the judge from one of his many enemies?"

"Very funny. Ha. Ha. As a matter of fact, believe it or not, I am here to perform a good deed for your husband. The judge doesn't know anything about this visit, and I prefer that it be kept that way. I happen to be fond of Tripp from his teenage days when he practically lived at the mansion. He used to fool around with my weights, and I showed him how to develop film in my darkroom. We talked football and I even took him with me to the shooting range. Ask him about this and he'll say that is all true. No, I am here to ask for a private meeting between the two of us alone. He's placed himself in a position of serious personal danger but there's a way out if he'll listen to me."

"Two Gun, surely by now you know that Tripp and I are separated. I am no longer speaking to him so I can't and won't give him your message. Besides, I don't believe a word you're saying. I'll be leaving now and don't contact me again, or I *will* call the FBI because I sure don't trust the sheriff or any other law enforcement office in Ector County."

"Ok, sister, but I promise you that he'll meet with me one way or the other." Both cars peeled out of the parking lot.

Patricia went straight to Tripp when she arrived at the ranch, and after describing in detail all that was said, Tripp asked if she had been threatened or felt the least bit threatened. She said no.

Tripp reacted just as Two Gun anticipated. He was irate and was ready to confront him. Patricia countered, "I honestly believe he knows how hot tempered you are, and he is baiting you. I fear for your safety. There is nothing bigger in the judge's life than his movie star princess granddaughter. His only child is a worthless drunk and he lives only for his granddaughter. He'll do anything on this earth to protect her from prison and to save her career, including killing you. If I can see this, why can't you?"

"No, I don't think so. They have offered a deal and I think Two Gun is trying to sweeten the offer. Vita brought me a bribe of $50,000 and an offer of one mil to the Devereaux family, which was rejected. I don't believe the judge would chance murder, but I will not go to them. They must come to me with witnesses present. They will eventually offer considerably more money to the family, and Zip will keep me informed."

"Another thing," Patricia replied, "That rumor about charging you with murder is still floating around."

"That won't fly. Trust me. Now you go on and keep me informed. You do know, I hope, that I would still like to have a sensible conversation with you about our getting back together. It appears that you still have some feelings for me after all."

She responded, "You are the father of my daughter and nothing more." With that she walked out the door.

Two Gun waited two days, and having heard nothing from Tripp, made his next move. Patricia's threat about contacting the FBI troubled him. He considered it a bluff but decided to force the action. He followed Patricia's car well clear of town before showing himself with his blue lights and forced her to pull over. He wasn't expecting to hear such foul language coming from the mouth of a traffic speeding violator. He never had before.

He issued his genuine threats between her shouts. He informed her that Tripp's life would be in serious danger if he didn't agree to meet. Possible collateral damage might accidentally spill over to his family members as well.

Patricia drove away with an eye on the rear-view mirror, half expecting him to follow. She was truly frightened now. She and Tripp and her family had all been threatened. To her, this included little Mary Mae. This was overwhelming. She dared not tell Tripp lest he go after Two Gun and the judge and fall right into their trap.

She decided to call the FBI but had a hard time convincing an agent that she had a serious complaint based on a law enforcement officer pulling her over for what appeared to be a traffic violation and issuing her a warning for cursing. He clearly did not believe the part about the threat on her husband's life. Her instructions, if she wanted to pursue the matter further, would be to come into his office and fill out and sign a complete report. She informed him that she would do just that, but she was still undecided about what to do.

By the next day Two Gun was getting desperate. He had expected Tripp to show up by now and the wear and tear on his nerves from being on high alert was making him edgy. No more 'Cool Hand Luke' warrior mode. He wanted it over and done with. In his mind, time was running out. It was time to put the fear of God into that woman in order to pull Tripp out.

Patricia played right into his hands. It was near dark when she left work. She had picked up Mary Mae after school for a dental appointment and returned to her office to finish up paperwork and to check on a seriously ill puppy.

As fate would have it, Two Gun's desperate move would be made against a car with a small child inside. He waited at a distance for Patricia to exit the parking lot. She instinctively looked for Two Gun's car. It was not in sight. The only vehicle she saw was a parked pickup truck far down the street. She didn't notice that the truck pulled out as she did and remained behind her.

She was several miles out of town when she noticed vehicle headlights coming up behind her. She expected the vehicle to pass, but instead she felt a bump against her rear and then felt her car being pushed at an accelerated rate down the now darkened highway.

She tried the brakes, but the more powerful vehicle was speeding up even as her tires squealed and rubber burned. Mary Mae began crying as the car began to weave and lose control. She tried driving faster but to no avail. Then the spin came. She came to a stop after several turns, with her rear wheels on the shoulder, the front wheels on the highway and the truck blocking her movement.

Two Gun exited the truck from the door close to her front bumper. Patricia's instincts told her to flee for their lives, so she pressed on the gas pedal and ran right at the startled assailant. He leaped out of the way as she crashed into his truck door. The severe impact moved the vehicle a few feet and she took advantage of the ample escape room and sped

128

away back towards town.

Two Gun was unable to open the smashed door and ran around the truck to the passenger's door. Finding it locked, he broke out the window to gain entrance. By the time he was able to pursue, Patricia was well down the road, but she was driving a damaged vehicle. He overtook her in minutes.

He was now enraged to a point well beyond reason, with his sole thought to crash the other vehicle. He used the usual police hook move on her left rear bumper and put her car into a violent spin that threw it off the shoulder embankment and down a 10-foot drop, where it landed upside down with the roof smashed down, crushing the two people inside. Patricia's skull was broken, and she was passing through delirium into unconsciousness.

Her only, brief thought was Mary Mae. Patricia was relieved by the sound of a tap, tap, tap and "To the river and back," which were actually the sounds of damaged spinning wheels and a moaning radiator, not the playful song of Mary Mae. She would not learn for more than a week that the red tap shoes would forever remain in their special place beneath the red jumping rope with the blue handles. Her darling daughter was dead, her tiny eight-year-old body crushed in her seat.

Two Gun hesitated and tried to clear his mind as he exited his truck and made his fateful decision. He decided to separate himself from the crime. He drove away before anyone came on the scene. He headed towards town and forced himself to stop at a phone booth to report the accident without giving his name. His conscience, honed over years of law enforcement and helping others, got control over his better judgment.

He then headed towards Midland with a plan. He knew of a chop shop, owned by a distant cousin who was suspected but never convicted of modifying stolen cars by inserting parts containing serial numbers from wrecks. He had no trouble persuading the man using a combination of cash and blackmail to modify his truck.

Most of his original vehicle was demolished in a crushing machine and on its way to a scrap yard within a matter of days. His rebuilt truck was equipped with old parts purchased in Amarillo.

Tripp Joiner was in his truck more than 20 miles away when his ranch family reached him on the radio and told that the accident had occurred, and Patricia and Mary Mae had been taken to the trauma center. He flirted with danger as he sped to their bedsides. He parked illegally at the ambulance entrance and left the keys in the ignition as he raced inside.

He was told that Patricia was in surgery, but no one knew or was willing to tell him where Mary Mae was. Finally, he was told that she had not survived and was in the hospital morgue. He demanded to be taken there but was refused. Tripp grasped the nearest doctor by the collar and demanded, under the threat of bodily harm, to be taken to her.

A small procession moved down the stairway to the basement as keys to the morgue were located and a security guard was called. Tripp entered the dark room alone. Someone turned on the lights and Tripp spotted the tiny body under a sheet. She was all alone. That set his tears flowing and he burst into uncontrollable weeping as he pulled the cover from her face.

The security guard arrived but Tripp informed him to leave the room. He told the guard told to get out and "get out now."

The guard complied, closing the door behind him. Tripp picked up his daughter and held her tiny body to his chest as he begged God over and over again to bring Mary Mae back to life. Finally, he got reasonable control of himself then raised her over his head and said "Oh, God, this is my angel. Take her into heaven now and introduce her to all the other angels. Her name is Mary Mae Joiner. I am her father and her mother is fighting for her own life. Please, God, keep her alive for me. Amen."

He then gently lay her body down and neatly wrapped her in the covering with her face exposed. He caressed and straightened her hair, carefully arranging each curl in its proper place. Then he stood erect and walked out of the room past the gathering crowd without saying a word or taking notice of their tears or words.

"We are praying for you."

"We love you."

"God be with you."

Back upstairs, Patricia was still in surgery, so Tripp sat down to wait for family members to arrive. No previous pain had ever felt like this. He silently prayed "God, help me," over and over. "Spare my Patricia."

CHAPTER EIGHTEEN

Death Comes Calling

The waiting room for the intensive care unit became the new home for Tripp Joiner and his grandparents as well as for Patricia's mother, father and other family members who rotated in as Patricia, still unconscious, struggled for life. Each took turns in the bedside vigil. One thing was clear. No one wanted to be the one to break to Patricia the news of her daughter's death.

Tripp felt that it was his responsibility, but he was finding it harder and harder to stay in the room. He could not stay seated for more than a few minutes at a time. He kept an unwanted feeling in the pit of his stomach, far worse than when he was trying to execute a football play from behind his own goal line on third and long with his team behind, time running out and no open receiver. Panic was eating at his soul. He needed to do something but could not decide what the best next move was.

A public announcement had been made that funeral services for Mary Mae would be private and held at a later date. A traditional wake and viewing would last for three days at the selected local funeral home, but formal services had been postponed indefinitely. After seven days without significant changes in Patricia's condition, Mary Mae was interred in a vault near the graves of Tripp's parents to await the hoped-for recovery of her mother. Patricia was expected to live but with some degree of brain damage. Only time would tell, and this fact alone was the primary concern of the moment.

The FBI was contacted shortly after all agreed that this car crash most certainly was the work of Two Gun Malham, just as Patricia had warned. Tripp's conversation with the agent who took his call became heated as he stated that his daughter would have been saved from death if the FBI had responded promptly to his wife's complaint of harassment by this uniformed law officer in his patrol car. He was promised an investigation to be initiated with an interview. No one had shown up for the interview after two days, and now Tripp was being restrained by family members from putting his revenge into personal action.

Recognizing his frame of mind, his family members assigned him an escort whenever he left the hospital, but without his knowledge. There were times when he wanted to be alone but found this hard to do. He decided that he could wait no longer on the FBI. He insisted on starting an investigation into the activities of Malham, and in particular, the condition of his truck.

The examination of Patricia's wrecked car showed that the culprit was driving a white vehicle and that it most certainly had suffered extensive damage. He could also turn to state police. Local and county law enforcement could not be trusted for obvious reasons. Even then, if rumors were true that Judge Parker "owned the current governor," calling the state police would not be wise. He hired a private investigator, and his first action was to search for Two Gun's truck and deputy's car.

No truck was found at his residence and his police car was undamaged. A search of every repair shop in the county turned up nothing.

Tripp had now accepted the gracious offer to use the hospital ICU private staff lounge as a refuge from autograph seekers and conversations with well-meaning football fans. Patricia's parents were troubled by the terrible irony of having Patricia's struggle for life take place in a building named for Judge Horace Parker. They located an alternate entrance without that name posted above the door. Their discomfort would have been much greater had they known that Judge Parker asked for and was granted daily condition reports on their daughter from the hospital administrator. Another example of the unlawful use of Parker muscle. No administrator would dare risk the loss of charity funds from the Parker Foundation.

Tears of joy came to the family of Patricia Joiner on the first unclouded day in a week. An omen perhaps. Patricia experienced a conscience moment for the first time since the tragic car crash. The moment was brief but was followed by another a few hours later. The doctors had recognized positive signs for a couple days and were cautiously optimistic but suppressed their optimism until they were sure that the she was totally out of the coma. Now was the time for celebration.

Patricia was making attempts to talk but the tubes in her throat and drugs in her system made her words unintelligible. This came on the eighth day after the car crash. Tripp was at her bedside. Her eyes told him that she

133

recognized him, and she smiled. It was clear that she had no memory of the accident. The tubes were removed, enabling her to speak clearly for the first time. Her first question was, "Where is Mary Mae?"

She was struggling to get out of bed but restraining straps held her firm. Her thrashing caused her great pain and she had to be sedated. She then drifted back to sleep.

Key members of the staff assembled to discuss her next awakening, which was expected in a few hours. They were ecstatic that her speech had been clear and coherent. But it was agreed to by all that news of her daughter's death must be withheld for a while longer. No one would speculate as to how much longer nor could they decide how to break the unbearable news. She did come awake again that afternoon and was told that Mary Mae could not be brought to her in her present condition.

She detected by the look on Tripp's face as tears welled up in his eyes that something was wrong. Her mother and father turned away. "Something is wrong. What is it? Is it … it's Mary Mae, isn't it?" She paused momentarily as memories of the terrible encounter on that fateful night unfolded in her mind. She screamed out at the top of her weakened voice. "Oh, God, no, no, no! Mary Mae is dead. I can see it in your eyes!" She fainted. More sedation followed.

Just over two hours later she awakened again with, "Tell me it isn't true." But no one could. Her restraints now removed, she could reach out for the hugs and kisses and weeping that come with this kind of realization that his world had come to an end. She was finally able to blurt out, "It was Two Gun. Two Gun killed my daughter and tried to kill me. I tried to warn you. I tried to warn everybody, but no one listened." She then began to weep again for Mary Mae.

As she again tried to get out of bed, family members were ushered out of the room. Restraints were replaced and an attempt was made to calm Patricia down without sedation. Her helpless cries continued to be heard in the private waiting area, where the families held each other and wept uncontrollably.

In less than an hour, details of this scene were being given over the phone to Judge Parker. The speaker was obviously having trouble with some details and refused to answer some of the Parker questions. He

134

remembered something being mentioned about calling the FBI immediately. Concern for this clearly showed in Parker's voice and brought another barrage of questions. With this the caller hung up the phone and left the judge cursing to himself about the stupid mistakes of Two Gun Malham.

Tripp was already preparing his next move. Confirmation of his suspicions by Patricia that Malham was the killer pushed him over the limit of his patience. He had a rough plan in mind to deal with Mr. Malham. In his fantasy world, his aim was to make a citizen's arrest, disarm him, beat him to within an inch of death and drag his body into the lobby of the local office of the FBI.

His plan was simple, but the execution would be very difficult. He must catch him alone and use complete surprise because he would surely be the loser in a shootout with this sharpshooter armed with two pistols. A straight fist fight would be no picnic either. He must avoid a wrestling match with this powerful weightlifter. His plan called for him to restrain Two Gun in his own handcuffs before he beat him. The thought of a fair fight never entered his mind. This would be a life or death struggle, and it would be his life at risk just as Patricia had warned. He now knew that Judge Parker had ordered his death.

Tripp did have one advantage. Two Gun was a creature of habit. He followed a set pattern of routines in his off-duty times. He learned this back in the happy teenage days and later when he had been engaged to Lavita Vorhees as he was befriended by Two Gun and went with him to his favorite eating place. He always ordered the same meal -- two cheeseburgers with fries and a beer with a pickled pig's foot for dessert. He always used the same shooting range and followed the same pistol routine and target distances. His photography and birdwatching spots were attended precisely in order. He even shared his secret that, contrary to public belief, he did indeed enjoy female companionship and showed him his favorite roadside motel, where he always reserved the same room. All of this was a bit much for Tripp at the time, but he was in awe of the deputy and his brother-like persona. Now he intended to use this against him.

Tripp prioritized his ambush places. The barber shop parking lot would be number one. He would be alone and no one there would interfere. The bar and grill would be a close second, but it must happen on the parking lot as Two Gun left in order to avoid a crowd of possible strangers. If he could not find him alone, the judge's office would work fine after the two gin players became sufficiently inebriated with the help of Jack Daniels whiskey. The game never ended until one or the other fell on his face amidst the cards. An unnoticed entry could be made by the back door of the Parker mansion, which was never locked until a servant made final rounds late at night.

His rage was building to the point of explosion. The opportunity to use option number two was at hand if Tripp left immediately. Two Gun was probably at the bar and grill now. He could hide behind his vehicle and nab him there. With his truck unavailable, he would be in his patrol car. The danger would be if a bystander who did not recognize him caught him with a gun pointed at a uniformed cop beside a marked police car. Maybe he should alter his plan, he thought, but he could do that on the way. He was running out of time.

When he arrived, the expected vehicle was not there so Tripp parked behind the building and decided to wait, but Two Gun did not show up. Tripp decided to check inside. He entered through the back door into the kitchen. He held his 30/30 saddle rifle beside his leg as he positioned himself to have a look at the occupants. His man was not one of the six customers present. At this point he stepped out and confronted the bartender owner, who greeted him immediately with, "Hey, Tripp, what are you doing in here with a gun in your hands? This isn't a pawn shop. Ha Ha!"

Others recognized him and called out his name. Tripp responded, "This is no joke. I am looking for Two Gun Malham. He killed my daughter and almost killed my wife. Have you seen him today?"

"Surely you are not planning to kill him?!"

"Only if I have too. You would do the same if it were your daughter. It looks like I've missed him here. Do me a favor, will you? If he shows up here later, don't tell him that I am looking for him." With that, he turned and walked out.

He heard a voice behind him say, "Do you know who that is? That is the *man*. That is Tripp Joiner, the greatest quarterback in America. He is going after Two Gun Malham. Let's form a posse and go with him."

136

"Are you crazy? I ain't going," someone shouted. No one followed Rusty Flake as he ran for his truck.

"I know where he's going. I'm goin' to get a posse and join him there."

On the day of the tragedy, Judge Parker, Lavita Vorhees and her husband, Tony Bender, had left on a family outing to Ruidoso Downs racetrack to watch a promising new colt from the Parker Racing Stable make his debut. They returned the next day and were blasted with the news that the daughter of Tripp Joiner had been killed in a car crash and her mother had suffered life threatening injuries.

Judge Parker, suspecting that Two Gun Malham was involved, called him in for questioning in private. "Were you involved in this?" he asked. Two Gun responded, "Boss, you need to stay as far away from this as you can. I promise you that there is no evidence that I, you or anyone else we know was involved. Take a look at my patrol car. There isn't a scratch on it." Concealing the fact that his truck was involved was easy. He had always used the car when harassing Patricia in the past, so no more questions were asked at the moment, but suspicions remained in Parker's mind.

Word that Patricia was conscience and naming Two Gun as her assailant prompted new action by the judge. Two Gun was now in serious trouble and the FBI would most certainly come calling. It was time for planning. He needed an alibi. The problem was that Two Gun expressed his belief that no alibi was needed. He argued that there was no evidence except for the illusions of a brain-damaged hysterical woman who had falsely accused him of harassment in the past. A fabricated alibi, if uncovered, would certainly cook his goose.

An argument between the judge and Two Gun had ensued and was becoming heated by the time Tripp began searching for Two Gun. For the first time in more than a decade of dedicated protective service to his boss, Deputy Sheriff John Malham was on the verge of losing his temper in a conversation between the two. He had come close to it a time or two in the past, but he had become, in his own mind at least, a close friend to his boss. Maybe the only friend he had.

The judge began to use demeaning language, pointing out his stupidity and reminding him that he was, after all, only a servant. Finally, Two

Gun exploded, "I have protected you countless times from your many enemies. I have always been prepared to give up my life in order to protect yours. I have done your illegal dirty work so many times they cannot be counted."

Both men were red in the face as they stood face to face. Two Gun made the first physical contact as he pushed the judge out of his face. He was rewarded with a strike of the judge's cane. He fended it off with his arm, but the second strike left a bleeding dent in his scull caused by the sharp nose of the wolf's head grip. Two Gun drew his pistol and ordered the judge to stop but the downward motion of another strike was on its way.

Tripp parked his truck up the street and out of sight, checked again to make certain that a shell was in the chamber of his 30/30 and exited the truck as quietly as possible. A quick scan of the area confirmed that no other person was near as he made a wide circle to the rear of the mansion.

Standard household lockdown procedure had always been to lock the front and side doors at the close of business hours and the rear door after completion of servant activities late at night. Tripp's plan called for him to slip in the back door, giving complete access to the interior, where only three people should be. He was surprised to find it locked. This set off an alarm in his mind. This meant that extra precautions had been taken.

The possibility of a trap had always been in his mind and this could be a sign of that. He hesitated a moment to think and withdrew to the side of the house in order to plan his next move. The wise thing to do would be to fall back on his option to wait and catch Two Gun alone. There could be two people with loaded guns waiting on him inside if they somehow knew that Patricia was talking.

He decided to walk straight back to his truck, but heard a shot fired inside the house. The noise stopped him in his tracks. He moved into the front yard, where he saw two men approaching from the direction of his truck. One carried a shotgun and the other a pistol.

"Tripp, don't shoot. This is your posse from the bar and grill. Remember me? I'm Rusty Flake and this is my brother Dusty."

138

Tripp answered, "Get out of here. Go home. I heard a gunshot fired inside the house a moment ago so I'm leaving. I will come for him another day."

Just then, a woman's hysterical screaming could be heard. Tripp stopped for a moment and announced "I am going in to find out what that screaming is all about. You guys stay outside. Do not come in. Do you hear me? *Do not come in*!" He bounded up the front steps as the two brothers remained frozen in place. He used the rifle butt to break the stained-glass door window, reached through the broken pane to unlock the door and cautiously entered.

Lilia Parker Vorhees had been well into her evening routine with Jose Cuervo and had reached the point of inebriation where she always began to drink straight from the bottle without a chaser. She had sat up on the bed in order to light another cigarette and take another swig from the half full bottle. Raised voices coming from the front of the house attracted her attention. It was obvious that an argument of some sort was in progress. She had eased out of her room with bottle in hand. Shouting continued. It was obvious that something big was coming down. She had held tightly to the rail as she descended down the stairs and staggered close to the office door, where she could hear the heated conversation. A shot rang out and she had opened the door slowly to find Two Gun Malham down on his knees with his arms around her father crying, "I'm sorry, I'm sorry, I didn't mean to do it, I'm sorry!"

Lilia screamed loudly and made her way to the two men. Blood was everywhere and spurting from a wound in the side of Judge Parker's neck caused by the bullet passing through and exiting from the house via a windowpane. Blood was also flowing from Two Gun's forehead. His pistol lay on the floor.

She picked up the gun, pointed it at him, grabbed his arm and shouted, "Go call for help and bring some towels. She removed her robe and wrapped a sleeve around his neck trying to staunch the flow.

"It was an accident. I didn't mean to do it. He was beating me with his cane. I pointed my gun at him to stop him, but he hit me again and my gun went off. It was not my fault. I'm sorry!" he shouted as he ran from the room.

She screamed again, "Hurry, *hurry!*" The pulsating flow of blood ceased quickly. The King was dead, killed by his own protector, not by one of his countless bitter enemies who would surely celebrate the news.

Lilia screamed once again. "He is dead!"

Two Gun hesitated outside the room with a phone in his hand. He had just committed a crime punishable by death and there was a live witness to his crime, holding a gun, his own gun. He was thinking the unthinkable thought of killing Lilia or maybe fleeing from the scene. Then he heard the sound of someone breaking the glass in the front door. His instincts pulled him in. He drew his remaining gun from its holster and held it in the firing position as he rounded the corner and entered the office door just as Tripp entered from the opposite direction.

Seeing the pistol aimed at his head caused Tripp to throw up his hands, with his rifle in front of his face as his assailant fired. The bullet struck his rifle, dislodging it from his hands and onto the floor. The bullet ricocheted downward under his armpit creating a minor flesh wound in the pectoral muscle. He grabbed the pistol trying to push it away just as Two Gun fired a second time. This bullet went harmlessly into the wooden floor. This repeated gunfire attracted the attention of those in the servant's quarters. They made an emergency phone call and the servants gathered together, but they were too frightened to approach the main house.

The winner of the battle for survival would be determined by who would ultimately gain possession of the weapon. Two Gun was considerably larger but much older. He was also stronger as a result of his obsession with weightlifting. Tripp was in football playing shape and much more agile. Football, steer wrestling, calf roping and ranch life in general evened the score. He was as tall as his opponent and weighed more than 220 pounds himself with larger and stronger hands. These strong hands remained fixed on Two Gun's pistol in spite of kicking, head butting and knees to his groin. Tripp had more stamina and Two Gun was quickly showing signs of shortness of breath.

Lilia was now pointing a gun at the two struggling men, yelling for them to stop. Both men noticed and attempted to use the other one's body as a shield. Tripp needed to find a way to end the fight quickly. He had only one weapon left to use, his teeth. He waited for the next head butt and

140

managed to bite down on Two Gun's nose with all his jaw strength. Two Gun roared like a lion and all four hands on the pistol came up to the face of the agonizing man.

Tripp jammed his powerful thumb into Two Gun's eye socket. His fingernail acted as a blade point, deeply penetrating to cause partial blindness. A hard jerk of the gun barrel loosened it from all hands, and it went sliding across the wooden floor and under the couch. Both men dove for the life or death weapon.

The quicker and more agile Tripp was first to reach under the couch but he didn't reach the gun. This turned out to be a fateful mistake. The larger man landed on Tripp's back with his hands around his neck in a choke hold. He jerked Tripp from the edge of the couch and applied all his strength and attention to choking him to death.

Tripp managed to momentarily break the grip, long enough to gasp a breath on several occasions and tried to cry out for his two-man posse, but the Flake brothers had fled. He had lost the fight and was drifting toward unconsciousness. He did not hear the explosion just above his ears or feel the pain as Lilia Parker Vorhees fired a bullet into Two Gun, grazing Tripp's shoulder. The last muscle reflex of the dying man was to maintain the choke hold as he slowly bled to death, but he did feel Tripp's body as it went completely limp before he fell over himself. Lilia intended to put a bullet into his limp body, but a better plan changed her mind. She placed the gun into her longtime enemy's hand and carefully wrapped his fingers around the trigger. Let Tripp Joiner take all the blame. She was in the clear now and final revenge had been rendered.

Sirens were now heard, and Lilia had just enough time to retrieve her precious Jose Cuervo before the first responders began arriving. The medics made a fast but routine examination of the casualties as law enforcement searched the house for shooters. Lilia was shouting that Tripp Joiner had killed her father, Judge Parker, and his bodyguard, Deputy Sheriff John Malham. She repeated this several times before she was asked to be quiet.

"We have two dead and one nonresponsive," shouted the head medic. "We will try resuscitation on the non-responsive." Then, "We now have a pulse," one said shortly thereafter. And then, "We now have breathing." They had saved Tripp's life.

141

He was immediately transported to a hospital. A uniformed deputy was assigned guard duty and rode with the medics. Tripp awakened to find himself shackled to his bed. The shocking feeling of this sudden loss of freedom was unfathomable to his damaged brain. Perhaps it was like the helpless feeling of a bird with a broken wing. No movement of his arm was necessary to feel the ring of steel around his wrist. It was always there, awake or dreaming. However, this feeling was nothing compared to that which came later with the sound of the key being turned in the lock of his jail cell door.

The first attempt to question Lilia was unsuccessful so the sheriff captain in charge began to question the servants, who all were now in the kitchen. Lilia's personal attendant was asked to make coffee and attempt to sober her up. She was allowed to take her for a bath and a change of clothes. Her bloody clothes were placed in a washing machine and washed.

This mistake, allowed by the police, would be one of many made during the investigation. Two hours of coffee drinking was required to bring Lilia into reasonable condition for questions. She was not a suspect, so she was not read Miranda rights nor offered a lawyer. She told a rambling story about the breaking and entering of Jimmy Jack Joiner and how he cursed and shot her father. How Deputy Malham, her father's bodyguard, came to his rescue and a fight over his gun ensued. Joiner was able to get control of the gun as he was being choked and shot Malham in the chest. She was pressed for more details and contradicted herself several times. The captain gave up eventually and a detective made a failed attempt to do much better. Too many questions remained unanswered.

Law enforcement personnel continued to arrive from the city, county and state. Even the serving county judge showed up. The celebrity level of the deceased and as well as the declared cop killer drew officials like flies on stink. The room and entire house were overcrowded with too many experts wanting to help. The crime scene was contaminated before control was finally established. The best crime scene expert witnesses in the country would have a field day at trial as they contradicted each other for the prosecution and defense. The house remained locked down for more than a week as the search continued for the bullet that killed Horace Parker.

CHAPTER NINETEEN

More Than a Simple 'Quid Pro Quo'

Recovery time in the intensive care unit was far shorter than normal for a patient being treated for a gunshot wound and near death by choking. But after all, Tripp Joiner was already branded as a double cop killer by the authorities. "This is to be expected," Mule Sherman advised him and his family. "Things will get much worse once they transfer him to a county jail, so we must do everything possible to keep him in the hospital as long as we can, with 'round the clock guard by armed county deputies. There will be very few visits allowed by family and attorney. There will be nothing private and confidential in our conversations."

Very short notice of the transfer was given, but Mule, expecting this, was well prepared and had a strategy to create an atmosphere of reluctance by jail personnel to take revenge on the "cop killer" during his confinement. He also had a more sinister motive in mind. His staff had alerted the media that an incident of possible interest might occur, and if it did, he would address it with a statement to the press. The large crowd of reporters were not disappointed.

Mule delivered on his promise when he demanded that his own technician be allowed to electronically sweep the jail conference room to make certain that no listening devices were hidden. His request, as he suspected, was denied. A microphone was already set up outside and T.V. cameras were rolling when he broadcast to the world that his client was being denied the right to a private meeting with his counsel as guaranteed by law and his constitutional rights. He reminded all that, "This county was brought to court a few years ago with a complaint that a recording of a lawyer and his client was illegally made and that the information was used against him, and I will make certain that this doesn't happen in this case. We are now attempting to reach the judge for a solution to this problem. We will keep you informed as progress is made and I will take questions at that time." With that, he turned and entered the building where he awaited word from the judge.

The judge made a quick decision. He suspected that Mule was playing a game that he himself wanted no part of and must be stopped immediately. Out of sight of the media. He ordered the jail supervisor to escort Mule and Tripp to his own private chambers behind his bench in the courtroom, where they could conduct their meeting in his empty chambers. This would have to suffice until the issue of the conference room sweep could be resolved. The defense meeting was to be held in two parts. The first was to be between the two of them only and the second with the entire defense team.

As they entered the room, realizing where they were, Tripp mused, "This must be some sort of special treatment."

Mule replied, "This is a first for me. This judge is known to a bit of a maverick. I'm not sure if that bodes well for us, but one thing is certain, there will be no listening device planted here." Mule continued, "It's standard procedure for me to have this private meeting with my clients in what I call a knee-to-knee session. It's important that we establish complete trust in one another, and direct eye contact completes the bond and assures that the complete truth is shared."

Two chairs were positioned properly, they were seated, and eye contact was made. Tripp had never looked into such penetrating eyes in his life. He was actually squirming in his chair as he felt his mind being exposed. Mule had done his homework. He already knew everything that Tripp knew about the case and much more. He had in his hand the completed questionnaire given to him earlier by Tripp and had put it to memory. Included were the contents of all conversations with other attorneys regarding this case.

"This private meeting has several purposes and it is necessary that our conversation be kept entirely between us. Do you understand that?"

"Yes" Tripp replied.

Mule's eyes were burning a hole through his. "At the risk of giving you too much information as opposed to too little, I am going to lay out all my thoughts and plans on the table based on our current knowledge. Strategies obviously change as events unfold. I would prefer that you hold your comments and questions until I am finished. You will have more questions than answers after our meeting and the meeting with the entire team.

144

"First, I want you to try to put your mind at ease. We *are* going to win this case! I will explain all the reasons why in a few moments but let's talk about what is facing you while we are winning. This is a fight for life. It will be tougher on you mentally than the most brutal football game that you have ever played.

"You have been labeled a double cop killer. Your jailers will hate you and they will find ways to make your life miserable. They will not apply physical torture directly to you, but the mental torture can destroy your body as well as your mind. Sleep deprivation will be their basic tool. They will pull very frequent cell inspections when they know you are asleep. They will assign the cells next to yours with the screamers, insane and troublemakers. They will play games with your meal schedule and even the food itself. You must be alert to contrived accidents when you are being moved about. Cop killers and child pedophiles bring out the bad behavior in what are, otherwise, normal human beings. You may be lucky enough to find one or two who play by the rules or even believe in your innocence. If so, they have a tendency to let you know who they are. Let's hope there are some N.Y. Giants football fans in the mix.

"Now. I am going to spell out in detail how we are going to win. The constitution guarantees equal justice for us all. Right? That is what is promised but it is not the truth for the vast majority of people brought to trial who are presumed guilty by the jury until proven innocent. Just ask the defense lawyers. You, however, are lucky. You fall into the class of people who are guaranteed innocence until proven guilty. You, my friend, are an American hero, a celebrity whose name is heard in the house of every football fan in the world. Juries don't want to kill their heroes or even punish them. Better than that, surveys of jurors show that even when leaning towards guilty, they tell themselves that their hero would not kill another human being unless they deserved killing. You not only didn't kill anyone; you did have justification by the murder of your daughter and the attempted murder of your wife to be lured into the trap that ended with the death of the real killers. Let me give you some more reasons we'll win.

"I win because we call the very best expert witnesses and pay them well in order to keep them available, and in this case, the forensic evidence is on our side. The state will get second pick and our list will be longer. We have Will Clarkson on our team, and he is the best that there is in destroying the credibility of witnesses. We will make the judge and Two

Gun look like scumbags who needed killing. The state's case depends entirely on the testimony of a so-called eyewitness. One who is a confirmed alcoholic, who was drunk at the scene and who could not be more biased. Under most circumstances, eyewitnesses are winners for the state, but with the baggage she carries, I am not overly concerned.

"Your conversations with other attorneys show that you were informed that certain key pieces of evidence might not be allowed into evidence at trial. This may or may not be true but let me assure you that the jury pool and jury members will have knowledge of everything that we want them to have through trial testimony or prior to trial with the help of the media. The overwhelming majority of pool members will have been attracted to the high-profile nature and sensationalism of the case to follow it every step of the way. We will see to it that the press has the facts. We are experienced at walking right up to the line of legality. This is another example that you have in the area of justice for all."

Mule continued to spell out his plan. "Now, I am about to tell you about our secret weapon, and we do, indeed, have one. We do something that comes with a high price tag, which most clients aren't willing to bear. My competitors don't use it because they consider it to not be cost effective. Not enough bang for the buck. That is because they don't know how to use it. Here is how it works.

"We have a husband and wife team who are trained and skilled psychiatrists and who assist in jury selection. They observe all testimony and read the reaction of juror's body language and facial expressions to all testimony. They submit a written report on their findings to me daily. Statements we make and questions asked to witnesses can be tailored to reflect their findings. These can be and are directed to specific jury members. We try to determine ahead of time who will be elected jury foreperson. Sometimes that's an easy read. As an example, if we have a jury member with advanced college degrees, that person will almost always seek the position and dominate the jury room conversations. That person may get more attention and eye contact in closing arguments than any other.

"You will be introduced to this pair in our meeting. They are assisted by our PI and others as needed. We will have a lot to work with as soon as we have the names of the pool members. Your friend Hal will be assigned to this group during the jury selection process. His expertise in case law may not be of much help to us but his phenomenal memory will come in handy as he scans the jury pool, because the barber shop gossip will tip us off to local misdeeds and tragedy. Some of this might have involved the family of a potential juror. Keep in mind that it takes only one juror to hang a jury. Simple logic tells us that this one juror can prevent us from losing and therefore produces a victory of sorts. Our practice is to lock and reload one juror at a time. Jeb Cassidy will be working with them early on as we investigate leads from the jury pool names list."

Mule suddenly stopped talking as he noticed a smile on Tripp's face. The first one that he had seen since forever. He did not need his psychiatric instincts to recognize that symptoms of tension had completely disappeared. This was his goal from the outset. Now it was time to shift gears and offer Tripp an option of a lifetime.

He stood up, took two bottles of water from the judge's private stock and offered one to Tripp as he pointed to the private restroom door. Tripp shook his head no and the two of them sat side by side on the couch. It was time to turn the briefing into a two-way conversation.
Tripp opened. "It appears from what you say that we are in the driver's seat. It feels good to actually relax a little. Every muscle in my body is sore from the constant tension that began when I woke up from my little trip to La-la land and found myself shackled to a hospital bed with armed guards in my room. Overall, I guess I'm doing OK. I'm looking forward to the next meeting, but I do have one question for now. Is there anything that troubles you about the case?"

Mule replied, "It would take a real bombshell to alter my thinking or change our basic strategy. I have beat the bushes over and over again and the only thing that appears remotely possible would be that the DA would attempt to indict you in the death of Debi Devereaux.

"I consider this a virtual impossibility for several reasons, in spite of what my inside sources are telling me about outside political pressure being put on him. That pressure is coming all the way from the governor's office down through influential locals and even from some members from his own office.

"You may or may not know that the sitting governor was hand-picked by Judge Parker, who also backed him financially with scandalous sums of cash. It appears that the Parker family is continuing to do everything possible to keep their princess out of jail and to save her career. That appears more important to them than your conviction in the killing of her grandfather. She is the eventual sole heir to the fortune and her husband is the new head of the empire.

"Even an indictment by a grand jury would prejudice the jury pool. I don't believe that this totally honest DA, without a single blemish in his 20-year career, would take this to a grand jury without utter conviction that you were guilty of a very serious crime. Nor do I believe that he has the time right now to be distracted from preparing this case. Also, he would have everything blow up in his face if the grand jury failed to indict. The two companions of Devereaux at the death scene would have to perjure themselves in order to frame you and that would still be a real stretch for the prosecution. No, I can't see this happening, but I plan to get a meeting with the DA and our judge to set the stage for the DA to become receptive to something else that I want to talk to you about now.

"I see the possibility of an exciting alternate pathway opening up that may be a shortcut solution to this whole mess, stopping this trial before it starts. This is based on the assumption that freedom for the princess is more important to the remaining family members than is their hatred and revenge for you. They would give you your freedom in exchange for hers."

Tripp was momentarily silenced by this, then he cautiously asked, "What are you talking about?"

"This is much more than a simple quid pro quo. This is a Texas-style horse trade of famous thoroughbreds! A movie star for a sports star. And it must be done in complete secrecy."

"I still don't understand."

"It would happen something like this. We would fabricate an accidental hallway meeting with one of our people and a Parker company lawyer. Our guy would probably be Hall, because he knows some of the Parker lawyers through his barbershop. There would be an exchange of greetings and our guy would say something like, "It's a shame that the two sides in the Joiner case don't settle this prior to trial." Their guy would likely comment that he couldn't see how this could be possible."

Mule continued, "But there is no way that this conversation would not be passed along to his new boss, the husband of the princess. I am betting that their star eyewitness, Lilia Vorhees, can be convinced to save her daughter by developing a fuzzy drunken recollection. She killed the man who had just killed her father."

Tripp had moved forward to the edge of his seat as he listened to the unbelievable fairytale plan to avoid trial. Suddenly he sat back in his chair and muttered, "I can't make this decision alone. This is a decision for Debi's parents. The killer of their daughter would receive no punishment. Her part in the eventual death of my daughter would be forgiven. My answer, at this moment, would be no."

Mule responded, "Be reminded that the real killers of your daughter are dead, and nothing can be done to bring her and Debi back alive. Her parents and brother will surely have some sympathy towards you and the brother has a strong desire to have you join him soon with the Giants. The terms of the trade will, of course, include a very large financial package for pain and suffering to Debi's family. I ask you to give this some thought, and we will bring it up with the family if you so allow. Now we must move along with our meeting with the rest of our team. For the moment, let's keep this trade plan just between the two of us. I will share it with Will Clarkson in private."

The other team members entered the room with the expected chatter about the unusual choice of the judge's chambers for a defense team meeting. Fresh introduction and role assignments were made by Mule and rough outlines of evidence and strategy were discussed. Each team member was invited to make a brief statement and to ask questions that he or she needed immediate answers to.

The meeting broke up after just over two hours and Mule asked Will to remain behind for further discussion. When the two of them were left in private, Mule stunned Will Clarkson. "I have inside information that the Parker people are up to more of their dirty tricks. A recent strategy session has apparently produced a plan to put pressure on the DA to file charges against our client in the Devereaux death for the obvious purpose of branding him as a criminal prior to this trial. Just one more way to taint the jury towards a guilty verdict in the death of Judge and Deputy Malham.

"They are calling favors up and down the line from selected politicians, reaching all the way to the governor's office and others that they have made financial contributions to, asking them to join the squeeze. One of those contacted is my informant. This has the potential of a major scandal, but my only goal is to make sure that we get assurance from the DA. And I want Judge Sullivan as our witness. The DA has a strong reputation for honesty, but we can't take any chances. He probably will have no other choice but to grant us the assurance in the presence of the judge. We must get the DA and the judge to agree to a private and secure meeting for obvious reasons. This can't be any kind of formal court hearing.

"There is also a second reason for this meeting. Let me spell it out for you. I believe that I see an opportunity to end this trial before it begins. It won't be easy to pull off, but it has enough of a chance that we must offer it to our client. I need your thoughts on this. I have never attempted something like this before but that is because circumstances have never lined up like this before."

Mule repeated all the details of the plan he had spelled out for Tripp earlier. Will had an immediate reply. "I agree that you must present this to our client, but I believe that you will have difficulty selling it to Lilia Vorhees because her personal attorney will most certainly advise her against it. I certainly would. No doubt, her daughter and her son-in-law will apply great pressure, but she has earned the reputation of being a very strong-willed person."

"I would like for you to witness my call as I ask for a meeting ASAP."

"OK, let's do it."

Soon thereafter a phone line was arranged, and Mule got right to the point. "Windy, I have it on good authority that a conspiracy is cooking that has the potential of creating a scandal of giant proportions. It includes some of your people, and it could blow the lid off this trial. Will Clarkson and I would like to have a private meeting with you and Judge Sullivan at your earliest convenience. I would prefer that you set this up with the judge, but If you prefer, give me your schedule and I will call him."

Windy started to ask for more information but Mule cut him off. "This is

150

too explosive to discuss on the phone so please give me a yes or no answer. If it is a no, I will call the judge, and believe me, you will be hearing from him real soon. This is very serious."

The DA responded, "You leave me with no choice, but I bet that he'll be calling you immediately, wanting more details than you are willing to provide me."

"Well, he won't get them until our meeting."

Judge Sullivan met them in his chambers with a scowl on his face. "I am a very busy man. Please tell me, counselor, that this is not another of your so-called legal tricks."

Mule replied, "Good morning to you also, Judge. Looks like we have found you in a bad mood, but I believe that what I have to disclose could greatly damage our client's chances of a fair trial. Thus, it is necessary for Mr. Clarkson and me to stop it in its tracks by getting assurance from Windy that it will not happen."

He then repeated the whole conspiracy story. The judge, as expected, started asking for names, and of course, Mule refused his request.

The DA interrupted, "I am highly offended that you would believe that I would let outside political pressure influence such a decision.

Mule replied, "Honestly, I didn't believe that, Windy. Just making sure."

"There. Now that we have Windy's assurance, get the heck out of here and let me go back to work."

Everyone was moving towards a hasty exit when Mule turned to the DA and said, "Windy, I am in the process of pulling together some evidence that suggests that your so-called eyewitness to the shootings did not actually see the shooting of her father but was attracted to the scene when she heard the shot fired. When I get those details, with our client's approval, we will offer up a plea bargain. A trade of guilty plea to threatening to kill Mr. Malham in exchange for dropped murder charges in the death of Judge Parker."

Angry now, with face red and arteries protruding from both sides of his neck, Windy exploded. "I have heard enough. Let me remind you of something. Outside of a confession by your client, I have the best case that a DA could wish for. I have an extremely reliable eyewitness to the killings, and I have several witnesses to the virtual testimony of your client's intention to kill. What more do I need?"

"I am sure that your very capable detectives have shown you all the evidence that solves this case, so you know what we will bring to the jury. But just in case you haven't studied it thoroughly, I've brought you the file prepared by our own investigative team that completely solves the crime. Of course, you know my chief PI. He was honored by your own police department for his outstanding service in solving murders, even some of your own, before his retirement."

The DA slapped away the envelope as he left the scene. Mule Sherman winked at Will Clarkson, and Will left with a smile on his face. Their mission was successful.

Mule lagged behind as he got from the judge exactly what he was expecting. "Just a moment, Mr. Sherman. I would like to have a few more words with you please." The judge then locked the door with a greatly exaggerated gesture, which reminded Mule of his father locking the tool shed door to prevent his mother from coming to his rescue as 10 licks, always 10, were applied to his bare bottom.

"There are reasons why lawyers refer to me as Honest Abe Sullivan, and I am about to give you a little taste of the kind of justice that I stand for. You have just run out of your allotment of games and dirty tricks that I will allow during the trial of this case. You just played this DA, another very honest provider of justice, like a violin. You took advantage of his proud reputation for honesty to elicit a fast assurance to a request to prevent a stupid move that you knew ahead of time that he would never commit. To seek another indictment of your client at this stage would be prejudicial to the point of causing a mistrial in our case and we all know that.

"No, Mr. Sherman. There is more to this. I smell a rat and I intend to find it. Do you want to make it easy for me?"

Mule replied, "There is no rat odor here, your honor, but I did have a second motive hidden in my request. I will get to that as soon as I respond to your dirty tricks allegation. As you know, I, too, have an obligation to my client to defend him with every means available within the law. The law has been interpreted by various courts and judges since the beginning of time. The line that I try not to cross is very fuzzy, to say the least, and I try to use every word of it to aid my clients."

Judge Sullivan interrupted, "I am the one who draws the line in my court, and that is how we will operate. I will let you know when you cross my line, and when you do, I will see to it that you have time to reflect on that line as you sit in a jail cell. Do you understand that?"

"I hear your threat, Judge, and now, if I may, I will explain my motive. I believe that the Parker family conspiracy to influence the outcome of this trial is very real, and it does reach all the way to the governor's office. I did, indeed, have an obligation to ask for an assurance, but my client needs something far more important. He needs a life insurance policy, and the DA can provide it for him. It is true that the man who ordered his execution and his deputy sheriff bodyguard are both dead, but the evil thinkers and planners remain. The revenge that caused all this mess still exists. Today I planted a seed in the mind of Mr. Warren that is at this very moment taking root. Our very honest DA is sorting out prospects for conspirators, and he will begin a quiet investigation that he will pursue with vigor after our trial is over.

"He will pursue it for two reasons. One, because of his pure honesty. And two, if it does lead to the governor, it has the possibility of creating the biggest stage of his lifetime on which to perform. If he could put the governor on trial, it would make him famous and catapult him right into higher office. His quiet probe will be reported to the Parker family, and it is my bet that no more attempts on the life of my client will be made. The Queen and the Princess will be stopped forever."

Judge Sullivan replied, "You are making a lot of presumptions here, counselor. I will say that you do have a very fertile mind, but nothing matters to me except what pertains to this trial. I believe that I have made that very clear."

Mule nodded slightly. "If you have finished pounding on me, unlock that door and let me be on my way."

"Dear friends, never take revenge. Leave that to the righteous anger of

God. For the Scriptures say, I will take revenge; I will pay them back, says the LORD." It took Mule much longer than expected to find this particular Scripture passage from Romans 12:19. He had not searched the Bible for a scripture since the days of his youth when he served his mandatory parental sentence to several years of Sunday school at Burchill Baptist Church in Fort Worth.

He was preparing his approach to the family of Debi Devereaux regarding the trade. He was troubled by the nagging, guilty conscience as he searched for his scripture. A guilty conscience was something of the past. He had not felt this way in recent memory. Was it because he was about to use what most people considered to be a sacred book for unsavory purposes or was it something else?

A burning question was attempting to creep into his agnostic mind. "Could there actually be a living, all powerful …?" He brushed aside the thought and continued to jot down some points. Talk to Zip Devereaux first and separately. Let him open the door to his parents. Massage words carefully as Zip is told that Tripp feels he can take the Giants to the playoffs next season. But avoid this subject with the parents. Tell Zip but not the parents that the lawyers will take no fees from the expected "pain and suffering" money. Make certain that there is absolutely no mention of money to the parents. Remind all that nothing can be done to bring back the lives of Debi and little Mary Mae, but life must go on. The Devereauxs are devout Catholics. Her brother is a priest. Find a delicate way to use Romans 12:19. Let them know that Tripp considers that the decision for the trade is theirs, not his. Decide if the meetings must be held face to face or by phone.

Hal Hall was working on his assignment to arrange an accidental encounter with a suitable attorney to act as messenger to Tony Bender, the Princess's husband and new head of the Parker companies. The ideal messenger was right in front of his mind. He held a standing appointment at the barbershop for a weekly hair trim. Hal selected an appointment day and did his thing as the man left the shop and the two of them talked on the front porch.

Hal was confident he had taken the bait and that Tony Bender would know about the potential trade before the day was over. He was right.

Bender called Mule the next day to set up a clandestine meeting to

154

exchange trade terms. Mule offered a slight change in Tripp's police report to say that he did not see the actual blow that killed Debi Devereaux in exchange for the full truth by the eyewitness, Lilia Vorhees in regards to the deaths of Judge Parker and Deputy Malham. He also asked for three million dollars in cash for "pain and suffering" for the Devereaux family.

Bender countered with an offer of a change in Vorhees' testimony that she did not actually see Tripp shoot her father for Tripp's testimony that Lavita Vorhees was not even present at the scene of Debi Devereaux's accidental death. He had no problem with the amount of the pain and suffering money. No agreement was reached, but they parted company with promises to continue working.

It took a few days. All of Mule's assigned people except Debi's father had given in, Zip had been assured by his mother that she would find a way to persuade her husband to change his mind. He did, reluctantly. Mule updated Tripp in their daily jail house visit and called Will with the good news. Their half was in the pot. Now it was up to Tony Bender to present his half.

In moment of celebratory glee, Mule said to Will, "You are the only Bible-thumping lawyer I know who carries his Bible in his briefcase, so you will enjoy the fact that I used a Bible verse to persuade Mrs. Devereaux to go along. I used Romans 12:19. Go look it up, and while you are at it, find one that we can send to Lilia Parker Vorhees," he laughed.

Will replied, "There is a verse in the Book of John that states that the truth will set you free, but I think it is going to take much more than a Bible Verse to break that woman loose."

They had no way of knowing that Lilia was on the fence with her decision. It depended on which end of the tequila bottle she was into when she was contemplating yes or no. When drunk she was feeling liar's guilt and compassion for her daughter. When on the sober side, she was heeding her attorney's advice. He pointed out that if she told the truth that she saw Two Gun shoot her father and that she then shot him after he had choked Tripp Joiner into unconsciousness and feared that he would probably kill her next in order to eliminate all witnesses, she would most certainly face perjury charges. Furthermore, one party would have to move first and trust the other to follow suit. True, if she went first, Tripp would have to follow suit in order to for the three million to be paid, but there was no absolute guarantee. Of course, this type of arrangement forbade any type of legal contract being put in writing.

Mule reached Tony Bender on his private line to tell him that all on the Joiner side of the trade were in full agreement and ready to go. He wanted an update from the Parker camp. The briefing was hopeful but not what he wanted to hear.

"Lavita believes that her mother will eventually agree to the trade, but being the drama queen that she is, she wants the confession to be made on national television as she takes the stand for the prosecution. Lavita gave her a brief statement structured around the words 'I shot the man who admitted to me that he killed my father after being struck by his cane because I knew that he was going to kill me, the only witness. I placed the gun in the hand of the unconscious Mr. Joiner out of revenge because he was the one who created this awful mess in the first place."

Bender continued, "I believe she'll try to have it both ways by sticking to her story with the expectations that your client can be bought off in some other way if the Devereaux death makes it to a grand jury. She believes that there are ways to prevent a grand jury from taking it in the first place. Please remember that she has been raised and schooled in her father's philosophy that everything and everyone has a price tag. Her own daily income comes from the many charities set up as a means to buy influence and favors from politicians and other power brokers. She rightly points out that Mr. Joiner has shown us that he does have a price tag in this trade offer, which means that he can be bought in the next trade. No, Mule, I don't believe she'll take the deal, and in any case, we will not know until she takes the witness stand."

Mule responded, "You do understand that the timeframe we have agreed to is for this trade to be made before the trial begins -- for obvious reasons. My client must be freed before trial. That is what he has agreed to."

Bender replied, "I don't believe that any sane man would turn down a dismissal of charges of double murder regardless of the timing. I believe that we'll not have our answer until Lilia Vorhees takes the stand."

Will Clarkson took the news without comment. A decline by the queen was what he expected all along. He was already deep into his study of the woman, starting with the contents of Judge Parker's will.

Lilia Parker Vorhees was now one of the world's richest women. She was already showing signs of being emboldened by announcing major changes to be made to the charity foundation, including a massive increase to her salary. More disturbing, she ordered a dossier on all senior executives in the Parker companies. Most damaging to her and the most interesting to Will was that she had fired some of the domestic staff at the Parker mansion. This was fertile ground to be plowed for inside information on his subject.

He was determined to know more about the woman than she knew about herself. He would know how often she brushed her teeth and changed her underwear. He also knew that the Princess Lavita was unhappy about the terms of the will. She was expecting half of everything but had to settle for a trust fund and no management control, not even the movie production business. There had to be fire developing in her relationship with her mother.

Will went about his task, believing he had the outcome of this trial in his hands. He must destroy the credibility of the star eyewitness in order to win the case. He had done it many times before and he could do it again.

CHAPTER TWENTY

Steal a Pig and Spawn a Dynasty

The jail conference room was small, plain and sparse, with only a four-by-six-foot table and six straight-back chairs for furniture. An observation window in the only door with one-way glass reflected like a mirror, adding to the claustrophobic atmosphere for the legal team as they awaited the arrival of Tripp Joiner. He was soon escorted in by two guards who removed the handcuffs and departed behind the soundproof walls.

Everyone stood and Tripp shook hands all around. After everyone was seated, Mule Sherman, chief defense council, began to speak. "If all agree, I will say a few words and Will Clarkson will speak next, then Hal Hall if he so wishes. Tripp, you jump in at any time with your questions and comments.

"I would like to begin this meeting with our feelings of the general lay of the land, so to speak. Give me your thoughts and opinions of how we should fight this battle based on the evidence available to us and the prosecution, keeping in mind that much of the evidence is not yet in.

"As I see it, the state will try to make the death of Judge Parker out to be an assassination of a king and his brave bodyguard, defending his life by a vengeful assassin." Mule suddenly paused. He had felt early tension in the room, and it had slowly increased to a point to where it could be cut with a knife. Tripp's face was flush and the veins in his neck were protruding. His fists were clinched so tightly that his knuckles were white. Mule had seen similar signs in defendants before as they realized that the race that would determine their life or death had left the starting line. He could see tension in the face of Will Clarkson even though their earlier differences had been swept under the rug. Hal was showing tension also. Probably more out of fear of this awesome responsibility than of anything else. After all, he was helping to defend his lifelong friend.

Mule stood up and began to chuckle. "Tripp, as I look around the room,

158

what I see would frighten me to death if I were looking from your eyes. What a motley looking bunch of warriors are we. Look at me. I'm a big lanky man in a Buffalo Bill cowboy suit with long hair down to my shoulders hiding oversized ears but with nothing to hide my grossly oversized hands and with expensive boots designed to minimize my huge feet." He shifted his eyes to Tripp and caught a slight smile, an indication that the tension was easing, then on to Will Clarkson.

"Look at ole Will there. He's wearing a dime store outfit with a used car salesman suit, an out of style tie and un-shined shoes. He is, without a doubt, the best in Texas in destroying the testimony of expert witnesses. From history, he knows all the expert witnesses that this prosecutor has a tendency to use. He uses people with long resumes and encourages them to embellish as they see fit. By the time it becomes Will's turn to cross examine, their egos are so inflated that when they see him approach with a dumb expression on his face and dressed like a country bumpkin, they are easily led into his trap. This costume gives him an edge similar to mine. Have you noticed? The prosecutors lead their experts through a list of credentials long enough to choke a horse in order to convince the jurors that he or she is the most knowledgeable about the subject matter. Mr. Clarkson steps up in his camouflage. They will never know that he has four or five suits exactly alike in his closet to go with several pair of identical shoes. He does have several ties, but all are out of style. His wife has some difficulty finding him out-of-date ties. He sometimes wears unironed shirts to further the image. That outfit he's wearing is pure show, designed to create an image of a person of superior intellect being questioned by a dumb lawyer. By the way, you should see his wardrobe when he's stepping out in New York or Paris." Then to Hal.

"Now let's look at Hal. The barber that has never set foot in a courtroom before. From the look at the early reports we asked him to prepare, he has established himself as an expert on case law. His barbershop knowledge of our jury pool will, I believe, give us at least one juror who will be on our side from the outset, and he will know something about others that the prosecution will not. His after-work business of providing free aid to the poor and indigent has established a large clientele in the Hispanic community. If any Hispanics are seated on the jury, and we will work to see that it happens, they will have heard about Mr. Hall's good deeds.

"We are all that stand between your life and death. Yeah, I would be

159

tense too." He paused for reflection, the continued, "But now, let me give you the good news that should take all your fears away. This Wild West outfit I wear is a costume that makes me a memorable character and gives me an edge. It has made me famous or notorious and people remember me because I look different. Almost every juror who sits in that box will have heard of me. He or she will believe that since I'm famous, I must be a good lawyer, and believe you me, I am a good lawyer. I have never lost a capital murder case. I have had two hung juries that were never retried.

"So, Mr. Joiner, rest easy and relax. You have a team that is pretty dang good. Let's not forget that the name Tripp Joiner is known by every football fan in America. Your recent MVP award, being selected All-Pro five times, and having been seen by millions in the Super Bowl, combined with your well-publicized contributions to charities everywhere gives us a huge edge."

Tripp Joiner spoke up. "Thanks for the assurances, Mule. I do believe we'll win. The confidence is there, but I know that I'll always be a little apprehensive, no matter how good we are looking now or in the last proceedings. I repeat what I said earlier. I have all the confidence in the world in this team, but you failed to mention our greatest advantage of all. I did not commit either of these killings and history tells me that very few innocent men have been convicted of murder. I am, however, literally fighting to keep my sanity as I fight sorrow and loneliness locked up in that tiny cell. I plead with you to continue to try to get me released on bail."

"Ok, Tripp, I hear what you're asking. We're asking for another bail hearing next week. What you are saying about the conviction of an innocent man is the gospel truth. Now we must go on with business with a confident mindset.

"As I was saying, I believe that if the prosecution wants to make the victim a mythical king then we must destroy the myth and show him for what he really was. He has made himself a political kingpin for a reason. He wanted influence with the most important people in D.C. in order to get something in return. There has to be dirt somewhere and we will find it. We will then find a way to get some of it before the jury and we will find other ways to use it.

"We will need to know everything not only about Mr. Parker but about his family history. How was his family fortune made and where were the profits spent? We will also need to know who the key players are and what role they play. In effect, we want to kick over every rock that has a Parker near it.

"I want to assign Hal to this project. I'm convinced that he can handle this project and we will give him the best PI I've ever known as his helper. His name is Jeb Cassidy, from Houston, called Hoppy after the old cowboy star Hopalong Cassidy.

"Hoppy became a household name in the FBI after he took a slug in his knee during a shootout with some bad guys and was left with a bad limp. He was decorated for bravery in the line of duty on three different occasions and became a cult hero among the agents. His personality is magnetic, and this has expanded his legion of friends and contacts. Some of his friends have been promoted to high level positions in the bureau. This gives him information sources in high places like no other PI ever had. Fortunately for us but unfortunately for him, he challenged the authority of his superiors one too many times and was canned. He is truly unique. The only one of his kind to come out of the FBI into this line of work. His price tag is right up there with his worth, which is tremendous, so we use him as sparingly as possible. He will work through Hal and receive all his instructions from him. We will pass our needs through Hal."

Mule continued, "The prosecution will want to balance our super star athlete with their movie star, Vita Vorhees, but they will find themselves caught between a rock and a hard place because her testimony will open the bribe attempt and perhaps even testimony in the death of Debi Devereaux. Wouldn't we dearly like to put her on trial for murder right there on the witness stand? Of course, the judge will not let us get near that. The only really big thing that the state can hang their case on is the eyewitness to the killing of Mr. Malham. This is, as we all know, Lilia Parker Vorhees, daughter of Parker and the mother of Vita. We must destroy her credibility and establish her obvious motives for fingering Tripp. The search for dirt will not end here. There is plenty to look for in the life of Mr. Malham. He was much more than a bodyguard for the judge. He was a confident and a strong man enforcer who was up to his elbows in bribery and possibly blackmail. Our investigation will start with these people and go as far and wide as necessary, even to

161

Washington, D.C. Now, Will, step up and lay out your thoughts."
Will began, "I didn't realize that my 'camouflage' suit was so obvious. Maybe I need to make some changes. I do believe there was a backhanded compliment there someplace in that long-winded commentary, but I was raised on a farm. I'm a country bumpkin and am proud of it. I want you to know that I showed considerable legal talent as a young boy when I learned to mimic the whinny of a horse and the braying of a mule. No pun intended Mr. Sherman."

The room erupted in laughter that produced a quizzical expression on the guard's face as he looked through the one-way glass and a profound "Touché!" by Mule. It was now established that the staid Mr. Will Clarkson had a sense of humor.

Back on subject, Will continued, "Now, I am working, as we speak, on the blood transfer evidence in this case because it is my belief that it clearly shows that Mr. Parker and Mr. Malham were killed by two different people, and most importantly, that Parker was killed by Malham. The significance of this, if true, is that it can make our case. The expert witnesses we bring in on this must be the very best available and I have them in my sights. Obviously, they will bring in witnesses who will counter ours and we must be prepared to shoot holes in their interpretation of the evidence.

"We have an accurate description of the crime scene from the time our client arrived until he passed out, but we must rely to a great extent on the blood transfer evidence to fill in the rest of the picture. I would like for Mr. Cassidy to give his evaluation of the scene independently and compare it to mine in report form before he goes on the goose chase. I will have more to say later but I would like to hear what Mr. Hall has to say. By the way, I know this judge, and it's my opinion that he will never let any evidence in about past bad acts by the victims. We are about to waste a lot of money and resources on a search for dirt."

Hal spoke in a voice steeped with sincerity as he said, "I want to thank you for allowing me to help in any way you wish. I've known Tripp since we were six years old. I gave him his name, Tripp. I would stake my own life on his innocence. I believe him when he says that Parker was dead when he arrived, and I believe him when he says he was unconscious when Two Gun was shot. I also believe that he was in a life or death struggle at the end and that he would have killed in order to save his own life, but he did not have that opportunity. I have given notice at my shop that I will spend all my time working on this case until its conclusion, and I will continue to work on this case for free. My research starts today."

The session ended when two jailers escorted the legal party from the room, then Tripp was cuffed and thoroughly searched before he was returned to his cell to fight yet another round with his demons.

Hal Hall returned to his assigned legal office as he tried to deal with a strange feeling that he could not remember having before. It was a feeling of apprehension crossed with some euphoria. He was excited but was also pushing back self-doubt. He calmed himself somewhat by realizing that he would have all the help and guidance he needed. By the time that he was seated behind his desk, he was pumped and ready. He began to make the outline of a plan.

His search for data began with the evidence list compiled by the investigators. This list had been copied to the defense earlier and it provided some items that he needed for further review. One was the file on Judge Parker's unfinished memoirs. He went through the necessary procedures and obtained a copy. This file contained a partially written manuscript and dozens of loose notes and papers. One such list contained the names of many very important people and world leaders. Some names had small notes and dates written in the margins. If this list was indicative of people Parker knew personally and had developed relationships with, then he truly was a very powerful man. It was, in Hal's mind, an indication that he wanted the world to know it. Some interesting marks appeared on the list. There were a series of random numbers appearing to rank them in priority. There were circles around four of the names and one name had been crossed out. Hal's curiosity led him to focus on the crossed out one, Senator Lester Hartley of Texas. Research showed that he had served six terms in the U.S. Senate after two terms in the House. This name went to the top of his interview list.

In addition to the VIP list, a Robert E. Wright was described as his college roommate at Columbia University and later as one of his key business employees and lifelong friends. This name was added as a high priority interview. He sent these names and a few others to Hoppy Cassidy so he could develop contact information and locations of these people. Hoppy was due in town in two days, and arrangements were made for him to tour the crime scene according to legal guidelines. Hal wanted the info before Hoppy became engrossed in the evaluation of the actual crime evidence, and in essence, attempted to solve the crime.

Cassidy arrived on schedule and Hal accompanied him to the Parker mansion in order to do some more snooping for dirt. The only interesting thing discovered was a book entitled *The Early History of the Parker Family*, written by Loucetta Givens Parker in 1931. It was a thin book filed away on the top shelf of the library. A quick thumb through indicated interesting reading and seemed to satisfy the need for reporting how the family acquired its initial wealth but it contained far more material than would be included in this report.

Hal initially labeled his report "The Dirt Search" and began work in earnest on the most important task ever assigned to him. He rejected the temptation to mimic the writing style of his favorite author of mystery stories or to somehow create his own personal touch. Mule's instructions were very clear. "Make the report short and sweet but include all pertinent facts and rumors involving Mr. Horace Parker and his family. Do not attempt to write a book. This report will not be published for use outside our defense team.

He attempted to cross out irrelevant parts of the book and reduce the remainder into short story form. After three reductions, it still contained too much content, but he became engrossed in this remarkable story about the patriarch of the Parker dynasty, Solomon Parker, and kept feeling something tugging at his conscience. Finally, the light came on. The actions of Solomon and the other early west Texas settlers and the trying times in which they lived before and after the war produced a special breed of people never before seen in American history nor seen since. This created the opportunity to develop a great trial defense strategy. He would need all that he had written in order to make his point to the defense team, especially Mule Sherman. Wouldn't it be ironic if the life of the patriarch helped to free the accused killer of the last male member of the Parker dynasty?

CHAPTER TWENTY-ONE

Home for the Ranger

The story began in 1825 when the government of Coahuila y Tejas created the Empresario System as a means of establishing colonies of immigrant Americans in Mexico. Moses Austin, and later, his son Stephen became Empresarios and brought families into the country. The family of Solomon Parker, which included his parents, a brother, two sisters and an uncle, was selected by Stephen F. Austin. They, as all colonists were required to, converted to Catholicism as a term of immigration. Many reverted to their original religious beliefs but Solomon and his family did not. He and his decedents remained devout Catholics throughout history.

The Texas Rangers were formed by Austin as a means of maintaining law and order among the colonists and for protection from Indians. Young 17-year-old Solomon volunteered his services to the rangers, and when the Texans declared war on Mexico in 1835, he left with his ranger company for scouting duties with the fast forming rebel army.

Each proudly wore a badge hammered out of a Mexican peso. They were promised about 10 pesos per month in wages. Their assignment was to set up an outpost on the Pecos River at a shallow water crossing and to mount scouting patrols in order to sound the alarm of any signs of a Mexican army approaching from the west. The company consisted of 47 men and was commanded by a captain with two lieutenants as the only other officers. They were provided with basic provisions and were instructed to "live off the land." This meant that they must seize supplementary foodstuffs from the local population, which was sparse and scattered.

The officers and sergeants were armed with swords and two muzzle-loaded pistols and the men were armed with two muzzle-loaded pistols and a rifle. Two wagons pulled by mules carried powder, lead pistol and musket balls, medical supplies, blankets, clothing, cooking and eating utensils, flour, sugar, dried beans, beef jerky, horse rations, repair tools and other supplies. Each man was mounted on a horse that was personal property brought from home. Two spare mounts were available and traveled with the wagons. The seizure or "scavenge" of fresh food and especially meat, mostly by force, was aided by the taking of wild game when available. Virtually all of these residents were Mexican citizens and were very hostile. The rangers never left the victims without food and were ordered to be humane and to never fire a shot unless absolutely necessary.

Solomon was assigned to "scavenger" duty with a sergeant and nine others on one cloudy day that unknowing to him would end up being one of the most fateful days in his life. He was soon to come face to face with Gilberto Diaz Garcia.

The frequent mention of "El Grande" by locals prompted a plan to find this wealthy ranch with expectations of a very successful food source. The words El Grande was a description, not a name. No one seemed to know the true name of the ranch, but rough directions were converted into a crude map. The location was estimated to be just under 10 kilometers upriver, with the main house being about 4 kilometers north of the river itself.

The scavenger party mounted up at sunrise still grumbling about this distasteful duty and the displeasure of being led by the despised Ranger Sergeant Millard Jefferson Braden, Jr., a veteran of Indian fighting in Tennessee as a member of the U.S. Calvary. He had been cashiered out of the army for drinking on duty and for striking a superior officer. He managed to cross over into east Texas, still wearing his uniform, and presented himself to Stephen Austin at the time that any man with military experience was desperately sought. He was rejected for army service but was sent to the rangers with the rank of sergeant. He ate alone and generally kept to himself except to tell stories of his past bravery and to brag about how many Indians he had killed. He was disrespectful to his superiors, which earned him perpetual scavenger duty. He actually liked this duty because it kept him supplied with alcohol.

One day, on the way to the intended goal, the group came across another ranch that provided enough supplies to cause Sgt. Branden to send three overloaded men back to camp, making certain that the confiscated jug of homemade wine was left behind for his personal consumption. Everyone in the group but him could converse in Spanish, so his role was limited. But his old U.S. Army uniform was useful in making him stand out as a person of authority enforcing law and order.

As they approached the target destination, the alarm of their approach was sounded first by a peacock then by dogs and guinea fowl joining in the din. They followed the approach protocol, with one man out front by at least 100 feet and the others spread out on guard for any unusual activity. They needed to know where the men were because each would be a weapon threat.

As usual, the family women and children came out on the front porch and the all others stopped their activities to watch them ride in. Only one very old man was visible standing near an out-building. He was holding a musket. Guns were trained on him as he was instructed to lay the weapon on the ground, and he promptly complied.

Corporal Ruiz, the point man, removed his hat and extended greetings to the obvious matriarch standing on the porch as he explained who they were and what their mission was. She became clearly upset and ordered the three young teenage girls to go back into the house. By then, as part of a well-rehearsed plan, two riders had ridden to the back of the house and one had entered the back door. Two others went to the out-buildings for a closer look. Anything on their memorized list was fair game if it could be carried on horseback. With all clear, the confiscation began.

The smokehouse yielded a cured ham and a side of bacon. The fruit cellar produced some dried and preserved fruits. Sgt. Braden burdened his horse with bottles of wine. Solomon Parker tied on a large pig, a duck and three chickens. Others tied on a young goat and other poultry. Some fresh garden vegetables and a melon were still in a basket and were taken, basket and all. The treasure trove was so abundant and unusual that the temptation was to carry away more than should be tied to saddles, and they all yielded to temptation.

The operation was swift and efficient, and they were mounted and on their way in little more than half an hour. In spite of their vigilance, no one noticed that the larger of the three girls had slipped away until she was seen fleeing from behind the main barn, mounted bare back with flailing reigns and riding due north at full gallop. No one needed to say a word. All knew that she was riding for help from the men of the ranch. The scavengers' pace was quickened as they knew not how great the danger was, nor how long it would take them to arrive. But they could

167

not proceed faster than a trotting pace as they headed for the river. The sergeant was well into the sauce by now but still sober enough to recognize danger. He might soon be required to make the decision to abandon the goods or to stand and fight against an unknown enemy. His precious wine cargo was certainly worth fighting for against what he thought would be a few poorly armed peasant vaqueros. They would, he told himself, be turned back at the sight of the well-armed rangers and a U.S. Army uniform firing a few well-placed musket rounds.

A shout from Solomon, who was the most burdened with the load of a heavy goods and who was trailing, caused every head to turn towards the approaching riders, who were well back but closing fast. There appeared to be far more than Braden expected, perhaps twelve to fifteen. Heavy dust made it impossible to determine how well they were armed but he could see that a few had muskets held above their heads.

Common sense trumped drunken bravado and he started searching for a defensive position. A large outcropping on some higher ground lay to his left about 400 meters away. They should easily make this, but it would require a sharp turn, and this was bad news because it would place them broad side to their aim. A suitable turning place was found, and the rangers wheeled left with Solomon trailing behind.

He had made the decision to cut the pig loose but delayed when the lead horse turned left. Sure enough, musket and pistol fire erupted as they came broadside. The shots were fired from about 80 to 90 meters away and drew return fire from several rangers. No one was hit but a slug passed through the neck of Solomon's mare and she pitch-polled headfirst with blood spurting from an artery. She had managed to make three good jumps before going down and blood covered his face and front side. Sweet little Dimples, Solomon's pride and joy, a gift from his father, lay on top of his lower body as she gave her last kicks in a death spasm.

The unconscious Solomon lay unmoving as the assailants rode up and past, with Gilberto Diaz Garcia signaling forward. He awakened to the sounds of gunfire coming from the area of the rock outcropping. A quick look around showed that he was alone. He was battered and bruised but could feel no broken bones. A cut on his forehead was bleeding but not seriously. One of his legs, still trapped under his horse was numb. He managed to free his usable leg and use it to push the dead horse off the

168

other. A quick rub of the leg brought back circulation and feeling.

Solomon retrieved his loaded pistols but nothing else as he crawled into nearby bushes. The cargo was scattered and the pig had vanished. His first option was to find a better hiding place until he could figure out how to join his comrades, which would not be easy since the enemy was blocking the way. He began to crawl closer to the firing, making certain that he remained well hidden. The firing had subsided to occasional shots as the reloading of powder and ball was a slow process. A few large rocks on the extreme edge of the large outcroppings came into view and he used these as a stopping point to sit up and catch his breath and reconsider his options.

He could now make out the back of the enemy position and could see a few of the vaqueros facing away. He noticed movement that indicated they were spreading out and probably looking for a way to surround the rangers. He saw the movement of a horse to the side and behind the men then he could see a rump of another. "This must be where the horses are tied," he thought. A man dressed in black clothes and sombrero came into view walking towards the horses. This was the outfit worn by the wealthiest Mexican ranchers. Solomon knew he had located the leader. The man returned to his position with a small telescope.

Solomon abandoned the idea of joining his friends. He now knew that would require making a very large circle around to the backside over exposed ground and could not be attempted until darkness. Even then, he might not be able to slip in because they might be surrounded. If he could steal a horse, he could ride for help back to camp or at least get close enough for gunfire to be heard there. He chose to steal a horse. He would probably have only one guard to deal with and he would likely be the youngest. Maybe a teenage boy or an old man. His confidence grew.

Sgt. Braden was also considering his options. He was hopeful that a scout from the base camp would hear the gunfire and go for help, but if that happened, it would be hours before they arrived. If they did not return by dark, a large search and rescue party would be sent out at first light. He could abandon his cargo and run for it, or he could attempt to send a lone rider on the fastest horse to the post.

This idea was abandoned as a shot was fired from the rear. This prompted him to order more protection for the horses who were out of

169

sight in the gulley, a very nice feature of their well-chosen defensive position. A try at negotiations would be very tricky.

He was in the act of retrieving another bottle of wine from his horse when he heard shouting from the enemy position and noticed a makeshift white flag mounted on a musket barrel being waved. Someone shouted that this meant they wanted to negotiate a deal. Braden suspected a trap, but Corporal Ruiz assured him that Mexican blue bloods were honorable people, and this was probably on the up and up. Gilberto Garcia requested that the adversaries each send one man out for talks, but Braden didn't trust this, and his few numbers did not allow him to risk a single man. The shouting back and forth had attracted the attention of all of the combatants. A cease fire was in place, but no one was exposing himself to possible gunfire.

Solomon had crept very close to the horses and could plainly see an old man guarding them. He was turned toward the shouting with his back to Solomon. He recognized his chance to slip up behind the guard, knock him unconscious with the butt of his pistol and escape unscathed. He hesitated as he could clearly see the backside of the leader who was doing all the shouting. Everyone in sight was deeply engrossed in the attempted negotiations.

Without really thinking, he raced across the ten paces to Gilberto Garcia and had a pistol to his head and a choke hold around his neck before he could be stopped. He pressed his head against the back of his captive's head lest someone be tempted to shoot, as he shouted for all to throw down their weapons and lie face down on the ground. He told Gilberto to command them to follow instructions.

Solomon turned one way then the other in order to give a moving target as the vaqueros slowly complied with orders. A young man dressed in similar attire as Gilberto was the last in sight to lay down his weapons. Solomon moved Gilberto into sight of the rangers and three of them immediately began to run to his aid. Soon all of the enemy had been rounded up and gathered into a small area, searched for knives and other weapons, which were piled up well away from the captives.

The capture was complete, and Sgt. Braden took charge and began giving orders. They would leave the unarmed vaqueros in place under guard until all weapons and horses had been collected. Gilberto Garcia and his son would be bound by rope and taken to the riverbank, with the horses scattered out of sight and the weapons left at river's edge down river from the two men. They would eventually be released and able to catch all the horses and retrieve all their weapons.

Solomon, having no mount, was allowed to select one of the captured horses. He chose the magnificent stallion being ridden by Gilberto, much to his chagrin and in spite of his pleas and an offer to give him anything else that might want. He rode the stallion back to the dead body of Dimples, removed his own saddle and replaced the saddle on the stallion. He seriously considered searching for the missing pig as a matter of principle but thought better of it and rode away.

Now intact, the scavenger party set out for the river, expecting an easy ride home. But thanks to Sgt. Braden, this was not to be the case. He had taken the lead rope on Gilberto's mount and could not resist taunting him. He received a cursing in return but could not understand what was being spoken in Spanish. When his men began to laugh, he asked for and received a translation. This so incensed him that he snatched the silver cross from the neck of his captive, whose hands were tied behind his back.

Gilberto Diaz Garcia spat in the face of Sgt. Braden and was immediately sentenced to death by hanging for his act by the intoxicated Braden, who of course, had no authority to do so. He ordered someone to produce a rope and to find a suitable tree.

The men began to murmur among themselves and no one complied with his orders. He removed a lasso from one the captured horses and placed the noose around the neck of the clearly frightened Gilberto and led him to first thing that resembled a suitable limb in a mesquite tree. Corporal Ruiz was telling him to stop. Private Solomon Parker pulled his pistol, disarmed Braden, removed the noose and pushed the sergeant with his foot, out of his saddle and onto the ground. He then bound and gagged him and tied him in his saddle where he remained until they reached camp well after dark.

They kept their bargain with the Garcias, and he and his son were released as planned on the riverbank. Solomon promised Gilberto that he would return the horse after the war was over and asked for the horse's name. It was obvious that this promise was not believed when Gilberto turned his back and walked away.

Most of the rest of the night was spent by the captain and lieutenants taking testimony from all participants and witnesses. A decision was made that resulted in the next day's departure of Sargent Millard Jefferson Braden Jr. under escort from the camp on the Pecos to the nearest Texas army headquarters, though no one had the slightest idea where that might be. Solomon Parker, "for bravery and the execution of uncommon quick judgment," was promoted to sergeant.

Santa Anna led his Mexican army across the Rio Grande River in January 1836 and moved towards San Antonio. Solomon's company was ordered to move to the rear of Santa Anna's Mexican army so as to harass its supply lines and to help protect the Anglo-American settlers against the Indians. The fear of raids and death by Indians was by far the biggest concern of the settlers, not the revolution.

One particular band of Comanche raiders was led by a young chief who was always seen on an Appaloosa horse with unique leopard spot arrangement. The head was solid colored and the remainder of the body spotted. No one ever learned his name, so he was called Spotted Horse Chief. His band was known and feared by its brutality. No victim's life was ever intentionally spared. Sightings were scarce and usually from considerable distances, but the uniqueness of the horse's markings made identification unmistakable. His torture methods were always the same and were only applied to the oldest male captured. His fondness for fruit preserves presented another clue to his presence. His habit was to hit two or three homesteads close to together and in a very short period of time, then disappear to the north. The rangers made several unsuccessful chases without ever catching sight of this particular band.

The revolution ended in April 1836 and Solomon Parker's one-year enlistment ended a few months later. He made plans to return home to his family.

The war was short, and victory was sweet and celebrated by all the Anglos. There were very few protestant churches in Texas at this time, but every town had a Catholic church. Bells sounded in all churches that had an Anglo as a parishioner and thanksgiving prayer services were held in most. Later in life, Solomon gathered his children and grandchildren around him on every possible occasion in order to tell and retell the

172

details of every event, significant or not, about ranger life and the war-ending celebrations. But there was one short period about which he never disclosed the details to anyone except his wife, and then on only one occasion after a few years of marriage when he was awakened by a nightmare. She recorded every word in her diary and no one read the entry until after her death.

Solomon had saddled up before good light and gathered his belongs, shared goodbye hugs with his closest friends and waved adios to rest of the rangers as he rode out of camp. Mixed emotions were playing tag with his brain. Excitement and sadness; two-way home sickness as he was leaving one home for another; yearning to see one family while leaving another; and resuming the life of a rancher's son while leaving his warrior self behind; brave in battle but apprehensive about riding alone for more than two days in hostile territory.

The jingle of pesos, one month's pay, tied in his rolled-up kerchief cheered him as he made a decision to ride about 12 kilometers out of his way to visit the trading post and purchase gifts for his family and maybe a stick of candy for himself. He planned the gift selections as he envisioned the smiles on the faces of his little sisters and brother. Tears wet his eyes as he imagined hearing his mother's voice. These thoughts caused him to push his horse, now renamed Comet, to a faster pace. He dreaded to tell his father about the death of Dimples but "his eyes will jump out of his head when he sees Comet. He has never before seen an animal like this mount."

After a good morning greeting was exchanged with the proprietor, the collection of gifts was placed on the counter and the bill was paid. The man introduced himself and asked Solomon his name. Upon hearing "Parker," his face paled as he asked if he were related to the Parker family who lived a ways northeast who had been massacred by the Cheyenne last month. Solomon asked for more details then bolted out of the store, leaving his paid-for goods behind. He leaped into the saddle and rode away at full gallop. He got all Comet could give until he dismounted at the homestead.

All buildings, a wagon and the corral fence were burned to the ground. He stood motionless and could not force himself to look around for fear of seeing what he knew would be there. Finally, he turned, and there, looking like the entry to Hell, were six mounds of dirt. The obvious graves were arranged purposely in order of two long, three short and another long a few yards away. He flung himself face down between the two longs as he attempted to hug his mother and father. He wept and wept and wept some more until there was no moisture left in his eyes. Then he forced himself to stand over the graves of his sister and brother, still sobbing. He said a few words to all six as he called them each by name. No more tears came that day or that week or that month or that year or ever again.

The air was still and even the birds were silent. No animals were in sight, but a few chickens were scratching for food in the nearby fields. He and his ranger band had come on these scenes before and as shocking as they were, heads had to be cleared and business taken care of.

A thorough examination of the clues confirmed that these Indians were Cheyenne. The fruit cellar showed that his mother's fruit preserves, sealed in small homemade pottery jars, were missing. This may or may not be proof that the Spotted Horse Chief was responsible. A wider search turned up some cows but no horses. He expanded his circle until he came to the nearest neighbor and had to face a duplicate tragedy with eight graves.

Without hesitating, he whirled his horse and rode hard past his home to the nearest neighbor on the other side, where he was relieved to find all was well. He was talking to the people who had discovered and buried his family. They offered details but he refused to hear. No one had seen the raiders nor the suspected Spotted Horse Chief. Solomon was asked to stay as long as he wished until all business had been attended to.

Three days later, he rode out to return his borrowed horse. He pinned on his crude ranger badge. It just might just provide a little protection along the way. He didn't want to admit to himself, but he was a little frightened and less confident of his abilities after experiencing the tragedy of the last few days.

He rode until he came to the Pecos and followed its banks until he recognized the trail that he and the scavengers had taken not many months before. This would lead him to the main road to the ranch headquarters. The ranch name, he now knew from the details of the written incident report made by his captain regarding the cashiering of Sargent Braden, was Arcoiris [Rainbow].

174

Comet's pace picked up as he recognized home territory, and Solomon had to hold him back with a tight rein. A lone rider did not bring out the large alarm committee of wailing creatures as had the larger group of scavengers. In fact, they were close enough to see three girls and a woman picking beans in the garden before they were discovered. Then the alarm sounded, but the dogs, recognizing the horse, were less hostile.

The girls raced to house shouting "Rojo! Sus Rojo Papa!"

Señor Garcia came out the front door and ran towards the horse. Solomon dismounted at the well, removed his hat and proudly said, "Señor, as promised, I return your horse."

The man, now with arms around the horse's neck, said nothing but "Rojo, Rojo, mi Rojo," as tears formed in his eyes.

The woman, clearly his wife, and the three girls gathered around as their husband and father said, "This is the man who saved my life. I do not know his name."

"Sargent Parker, er Solomon Parker," blurted out Solomon. "Nice to meet you," proudly spoken in pretty decent Spanish, he thought.

The woman, Adora, held out her inverted hand as she introduced herself. Solomon knew enough to kiss the back of her hand as she introduced her daughters, Rosita, Sofia and Pepita. When asked about her son, Gilberto Garcia answered, "Alberto went off to fight for Santa Anna and has not yet returned, but we expect him any day now."

A servant watered the horse and led him away to be unsaddled and fed. Solomon was invited into the house where a quick meal was served and a jug containing cool water was brought up from the bottom of the well. After a lengthy conversation, Solomon stated that his plans were to first obtain a replacement horse for his Dimples but that he was not sure what his plans were next. He said, matter of factually, that he had no family to return to as they were killed by Cheyenne. One option would be to reenlist in the rangers. They wanted more details on the Indian raid, but it was clear that he did not wish to relive that pain. Death by Indians was the most feared means of dying by the remote west Texas residents.

It was clear that a free horse was expected as compensation for Dimples, but since the rangers had taken loot from the ranch, Señor Garcia, when dealing in horses, was all business. Solomon would be allowed to select one from hundreds on the ranch. Garcia was in the business of raising horses and many were nearby and broken to the saddle. He could purchase one with coin or in exchange for work. Solomon, stating that he was a pretty good wheelwright, agreed to replace or repair all the spokes in their wagon wheels. A deal was struck and then Gilberto rewarded him for saving his life by offering to let him stay on the ranch for as long as he liked. That deal would be confirmed by Alberto, the crown prince in this Spanish land grant aristocracy, upon his return.

Solomon Parker settled comfortably into his life on this ranch, ruled with an iron fist by a pseudo king over almost slave-like servants. He was assigned quarters with the vaqueros and set about repairing wheels and doing odd carpentry work. The women of the house asked him to teach them English and this became a nighttime routine. Rosita, the oldest daughter, started serious flirtation. Solomon was unsure how to deal with this, especially since he was learning to like it and feeling the urge to reciprocate. However, it became clear that Señor Garcia disapproved when English lessons were halted for a time.

Alberto never returned from the war and, after several months, an appeal was made through the church to find out why. Records were searched in Mexico City by an emissary and it was learned that he died in an accident crossing the Rio Grande as Santa Anna's army retreated back to Mexico. A mourning period was declared by the family and no family member left the home for 30 days except for emergencies.

Some gratification came to Solomon with knowledge that Alberto was not killed by a gringo bullet, but he still felt the sting of being treated as an enemy combatant for many weeks. Word came that a strong move was underway in the Texas Congress to seize lands from the Spanish land grant recipients. A plan formed in Gilberto Garcia's mind to protect his property from this move if it came to pass. Why not have a soldier from the rebel army, a gringo, as a family member?

He began to condone and even encourage the flirtation between Rosita and Solomon. This soon developed into serious romance then a short engagement and marriage with conditions regarding Solomon's position in the family aristocracy. He would not inherit the estate, but his oldest son would. The oldest son's name would be Gilberto Diaz Garcia Parker.

176

On the death of Gilberto, Solomon would rule the dynasty until his death and full control would then go to his son. All other heirs would share in the estate, but all land titles would forever continue to be passed to the eldest Parker son. The "Parker Dynasty" was spawned.

One year into the marriage a son was born, and two years later a second son was born.

By then, Spotted Horse Chief was raiding again, and more ranchers were killed. Horses were also taken from the Arcoiris ranch and ranchers from far and wide were demanding action from the new government. The rangers were busy elsewhere, so the local ranchers organized a posse and asked Solomon Parker to lead it since he had experience as a ranger. He agreed in spite of the objections of Señor Garcia and began to make plans to dispose of the renegade killer of his family.

He cut a deal with the Apache enemies of the Cheyenne for them to provide three trackers to back track the quarry to their hideout and to lead the posse to the prey. Solomon needed only about 20 fighters because the Cheyenne lived in small bands unlike all other Indians who lived in large tribal villages. Having superior weapons was a major factor, as well. Each member of the posse carried two pistols, a rifle and a Bowie knife. Many also carried swords.

The village of the Spotted Horse band was located in Palo Duro Canyon at the Caprock escarpment on the high plains of the Texas panhandle. The well-armed posse of 21 gringos, Hispanics and Apache braves rode out a first light on a cloudy fall day.

Their plan was to attack as the morning meal was being prepared, before the male fighters had begun to stir. The Apache scouts quietly disposed of the unsuspecting sentries and the posse rode in to begin the turkey shoot.

Completely surprised, many Indian men were cut down by the first volley before they could wield a weapon. Rifles and pistols, kept reloaded by a special few, enabled a constant stream of lead slamming into the bodies of all armed males. Arrows, spears, war clubs, hand axes and knives had no chance to stop the slaughter. No woman, girl or unarmed boy was touched. The teepees were set afire but Solomon allowed no looting. Only replacement mounts and the scalps of the 39

Cheyenne men taken by the Apaches were allowed as spoils of war. Spotted Horse Chief was not identified but his infamous horse was killed so as to never be seen in a Texas raid again. The corpse was left for the women to add to the food cache.

The fight lasted less than two hours and the posse departed with four dead and six wounded fighters of their own. Solomon Parker suffered cuts on one arm and hand and a war club knot on his head.

The long ride home was filled with sorrow for their own causalities but with complete pride in their accomplishment. There was no celebration. None was wanted or needed. Each man felt that fair and warranted Texas justice had been served.

Details and memories of this massacre were passed on for many generations by the riders but not by Solomon Parker, who filed them away in the same dark closet with the memories of the deaths of his family, never to be spoken of again. When grandchildren asked the question "How many Indians have you killed, Grandfather?" his answer was always tersely and simply, "Too many."

CHAPTER TWENTY-TWO

The Apple Falls Close to the Tree

The Parker dynasty remained intact and managed to hold on to its vast land holdings through the major landmark changes in Texas history. Being a part of a Mexican state then an independent nation, part of the U.S.A., to a Confederate state then back to the U.S.A. brought little hardship to the family. Two sons returned safely from service in the War Between the States with battle wounds. Most of their horse herd was taken without final payment by the Confederate government and raising horses never returned as a vital part of family business.

The coming of the railroad with the opening of Midway Rail Station [Midland] in 1881 enticed the Parker family to relocate ranch headquarters near rail transportation so as to provide for easier travel across the country and to Europe. They traded for additional land in Ector County and built a new home featuring Victorian architecture -- a dramatic departure from the Spanish adobe design of the original headquarters home. This move also made it easier for the family to send their children to the best schools in the eastern part of the country.

Black gold was discovered in the Permian basin in 1921. The oil was a God-sent bonanza to the Parker dynasty because all of their land holdings fell within the basin. Drilling began immediately on the ranch.

The first well drilled on the small portion of land leased to a driller produced oil. The second move was to hire a driller on land not leased out, and the final move was to form a Parker-owned drilling company for the purpose of drilling thousands of new wells over many years. Each step produced a large increase in income, giving the family more cash than they could spend. Without knowing it immediately, the family became one of the wealthiest in the country.

Fame and notoriety came with wealth, and they found that management of assets and investments required more and more expertise as the fortune grew. The stock market crash in 1929 created a great loss in family wealth and a decision was made to send the eldest son, the legal heir and the family's crown prince, to an Ivy League school. After graduation, he moved to Europe for a substantial period in order to further his cultural education. This became a tradition that prevailed through the end of the life of the last male heir, Horace "Judge" Parker.

Hoppy Cassidy had located Senator Lester Hartley and Professor Robert Wright. Senator Hartley was enjoying retirement in his home on Lake Texoma in Texas and Professor Wright was teaching at the University of Central Arkansas in Conway, Arkansas. Cassidy informed them the nature of his business and got permission for him and Hal Hall to interview with each.

Before Hal made the calls, he had some difficulty deciding who to interview first. He decided to speak with Wright first because he had known the judge in his youth and was close to him for many years, from his college days through the years that he served as his top assistant until a much-publicized split that got splashed around the media. Hal believed that if bad blood still remained, the chances of finding the dirt that they were seeking were good. He was right. The good and the bad came out in buckets.

Hal reviewed the Robert Edward Wright bio, which had been prepared by Hoppy, as the two flew on the commercial flight to Little Rock in route to the prearranged appointment with Wright. It revealed a fascinating story of his entire life.

Wright was raised on a 60-acre hard scramble cotton farm in the community of Beryl in Faulkner County, Arkansas, near Conway. His father farmed the land with a team of mules while his mother taught school in nearby Vilonia. Young Robert chopped cotton, picked cotton, milked cows, slopped hogs, cut firewood and performed many other farm chores beginning at a very young age, and according to him, without complaint. He was blessed with a good mind and his I.Q. test scores encouraged his mother to push him as hard as she could to higher things other than small time cotton farming.

He ended up being a presidential scholar with a full ride scholarship to Columbia University, where he met fellow student Horace Parker from Ector County, Texas. After obtaining his master's degree in economics at Columbia, he enrolled at the University of Arkansas to complete his doctorate. From there he realized his lifelong ambition to teach at

180

Hendrix College in Conway. He left Hendrix to go to work for Horace and the Parker companies in Odessa, Texas, accompanied by his young wife, Myrtie. It turned out to be a good career move. It took him only three years to move up to the number two position under Horace, where he remained until the messy split several years later.

Hal rented a car at the airport and the pair drove through Conway, turning east on Highway 64 towards the community of Beryl 12 miles distant. A stop at the only business in Beryl, Avra's Grocery, got them directions to the Wright home. "Just up 64 a piece and turn right on the lane across from Beryl Baptist Church. First brick house. Can't miss it." They had seen no cotton growing since leaving Conway, yet they were still looking for a small cotton farm. Instead, they saw only a grass pasture with a few Black Angus cattle grazing, but the nice brick home came into view as they made the turn down the lane.

They were a few minutes early, so they parked to wait before leaving the car. Almost immediately, a tall balding man with a smile on his face walked to their car, saying in a loud voice, "Come in to this house. This isn't Texas but it's pretty dang close."

Hal had learned in his barbershop to be prepared as you shake hands with a rancher or farmer because they will put a handshake on you that can render serious bodily harm. The pain did not keep Hal from laughing as Hoppy and Robert compared and commented on their shiny bald knobs. This ritual seemed to be standard greeting protocol among bald headed men, but he never understood why. "Another of the great mysteries of life, I suppose," he thought as he followed the two equally gregarious yakers into the house.

Robert apologized for his wife's absence and directed them to the chocolate chip cookies and a pitcher of lemonade made from hand-squeezed lemons, with slices still floating Arkansas style and with coffee as a backup. Taught since childhood to never insult a host by refusing to partake of refreshment, both men reached for a cookie at the same time. Hal drank lemonade while Hoppy and Robert chose black coffee.

After making certain that Robert was informed again that they were there on behalf of the defense of Jimmy Jack Joiner and were fitting the pieces together of the entire life of Horace "Judge" Parker in order to avoid all prosecution surprises and to seek any and all information that might

181

benefit their client. They asked that Robert tell his complete knowledge or hearsay of all Parker activities that he was willing to share. This was not a deposition, after all, so no one was under oath.

Robert said that he fully understood their request and opened his story. "I may have been the closest thing to a friend that Judge ever had, or at least, he said as much on several occasions. In later years, he told the same thing to Two Gun Malham. He just never trusted very many people. He loved his daughter immensely and worshiped his granddaughter. He contributed much to society as a whole. He and his family gave millions to charity and worked behind the public eye to help a great many people. Many politicians owed their careers to him. He was, indeed, a great man in many respects. But he lived a double life and spent tons to keep the bad side secret. He was taught by his father that everything in life had a price and could be purchased. That included people. But there was an invisible line, when crossed, that constituted bribery and thus must be dealt with carefully and skillfully. I am reluctant to expose it all just now, but we will see where we wind up at the end of the day, so to speak. By the way, I do have the rest of this day available to talk but I must join my wife for dinner in Conway at 7:00."

The first time Robert Wright met Horace Parker, the two disgruntled and mismatched strangers were thrown together in the same dorm room. Horace began tossing bags through the door then announced that he preferred the bed already occupied by Robert. Horace seemed shocked when Robert refused his request, and he began to make a scene. Horace's father invited him out into the hall, and he returned with a change of attitude and soon smoothed everything over.

Their conversations became cordial, with Robert feeling sorry to learn that Horace enrolled at Columbia after flunking out at Harvard. His father, himself a Harvard grad, had dropped a wad of donation money in the right places in order to get his indifferent son in to that school, only to be rewarded with his son's desire to be a playboy instead of a student. Columbia didn't want him either, but again, money talked.

Horace soon discovered that Robert made a willing tutor. He began longtime plans to take advantage of that fact. They were both seeking degrees in economics, creating a perfect situation. Robert was short on cash and Horace had a pocket full, so he hired Robert as a tutor at 50 dollars per week. He also promised to take Robert in rent free when he

182

left the campus and rented an apartment.

Robert was hooked and happy to be so. The two actually began to like each other and to have long personal conversations, developing a friendship that lasted for many years. Robert enjoyed hearing the details of the fairytale life of the Parker prince, and Horace seemed interested as he listened in almost disbelief at the childhood chores assigned to Robert. He did not believe that a five-year-old boy had an assigned cow to milk or that he began to bust the middles of cotton rows behind a mule at age eight. But he never called him a liar. Nor did Robert call Horace a liar when he claimed to be heir to the largest ranch in Texas, one that floated on oil. After all, friends are allowed to brag to one another every now and then.

The move to a very expensive apartment happened as promised, marking the beginning of a very different lifestyle for the two roommates. Horace seldom attended classes and attempted to repeat the playboy lifestyle that caused his failure at Harvard. He now had Robert, who never skipped a class, covering all the bases for him. All he needed was for Robert to pull him through the cram sessions prior to tests. All he wanted was a passing test score. The only notes he kept were phone numbers of college girls and the train routes to the bars and clubs that sold liquor to underage college kids.

However, Horace discovered early on that his money was not enough to lure in the cream of the campus beauties. His rotund body and swarthy looks turned them off. Even penniless Robert managed to do better with women that he did, creating some jealousy. Horace made a rule preventing Robert from bringing women to the apartment. Since Robert was spending most of his time studying and reading, this wasn't a major issue.

Horace approached a few friendly bartenders about possible contacts with hookers and was rewarded with almost instantaneous service. One after another seemed to appear from nowhere, and Horace's hooker habit began in earnest, but he wasn't satisfied with the age and quality. He soon learned about the more expensive call girl pipeline. He was able, over time, to find just what he was looking for, beautiful young natural blonds who could be hired by the hour, by the day or by the week and even longer under certain circumstances.

Robert noticed that there seemed to be a girl in the house most all of the time, much to his dismay. One morning, he found a young teenager, clad in her undies, having breakfast in the kitchen as he entered to prepare something to eat for himself. He spoke to the young lady, a bit unsure as how to handle this encounter, expecting her to flee for some article of clothing, but she did not. Instead, she introduced herself and carried on a pleasant conversation throughout the entire meal and then departed to Horace's bedroom.

This meeting wouldn't have disturbed Robert at all had this girl not appeared to be underage for a prostitute and most certainly too young to be shacked up with Horace. He was informed later in the day that she was indeed 19, and he accepted this for the time being, but a few days later, the opportunity presented itself for Robert to have another conversation with her. Horace was out on an errand, and three bloody Maries had loosened her tongue to the point that Robert found himself listening to the girl's life story.

She was a runaway from New Jersey and had been taken in by a pimp. She was elevated from street work to the call girl circuit and was enjoying the high life of drugs and alcohol. She was hoping to find a John or someone who would take her in so that she could pursue an acting career. She admitted to being much younger than stated earlier. Robert felt sorry for the girl but made no commitments. When Horace returned, he was met with an ugly confrontation. Robert pointed out, "You are breaking the law with this underage girl, and it exposes me to your liability. I don't do crime and I can't stay here if you don't send her away.

Horace conceded, "OK. She is paid up through two more days, then she will be gone." Robert persisted and the girl was sent away in a taxicab. None of the women who came later stayed more than two days.

Time passed quickly and Horace managed somehow to make passing grades and graduate with a degree but did not stick around for the graduation ceremonies. He did take with him a pretty good education and actually enjoyed learning from some of it. He especially liked the brief lesson on the details of day trading on the stock market. Robert, on the other hand, enjoyed the celebratory moments of the graduation events with his parents and sister and took an excellent basic education with him to graduate school.

Horace spent a month at home before dashing off to Paris to begin his anticipated cultural education, following in the footsteps of his notorious father, James Parker. He was determined to become another dashing cavalier. He was a Don Juan wannabe with the intent of lifting more skirts of European royalty and blue-blooded lassies than had his father. This seemed to be his definition of cultural education. The problem was that he possessed none of the good looks and charisma of his father. The apple had not fallen far from the tree, but the fruit was not so sweet. He and Robert corresponded regularly, and Horace persuaded Robert to come over for a visit. It took less than a month for Robert to take in all the major tourist attractions and return to school.

A short time later, Horace managed to run up a large gambling tab at a Monaco casino, and Papa had to bail him out. This was an unforgivable sin in Papa's eyes. In fact, it had been made very clear to Horace before he left home that no serious gambling would be tolerated. In fact, gambling and serious criminal acts were about the only things that were off limits. Papa's European sojourn was the template by which standards were set. He cut the purse strings, and young Horace was forced to return home well short of the 10-year record set by his father. In fact, he lasted less than four years. Not only that, he had received the cold shoulder from the royalty and most of the blue bloods and had renewed his old habits of hiring call girls in his search for beautiful women.

A large welcome home party was given in Horace's honor and nothing was spared in the effort to make it a success. Robert was not invited. After the celebration, mother and father sat their little crown prince down for the serious introduction to real life. The entire scope of the Parker Empire was laid out, along with a written agenda that detailed how and when Horace would take control of the businesses.

He was awed yet somewhat apprehensive with what was expected of him. He would be paid a handsome salary and his title was now executive assistant to the CEO. He would spend training time in each of the corporate offices so as to understand the nature of each business. After training was complete, he would be assigned supervisory duties. He had no doubts that his feet would be held to the fire. More so by his mother than his father. Geraldine had, long ago, shown her ability to handle the Parker men.

It started when the dashing debonair, James Parker came home from

Europe and shocked the family and the community by marrying Geraldine, plucked right out of the barn of a nearby dairy farm owned by the Parkers. She was stocky but cute and had a beautiful smile. The marriage to a milkmaid set the gossip tongues speculating that James must have needed a change in lifestyle from "wild" women. It did not take her long to "tie him to her bed post" and drain him of all desire to pursue other women. In fact, he soon took full control of the dynasty holding company, Parker Enterprises Inc., and immersed himself in managing the vast business holdings.

Geraldine did the childrearing. She was very strict with Horace and his three siblings, but she tempered her discipline with genuine love and had a special place in her heart for Horace. She ignored the gambling habit he brought home with him. She did not believe that spending a few hundred dollars on stock market day trades was real gambling. His father had broken him from serious casino gambling and that was that.

Horace always had the ability to maneuver her, somewhat, with his pleas. There came an opening in the servant staff, and he told her about the pipeline of young women arriving in the U.S. from Scandinavian countries with the sole intent of working as domestics. He knew people in New York who could tap him in to the pipeline and produce a list of young women who were guaranteed to be young, intelligent, with good personal hygiene, trained in housework, and he thought but didn't say, blonde and beautiful. Let him, he asked, take on the task of getting this list for review.

Mom agreed but made it clear that the hiring decision would be hers alone. When the prospects folder arrived with resumes and pictures, Horace made his pick then told his mother that only one candidate had applied and Erikka Elstad was presented to Mom with Horace's plea, and she reluctantly agreed. The resultant hire was an 18-year-old blonde Norwegian girl who was enamored with the prospects of living in Texas so as to experience life in the "wild" west.

Though her command of the English language was very good, Erikka's only exposure to the west was through western movies and a few novels. On her arrival, she was somewhat surprised and disappointed to find no cowboys or Indians. Horace found it difficult to conceal his delight, as she was absolutely gorgeous in every respect. He began immediate plans for victory.

The advances by Horace started in a few weeks but Erikka held out for several months before she caved. She was showered with expensive gifts and grand promises. After understanding the immense wealth of the family and with the veiled promise of marriage, she agreed to a secret engagement. Horace had no real plans for marriage. His only desire was to start a romantic relationship with her, which he now was able to do.

A few months later, the family driver was carrying on his running conversation with his favorite bartender and the other regulars in his usual watering hole when he blurted out, "A big event is about to come down at the ranch. It seems that Junior has knocked up the maid and we are about to have a shotgun wedding." This premature announcement traveled fast via the grapevine of beauty salons, barbershops, bridge clubs and street gossip. This brought out media questions to the family and speculation in the gossip columns. Things never seemed to go right for Horace Parker.

The marriage produced one daughter, Lilia, and after three more years of trying for a male heir, Erikka had about all that she could stand of Horace and his philandering habits. She fled back to Norway, taking Lilia with her. Horace, now County Judge Parker, divorced Erikka but was unable to gain custody of Lilia or even get her back in Texas for a visit. He had to travel to Norway for that. Finally, enough money changed hands in a deal, and Lilia was allowed to attend selected private schools in the U.S. After college, she married a law student and settled down in Dallas.

Horace's economics education helped him to determine right away that some of the PEI companies were being poorly managed, and he turned to Robert Wright for help. First on a consultant contract, he wrote an evaluation on the biggest loser, a company that had never turned a profit. His father nor anyone else seemed to be concerned because of the flood of cash coming in from oil revenues. There was plenty of money to be blown by everyone.

Robert wrote the evaluation and added a plan for turning the sick company around. It included an incentive-based bonus plan for executives, later to include all employees. This company was a manufacturing company whose line workers were set up to be paid on a piecework basis with profit sharing. The plan included a system that reported budget variances in detail and real time. This system let managers set corrective actions in place almost immediately instead of

187

waiting for the monthly P&L weeks after.

This piece of work so impressed Horace and his father that Robert was asked to come aboard full-time to implement the plan there and in all the PEI companies except Arcioris Oil. Robert was reluctant to accept the job but the lure of the big bucks and pleas from his personal friend finally persuaded him and his wife to make the move. All the companies became profitable and Robert became a true insider, almost but not quite part of the family. It would be years before details of the double life of Horace, then Judge Parker, became known to Robert.

The variance monitoring system allowed Horace to control his companies without exerting direct, hands on management of every detail, a practice that had hampered his father. Horace managed by reading his daily variance reports and heeding only the items flagged outside the specified limits. Then he held daily conversations with each of his company heads who had also read the report and were expected to present corrective actions to the big boss. If the corrective actions were not effective, then a more detailed conversation was necessary.

Once a quarter, certain portions of budgets were adjusted to allow for changing economic conditions. This management-by-exception style gave Horace plenty of spare time on his hands. He was itching for more power and recognition, so he decided to get into politics. The position of county judge came open and he won the election without opposition.

This job, in Texas and in most states, is an administrative position with this misnomer of "judge." There would be no presiding over courtroom trials. He liked the job and the perks that came with it, including a county deputy sheriff as a bodyguard and driver. He selected John "Two Gun" Malham from a list of all the senior deputies, which turned out to be a perfect fit. Malham was unmarried, intelligent, soft spoken, subservient yet intimidating in size. Weightlifting and photography were his hobbies. The fact that he qualified as an expert pistol marksman was a bonus. The judge felt safe wherever he went. Living quarters were immediately provided in the Parker mansion, where Two Gun remained until his death.

Judge served three terms before his move for higher office, that of governor. He failed twice, narrowly losing on the second attempt. When U.S. Senator Lester Hartley announced his planned retirement, Horace decided to run for the Senate but changed his mind when he failed to obtain the senator's endorsement. That was the end of his political career but the beginning of what became known as the Parker political machine.

****

At this point of the report, Hal Hall included details of his interview with retired Senator Hartley.

Hal and Hoppy had arrived late at DFW airport. This was planned as a one-day turnaround trip so they were traveling light, with one carry-on bag and a briefcase each. They picked up a rental, caught a few hours' sleep in the airport Marriot. They arose very early, grabbed a fast food breakfast, and with the senator's precise directions in hand, headed north on I-35 then over to 377 and again north to Lake Texoma.

The gated community guard cleared their IDs and offered further directions to the opulent lakeside home. No bio on the famous senator was needed. They were forewarned about his aggressive and gruff personality and were prepared for it, or so they thought. They discussed their interrogation strategy. The unusual request by the senator that they bring swimsuits came up again. They were amused by this obvious ploy by the senator to make certain no recording devices were concealed in their clothes. Would he have them enter the water? Would they or would they not comply with his request? Of course, they would.

They arrived precisely on time at 10:00 and were admitted by a middle-aged lady in uniform, who escorted them into the senator's study.

The senator greeted them with only one word. "Gentlemen," he said in a deep, gravelly voice. The senator was a short round man with a full head of white hair. Yet they could feel a strong sense of presence about this great man. This feeling intensified as he continued to speak. "Ann, who admitted you, has promised to prepare a varied selection of sandwiches and sides for our lunch. I guarantee that you will find something that you will like. She never fails to please. The bar behind you is well stocked with whatever you need to wet your whistle."

The meeting moved to the veranda overlooking the lake. "It's a beautiful day for sitting outside, so let's sit on the porch. I like to show off this view."

Now, looking very intimidating, he drew himself up close and made eye contact with Hal and Hoppy, speaking with a voice that was a graveled growl. "I want to make it very clear at the outset that I have agreed to this meeting for two specific purposes. I believe that Tripp Joiner is an innocent man in spite of the promised testimony of the eyewitness to the shooting of Judge Parker. I might add that I hope the shooter, whoever he is, gets off scot-free, because if ever a man needed to be removed from the face of the earth, Horace Parker did. He was the vilest of scoundrels, an evil man, and there will be much less pain on this earth without him. More importantly, the Parker dynasty must be ended completely. It stands now like the headless rattlesnake with the unbelievable ability to continue to strike without a head. It must not be allowed to grow a new head!

"First, I want to establish ground rules that I insist we follow in this meeting. I believe I know exactly what you, representing the defense in this case, are looking for. Before my time in the Senate, I was a defense trial lawyer and a prosecutor in Midland County. I'm going to give you what you came for but under my conditions.

"Even the great Mule Sherman will find it hard to get any of this dirt into the minds of the jurors, but if there is a way, he will find it. Either way, I am convinced it will prevent the snake from growing a new head. I am going to tell my story without interruption from either of you. There will be no questions. Let me throw in a little warning. If my name ever comes up in the media tied to anything that comes out of this meeting, I will sue you 'til the cows come home, and I'll do everything within my power to get any operating licenses you may have revoked. I will not agree to be a witness in any courtroom unless forced, and I will remember none of this conversation. Now, if you understand and fully agree to my conditions, I will proceed with my story. Do we have an agreement here?" They both nodded yes to the terms and Senator Hartley began his story.

"I came out of the Permian Basin with the best interest of both the cattle and petroleum industries in mind. In fact, most of my campaign was financed by these two entities. I told myself that I wanted to be elected because I wanted to do my duty and make a contribution to society. In truth, I probably was on a quest for fame and power like the vast majority of public office seekers. Thank God that all are not motivated by only this.

"The Parker family was a major contributor to all my campaigns but seldom came to me for requests. Social activities brought me into contact with them all and we were on a first name basis. I had very few long conversations with Judge Parker himself prior to announcing my retirement. However, I was not surprised by his phone call. I knew his purpose before I answered the call. His was the third of five calls from people with the same mission. Every call began with the expression of regrets about my retirement. Did they really believe that I swallowed their pleas to reconsider? Of course not. They were seeking my personal endorsement.

"I did not commit myself to anyone, but I had to give serious consideration to Judge Parker because of the past campaign support by him and his entire family. I had serious doubts about his electability, but I had decided to take a hard look. I had decided to hand pick my successor, endorse him and hope for the best.

"It was obvious that the judge had expected a simple phone call was all that was needed to gain my endorsement Instead, I requested that we meet at my Washington home at my earliest convenience, the following Sunday. I asked him to leave his aide, bodyguard and pilot at the airport so that we could have a totally private meeting. He began to grumble and growl about how busy he was and that he wished this could be handled over the phone, given the close personal relationship between our families over the years and in view of the fact that the Parker Foundation was of course going to support my favorite charities. I explained that I had suggestions requiring a lengthy conversation. An exchange of ideas in a face-to-face meeting was required. He agreed to my time and date.

"Now, I want only one witness to the rest of my story as it contains a bit of what some people might consider to be self-incrimination. No second collaborating witness, if you know what I mean. So, you make a choice as which one of you it will be. The chosen one and I will don our swimsuits and take a quick dip in the pool in order to cool off. The other will remain here and be comfortable until we finish. I promise that I will keep it short from here on."

Hoppy was selected, and after a brief dip in the water, the senator continued his story. "I can still remember the conversation in the meeting with Parker almost word for word. The judge began that tripe about wanting me to stay in office. I cut him off in mid-sentence by telling him

191

to cut the crap. He was taken aback by my bluntness but continued to pay eager attention.

"I had decided not to give him my endorsement, but I did have a positive plan in mind. I also wanted to throw him a bone and stay off of his enemies list. He was a very vindictive man who might still oppose my pick, whether or not he still decided to toss his hat in the ring. I knew that he was on an ego trip like none I had ever seen. My staff had done their homework and had prepared a dossier with his complete personal history. That, coupled with my own past experience, showed that he had never gotten over his failure to conquer Europe. Most importantly, he had converted his judgeship into a dictatorship, with complaints and lawsuits being heard all over the county. He simply was not fit for office.

"I had to come at him from around the North Pole and use the back door. I told him that I had worked very hard on a positive plan for him, and I wanted him to hear all of it before giving a decision. The expression on his face told me that he thought that he was about to receive my endorsement. This assured me that he would hear me out."

The senator recited the sermon he had given Horace. "You have become a famous person with a very high public profile. You have taken your considerable inherited wealth, spent it wisely as you diversified your oil-based income by founding many new companies and other entities. You have contributed more to charity that anyone else that I know. You have created a powerful empire. You have great influence in the highest seats in the world. I do not believe that you even realize where you sit today. You, my friend, sit on the periphery of a small group of people who really decide who occupies the White House and many other elected offices on down the line. I believe that you will eventually move into that inner circle of king makers on your own, but I am in a position to help you get there sooner.

"As you know, I have considerable influence and powerful friends of my own. King makers are more powerful than the people that they put in office. Even the president shrinks back into the masses after one or two terms, because it is the office itself that holds the power, not the man. Real power brokers are not restrained by term limits and remain powerful as long as they want play the game."

The judge's facial expression had changed completely. The smile was gone. He was tempted to speak out but somehow remained silent.

"You and I and your father always supported the same interests, with cattle and oil being the base. Our next senator must follow suit but what we really need is for whomever sits in the White House to champion these same interests. Only the true power brokers can see to that. Judge, I have offered my help as a way saying thanks for your years of support. It is a freebie. Now let us get down to the true business of the day.

"I asked you to come here because I want to do some serious horse trading, the kind that our grandfathers would have made. The kind that requires the bending of elbows for a drink of good Tennessee whiskey and a chaw of chewing tobacco."

A smile had returned to the judge's face, thinking that the senator was about to set the price for his endorsement, desperate to go out of office as a rich man. He was wrong.

"You are aware, of course, that this campaign will be tough and very expensive. Much tougher than your last race for governor, which you narrowly lost in spite of out spending your opponents by more than three to one. You will have at least one very powerful opponent.

"Wealth used to buy elections, but the explosion of television has turned far too many voters into movie star wishers. Unless you seek office with serious name recognition of a war hero or a sports star, that growing segment of voters mostly under the age of 40 almost require a candidate to be handsome and have a great deal of charisma. There are very few exceptions to this rule. If I were running for election as a first timer, I honestly doubt that I could be elected. Instead, I would be looking for a good law practice. I don't have the looks or charisma required. Further, every candidate in today's world has to run in the face of total and I mean *total* exposure of one's personal life. If there is any dirt on one's underwear, it will be exposed. I am sure that you know that my endorsement will not be enough alone to guarantee your election." The senator paused his recital to explain to Hal what came next.

"At this point, I could see that the judge was nearing an eruption. His face was red, his eyes were bulging and the veins in his neck were protruding. I decided to shift gears a bit and talk about money. He might think this was a continuation of talk about campaign financing but in fact

I was about to lay out my own horse trade plans and the real reason for the meeting."

He continued repeating his Judge Parker script. "Money on Wall Street is flowing today, big time. Would it surprise you to know that I have the key to the secret code known only to the Wall Street inside traders? I called you here today to offer you a trade that you did not expect. I am offering you this key in exchange for your promise to stay out of the Senate race."

The Senator explained that at this point, Horace leaped out of his chair, shouting and cursing and pointing his finger, calling him vile names. "I finally calmed him down by telling him over and over that I could prove it all to him right then. I was counting on his gambling instincts overcoming his anger. I told him that he would be gambling in the world's largest casino with a stacked deck that made it impossible for him to lose. He calmed enough to speak coherently."

"You have committed an unspeakable act of treachery by luring me here, knowing that I came to ask for your endorsement. One that should have been granted over the phone, given that I and my father have poured tons into your election campaigns and your charities. But no, you bring me here in order to attempt to bribe me to stay out of the race. Please tell me why you are doing this."

"If you will be quiet for a few seconds," I told him, "I will do just that. First of all, I don't believe that you can win under any circumstances so my endorsement would be wasted. You have made far too many enemies with your scandalous behavior. You live on the edge of the laws that you took an oath to protect. You are a notorious gambling addict with residences in Monaco, Aruba and Mexico. You are a silent partner in a Las Vegas casino with some very savory characters in that venture. You own a string of racehorses on which you bet almost daily. You are a notorious womanizer as displayed by the scandal sheet tabloids on a regular basis.

"Senate rules would force you to give up control of much of your holdings, including your off-Wall Street trading company. Your name will be muddied from every evangelical pulpit in the state. The list goes on, but I will stop here.

"Judge tried to convince me that as the last male heir of the great Parker dynasty, he wanted to make his mark with high political office, serve one term and step down. He explained that his holdings would be put into a blind trust while he held office. He called my offer a charade of a horse trade and refused what he referred to as a bribe stopping him from a lifetime goal. He was convinced that everything, including that office seat, could be purchased. 'Money talks and bull-shit walks,' he reminded me. With that, he gathered up his crew and went back to Texas. Then exactly four and a half hours later, he called and asked me to explain more about the secret code on Wall Street, and I did. This is how I described it to him.

"There is one segment of the market that is vulnerable to organized insider trading. A major event occurs in the accounting department of every corporation that qualifies to have its stock traded on Wall Street. A P&L report is created every month, every quarter and every year's end. It is held and reviewed by very few people before it is forwarded to receiving channels on Wall Street then sent out for public consumption. This means that there are precise times after each financial report when this motherlode can be mined. It's no wonder why that is the exact term used for the information, *motherlode*. I happen to know one of the inside traders who serves as a miner. He's a former aide of mine who owes me some big-time favors.

"I'm prepared to call in those favors in order to make this trade. I am also prepared to let you taste the water in plenty of time to still make the race if you don't like the taste. Just skip this race and run for something else later.

"Keep in mind that insider trading is considered a victimless crime, and law enforcement agencies view these crimes as low priority budget items. Just like with prostitution, there are middlemen called pimps who match up the information sources, or whores, with the buyers for a percentage cut.

"I gave Judge Parker the name and phone number of my source, certain of his being hooked on playing in the world's largest casino with a stacked deck that would compel him to wait for another race in which to live out his dream. But to prevent a double cross, I had an ace up my sleeve.

195

"I once was invited to a certain judge's hunting lodge for a three-day deer hunt which turned out to be a three-day party. On the first night several scantily dressed girls showed and started mingling with the guests. As soon as I figured out the score, I left and even now wonder where and when the photos might start showing up. Since I could not have been in any of these, I had no worries. Other prominent guests were not so lucky. When I reminded the judge of this, he mumbled something about my adding blackmail to bribery and hung up the phone."

With that, Senator Hartley invited Hal to rejoin them. "You gentlemen are free to discuss the details I have shared. I would truly like for you to know the rest of the story, which I will give it to you in the form of a riddle. Solve the riddle, and you will have the end of the story. Here it is: I did; he did; he did; he did; we won; he won; he didn't.""

Senator Hartley's leaned in the car window before they left. "All I have given you is dirty laundry worn by a very dirty man shielded by a law enforcement badge as he tried to steal a sacred Senate seat. In the end, thank God he failed. I know that Mule Sherman and his team will find a way to put my information to good use. I pray that it will help free Mr. Joiner."

True to the Senator's prediction, Hoppy began trying to solve the riddle, but his thoughts changed as he felt a creepy feeling overcoming him. He had the strong urge to wash his hands and became anxious to reach the airport lavatory. His whole body felt dirty. His head was spinning. Too much data for his brain to handle. Too many questions. Could the Wall Street information really be "mined?"

He had heard of a corporate CFO being charged with selling P&L information and knew that far too many traders had been suspected with having inside information when they amassed huge fortunes overnight, but no one seemed to be investigating them. Suddenly it hit him. He had been exposed far too long to an evil atmosphere. The whole conversation had been about corruption everywhere.

He was not a young man anymore and had witnessed many things as a detective and FBI agent. He thought that he had been exposed to every vile thing life had to offer, but he had never before doubted our democratic system of government. Was this the same government that he volunteered to go to 'Nam for? Is this the government that he took a

196

bullet for? Is this what his buddies died all around him for?

No, it was still the best government in the world, but he was sickened with what he had just learned. Had this revered senior senator turned into a clown with his juvenile riddle and his admission to breaking the law? He had to fight back nausea and screamed, startling Hal. "Take me away from here, dear Jesus."

The stunned Hall responded, "You must be thinking like I am. Our honorable Senator Hartley has dirty hands like we suspect of many politicians, but never him. There is deep revenge at play here." He then muttered to himself, "I know most politicians are devoted and honest, but I need someone to show me a few right now."

CHAPTER TWENTY-THREE

Pay Dirt

Hal Hall continued writing his report about Judge Parker and his interview with Robert Wright, still puzzled as to what all this dirt could possibly be used for. He made a mental note to talk to his friend Tripp about the cost/benefit ratio of all this research being conducted by several people. He was aware that Mule Sherman had been given free spending authority, but he was seeing far too much waste.

But from his research Hal knew that as a direct result of the meeting with Senator Hartley, Judge Parker had abandoned his career plans as an elected official beyond Ector County. But he continued to retain the title of "Judge" as he introduced himself and as he insisted that he continue to be known. He had turned the county judge's position into a mini dictatorship and as a result, created a lot of ill will and animosity throughout the county organization.

Even Two Gun Malham had been feeling the heat from his fellow deputies. His privileged status and extra pay as driver and bodyguard for the judge had turned them against him. He was elated when the judge struck a deal with his handpicked successor that enabled him to retain Two Gun as his bodyguard. The salary was reimbursed to the county. Two Gun technically remained on the force as a deputy sheriff lieutenant. It so happened that the new sheriff, Tom Rivers, was Parker's first bought and paid for politician. His campaign for the office was fully funded by the new Parker machine. If grumbling about the deal came up, and it did from time to time, the public was reminded that one of the Parker charities was set up to help families of all fallen and disabled policemen, firemen and first responders. Their unions were strong defenders of Judge Parker and his deals with the county. He had become a true philanthropist and business mogul in the eyes of the citizens of west Texas.

Two Gun, in uniform with his always present twin pearl-handled Glock pistols, continued to drive his law enforcement vehicle with full markings and siren as he transported the ex-judge and now private citizen Horace Parker wherever he wanted to go. Over time, he became the judge's closest friend and confidant. He and the judge developed the habit of engaging one another in a game of gin rummy, and on occasion, Lilia or Robert would join in.

Two Gun also became the only witness to most of the unlawful activities orchestrated by the judge, which became more and more plentiful. Big time entertainment for the "clients" of the Parker machine became one of the necessary tools for gathering information. The old Acoiris ranch headquarters became a hunting lodge, and a leased condo in Brownsville became a fishing lodge. In fact, they served as sites for lavish parties for invited and selective VIPs from politics, government and large corporations. From time to time, visiting VIPs from foreign countries were present.

Obviously, hired hookers were needed for the type of parties being thrown. Women from Las Vegas were brought to the ranch and from Mexico for the fishing lodge. Robert Wright was in the dark for some time about the parties, until bits of conversations in gin rummy sessions between the judge and Two Gun led Robert to start asking questions. Most of the truth began to leak out.

Robert had been aware for some time that after the judge divorced his second wife, Eilene, who had tried for three years to produce a male heir to the throne but failed, he had returned to his old habits of using call girls for female companionship. Of course, plenty of very eligible and attractive women other than the hookers were available to him because of his wealth and power, and he did date some of them on special social occasions. But with the time needed for developing his new political machine, he had no time for cultivating romantic interests. Call girls were in and out in a hurry and carried none of the baggage of lingering obligations. He and Two Gun began to make frequent "fishing" trips to Brownsville and on into Mexico. The Boy's Town brothels in Matamoros were always on the agenda. Some but not all of the information about these trips was shared with Robert in the days before the entertainment parties were started. Robert even joined in two of these fishing trips and was able to hang a nine-pound bass on his office wall as a result.

One of the trips resulted in unforeseen long-term consequences for the judge. He and Two Gun were in the process of selecting their companions for the few minutes of pleasure in one particular Boys Town brothel when Judge looked in the eyes of a very beautiful young woman and hesitated as he was struck with the thought that he knew her. Impossible, he knew, but a strong feeling of magnetic attraction came over him and he selected her for his tryst. Robert became aware of this encounter while he was in a business meeting with Judge in his study when he noticed him staring at the decade's old portrait of the matriarch of the Parker family, Rosita Garcia Parker, wife of Solomon. The judge was distracted to the point that his actions prompted Robert to inquire why he was suddenly interested in the portrait, which had been there since before his birth. The judge now knew where the magnetic attraction had come from.

The girl, Risa Morales was her name, bore a striking resemblance to Rosita Parker. Judge seemed to let out a sigh of relief as he said, "Good. In a weak moment when I first laid eyes on that girl, I thought it might be love at first sight. I guess I don't know what real love for a woman is because I have never truly loved one. As you know, there have been hundreds of women in my life and now you know that I have never loved one, not even Erikka." The confession, not the fact, stunned Robert.

Whatever the true nature of the attraction was, it caused Judge to take much more frequent trips to Matamoros, and after his return from one of these trips, a picture of a beautiful young Mexican woman suddenly appeared on a bookcase shelf behind his desk. She became known as the Mystery Woman to the staff. This set their tongues to wagging.

It was apparent to Robert why her beauty had made her the top attraction in the most upscale bordello in her town. English lessons were mandatory for girls in this particular bordello as well as lessons in poise and personal manners. She was fast developing some class to go with her good looks and personality and her price rose accordingly. She became, in Judge's mind, the future star of his VIP entertainment plans in the Brownsville condo. He began to take her with him on trips around his travel circuit. She was seen in New York, London, Paris, Rome and Houston but never in Oslo, the home of Erikka.

Robert and his wife, Myrtie, joined Judge and Risa at a petroleum producer meeting in Dallas and went to dinner together at The Cattleman's Club. While dining, Judge asked Myrtie to take Risa shopping for a new wardrobe at his expense and told her to buy some things for herself as well. Myrtie gladly obliged. Risa came back with six complete outfits from Neiman Marcus. She now had plenty of expensive clothes to accent her beautiful body. This act of kindness by Myrtie created a bond between the two and resulted in continued correspondence between them. Risa would always send a post card from her favorite travel cities.

Judge began to use Risa to entertain his most important clients and on a very selective basis. If you got a date with Risa Moralas, you were someone very important to the judge, indeed. Risa used these meetings as a means of developing her own clientele book to be used apart from Horace Parker. She was climbing her own ladder to success. Judge was inadvertently pushing her up the ladder without his knowledge. The lethal combination of brains, beauty and charm had rapidly propelled her to the top of whoredom. Her correspondence to Myrtie reflected this when she wrote that a Saudi prince had offered to buy her a home in Dubai if she would move there. The real irony was that Risa had conquered Europe and beyond, where Horace Parker had failed. One day Myrtie received a rare phone call from Risa, who expressed alarm about the discovery of a lump in her breast and asked for her help in getting into a good American clinic for an examination. Myrtie, in a few days' time, had her checked into the MD Anderson Cancer Center in Houston and joined her there since Risa had no one else in this country to stand by her.

After the initial examinations, a lumpectomy was performed. She was then informed that a mastectomy was necessary; her whole world collapsed around her.

She was one tough cookie, having been raised in a scrubby corn patch on the side of a steep Mexican mountain in a shack with no door and having been delivered to a whorehouse by her own father, but this bad news was almost too hard to take. She once blurted out to Myrtie, "There have been times when the judge promised to marry me some day, but I never truly believed it. Those promises sometimes come with the profession but I stored these from Judge in my mind and used them to pull out a tiny bit of comfort from time to time. I do truly hate men but sometimes I did have good feelings about Judge. Sometimes I may have loved him more than I hated him."

It was clear to Myrtie that Risa was about to crack up. Had not Myrtie been there, she would have broken but she stayed there, had her surgery and returned to Mexico. It had taken her years to climb the ladder to success, to dance with movie stars, to cavort with the world's richest and to travel in their private jets, but it took only a few minutes to fall to the bottom.

She cried out for help to the judge but her pleas fell on deaf ears. She was, after all, of no further use to the Parker machine. She became just another member of the enemies list. This sad story was discussed many times between Robert and Myrtie, with Myrtie saying, "Those people live in a world that I never knew existed. It must be like living in a large sewer. I can understand how Risa got there but the judge could have lived in a world like heaven on earth."

Robert replied, "The lust for sex has taken many a man down a road best not traveled." This part of Robert Wright's story, as it later came to pass, would lead to the most important facts in Hal's report. Hoppy Cassidy read the insights and immediately knew what his next assignment would be. He would be on the next flight to Brownsville.

"Ya' know guys," Robert was ending his story, "we ole boys who were raised in a small rocky cotton patch in Arkansas are like blackjack oak saplings. It takes a lot to break us, but when we snap, the loud noise is heard faraway. I suspect that a little girl raised in a rocky corn patch on the side of a hill is also like a blackjack sapling.

"For every Judge Parker in this world, there are 10 powerful but honest people with impeccable credentials. There are many elected office holders and civil servants who are not influenced by the temptation of illegal or unethical wealth. The real backbone of our society are the millions of common people who are taught by their parents and others that they must earn their way in society by trying, every day, to make their neighborhoods and their country a better place to live."

Robert saved telling his true reason for the noisy split with the judge with a lengthy explanation. The judge had set up his machine in order to gain himself fame, power and influence and had succeeded beyond his fondest dreams, but he also discovered that he was receiving valuable knowledge of coming events controlled by Washington, and in particular, Congress, which would have a major impact on the stock market.

He fed this inside info to the family-owned brokerage firm and used it to give him an edge in his game of day trading. He was making a lot of money in this manner, but serious greed got to him as he began to learn how insider trading was being conducted on Wall Street, where more money was gambled in a day than in most casinos in a year. Wall Street was the world's largest casino. The insiders were rich and getting richer without much interference from the Justice Department, and he wanted to share in this. He surmised that the information that drove the market up and down had to be compiled by humans before it was announced, and humans can be separated from that knowledge when the price is right. How else could have the insiders gotten their information?

He instructed Robert to study the ways and means and the who's of this information flow. Robert knew that his personal actions were about to enable the judge to commit a crime, so he refused. After receiving a strong tongue lashing and cursing, he was fired and threatened. He never knew, for sure, if the judge made it to insider heaven.

Hoppy took a plane to Brownsville and a cab to Matamoros but he should have taken a dump truck. Pay dirt would be struck at last and it would, indeed, fill a dump truck. Using Robert's instructions, Risa was easy to find. She was working as a hostess madam in a nondescript bordello in Boys Town. Hoppy had no problem getting her to spill her guts for a price. She asked for a $20,000 fee but eventually settled for $3,000, all that Hoppy had on him or all that he admitted to having.

Her story pretty well paralleled Robert's version, but she added some important details. Her poverty-stricken childhood was shocking. She and her family members, especially her six siblings, were often sick and always hungry. None died but most of their neighbors were not so lucky, including her closest little girlfriend. Every family member labored in the corn patch and the garden and tended to the pigs and goats who wandered at will in and out of the door-less shack.

It was common knowledge that these poor peasant families prayed for beautiful daughters to send to the "houses" to become rich and to share those riches with the family. Every father looked forward to returning with many pesos in exchange for his daughter. She had to be very pretty with good teeth and at least 18 years old, but birth certificates were rarely checked. These girls were taught that this deed was mandatory and a giant step up to a better life. Most girls did not object, but Risa did. She ran away twice before giving up the fight and began to hate all men.

She had been working in the bordello only a few weeks when she first met Judge Parker, who was very kind to her and gave her a large tip that she had to share with the house. All the working girls resided in the house and were initially confined there. They felt like prisoners even though there were no bars. Freedom came with time and trust. Risa learned what the American clients already knew. Some of the most beautiful women resided in these bordellos. She also learned that most of the business came from north of the border and these customers wanted to hear the English language spoken. She was tutored in the house and learned to speak passable English in a few months. Some foreigners came but not many.

Hoppy pressed her for information about the judge and Two Gun and she gave him what he was searching for. She pulled out her little black book and disclosed many names of people, important people, who had been entertained by the judge. She spared no details, and even Hoppy became a little embarrassed, occasionally breaking eye contact.

The judge and Two Gun did not share in sex acts but kept the liquor flowing and the girls matched up. Over time, Risa began to take notice of the unusual movements of Two Gun and finally determined that he was always moving about taking pictures, or so she thought. But no camera was visible. He must be holding a very small camera in his huge hand, she thought, and this need to fulfill her curiosity compelled her to sneak a peek in his luggage.

No camera was there but she did discover a tiny roll of film, which she took home with her. After a few days, she had the roll developed into negatives only; no pictures were printed.

She examined the negatives and could tell that most of the roll was taken not at one of the VIP parties but at one of the private parties with Judge and Two Gun. She still possessed all the negatives and three photographs that she had printed. Showed them to Hoppy.

The most revealing photo was of the judge with Risa and a young woman lying in bed nude, apparently unaware of the camera. One was with the same girl sitting on the judge's lap with a bottle of tequila in her hand. To Hoppy, this meant that Two Gun was attempting to create a little liability insurance protection for himself in case the judge ever turned on him.

Hoppy knew it was time to end the interview and move on. He asked if the photographs were for sale and she said yes because the judge's death took away her need for them. Hoppy knew that she had been holding on to them to use for extortion. He told her he would send a newspaper reporter by the name of Chic Rowler to her and that he would pay top dollar for her story and more for the photos. He advised her to strike a deal that made certain her name not be used.

Chic did not yet know about any of this but Hoppy and he had worked together before. He always followed Mule around to his big cases involving celebrities, knowing that there would be a good story for his scandal sheet and that a sensational story would be tossed to him if something needed to become public knowledge that could not be used in court. He always came to Hoppy with questions and to be guided to the source of meat.

Based on the pay dirt delivered by Risa in Matamoros, another search of Two Gun's rooms was needed. Proper protocol was followed and Hal and Hoppy returned to the Parker mansion. There must be a hiding place someplace, but the question was where?

A thorough search had conducted once before. While Hal was going over the walls, floor, ceiling and so forth, Hoppy reexamined the large bookcase. In his earlier search, he had been looking for a large hollow cavity that could hold notebooks, pictures and other incriminating documents, but now, in light of the discovery of a tiny roll of film by Risa, he understood that a smaller cavity could possibly have been used.

He tapped on the tops of all shelves and the sides and back of the case with his pocketknife, listening for a hollow sound. He had expected one of the panels to be thicker than the others, but his earlier examination had proved this not true. Now he was expecting the cavity to be thin with room enough hide developed negatives and pictures.

Tapping on the top of the case seemed to produce a slightly different sound than the other panels and as he stood on a chair, he was able to slide his knife blade along the edge of the panel and lift it up. Bingo! He exposed a thin layer of negatives and developed pictures. More pay dirt.

Hal took a look and discussed what to do next. Both were elated but they knew that this material, by law, must be turned over to the prosecution, then in turn be shared with the defense if the prosecution deemed it to be relevant trial evidence. They needed guidance from Mule or Will and put in some calls.

While waiting to make contact with one of them, Hal went back to the desk drawer that contained Two Gun's cameras and found the inventory to be the same as his earlier discovery. Three cameras and six assorted lenses and an antique European style cigarette lighter. There was no sign of a small camera that used the tiny rolls of film as had been described by Risa.

He reexamined the cameras and toyed with the lighter trying to make it light. Hoppy spoke up. "Wait a minute. Let me see that lighter. I once saw a lighter similar to this that turned out to be a disguised miniature camera in a CIA exhibit of the former East German Stasi secret police toys."

He began to look for something that would twist or open and he found the little camera lens and the shutter button. The rest was easy. It even contained a roll of unexposed film. Without waiting for instructions, Hoppy used his own camera to photograph the tiny camera and the pile of pictures and negatives and the written notes on backs of pictures. He photographed only face sides of the most incriminating photos of the judge that were in a separate envelope. As suspected, Two Gun had his little insurance policy just in case he ever needed it. It was very similar to the one Risa had discovered.

All items were returned to their original locations. Hal and Hoppy logged out and returned to defense headquarters feeling great self-satisfaction about their accomplishments and knowing that they could now wrap up the report.

CHAPTER TWENTY-FOUR

A Dump Truck Full of Dirt

Mule Sherman now had possession of Hal Hall's full report containing all the pertinent information about the victims as requested, or so thought Hal. In fact, much more was gathered than Mule had dreamed of. The team of Hall and Cassidy had done an excellent job. Far too much of early history, perhaps, but it made for interesting reading. He began the task of sifting through the dirt, looking for what Judge Sullivan might allow to be introduced as evidence in open court and what might be slipped in if the prosecution opened the door. But the goal was to make sure the jury pool got it all, one way or the other.

Will Clarkson summed up his review of the report. "This is a good short story about a great Texas hero, Solomon Parker, who is in all the history books alongside Sam Houston and Davey Crockett. And his pioneering Parker family that has established a dynasty, which has given millions to charity and ended up with one very powerful bad apple -- a very wealthy alcoholic heiress and wannabe movie star who was left to carry on the legacy. But we have nothing in this report that Judge Sullivan is going to allow in evidence unless one of the VIP partygoers is stupid enough to appear as a character witness. That might open up the sewer to impeach his testimony and allow our Mexican whore to testify. We would need answered prayer for the jury to believe her testimony."

Hal responded to his assessment with some history on court rulings on the admission of bad past acts of victims and defendants. In the early days, he explained, everything was admitted but now it was very restrictive. He offered to assist in the search of court rulings and said nothing more. They all agreed that if they put Tripp on the stand and they were able to elicit testimony about why he was present at the time of the murders, he would then be able to relate to the jury what his wife had told him about the death of their daughter. The prosecution would naturally try to keep this out.

Mule interjected, "I see it like this, we have two scum bags murdered, and according to the prosecution, by an all-American sports hero who is practically worshiped by millions of football fans. May God help us if we can't win this case? All they have, really, is an eyewitness who has a strong bias against our client. True, she may be a very formidable witness. She will come in fresh from that clinic, dried out and making sense as she speaks. She will reflect her good education and her intelligence instead of that of the slobbering drunk who told officers at the crime scene that she saw our client shoot Judge and Two Gun. We have been dealt a pretty strong hand of cards and we know how to play them."

He had told the defense team early on that this would be a "big boy" trial played by big boy rules. They would soon learn what that declaration meant without his having to say a word more. The dirt would be dumped in spectacular fashion.

A sudden thought came to mind. "I wonder if there might be a way to use this proof that her father was a pedophile to influence Lilia Vorhees to testify to the truth about who did the killings. Yes, this is obviously blackmail, but we just might pull it off. After all," he mused as he searched for a clear conscience, "the police and prosecutors use blackmail all the time when a partner in crime is bribed with the offer of a lighter sentence for testimony against his fellow perpetrator. This might turn into another defense team first."

He bounced this idea off Hoppy, whose first response was, "Are you crazy? That is a criminal offense that could get you disbarred and also cost me my license because you would ask me to deliver the goods to the witness. Besides, what makes you think she would change her testimony anyway?"

Mule answered, "She would probably escape with a slap on the wrist if she admitted to shooting Two Gun after he shot her father and after she thought Tripp had been choked to death. I'm not asking her to change her testimony. I'm saying she might do it on her own in order to prevent a family scandal and the tarnation of the great Parker dynasty. She could receive a note from an anonymous friend, a mole inside our camp, who says that we have plans to publish the dirt only if we lose the case vis-a-vie her father."

"It's blackmail, so forget it." Cassidy, ex-FBI and a lawyer himself, knew that scandal might sap some strength from the Parker machine and cost it some big-time earnings, but Lilia's goal was to protect her daughter from the Debi Devereaux killing by destroying Tripp with a conviction in this case. A grand jury will never believe the accusative testimony of a convicted murderer with revenge on his mind.

In spite of the objections from Hoppy, Mule was still considering the idea. It would certainly guarantee an eventual verdict of innocence, so he was not quite ready to throw in the towel. He then pitched the thought to his old law school roomie and first law partner, Charlie Horton, first with pleasantries, "Are you following my trial?"

"Of course, how could I not? It's eating up all the media. I'll bet you're making a pretty penny from this one. Tell me sometime how you landed it."

Mule answered, "As a matter of fact, I'm working for expenses only. You know I have a bone to pick with the Parker machine and I need the advertising, but there's no time for trivia now. I want to bounce an idea off your ever-numb brain." He pitched and Charlie's response was the exact same as Hoppy's.

"Are you *crazy*? I can see where you might be tempted to be the first ever to blackmail a prosecution witness into telling the truth. This is an ego thing for you. You're looking for bragging rights even though you can never use them. Drop it!

"But while I've got you, you owe me a sec so don't hang up. It sounds like you are going to need a big payday and I have something you might be interested in. I'm about to jump on the class action gravy train and I need your help. I have inside poop on a drug that is about to be recalled from the market because it's killing people by the scores. I'm preparing to run a nationwide ad campaign and I need a couple of mil. I have scraped up one, but I need one more. I need you to join up with me with your investment. I will do all the work. Guys are making killings with these things and I want my share. What do you say? Think about it and get back to me."

Mule responded, "I don't need to think about it, and I'll end this discussion with this. I don't believe in huge class suits because they knock out thousands of smaller cases for lawyers all over the country and they are driving up the cost of liability insurance and the cost of health

209

care. Count me out!" With that, he hung up the phone and momentarily hung up on the thought of blackmailing Lilia Parker. He must be needing rest. How could he have allowed this distraction? He would go to plan B. He knew exactly how the dirt would become public knowledge. Enough dirt would find its way into the jury pool that would influence the minds of at least a few of the seated jurors. As an afterthought, he placed the photos in his briefcase to use, just in case.

Once the sordid stuff, the real sewer crap, hit the scandal sheet tabloid news stands, the job would be complete. Mainstream media would begin to report quotes from these sources, then everyone would be exposed to it. The barbershop and beauty salon grapevines would do the rest.

Mule knew that Hoppy would eventually play by "big boy rules" and give some of the file's details to a selected scandal sheet reporter. He was already hanging around for some smut and had already written some fringe stories, including one that Tripp, the football superstar, was still involved romantically with Vita Vorhees, the movie star. He also knew that the crap would hit the fan with Judge Abraham Sullivan, but he would be prepared to truthfully answer, "I instructed no one to leak anything and I have no direct knowledge of who did. I suggest that you talk to some of the scandal sheet reporters who have been publishing the stories." Nothing untruthful was in the file and some of the stories would be backed up with interviews if the most responsible main media reporters follow the norm. The game was on, one that Will Clarkson would never have played.

CHAPTER TWENTY-FIVE

A Big Boy Trial with Big Boy Rules

Mule Sherman learned early in his career that defending celebrities gave a lawyer a tremendous advantage over that of defending average clients. Media attention and the resultant spreading of knowledge and interest to the potential juror pool offered the ability to try the case by tainted public opinion.

He began to play his pre-trial cards by arranging a jailhouse interview with one of the largest sports magazines, Sport Digest, which had the largest circulation in Texas. The interview was programmed to place emphasis on two main topics, Tripp's plans to return to the New York Giants as soon as possible and also the details surrounding the death of his daughter.

There were several questions from the reporter and Tripp briefly covered both topics. His surgically repaired shoulder was healing nicely, and the superficial gunshot wound received in his fight with John Malham would not be a factor. He was anxious to return to his team. And yes, he realized that he was very near to breaking several all-time NY Giants passing records but that had nothing to do with his desire to return. He followed by expressing dissatisfaction that law enforcement had done nothing in the investigation of his daughter's murder and the serious injuries to his wife. Questions about the death of Debi Devereaux were answered, "No comment."

Knowing that he had a couple of weeks before this interview would go to press, Mule played his second card. He called a press conference on the courthouse steps. Will Clarkson declined to be present but Hal and Miss Beaton, his veteran legal secretary, were standing with him. This public statement was intended to declare his commitment to an all-out effort to get all of the pertinent evidence introduced into the trial. It was his belief that his client could not get a fair trial if that did not happen. He wanted a grand jury to be convened in the matter of the death of Mary Mae Joiner, the daughter of his client, and also to be convened in the matter of the death of Debi Devereaux.

211

He took no follow-up questions, knowing that he had accomplished what he set out to do. He also knew that this incident and the playing of card number three would blow the lid off the prosecutor's office. The shit was going to hit the fan twice, but Mule wanted to face Judge Sullivan only once. He would be conveniently unreachable for a couple of days until after card number three had been played.

Card number three was played by Chic Rower, the big name in scandal sheet publications. But the card was not immediately played in Texas. Chic had followed up with the dirt file that had been given him by Hoppy and from the subsequent purchased interview and incriminating pictures from Risa Morales. He decided to throw in a layer of liability protection by having a friend break the story in a London scandal sheet. His piece, then, was theoretically the reporting of what was written overseas.

The Texas version carried everything except the claim of originality. The coverage had maximum size headlines and nude pictures of Judge Parker and his very young virgin fiesta toy. Extra copies were distributed to all the newsstands and grocery store counters in west Texas and as these quickly sold out, more were supplied. Gossip flashed through the beauty parlors, barbershops and bridge clubs throughout the county. The mainstream media began to report on the story but without the pictures and the sensational headlines. The jury pool had been poisoned. Had it ever.

The news sent Windy Warren screaming to Judge Sullivan like a banshee, slobbering and hardly able to state his complaint. He demanded that Mule Sherman and the whole defense team be called on the carpet and severely punished. The judge agreed to have a hearing but found it difficult to locate Mule.

Two days later and with all the relevant players assembled, the judge had his hearing. The now calm prosecutor and his team were prepared, but prepared for what? Other than a restraining order against future similar conduct, they did not know what punishment to ask for, but in their view, punishment was clearly called for.

Both sides were given a chance to speak and the judge asked Windy what action or punishment he had in mind. While Windy was mumbling about a change of venue, his young assistant DA blurted out, "Mistrial."

"You idiot," Windy said under his breath.

Judge Sullivan was not smiling when he replied, "Son, I might consider that if only we had a trial to deal with. I don't believe that we have seated a single juror just yet." He looked back to Windy. "You have opposed a change of venue from the start and now you have changed your mind. Please tell me how moving this trial to anywhere but Timbuktu will get us out of a tainted jury pool. We might lessen the impact some if we delayed this trial for 10 years or so, but we can't do that, can we? Any changes that we make now will cost the state tons of money, but if you so desire, go ahead and file your change of venue motion." The judge closed the hearing by slapping a restraining order on the defense team and promising Mule that he would come up with an adequate punishment for him later.

Windy did file for the change, and as a result, fell into Mule's trap. He had known two things. First, Judge Sullivan wasn't about to grant a change of venue, and second, a request alone would set the media in search of reasons, spreading more of the dirty laundry.

This big boy trial was being played by big boy rules.

CHAPTER TWENTY-SIX

The Cross

Will Clarkson was convinced, without doubt, that the credibility of the testimony of the prized witness for the state must be destroyed for the defense to have much hope for an acquittal. To save the life of Tripp Joiner. As a first witness, the prosecution had used their gem of all prizes by putting on the stand a credible eyewitness to the alleged crime. Lilia Parker Vorhees was more than credible due to her high-profile image created by the countless number of her pictures published by the media and all the publicity given to her charity work. Further, her eyewitness account was from the same room as both shootings. Very few prosecutions have been successfully defended against in these circumstances.

In spite of the enormity of the task, Will did not let the pressure bother him. He had ice water in his veins, and he was well prepared. He had done his homework. He probably knew more about this witness than did anyone else in the world. Mainly because of her celebrity status and the help of information that he was able to obtain from inside the Parker camp, her life was like an open book to him.

The ice water began to form in his veins at a very young age as he was required to take on the chores of a grown man far too early in life. He was raised on a scrubby piece of irrigated farmland in the Texas panhandle. His father was an ex-marine who had left an arm on the battlefield, and as a consequence, was unable to resume his career as a cowpoke. No one wanted a cowhand who couldn't rope a calf. But with the help of the VA and a friendly banker, he purchased a small farm.

His mother had worked as a seamstress while her husband was off to war and continued to practice her craft in her spare time as well as do her farmhand chores. Will came into the family after two sisters, who also were introduced to hard work early on. He liked to tell friends that he knew the exact day that he became a man. That day came when he was given the task of cleaning out the septic tank with a lecture and a promise from his father. "Son, the greatest rewards and therefore the greatest pleasures in life come from successfully completing a task. The harder the task, the greater the pleasure." Over time, he found that to be true … sort of. In any case, that became his work philosophy. Based on that, he could anticipate the great pleasure he was about to experience with the destruction of Lilia Parker Vorhees.

Will was blessed with a brain that allowed him to finish high school just after his 15th birthday and earned him a full scholarship to Tulane University. He boarded the Greyhound bus for New Orleans with his homespun suit in a cardboard suitcase. He returned home from Cambridge and Harvard Law with a store-bought suit in a used Samsonite suitcase. This diploma and a pocketful of job offers set him up for life. He wanted instant work as a litigator, so he took a job with the hometown prosecutor's office doing simple slam dunk cases.

He soon understood that our system of justice, "presumed innocent until proven guilty," was really a farce. When a defendant was paraded in front of a seated jury wearing handcuffs and dressed in prison attire, most jurors presumed guilt, and it was up to the defense team to prove otherwise. Will felt a calling to serve the underdogs even if it meant that at some point, he might be responsible for putting a guilty person back on the street.

He was ready to fight this battle with a rough but flexible plan formed in his mind. He would make the jury dislike this person first, show her to be a pompous ass, catch her in a lie and lead her into forbidden territory. Territory denied him by the judge's instructions. The fact that she was a complete alcoholic could be his ace card. He had defended enough alcoholics to read them like a book. He was betting that he could make her fall off the wagon.

District Attorney Warren had a difficult choice at the outset of presenting the state's case. Ordinarily, he preferred to present the crime scene evidence first, then drop the hammer with his prize of the eyewitness testimony, but now he hesitated for two reasons. Number one was that his crime scene evidence had flaws in the forensic evidence area. These would have to be explained away by his hired expert witnesses whose testimonies needed to be dominant over the defense witnesses. This would be difficult because the spending power of the defense enabled them to hire the best experts available.

Second, hours of schooling his witness had left her with strong but scripted answers to his basic questions if she remembered the script. But simulated cross examination often led to her confusion and breakdowns. Everyone on his team knew what the problem was, but no one spoke about it. So, the DA decided to use her powerful eyewitness encounter as the opener instead of the closing hammer. If he could make that strategy option work, then it was his belief that his weakness in the forensics would be overlooked. His top aides agreed with his strategy and so he proceeded with his plan.

Various media outlets projected speculations as to what the prosecution plan of attack would be. They were all wrong. None projected that the star eyewitness testimony would come first. Nevertheless, the crowd of potential spectators began to gather before dawn with hopes of obtaining a seat near the movie star main attraction, Vita Vorhees, or the great football hero, Tripp Joiner.

A cold front had moved in and the wind was fierce. In west Texas, where the wind blows most all the time, its mention does not become worthy of conversation by the local population unless it is not blowing at all or blowing hard enough to require at least one hand to keep one's hat in place. The pioneer cowboys called it a "grabber" wind and this colloquialism was passed down through the generations. A "grabber" was considered dangerous because most functions performed while on horseback required both hands, which left none to hold the hat on. The loss of one's hat was a mortal sin for a cowboy.

The jurors entered their room in the courthouse right on time, with the wind dominating their conversations. One commented to another, "Boy! She's a grabber out there today, ain't she?"

"She sure is, and my wife just bought me this Stetson to wear for this trial. Thought it was a goner once there."

Shortly thereafter, the bailiff began the parade into the courtroom. The last person allowed to enter the courtroom, led by her husband and with all eyes on her, was Vita Vorhees. She took her reserved seat next to other family members and special guests. A disruptive murmur arose.

The crowd was seeing the face of a movie star who they had never seen before on a theater screen or in public. She looked like death warmed over. Lipstick was the only makeup present. Her eyes were swollen, and her hair was a mess. It clearly reflected that she had not slept the night before. After being told that her mother was to testify first, she had announced her intentions to not attend the trial on this day, such was her anxiety about her mother's intentions. Would she save or destroy her future? She yielded to pressure at the last moment, arriving in the nick of time. The spectators were left to gape and wonder about her condition as Judge Abraham Sullivan gaveled the court to order at 9:00 sharp.

Two people in particular were dealing with far more anxiety than ever before. The big trade decision was the only thing that these enemies, Tripp and Vita had left in common. Lilia took the stand. Vita had her fingers crossed and her head in her lap as she prayed that the dramatic confession was to be heard. Tripp found himself holding his breath longer that he believed possible. All involved in the behind-the-scenes trade proposed by Mule Sherman and accepted by most of the Parker family stared intently as the DA began to talk. They anxiously awaited the first words from the mouth of Lilia, who had agreed to the plan then changed her mind several times. Would she change her mind again? Yes or no?

The usual introductory questions were asked and answered, and the DA began to put a greater than usual emphasis on the credibility buildup. He used practically everything in her scrapbook regarding her good deeds. She had made certain that there was a photo op with every established charity. Every building named in her honor had been dedicated with a ceremony filled with high profile politicians and VIPs. She had been recognized by the Chamber of Commerce as woman of the year. He read a long list of the active charities. Somewhere along the line, Tripp and Vita came back to the line of questions and suffered through the early remarks. The lists were long but soon the preliminary scripted questions began.

Lilia Vorhees, when asked to describe what she witnessed on that fateful day, needed only a few words. "I saw Jimmy Jack Joiner shoot my father and Deputy Malham."

The bold and risky trade created by Mule Sherman had failed. The bad news had a dramatic impact on all parties involved in the plan. This perceived betrayal by her mother was more than Vita could stand, causing her to moan and rise to her feet sobbing loudly as she pushed her way to the aisle to exit the room. To her, this was an unbelievable decision made by the one who had created a fairytale life for her daughter, pushing her through countless beauty pageants and eventually into movie stardom. Now, her mother was allowing for her life to be destroyed by not protecting her from certain indictment in the death of Debi Devereaux.

The commotion created by Vita drew the gaping stares of everyone including Lilia. Her eyes teared up as she shared her daughter's pain. She wanted to run after her and assure her that everything would be alright and to convince her that her plan would still keep Tripp Joiner controlled. After all, it had been established by this trade offer that he could be bought at the right price, and his price would be met again. If not, there were other ways to deal with him. The plan to bribe a juror was being developed by Tony Bender at her insistence and with her daughter's approval.

Tripp Joiner had attempted to brace himself against the possibility of a failure in the trade agreement by telling himself, again and again, that the odds were against it. But the failure still caused the feeling of a weight crashing down on his body worse than any pile-on of huge NFL linemen ever did.

Mule Sherman and Will Clarkson made instant eye contact, showing obvious pain in losing their miracle admission. Hal Hall was forced to hide his face with his hands in order to conceal his grief. Zip Devereaux felt a twinge of guilt of selfishness with his pain. This meant that his team, the NY Giants, his bread and butter, would be without their star quarterback perhaps forever and also that his parents would never receive the cash that would have made them financially secure for life. Even Tony Bender wondered if the rift between his wife and her mother would cause a split in the family, which might jeopardize his job as head of the Parker business empire.

The murmurs coming from almost everyone rose to a noise level that roared like a wounded lion as the crying movie queen departed and was suddenly joined by the sounds of a giant gust of a grabber wind, one made the ancient courthouse screech, crack and pop like a firecracker. The loud weird sound frightened many people, causing them to look around with widened eyes. Some cried out with alarm.

The deputy sheriff door guard had seen many disturbances in his half century of courthouse service. He turned to his cohort and attempted some nervous humor. "That noise must be the ghost of old Judge Parker coming back to punish us." The eerie sound even caused a delay in the judge's use of his gavel to restore order, but he recovered his senses and declared an immediate recess.

Lilia returned to the stand after the recess, still somewhat saddened but rested and refreshed. Still under oath from her direct testimony as the state's star witness, convinced in stating that she saw the defendant shoot and kill her father, Judge Horace Parker, and Deputy Sheriff John Malham. The DA milked her story of all the bloody details, but he felt a certain feeling of insecurity as he turned her over to Will Clarkson for cross examination.

Will approached her with his fake Howdy Doody smile on his face but not looking directly into her eyes. Just as he reached the witness stand, he shuffled through a stack of papers in his hands as he appeared to be searching for a particular note. He then turned, without speaking, to the defense table and began searching through a file.

This clearly disturbed Lilia, as evidenced by the look on her face. This also gave her time to notice the overall appearance of this "famous" lawyer. He wore a cheap, out of style, rumpled suit and an even older tie. His much too short trouser legs exposed white socks and worn brown shoes with his dark blue suit. Further scrutiny exposed his mismatched black belt. To her, first appearances meant everything. What flashed through her mind was wonderment as to how a celebrity football star like Tripp would hire a slob like this to defend his life. This was truly a lesser being standing before her who was about to do battle.

She had been schooled by the prosecution team at great length, of course, about the tactics of this great cross examiner, but in spite of this, she dropped her guard before the battle even started. Will started the questioning with the same smile on his face by deliberately mispronouncing her name as Lulu. This raised her up in her seat to her full seating height as she corrected him. "It's Lilia. L-I-L-I-A Parker Vorhees."

A glance at the jury showed Will that his first goal was being reached. They were not liking this woman. Will noticed another thing that helped

219

the cause. She was weighted down with expensive, gaudy jewelry. He had no way of knowing that prosecutor Walter Warren had asked her prior to taking the stand to scale back on the display, but she refused by saying, "This is some of my cheaper stuff. I *do*, after all, have an image to uphold."

"Miz Vorhees, you testified earlier that your title is president of the Parker Foundation, by which you administered all the charities funded by the foundation. Would you like to expand on that?"

As she did for several minutes, she bored the jurors to death, much to Will's delight. The key sentence was, "Judge Parker has me working very hard to satisfy his desire to provide a better life for the many, many underprivileged people who live all around us."

"Will you tell us how much you have given to these underprivileged folks?"

"Oh, many millions, countless millions over more than 20 years."

"Where does all this money come from, Miz Vorhees?"

"Well, from Judge Parker's pocket, of course."

"So, the judge himself determined on an annual basis, the exact amount of money that was to be distributed and to whom?"

"Well, yes and no. He had me and a committee to sort out the details."

"Then, he determined the total and you and the committee determine the split?"

"I guess that is true."

"Please don't guess, Miz Vorhees. If you don't know, then please say so." This question brought out a protest from Windy Warren.

"Your honor, he is badgering the witness and he has been allowed to spend far too much time on this subject."

"Do you have a purpose for these questions, Mr. Clarkson?" asked Judge

Sullivan.

"I sure don't want to hurt the feelings of Miz Vorhees, your honor, but I believe that this jury needs straight answers. We will, I'm sure, have more uncertain answers to many questions from this witness before I'm finished."

The judge did not wait for an objection this time. "That's enough of that counselor."

Will interrupted, "I withdraw my statement."

Windy jumped up and exclaimed, "He can't withdraw a statement. He can only withdraw a question."

With that, both parties were called to the bench for some strong talk from the judge. He finished by saying, "We both know where he is going with this line of questioning and I'm going to give him plenty of rope with which to make his points or to hang himself. Now sit down and behave yourselves."

Will had inside information that gave him the answer to the next question before he asked. "Miz Vorhees, isn't it true that the total monies given to charities is a budgeted item determined by a fixed percentage of the profits of the Parker companies and for the last several years has been fixed at 3 percent?"

"I'm not sure of that and I don't know for sure what you mean by the Parker companies. Some of his companies are corporations with a few other shareholders."

"So, let me understand this. You are the president and yet you do not know where the money comes from or how much it is that you have to spend. Am I correct?"

"No, you are not correct, and besides, I have a clerical staff who crank out the splits."

"I'm sorry, I thought you testified that you did that."

"I said that I called the shots, not that I did the clerical work."

"Now I am totally confused, so I will move on."

Lilia's blood pressure was rising as evidenced by her flushed face. She also appeared to Will that she was an alcoholic in bad need of a drink, but he was saving that for later.

"Are all the charitable donations made in Texas, Miz Vorhees?"

"Most are but some are made in other states and countries. We want to take care of our local folks first, ya know."

"Who determines who gets the out-of-state donations and how much, or do you know?"

"Judge mostly determined those things."

"As required by federal law, you have furnished a list of your donations to the IRS. We have prepared a chart showing some of your out-of-state donations." He had the charts brought out, introduced into evidence and set up so that the jury and Lilia could read them.

"The charts are numbered and dated, and you can see that number one has the current date and number two is dated 10 years ago. They display an area that encompasses a large number of states. The uncovered parts show the names of nine charities and their location by city and state. We will uncover the other parts in a moment, but first let me ask. Are you familiar with these charities? Did you go there to research the legitimacy and the needs of each of these? If not, who did?"

"I have already told you that Judge Parker handled these. I did not visit any of these places, but I did carefully review the requests and made approvals before signing off on them."

Will pointed to chart two. "Notice that I am uncovering these spaces that name by office the congressional official who resides in that town. Coincidence? Maybe, but watch as I uncover equivalent spaces on chart one. What do we see? We see the same congressional officers, but they are now in new locations. What does this one say? It reads chairman of Ways and Means Committee. This one reads chairman of Armed Services Committee and this one says chair in control of EPA. None of the donations repeat to the same charities but were changed to cities to coincide with resident location of new holders of the same chairmanships. This one here even bears the name of the chairman's mother. I repeat. Coincidence? Maybe. Can you explain this Miz Vorhees?"

"Yes, my father and other members of the family, including my daughter, have many friends in high places around the world. Society brings us together and we seek each other's company. There is nothing wrong with asking favors of one another."

"You are saying it's like you scratch my back and I'll scratch yours?"

"That's a very Gothic way to say it, but yes."

"When you approved, or signed off on these, as you say, Miz Vorhees, did not they smell a little like bribery to you?"

"Of *course* not."

Will uncovered the remaining charity name, Renewal Haven, and asked, "Was this one approved by you and did you happen to go there to check out their credentials?"

"Yes, I did personally check this one out and found it to be worthy of our charity."

"Have you personally visited the site of this charity?"

"Yes, some years back. It has been on our list for some time."

"Have you visited there more than once? If so, how many times?"

"I can't remember exactly but more than once."

"Have you been there for any reason other than to check them out for donation purposes?"

"I have been there to avail myself of their services."

"What services would that have been?"

"Recreation and rest."

"Do they dry out alcoholics and other addicts there, Miz Vorhees?" This brought another objection from the prosecutor's corner and the judge directed Will to clean up his question. "Do they treat patients suffering from alcohol addiction?"

"Yes."

"Were you there for the treatment of alcohol addiction?"

"Yes, according to the papers that I signed."

"Were you treated there on more than one occasion?"

"Yes."

"When were you last released from Renewal Haven?"

"A few weeks ago." It was now obvious to Lilia that Will had all the facts. She was growing tired of playing games, but surely he was about done. She was wrong.

"Who paid for your treatment, Miz Vorhees? My information shows me that their quoted fees range upward from 60 thousand dollars per confinement."

"I did, of course, and it was *not* confinement. I was free to leave at any time."

"But, if you left early, before the agreed to period of confinement … sorry, stay … was completed, you wouldn't be allowed to reenter without a new contract. Is that correct?"

"I don't know about that."

"These are discharge papers that show your charity donations covered your expenses. Did you just lie to this court or was that just poor memory on your part? Oh, don't bother to answer that, we will let the jury to decide for themselves." This brought another call to the bench, but Will could now strike another accomplished goal off his list. She had

224

obviously lied.

Will noticed that Lilia was becoming more and more nervous and was having to give more thought to the questions before answering. A bead of perspiration had formed over her upper lip. She clearly needed a drink of something besides water.

He stepped back to the defense table and took a long sip of water, hoping to stimulate her thoughts of having a drink. The questions about her problem and her last confinement might trigger bad thoughts and backfire on him, but everything worked as planned. She asked the judge for a "restroom" break and the judge agreed, "Let's stop here and take an early lunch break. You are excused until 1:00."

Lilia returned from the lunch break looking refreshed, and it took Will very little time to understand why. He detected alcohol on her breath. He moved closer to make certain. There was no doubt about it. He wondered if Windy had noticed also, but what could he do? A request for another break would have been denied. His only chance would have been to plead illness. If Will could keep her on the stand long enough, Lilia should become easy pickings. She was now back off the wagon. Booze had become the boss. He moved on to questions about her relationship with his defendant.

"Miz Vorhees, how long have you known Mr. Joiner?" His smile was back on his face. He wanted her to relax a bit before he started to lower the boom.

"I'm not sure. I believe I met him when he was in the fourth grade or sometime about then. My daughter had transferred to his school then. Lavita, my daughter, makes friends easily. She makes a point of knowing everyone in her classes. She became heavily involved in the horse culture and so was he, so they were drawn into conversations about their mutual interest. He was a ranch kid and so was she. They were performing in the same horse shows and rodeos. I think the note passing about who likes who began about then and she ended up referring to him as her boyfriend. This continued on and off for a number of years and became a serious relationship while they were in high school."

"Did this relationship meet with your approval, Miz Vorhees?"

225

"Yes, but not with Judge Parker."

"Why not with the judge, or do you know?"

"He said that left-handed cowboys are bad luck, so it took a while for Jimmy Jack to win him over. Jimmy Jack was winning rodeo events and so was my daughter. Judge liked to watch his granddaughter ride and win on horses that he had bought for her. She became a crowd favorite as was Tripp. Judge saw how much she liked him and gradually came around and even started attending his football games with Two Gun. The kid practically lived at our house when he wasn't doing his own ranch chores. He lifted weights with Two Gun and went to the shooting range with him. I simply could not understand why he later came to hate him so much."

"Well. Let's see if we can find out who the real haters were. Shall we?"

"I do believe that is obvious."

Judge Sullivan interrupted, "Don't take that any further, Mrs. Vorhees."

She obviously wanted to add more but bit her tongue and let the scowl on her face show her displeasure in being interrupted."

"So you are saying, Miz Vorhees, that everybody loved Tripp Joiner and he loved your family. He obviously loved your daughter enough to ask her to marry him, did he not? There was a formal engagement celebration at some point while they were in college. Right?"

"Yes."

"There was an incident that came about while they were in high school that displeased you very much. It angered you enough to forbid his seeing your daughter ever again. Isn't that right?"

"Maybe so, but we worked it out."

"Will you tell us about that incident?"

"That was a very private thing involving my daughter and I don't wish to air it in public."

"A man's life is at stake here. Everything is important here. I implore you to answer my questions unless Judge Sullivan forbids."

"Well alright, if you insist. I walked in on a teenage petting session between my daughter and Tripp in my house after I had initially retired for the evening. They were in an inappropriate position and I asked him to leave the house and never come back."

"Did that order stick?"

"Yes, for about a week, then I relented to my daughter's pleas."

"How and why did you let him off the hook?"

"I met him at his truck after football practice and made a deal with him. I carried a Bible to him and made him swear on it that he would never be intimate with my daughter until they were married, and he did as I asked. I then gave him a lecture and forgave him and sent him on his way."

"That deal was sealed with a kiss on the cheek, was it not, Miz Vorhees?"

"I don't remember."

"You still loved him like a son at this point, didn't you, Miz Vorhees?"

"Well yes, as much as I could of course."

"You have made that statement in public more than once, have you not?"

"Probably."

"Do you recall making an extended toast to the betrothed couple when you spoke about how much you loved Tripp and how you considered him to already be a son and you told the funny story about the bible swearing incident?"

"Some of it. Yes."

"Did your daughter ever tell you that when she and Tripp got together for the first time after the incident, she proposed that they exchange their own private wedding vows as a means of escaping the ramifications of

227

oath violation?"

"She did not, and I don't believe that. She would never do that."

"Did there come a time when elaborate wedding plans were started, to the extent that a date was set, deposits were made for venue rental, honeymoon location, limo rental, and so forth? The lists for bridesmaids and grooms were being prepared and even the bride's gown was being designed?"

"Yes."

"Then suddenly, all was called off in a fit of anger. Isn't that correct?"

"No, not exactly, my daughter made her decision over a period of time. After my daughter's first movie. Her picture and featured stories began to appear everywhere telling how she had become a big star and overnight sensation. Tripp did not handle this well. He became very jealous and began to sulk. He was accustomed to being the big star and he complained to me, and I quote, 'I don't like sucking hind teat.'"

This crude euphemism brought snickers in the courtroom as Lilia continued. "When they were seen out together, the media now pursued her and not him. God bless his soul; his little ego was bruised. She finally had enough and called him out to the house in order to break off the engagement."

"Is this hearsay, Miz Vorhees, or were you present?"

"I was in the house, but it was a private matter between them."

"You would think that, yes. Do you know if anyone else was present? Strike that. Let me ask it another way. Did your daughter have a house guest present at that time?"

Lilia's sudden body shift told him that he had struck a nerve, but there was as yet no sign of the meltdown he was trying to create. He did not know that the need for Jose Cuervo was doing his job for him. Now that she was off the wagon, Lilia was nearing the end of her normal break between drinks. The craving was intensifying rapidly.

228

"Er … I believe that she did. A friend rode out with her from SMU in order to satisfy his curiosity about ranch life and the horse world society in general. He was a journalism student and wanted to do a little story about her. She had a few meaningless dates with him and was weaning herself away from her relationship with Tripp. She was preparing herself to break the marriage engagement, and Tripp's jealous actions forced the issue."

"Was her friend present at her *private* meeting?"

"I'm sure that he wasn't."

"If not, then how did the fight between him and Tripp start, if you know?"

"Yes, I saw and heard part of it. He was shouting at Tripp to calm down. Tripp was yelling and cursing. He was taking the rejection very hard. Tripp grabbed him by the throat and pushed him against the wall and then left, slamming the door on his way out. He got in his truck and drove off."

"What was your daughter doing at the time?"

"She was upset and crying. I had my arm around her as he left. She looked at me and said, 'Good riddance,' and walked back into the house."

"She, of course, returned the very valuable wedding ring to him, right?"

"Not right then. She sent that back to him later."

"Have you forgotten that you organized a search party of some servants to find the ring that ended up lost in the grass near the driveway after it bounced off Tripp's windshield because your daughter chose this way to ease his pain of being rejected?"

"You can't prove that, Mr. Clarkson."

"You were there. But maybe we can jog your memory when the defense presents its side of the story."

229

Windy objected again and the judge advised the jury to disregard this statement, but Will had made his point. He continued, "You have now told conflicting stories again, Miz Vorhees, but I will let the jury sort it out. So now let me ask another question about this not-so-private meeting. Did you see your daughter kissing her male house guest and hear the rest of the words of the real breakup?"

This time, the objection by Windy led to a bench call, but the judge instructed the distressed Lilia to answer.

"I told you what I heard."

Will could now see some signs that Jose Cuervo was doing its job. But he backed off temporarily. "Once things calmed down, how did you react to the breakup? Did you suddenly hate Tripp as your daughter apparently did?"

"No one hated him. I still loved him. As a matter of fact, I tried to talk my daughter into taking him back. I wanted the wedding to go on. I tried several times, I really did."

Will felt a vibe that told him that this was the time to spring his trap, to force the meltdown. He began to speak in his best Texas drawl. "Let me see if I can string all of this together so that we can make sense of your story. Jimmy Jack Joiner came into your life when you moved here from Dallas and your daughter was enrolled into the fourth grade. In her classroom was an orphan boy being raised by his grandparents on a ranch. A shy young man who stood out because of his exceptional height. He was considered by your daughter as the big boy who was always kind to everybody. He was the class leader and made a good friend. They remained friends until they became engaged, in spite of many obstacles along the way."

Another objection from the prosecutor. "Is there a question in there somewhere, Your Honor?"

"Get on with it, counselor."

"Thank you, your honor. So, they planned their marriage and set a date. You say that she changed her mind, didn't want him anymore because he was jealous. You made several attempts to bring them back together because you loved him like a son, but to no avail. Then suddenly, your love turned to hate, Miz Vorhees. Why was that?"

"Because I believed that he killed my father."

"Before that, Miz Vorhees. You walked into the office of the county sheriff and demanded that Jimmy Jack Joiner be arrested and that he was a menace to society who needed to be taken off the streets. Why, Miz Vorhees? Why did you do that?"

"Because he accused my daughter of killing his little New Orleans whore, you two-bit son of a bitch!" She shouted at the top of her lungs.

Pandemonium erupted in the court room. The prosecution team moaned in unison. Judge Sullivan pounded his gavel. The jurors gasped and some spectators laughed and muttered. The defense team popped the corks on their imaginary champagne bottles as they celebrated the victory. He had led the state's witness into opening up forbidden testimony.

After a call to the bench, the judge admonished the witness for using foul language. He forbade Will from asking further questions about the death of Debi Devereaux. Will was anxious to ask Lilia how she had known the contents of a police report that had never been made available to the public, but he was denied the request. The judge adjourned court for the day and called the litigants to a meeting in his chambers.

All members of the two opposing legal teams gathered in the judge's cramped chambers as he took off his robe, poured himself a stiff drink of straight bourbon, opened a jar of pickled pig's feet and offered to share. There was an air of tenseness and apprehension. All were aware of his reputation for brutality towards those who, in his view, disobey direct orders.

"Well, Mr. Clarkson, you managed to do what I had explicitly forbidden you from doing. You managed to bring the death of Miss Devereaux into this trial. We are on the verge of having a mistrial here, and I may be the one who declares it without a request from either of you. I told you that I was not going to allow this court to become a grand jury or trial in the death of Miss Devereaux, and I meant it. I did make it clear that nothing could be brought in unless the prosecution opened the door. This prosecution witness has opened up forbidden territory in a limited way, but I intend to keep a lid on it. This incident can harm both parties but probably can be more damaging to the prosecution. Yet Windy, it was your own witness who did it. You should have warned her about this beforehand."

"Of course, I did, your honor," replied the DA.

"Mr. Clarkson, you may have outsmarted your own self here. You are on a slippery slope now, for sure. It would take several months to restart this trial. In the interim, unbearable pressure would be brought to take the Devereaux death to a grand jury. I have, of course, reviewed the conflicting statements there, and it appears to me that you now have two juries you must convince of Mr. Joiner's innocence. A loss there would certainly negatively impact your chances in this case. It almost takes on the odor of double jeopardy for the defendant who, let me remind you, is our subject of fair justice.

"I am considering a recess in this trial while I muddle my way through this. My role in this trial is to make certain that justice is served with a fair trial for the accused. Too much evidence is better than too little as long as it does not prejudice either side. It is my thinking now that this witness must remain off the stand."

Will objected, "I am not finished with my cross, Judge. She opened up a new can or worms."

Windy interrupted, "I must have my turn at rehabilitating my witness. Please be reminded that, by law, I have this privilege."

The judge asked Mule, "What is your response to this?"

Mule moved to the edge of his chair. "I will restate the defense's position in this case and my opening argument in very clear terms. The Parker camp feared what the accused, my client's, testimony in the Devereaux death would do towards sending Princess Lavita Parker, Judge Parker's only grandchild and heir to the throne, to prison. That is their primary motivation now, and the princess is calling the shots. She is a scorned woman whose grandfather ordered the execution of my client, killed his daughter and triggered his own death and that of his bodyguard. My client is falsely accused and charged with two counts of murder by this prosecutor. Your job of insuring fair justice will take an open mind and far reach. May God help you do that."

The DA, now standing, was trying to control his temper. "The defense obviously has forgotten what a jury is for and is looking for you to give them a gift of innocence. Perhaps this trial should have been delayed until after a grand jury met on the Devereaux death and until the investigation into the death of the Joiner girl was completed. Remember, there is an accident factor that comes into play in both of those deaths that cloud the water enough to cause a no-bill possible in both. The accused in the young girl's death is dead. The claimed motive for Joiner's rush for a confrontation with Malham was based solely on his wife's accusations, which were not the absolute proof of his guilt."

The judge stood up, an indication that he was finished. "We are done here, but you two can spend the rest of this day working on your written recommendations as to how we work through this mess with further witness testimony. Get it to me before we convene tomorrow. I will consider a request for a mistrial by the prosecution if it comes, but keep this in mind, Windy. The expense of starting a new trial will be immense and your star eyewitness, key to your case, will be subjected to another grueling cross examination. If you think she will be better prepared next time around and you want to take that chance, I am receptive to your request for a mistrial. I have not yet ruled out that option on my part, either."

Hal Hall and the others in the room remained silent but their thoughts were the same. There is more justice served in the judge's chambers than in the courtroom, more than ever imagined.

The prosecution and defense teams met, as instructed, taking the remainder of the day and part of the evening to reach an agreement. Details of the head injuries to Debi Devereaux would be avoided in all future testimony and Lilia Vorhees would be allowed to return to the stand next morning.

Court reconvened on time and Lilia Vorhees, back on the stand, requested and was allowed to make a statement. "I want to make an apology to this court for my poor behavior and language while on the stand yesterday. There is no excuse, but I was extremely tired and out of schedule with my medications. I assure you that it will not happen again."

233

Will Clarkson thanked her for the apology and continued his cross. "Let's shift gears a bit, Miz Vorhees. I have in my hand a copy of the police report filed by the first law enforcement officer to arrive on the crime scene, Deputy Sheriff Hanner. It states that you came forward immediately after he surveyed the room, grabbed him by the arm and pointed out Jimmy Jack Joiner as the shooter of your father and Deputy John Malham. He asked if you were certain, because Mr. Joiner was unconscious and being attended to by the medical personnel. He asked again and then once more, because as he states here, you were in an advanced state of intoxication. Do you deny or agree with that description of your condition, Miz Vorhees?"

"I do not deny that I had been drinking but I was far from drunk. I have a drink or two before I go to bed at night as a means of sleeping. Most people take sleeping pills; I have a couple drinks of tequila."

"Let me, with his honor's permission, give you a copy of this report so that you can follow along."

With a nod from the judge, she took the copy and focused on the underlined section.

"You see that Deputy Hanner reports that you were having trouble standing without the assistance of your female attendant who had appeared on the scene. He then escorted you into an adjoining room for more questioning. You were incoherent and having trouble understanding the questions, so he asked the attendant to sober you up with black coffee and bring you back in one hour for questioning. She asked for permission to replace your bloodstained clothing. This was granted and instructions were given as to how the clothing was to be handled and returned to police custody. Do you read that here, Miz Vorhees, and do you agree with his statement of the facts?"

"I was not drunk. I was overcome with grief."

"Do you ever get drunk, Miz Vorhees? How much booze does it take to make you drunk?"

Judge Sullivan interrupted again. "One question at a time counselor."

Lilia responded, "Since I never get drunk, I can't answer your question."

234

She was getting a little bit cocky now as Will approached with another document in his hand. "I am now showing you records from Northside Liquor Store, which I ask to put into evidence, that show an average of more than one bottle per day of Jose Cuervo tequila delivered to your home over any timespan that you choose. There are some time gaps in there that coincide with your trips out of town. Were these deliveries for you?"

The prosecutor objected to this slight discretion, but the judge said, "The witness may answer."

"There are several people in my house who drink booze, Mr. Clarkson."

"Do they drink Jose Cuervo, Miz Vorhees?"

"You must ask them."

"I have. Indeed, I have," he lied. "Now Miz Vorhees, I'm sure that you consider yourself to be a well-educated and intelligent person. Correct?"

She responded, "I like to think so. Yes."

"Then, I'm sure that you have been taught like the rest of us that the first instinct of virtually all of life's creatures is self-preservation, exceeded at times by the exceptions like the protection from harm by a child's mother. We also have examples of heroism when one risks personal harm in order to save the life of another. In view of this, I would like to pose a question containing a hypothetical situation. Suppose a sane woman is the only witness to the killing of her father. The killer undoubtedly knows now that his own life is in danger if this witness tells her story. The woman would reasonably expect that her own life was in eminent danger and that she must defend herself from certain death. She has the skill and the means in her hand to do just that. Then she sees the opportunity to save her daughter from harm. Natural instinct kicks in and she does both. Do you see any correlation in this hypothetical and your own tragic experience, Miz Vorhees?"

Her adamant answer was, "I see none because there is none. It's nonsense."

"Miz Vorhees, you shot John Malham in order to save your own life, didn't you?"

"Objection!" shouted Walter Warren. "Asked and answered."

Lilia gave no answer.

Will spoke, "I withdraw the question." He had achieved his intended goal with the question. No answer was needed. He had summed up for the jury, the defense case in a tiny package containing the what, who, when and how. He then informed the judge, "I am finished with this witness."

The DA attempted to rehab his witness, wasting his time with a few weak questions and finishing with, "Mrs. Vorhees, did you see, with your own two eyes, Mr. Jimmy Jack Joiner, who you have claimed to help raise as a son, shoot and murder Mr. John Malham, hired protector of your father, Judge Horace Parker?"

"Yes! I swear."

He then dismissed Lilia from the stand. She fled the courtroom as fast as her wobbly legs would allow and fell into her waiting limo. Her first action was to extract a bottle of Jose Cuervo from the backseat bar and take a long swig and then light a Marlboro. "I knocked 'em dead on national television in there today. You can watch it later on CBS if you like."

Her driver responded, "I'll do that," as he drove away. No instructions were needed. He knew she was headed for bed to watch television, smoke and drink herself to sleep.

CHAPTER TWENTY-SEVEN

Nightmares

Since the first day of his incarceration, Tripp Joiner had paced back and forth the eight feet from front to back of his Ector County cell trying to control his emotions. He was still chaffed about the demeaning body cavity search and the daily delousing wash downs, which magnified the overwhelming odor of disinfectant that permeated the entire jail complex. The undersized standard issue coveralls were pinching and rubbing as he paced, yet these were the least of his problems. He wanted out.

He now understood why the many birds and wild animals he had attempted to raise from babies never quit pacing in their cages and pens until he finally released them back to the wild. He had expected to be released on bail by now in spite of the seriousness of the charges and the adamant opposition formally expressed by the prosecution. Strangely, the thought that he could be faced with a conviction of two counts of murder one and several other lesser counts was not even in his mind. He had convinced himself, long ago, that if and when he came to trial, he would be declared innocent by any jury of his peers.

His ego led him to believe that his super star status and his standing in the community offered enough proof that he was not a flight risk to qualify him for bail. After all, he had played golf several times with the governor and other powerful people in Texas. He had participated in many charity fundraising events with and for these same people and many others. Just look on the streets. Kids and adults everywhere were wearing replicas of his football jersey. He had paid no attention to his lawyers when they warned that bail might not be granted, and if so, the amount would be set at an astronomically high figure.

For the first two days in jail he turned down the standard jailhouse meal in hope of that he would soon have something better outside. When a uniformed deputy entered into his cell on day three, a look of relief came over his face as he expected the good news about bail. Instead, the chief jailer introduced himself and asked Tripp to be seated.

He started the conversation, "You were given an explanation of our basic rules and procedures when you were received into our custody, but given the confinement status assigned to you, more details are required by my regulations. Please don't interrupt my short little speech before I'm finished and then I will answer all your questions.

"We call the assignment of special status 'red tagging.' You are marked for special treatment. You are to be given special protection because of your high profile. It is not unusual for a screwball in a place like this to have a perverted belief that he can make a name for himself by doing harm to someone like you. Every inmate and guard already knows that you are in this jail and what the charges are. The guards know that you are here, charged for the death of two of their own county sheriff department members.

"We all knew Two Gun Malham personally and Judge Parker was a famous former leader of our department. There is no prejudice allowed here based on race or religious belief, but there is prejudice based on behavior. We will be as nice to you as you are to us. Privileges can be taken away, and we do have means of solitary confinement and the ability to use it without a court order.

"You have been assigned to this particular cell at the end of the row and with an empty cell between you and the next occupied cell. You will be escorted everywhere you go outside your cell, but I would advise you to always watch your back. Some prisoners have earned trustee status and have free access in most all areas as they go about their work.

"This is not solitary confinement. This is an open cell but private to you only. It is subject to all the normal rules of inspection and cleanliness. You will not be allowed to keep anything in your cell beyond what is standard issue for all inmates. From time to time guards will enter your cell without requesting your permission. Showering will be mandatory twice a week except on court appearance dates when one shower per day will be permitted but not mandatory. Lawyer visits are unlimited, but family visits are allowed once per week unless mandated otherwise by a judge.

"You are not required to carry on casual conversations with the guards who like to talk to famous people, but most inmates become lonely and bored enough to seek conversation with most anyone. I want you to know that I, myself, would like to be available for a conversation now and then. I played a little college football myself. I am a sports junkie and a fan of yours. I would enjoy picking your brain about some of your big plays I saw on television. Of course, that can't happen because of your implication in the death of a deputy sheriff. Okay now, it's your turn, so fire away."

Tripp cleared his throat. "Thank you, deputy, for all the information, but I am not planning on needing it. I plan to be released on bail very soon. Probably sometime today. I do have a few questions. First, why the terribly strong odor of disinfectants, and second, what is the other strange overpowering odor?"

"The age of this jail makes it very hard to keep clean. I am a cleanliness freak. Before I came on this job, this place was a pit. There were outbreaks of disease, and rats and cockroaches owned this place. We even had lice. I have eliminated everything except for a few mice, and they will be gone soon. The county had been sued three times over these conditions and then a judge stepped in with instructions to clean things up here. He also ordered the county to build a new jail. You will get accustomed to the odors.

"The other odor that you asked about is body odor. It will be eliminated only when inmates are required to bathe more than twice a week. Right now, our budget prevents this.

"As to you getting out on bail. To my knowledge, no person charged with a double murder or with the murder of a law enforcement officer has ever been granted bail in this county, so I wouldn't hang my hopes on that. Your best bet for getting out of here is for you to be transferred to another facility near here. I would like that myself, very much so, because your presence here makes me nervous. Now, unless you have more questions, I'll go on with my chores."

Tripp knew before the cell door was opened and closed that he had been the victim of a cleverly designed scare tactic delivered as a gift from the Ector County sheriff's department for the sole purpose of making his life miserable. No doubt they believed that he had murdered Two Gun. He had no way of knowing that at that very moment, Mule Sherman was attempting again to have bail granted. He was making the argument that given the charges of double murder and the killing of a police officer, his life was in danger as long as he remained in the custody of the sheriff department or any other law enforcement group other than the FBI. Unfortunately for Tripp, bail was denied, and the bad news was delivered shortly thereafter.

Being penned up in a cage was, in itself, enough to drive him crazy. Ranch kids are accustomed to wide open environs. They do outdoor chores and play outdoors. Tripp still believed in Santa Claus when he received a pup tent on his fourth Christmas and spent many nights camped out with his grandfather on the river then alone countless times in his own backyard. He liked to take his meals and sit on the house steps just to enjoy the fresh air and openness.

He was now beginning to feel the harassment of the jailers. He was oftentimes brought cold meals delivered long after the sound of food delivery to the other cells had ceased. He imagined that the late-night screamers had been moved closer to his cell. He was subjected to surprise cell inspections, accompanied with a demeaning body cavity search.

Guards would not have a conversation with him, yet they would congregate outside his door in the wee hours for meaningless chatter. The old-style cell fronts, with bars only for a wall, enabled the mere presence of someone standing just outside to be a distraction. Very often, a guard would be posted there for no reason. Again, in the middle of the night in order to deprive him of sleep. More than once, he was summoned to the visiting area to find that no visitor was there and would be forced to wait there for more than hour before being escorted back to his cell.

His suspicions of harassment were confirmed one day when a trustee, who was cleaning the hallway, said to him, "I am not supposed to talk to you, but I hear things, ya know man. They've got you marked for the treatment cause you're a cop killer." He then rapidly departed the area because he knew that talking to a red tag could cost him his position as trustee.

Tripp became even more determined to force the issue of bail or a transfer. His lawyers couldn't get it done so he turned to his visitors. He prepared a list of some of the most influential people he knew personally and gave the list to several of his family and other visiting friends, asking them to spread his plight with phone calls and letters. Tripp impatiently awaited the results. It took a while, but he eventually got help from unexpected sources.

The trial finally got underway and the first few days of embarrassment created by the accusatory staring of a courtroom full of people gave Tripp an unexpected feeling of security back in the very hell hole that he had been fighting so hard to escape. That feeling changed over time and he began again to hate the courtroom less than the cell.

His dreams of getting out began to manifest itself into nightmares. Most were associated with the death of his daughter and his experience of seeing her mangled body in the hospital morgue. Then nightmares also came with totally unrelated incidents. In one, his beloved horse went wild and attacked him. In another, his grandmother, whom he loved with all his heart, spat on him and called him a murderer. He dreamed that Coach Carr withdrew his numbnuts protection and he was overcome with physical pain. There seemed to be a new nightmare every night during his only one or two hours of brief sleep.

He began to try to fight off all sleep in order to avoid the nightmares, and he began to pay attention to a mouse that came snooping around almost every night. He withheld a few scraps of food from his evening meals and began feeding the mouse. Little by little, the mouse would work himself closer to Tripp's outstretched hand. The goal was to teach the mouse to eat out of his hand.

He gave him a name. For some reason, his mannerisms reminded him of his childhood friend, Weezer Wilson, so Weezer it was. He began to talk to Weezer as he fed him. At first, the mouse would shy away, but slowly began to stand his ground and just look at Tripp as he talked to him in baby talk.

Finally, after a few weeks, Weezer did take the food from his hand but suddenly bolted out of the cell with the food in his mouth. Weezer never came back. Tripp kept food for him and called his name night after night. The nightmares had ceased during the friendship with Weezer, and Tripp desperately wanted him back. Despite the calls, he waited in vain and the nightmares returned.

The ones about his daughter returned first, except that now they were worse. She had no head and his wife had no head; no one had a head.

Tripp knew that now he was definitely going insane. His brain was behaving the same way as it did on the day that Debi Devereaux died. He was on the guilt trip again. He needed help.

Prayer didn't help. He tried that over and over, alone and with his pastor. He lost his appetite for food and lost more than 20 pounds and was feeling physically ill much of the time. There were pains in parts of his body other than in his recently surgically repaired shoulder. His old bullet wounds were hurting again and numbnuts could not stop the pain. He knew that narcotic painkillers were not available from the jail dispensary. He was suffering from mental and physical pain as he somehow fell asleep. Then Weezer returned in his dreams.

This time he was much larger in size. His body was the size of a mountain lion. He was frothing at the mouth and very ill. Tripp recognized the signs of a poisoned animal. He had seen poisoned coyotes before.

Weezer looked at him with hatred in his eyes. He began to growl and foam from the mouth as he leaped on Tripp, biting and clawing his nose and eyes. Tripp could not breathe and sat up straight up in bed and awoke screaming for help, which continued for several seconds.

The jailers were accustomed to nighttime prisoner screams but could tell by the direction of these that they were coming from their red tag prisoner. They raced to his cell. There they found him cowered in the small space between the toilet and the back wall of his cell. He was now silent but was shaking violently as they lay him in his bed and began talking to him. He was soon coherent and talking. They walked him to the dispensary cell and put him under observation but offered only aspirin and water.

This incident involving a red tag was considered severe enough by written guidelines to trigger a phone call to the sheriff's office at 3:42 a.m. The deputy on duty filled out his report of the screaming, reportedly caused by a nightmare, and deemed it not to be important enough to wake the sheriff. The sheriff would be calling in before preparing to come to work and could be informed then. According to protocol, he could then report the incident to the prisoner's lawyer or designee.

Later that morning, Mule Sherman, recognizing an opportunity to make a

242

point, called the jail and was allowed to speak to his client. He gave Tripp clear instructions. He was told not to shave or bathe or wear a suit or tie. He was to appear in his prison uniform. He wanted him to look as haggard as possible.

Indeed, Tripp came in looking terrible. His great weight loss caused the coveralls to drape off his body. The dark circles under his eyes added to his appearance of a zombie.

Mule advised the prosecution that he was going to ask the judge for a one-day trial recess but was secretly hoping that his request would be denied. He wanted the jury to be viewing an obviously ill defendant for the entire day. His request was denied. The press gave him a bonus by widely reporting a dramatic change in his appearance. This incident added fuel to the fire for those working far from the courtroom in the conspiracy to force the granting of bail.

An extremely high-profile trial created by famous defendants and famous victims causes shock waves and always affects people far away from the trial. New York Giants teammates, coaches, organizational personnel and team owners were prime examples of this. Zip Devereaux took his instructions from Tripp and called his head coach to report that his quarterback's health was deteriorating and that his very life could be in danger.

Dirk Stonner met immediately with owner Ralph Blakley with a plea for help. Blakely was obviously concerned about losing his all-pro quarterback with three years left on his contract and began to lead this new branch of conspirators working to free Tripp on bail. He knew immediately where to begin. There was a 20 plus-year Giants season ticketholder who had become a close personal friend. He just happened to be the senior U.S. senator from New York, Harlan Mickelberg. In less than an hour, he was asking the senator for his help. Harlan knew this request was a sticky wicket because of the laws against interfering with a judge, but he said that he would think it over. By nightfall, he had formed a plan and set it into motion. After all, these were his Giants too!

The next day, the senior U.S. senator from Texas and ranking member of Mickelberg's senate committee was called to the telephone. After a lengthy exchange of small talk, the conversation got down to serious business.

Harlan opened, "I have a request for a favor. If you refuse there will be no hard feelings, but I believe that you owe me one or two. I have to fly under the radar on this and you will understand why when you hear my request.

"I'm sure you are following the big trial down there and someone needs to get word to Judge Sullivan that there may be a move by very powerful people to ask the big guy at FBI to start an investigation into the inhumane treatment of the defendant that has already caused considerable damage to his health. This investigation, if discovered by the media -- and it will be -- will destroy his trial because there will be no way that it can be kept from the jury, even though they are sequestered. I believe that you know the judge well enough to give him a heads up and nothing more. Do you not?"

"Yes."

Nothing else was said. Nothing more was needed. Judge Sullivan granted bail that same day. It was set at three million dollars with some house arrest conditions. Tripp had suffered several weeks of confinement torture, but many more days were ahead. Maybe his sanity had been spared. Super stardom has its perks.

CHAPTER TWENTY-EIGHT

Fury of a Scorned Woman

The defense team was up tight but confident and anxious to try their case. This, the big day, was finally here. They were all gathered with the prosecution team in the judge's chambers to be advised of his promised ruling.

Feigned friendly greetings were exchanged between the combatants then Judge Sullivan spoke. "Good morning folks. Hope you all enjoyed a good night's rest. This is going to be a busy day. Since the state's witness opened the door a wee bit about the death of Debi Devereaux, I will allow the defense to offer limited response. If you take the risk of putting the defendant on the stand, I will allow him to mention it. I will not attempt to script his words, but he will not use the words kill or murder because we are dealing with an accusation and not proof. He will not go into a description of why or how, as this will open up a whole new trial by bringing in a raft of witnesses and experts.

"My ruling gives you a means of bringing in a missing piece of the picture that you are trying to paint. You are allowed just enough, in my view, to prevent an overturn of my ruling by appeal and nothing more. I have kept this simple and clear and I don't expect questions are needed at this juncture, so let's go out and start the proceedings. Mr. Sherman, will you remain just a second? I have something that I want to say to you in private.

"The state will have the opportunity to respond with testimony in the rebuttal segment following the defense. My crystal ball tells me that the state will bring testimony from the purported two other witnesses and will say that any altercation was started by Devereaux and her death was an accident. I will not let the coroner's report come in. Again, because it would open up the same can of worms."

When the others had left the chambers, he continued, "Your reputation for playing dirty tricks preceded you here, and true to form, you found a way to attempt to bias the jury pool. No one will ever know how much you succeeded. God only knows. You will not let in the slightest whisper of past bad deeds of the two victims that do not pertain directly to this case. Do I make myself perfectly clear?" Mule made no response and left to enter the courtroom. Judge Sullivan waited behind.

There was no question about it. Tripp Joiner must testify. There was no other way for the defense to connect all the dots and even then, there would be gaps in the story that somehow must be told. This fairytale narrative must convince an intelligent and probably skeptical jury that a man of Judge Parker's stature and wealth would risk everything by committing murder in order to protect his granddaughter's movie career and the possibility of her doing prison time. And to do it by using his deputy sheriff bodyguard to make it appear to be self-defense. This must be sold in such a way as to overcome the burden of the state's eyewitness. There was a near silent motive here also. Severe damage to the family reputation could rob the judge of his influence and high-level contacts. Then there was his paranoia about losing at anything and especially to a football player who had dumped his prized little princess and left her stranded at the altar. Actual revenge and the threat of revenge were always a part of his arsenal. Mule knew that he could not fill in all the gaps, but he was, nevertheless, confident of victory as he was asked to call his first witness.

He stood tall and resplendent in yet another new western outfit. His costume change would surely set off another round of jokes among the media as they speculated as to whom he was trying to emulate. Was it Davy Crockett, Sam Houston or perhaps Stephen Austin? They had written that while he was not Hollywood pretty, he could be described as ruggedly handsome. That is, unless his massive ears were visible. At the moment, they were well hidden by his long hair, coiffed such that not a single hair was out of place. He believed that his fame had given him the early advantage in the pursuit of another miracle -- a long-shot verdict not guilty on all charges.

His overall plan had flex as needed, but he decided to score points at the very beginning by attacking the glaring hole left by the state. That was the inability by expert witnesses to adequately explain the presence of John Malham's tissue and blood on the judge's cane head. He put three renowned pathologists on the stand that unequivocally matched the shape of the cane head to the wound in the forehead of Two Gun Malham. They, of course, could not say who wielded the cane, but there were no

246

other fingerprints on the cane handle other than Judge Parker's.

He would set the timeline of the onset of the crimes with the introduction of phone records. These showed the time of a call from the nurse's station nearest to Patricia Joiner's room to Judge Parker's private number immediately after she had awakened from her coma and begun her accusations against Deputy John Malham. Despite considerable efforts by law enforcement and the defense investigators, the caller was never identified.

A total of 29 witnesses were called by the defense. Several of these were for rebuttal purposes. Two testified that while theoretically possible, it was highly unlikely that Malham would have been able to finish choking Joiner to death after being shot in the chest. Both believed that the impact of the bullet would have knocked him away from a choking position. Three expert witnesses, all pathologists, testified to the same facts. The cross examination of each of these key witnesses by the prosecution was lengthy and brutal but none were discredited to any significant degree. Important testimony was given by the law enforcement personnel and others present at the scene about the degree of intoxication of Mrs. Vorhees. This included her own personal attendant, who had been given the task of sobering her up.

The rail birds were betting that Mule would close his case with Tripp Joiner on the stand, but they were wrong again. He planned to close with a tearful Patricia Joiner, who would describe the terrible death of her daughter at the hands of Two Gun Malham. He wanted the jury to go into their deliberations with tears in their own eyes. He was gambling that she would be in better mental and physical condition than she was at that moment. He continued by calling a host of character witnesses including Coach Carr and Zip Devereaux. He called New York Giants teammates, coaches and executive personnel. He called Tripp's pastor and the directors of several charities, including an executive from St Jude's who described Tripp's many visits to children ill with cancer. The list seemed endless and began to bore the jurors, who wanted to hear from the great man himself. Finally, Mule did call Tripp to the stand, where he was properly sworn in.

Asked to state his full name and occupation, he responded, "My name is Jimmy Jack Joiner but most people call me Tripp. I am a professional football player for the New York Giants, but I am now on injured reserve status. I am also a cattle rancher in partnership with my grandparents."

Mule started, "Mr. Joiner, I would prefer to call you Tripp, if I may." Without waiting for a response, he continued. "I would like for you to tell this jury, using your own words, the complete story of all events leading up to and including all the horrible details of the alleged crimes that you are charged with. Tell the complete truth as you know it. Keep your descriptions of the events short and succinct so they jury can fully understand. Refrain from allegations and speculation. Only facts, please. You may begin."

Tripp felt the butterflies in his stomach like he had dealt with hundreds of times before he handled the first offensive snap of the football in a big game. He prayed that they would disappear very soon as always. He cleared his throat and began his story.

"I have known the Parker family since I was nine years old. Beginning when Lavita Vorhees arrived at our school in a Lamborghini, a very expensive Italian sports car, driven by her mother, Lilia. We soon became friends and shared our mutual interest in horses and rodeo events. I taught her some rope tricks which always drew a crowd at school and we eventually began going to the kids' rodeo events together.

"Years later, Judge Parker bought her an expensive barrel racing horse that we kept at the ranch most of the time, and Lilia would bring her to our house so we could practice together. Lilia made my grandmother a little uncomfortable as she was always dressed to-the-nines and sporting large diamond necklaces and bracelets. She was flattered that the family of the 'king of west Texas' would visit us but didn't feel up to the task of entertaining them."

"I must object at this point, your honor. This is a lovely story, but it is hearsay and irrelevant," roared prosecutor Windy Warren.

"Your honor, may we approach?" Mule Sherman responded.

Judge Sullivan motioned with his hand and as the parties arrive at the bench, preempting their arguments, "Objection overruled. Now Windy, the defense is trying to spin their story a little bit to prove their revenge theory, just as you are trying to base your case on the same theory of revenge by the defendant. I am going to give them plenty of room, just as

I will you."

"But your honor," interrupted Windy. "He is wandering all the way around the North Pole and he cannot be allowed to do that."

"How about I give you the South Pole for your wanderings? I will keep things fair, so go sit back down and enjoy the show. Get on with it."

Windy was seething as he returned to his seat and he turned to his assistant DA and with hand over lips, muttered, "This clown is turning our courtroom into a circus. We have now added Roy Bean to Davy Crockett and Jed Clampett. If the defense wants to bring in a dancing bear, he will allow that also." Snickers erupted around the table which drew a scowl from the judge. He knew that Windy was talking about him, possibly even making fun of him.

Tripp continued, "When I first started serious conversations with Lavita, we began to share personal secrets and she admitted to me that she had developed a compulsion to perform in front of audiences, and most of all, to win. She had developed a paranoia about losing. She could not tolerate losing.

"Her mother had entered her in every tiara toddler beauty contest that she could find, and she had liked that because she was performing and winning more than her share. However, people learned to avoid her for days whenever she lost, and as she got older and into the awkward age, she began to lose most always. They left the pageant scene, but she still had the urge to perform. Rodeos gave her a chance to satisfy that need. She rode a beautiful palomino stallion in the parades and her black quarter-horse mare in the barrel races. Her grandfather began buying her the fastest horses in his vast reach regardless of cost and she started to win everything she entered; her ego was satisfied.

"I was 14 years old when I was first allowed to take a ranch truck to school. It eventually became my own to use. That was when we started serious dating, and I began to spend as much time with her as I could work in between my chores and football practice. At times, we were forced to hang around her house against my wishes. All I wanted was to find a quiet place where we could cling to one another or just hold hands.

"We were about 16 years old before we were allowed to truck date and to

249

hang out with the tailgaters who partied at the park. After that we practically lived there in our free time. I had very few conversations with Judge Parker but one in particular stands out. He called me into his office one day and asked me to be seated. He remained standing and stood over me with a very stern look on his face. He began a lecture about dating a member of a very powerful family. He said he had the ability to make my life very miserable if I in any way mistreated his only granddaughter. He made it very clear that he expected me to be a gentleman at all times and to treat her like a lady.

"I could read between the lines and knew that he meant for me to keep my hands off her, if you know what I mean. It was a threat, a very serious one, and I took him seriously. I'll admit, it frightened me. I was thereafter uncomfortable around him, but I was at ease with Lavita's mother. In fact, she treated me like a son she never had and told me that many times, and she led to believe that I could have a position with the company someday. I began to wonder what it would be like to be rich and married to a beautiful woman at the same time.

"Lavita began to enter beauty contests again, upon Lilia's insistence, and was winning most of them, again. It was obvious that Lilia was trying to relive her own youth through her daughter and savored the atmosphere of every victory and all the media attention.

"She began to set her sights on her daughter becoming Miss America. She persuaded her to enter the Miss Texas pageant and spent tons in the quick development of a talent. You can't win on beauty alone and Lavita had no talent except for cheerleader gymnastics. She couldn't sing a lick and had rebelled against piano lessons, so they decided to make her a ventriloquist with almost disastrous results. But they went forward as if they knew they could win on looks and poise alone.

"The interviews were also important, and she prepared diligently. She won everything but the talent contest and finished as first runner up overall. Their mourning over the loss was tempered somewhat when a famous Hollywood agent introduced himself and showed them a list of his famous clients. He wanted to be her agent. He also did some producing, he said. What sealed the deal was his plan to put Vita in a movie right away. He even had an acting coach lined up. He had done his homework well. He knew of Judge Parker's deep pockets and his worship of his granddaughter. He could and would take her to stardom with her first casting as soon as he completed the funding of a movie he had in mind.

"Half of the funding was committed and if Judge Parker would bankroll the remaining half, he could start the picture as soon as casting could be completed. He was gambling on the women's power of persuasion.

"The judge was a hard sell and did his own research. He could recognize a con when he saw it. But he agreed, provided the agent could produce a top line star actor and director from a list he provided. An agreement was reached, and the movie was made quickly. The judge took a tremendous financial hit but it was successful in creating a new movie star. Overnight. Vita, as she was now called, became a household name.

"This was the beginning of the end of our relationship, but she swore that I was the only thing in her life that really mattered, and I believed her."

Mule noticed that the judge was glancing at his watch, which probably meant that he was looking for a good breaking point. It was time for lunch. Mule was hoping that he would wait a little longer because the jurors were caught up in the story, and who wouldn't be? They were listening to a local football idol tell about his life with a beautiful movie star. No juror was squirming or looking at a watch. But Judge Sullivan called the lunch break.

A short while later, Tripp began again. "A beautiful piece of embroidery is displayed in an ornate frame behind the desk of Judge Horace Parker. In it, a phrase was stitched between rows of Texas bluebonnets. A date of January 1, 1900, was stitched in a corner. It reads simply, 'Go make a big splash.' As time went on, I began to realize that this phrase had become something of a family motto. Parker family members used it frequently as a parting expression.

"At my home, Granny's parting expression was, "I love you. Be safe." This was an example of the many differences in verbal exchanges between the Parker family and ours. I felt a remarkable difference in atmosphere in their presence. My belief was that it had to do with the way rich people lived their lives. Everything seemed to be about winning and never about sharing. I never heard the word love mentioned except to describe a possession or desire.

"Of course, I was normal in wanting to get rich someday. I began to wonder if I had to change my whole attitude on life, go against my family and church teachings in order to become wealthy. I believe that 'Go make a big splash' had a different meaning to Lilia Parker Vorhees. I believe that she took it to mean that she should make a dramatic production out of everything. Call in the media and toot your own horn. My first exposure to this behavior came on the day that her daughter was introduced to our society with her transfer to my school.

"I believe this episode of hell on earth that I am now living began the day that I broke my engagement with Lavita Vorhees. We seemed to be drifting apart for some time, perhaps weeks, prior to then. I was attending Texas Tech and she had enrolled at SMU after making her movie. We seldom saw each other but talked daily on the phone.

"The first time I became completely repulsed by her selfishness and paranoia about losing came with a long conversation about her fear about losing her barrel racing skills. She had heard about a trainer by the name of Justin McCormick in Vivian, Louisiana, who was training horses to round a barrel in one fewer step, saving valuable time. She wanted me to go find him and check it out. The whole world was at her beck and call.

"Then, what drove the nail in the coffin, was when I walked in on Lavita at the Parker house as she was locked up in a long kiss and some heavy petting with a guy she had brought home with her from SMU. I lost my temper and grabbed the guy and threw him down on the floor. He was considerably smaller than I and offered very little resistance as I held him down by his throat. I could see the fear in his eyes as I raised him up and slapped him hard across the face. I then asked Lavita what was going on. She offered no plausible explanation. I said something like, 'That does it,' and walked out the door.

"She followed me outside to my truck and attempted to open the locked door while cursing at the top of her lungs. She pulled off her engagement ring and hurled it at me. It bounced off my windshield and I stopped to retrieve it but changed my mind.

"Her mother had joined her and was also screaming. The ring had landed in the grass beside the driveway and I was in no mood to start a search. When I left, I was deeply troubled. I was certain that Lavita and her mother would let revenge rule the day, and if Judge Parker decided to become involved, the results could be devastating for me and my family. I knew we would have clashed sooner or later to the point of a broken engagement but she would have been the one to break it, especially, since she has a new boyfriend. When I grabbed the little fella by the throat, I started a chain reaction that eventually cost the lives of four people, including the live of my little daughter. I discovered the known truth as we all have read in classic literature, 'Hell has no fury like a woman scorned.'

"I received a message from Lavita several days later, asking to meet in order to return the ring. I refused to meet and instructed her to leave the ring with a mutual friend, which she did. A note came in the envelope with the ring asking, once again, for a meeting. Her mother called a few times after that to tell me that she still considered me as a son and encouraged me to contact her daughter and settle our differences. She stopped the calls after a few weeks. Except for an occasional sighting at rodeo events. We moved on with our lives and had no more contact with each other until a few months ago when she came to our ranch unexpectedly.

"Lavita had married her current husband before I met the girl I would pursue relentlessly for several months before she agreed to become my wife. Her name is Patricia. She was in a residency program seeking a permanent job as a veterinarian. She and I shared the love of horses and cattle but had very little else in common. She had no interest in football or rodeo events and her mind was focused on her future career.

"We assured ourselves that true love would overcome all our differences and so we married. We were blessed with a baby daughter soon after. We named her Mary Mae after Patricia's mother and my grandmother, who had raised me after my parents died in an auto crash. This little angel had me constantly seeking time to spend time with her. She was truly 'a daddy's girl' and I teased her mother about that. I trained her to say that she liked me best of anyone else in the whole wide world.

She once painted my face with her mother's makeup and Patricia photographed the event. Mysteriously, that photo was posted in the NY Giants dressing room, much to the amusement of my teammates. Only the fathers of daughters could appreciate the true significance of that event. Now my angel is gone." He paused and wiped tears from his eyes.

"I was fortunate enough to be employed as a professional football player and Patricia was a practicing vet in her dream job. We were living on top of Happiness Mountain and we thanked God every day for our blessings. We were planning a second child. This bliss was shattered by a stupid act on my part. I have been advised to testify about all significant encounters with any member of the Parker family regardless of the consequences, so I will share one of the biggest mistakes of my life.

"I served with Lavita on the fundraising committee of the Professional Rodeo Association charity that raised money for retired or disabled rodeo performers. We meet once a year to work out details of the annual fundraiser at a local hotel. She and I were considered high profile enough to lend our names and to perform for charity.

"At this one meeting, we came together, I am ashamed to admit, in what is commonly called a one-night stand. I take full responsibility, even though I did not plan nor initiate the event, which destroyed my marriage. My wife was informed by an acquaintance and given all the details the following day.

"Since I had not told anyone of the affair, the word had to have come from Lavita. I lied to my wife at first but eventually confessed after a nasty confrontation. I apologized and asked for forgiveness, but my wife split our marriage. By temporary agreement for convenience sake, she and my daughter continued to live in the home, and I moved to the bunk house and later into a double-wide trailer next to the bunkhouse. This allowed me to stay close to my daughter." Tripp tried to smile but couldn't hold back the tears. Judge Sullivan took this opportunity for a short break.

This break gave time for painful thoughts to play through Tripp's brain as he realized that he had just broadcast an image-destroying confession to the thousands of kids who considered him to be a role model. He was a marriage cheat, an adulterer. His role model image was one part of his life in which he made no effort to conceal his pride. Of course, none of this compared to his status of accused murderer, but he believed that stain would be wiped away with an acquittal by the jury. Thankfully, the break was short, and he was asked to continue his testimony.

Tripp began again. "My football teammate and road roommate, Zip Devereaux, is in the courtroom today. During the good ol' days, he was a frequent visitor the ranch. His teenaged sister, Debi, accompanied him once and ended up staying a month. She fell in love with ranch life, and in particular, horseback riding. I taught her how to ride and how to toss a few rope tricks.

"She returned for summer-long trips for a period of years. Her brother referred to her as Baby Sister, so we all came to do the same. She had a beautiful singing voice and liked to entertain us with my wife playing the piano. These visits ended when she attended college in New Orleans and joined up with a local band doing gigs on Bourbon Street. She had been singing with the band for several months when her lifestyle and the Bourbon Street club atmosphere led her brother to call me asking for help with finding her a job here. He had persuaded her that a country and western singing career would offer an easier way to stardom than with New Orleans style blues songs. Texas could provide this opportunity and she could live in the horse country that she loved so much.

"She bought off on the idea and moved here to start her new career. She moved into the ranch for a while until she found a more convenient apartment in town. Her parents added an unexpected burden to the deal by asking me to 'look after their daughter.' To me, this meant taking on the role of surrogate father and I was reluctant to take on this responsibility. My life was a real mess then. My marriage was broken, my daughter was crying herself to sleep every night, and I was recovering from surgery that might end my playing career. And besides, no young woman wants a second father. However, I made the commitment and took it seriously.

"This probably resulted in more phone calls and visits than Baby Sister liked. I began to catch her shows on a regular basis, and I swelled with pride when she began to get standing ovations from growing crowds. The media attention was totally unexpected, and her fame spread. Even the now famous movie star, Vita Vorhees, came for a performance and visited her in her dressing room afterward. She was flattered by this, but I suspected a sinister motive and advised Debi to beware. Lavita was there to size up her potential competition for the local spotlight." This comment brought an objection from the prosecutor and was sustained.

"One day I was working cattle on a piece of leased land that is about three miles from the main ranch. This land was originally used as a bull pasture by my grandfather, but I am now using it to develop a small herd of Santa Gertrudis cattle. I had loaded up a seriously injured cow, her calf and my horse into a two-horse trailer and was headed to my veterinarian by a route that took me past the canyon overlook park. I was in a hurry because the dust was heavy, and a bad storm was following close behind. Rain had begun to fall as I glanced towards the parking lot where I had shared many teenage tailgate parties years ago.

"I was surprised – no, shocked – to see the car belonging to Lavita Vorhees parked there. I recognized it by its custom blue paint job, the only one like in the county. It is a convertible and the top was down."

Tripp continued his story, "My curiosity was getting the best of me and I slowed down to look but saw no one. I took another look back as the road turned with the canyon to the right. I immediately spotted a bright blue object on the canyon floor. I stopped the truck and grabbed my binoculars. I saw Baby Sister in her Sunday blue dress moving slowly along the rocks. She appeared to be limping. I then spotted two women coming towards her down the main trail. I could see that it was Lavita and GiGi Smurl.

"Objection!" shouted the DA. "The witness has crossed the line with testimony about the death of Miss Devereaux."

Judge Sullivan replied, "It was your witness who opened the door to this testimony, and surely you have not forgotten my ruling. I will allow for now. Sit down and let the witness continue."

Tripp continued, "My instinct was to go back and assist if I could. I found a place to turn my rig around, entered the park and parked next to Lavita's car. I hurried down the trail to the canyon floor about a hundred yards and found the girls immediately. Baby Sister was lying on the ground with a very bad head injury and wounds to her face. It was obvious to me that an altercation had taken place. GiGi was over her with a bandana pressed against the wounds. Lavita was sitting nearby with her hands over her face. I could see that Baby Sister was unconscious and I pushed GiGi out of the way, cut bandages from my shirt sleeves and tried, with little success to stop the bleeding.

"I picked Baby Sister up and started back up to the truck. I yelled instructions for the two of them to go ahead of me and call for help on my farm radio and have whoever answers to send an ambulance towards the park. They were to wait for us and then drive Baby Sister towards the hospital, hopefully meeting the ambulance on the way.

"When I reached the top of the hill, both women were gone. I got on the radio and had the ranch foreman, Rod Rodriquez, call for an ambulance to head our direction. I met the ambulance about a mile or two from town and transferred Debi, who was still unconscious, then followed them towards the hospital. A police car joined us soon after and took over the lead.

"When I arrived at the ER, I expected to find the two girls there, but they were nowhere in sight. I called Zip, Debi's brother, and told him what had happened. I was then taken into an office down the hall and was asked a few questions by an Odessa police officer. He called in his superior officer and I told him my story and answered all his questions."

After a brief delay, with tears in his eyes, Tripp sadly stated, "Baby Sister was taken into surgery and everything possible was done to save her, but she never regained consciousness and passed away two days later. Her family had arrived the morning after she was taken to the hospital. Her parents, sister and two brothers were by her bedside when she died. They wanted answers, and I had none. None, in any case that would satisfy them. They were told that an autopsy would be performed and that would take several days so they returned home to mourn.

"A police detective came by the ranch with more questions. They had been unable to Locate Lavita and GiGi and were told by the Parker family that they were out of the country and had been since before the 'accident'. I could tell right away that I was a suspect of something, lying probably." This brought on a stern look from Mule, but he said nothing for fear it would appear as if they were hiding something, so he let Tripp continue.

"Their questions soon confirmed that they had not ruled out something worse, and they left telling me not to leave town and to be prepared to come in for more questioning after the autopsy became available.

"Several days dragged by before I was informed that the autopsy report was in. It did not completely confirm details of my statement to the police, but I was told that this was to be expected and was nothing to be concerned about. I tried to continue normal activities at the ranch.

257

"After I had become a full ownership partner in the ranch but continued to play pro football, I had taken on the project of modernizing ranch activities, taking advantage of my college major to blend in the latest science technology. I had established a routine that required a daily coordination meeting with Rod, again, our ranch foreman", he reminded the jury. "We met before sunup, five days a week.

"My practice was to walk outside, first thing, take a look at the sky then return inside to tune in the weather forecast and make coffee and breakfast. The door was left unlocked for Rod to join me.

"On this particular day, I had not finished eating when I heard someone enter the front door. I assumed that it was Rod and he was early for some reason. Much to my surprise, I heard the voice of the most despised person in my life, Lavita Vorhees, She greeted me in her best seductive actress voice, 'Good morning, Big Boy. Mind if I join you for a cup?'

I was angry but momentarily struck speechless with shock. I did manage to utter a refusal as I stood to escort her out. The use of the Big Boy term brought pain to my ears as it brought back memories of her nose thumbing words as she departed from the spot of our affair that had cost me my marriage. She stopped me in my tracks as she shouted out that a warrant for my arrest had been drawn up. She repeated it again then went on to say that the autopsy report had confused things somewhat and that the latest word was that a grand jury was going to be called by the DA. There was no need for me to ask how she had come to know all this because I knew that Judge Parker was wired into the law enforcement camp.

"She was talking rapidly now in an animated manner and I was listening. Her story was that she had come there to talk peace and to hopefully reach an agreement that would prevent the calling of a grand jury, which could cause great harm to both of us. Her movie career would be destroyed and probably my football career as well.

"I told her that I had nothing to fear and that I had no intention of changing my testimony. She was now shedding tears as she told me that her family had raised a large sum of money for my defense, knowing that I had hired a very expensive attorney. This offer of a …"

"Objection!" shouted the red-faced DA as he jumped to his feet. "May I

258

approach?" He was standing in front of the judge before he finished his question. "The witness has crossed the line and he must be stopped." A conference was called, and the judge halted further testimony about her visit, establishing new guidelines for the alleged bribe attempt.

Tripp continued, working to heed those boundaries. "Shortly after Lavita left, Rod knocked on the now locked door and entered carrying a briefcase, saying that my departing visitor had left if on my top doorstep. He had recognized her, of course, and had curiosity running out of his ears.

"I gave him a brief summary of the event as I opened the unlocked briefcase, which was full of money. I was about to count the money when he stopped me with a suggestion that I touch nothing and turn it over to law enforcement. I expressed my intention to take it directly to Judge Parker and 'stick it where the sun don't shine,' and I asked him to go with me to the judge's office.

"He argued that that move would be dangerous, but he agreed to go with me. He also suggested that we document everything with photos, which we did. The exact amount of the money was $49,400. We returned the money to the briefcase, drove straight to Judge Parker's office and deposited it on his desk. Two Gun Malham was present and seated on the couch. He was holding a cup in his hand, which he quickly placed on the floor and jumped to his feet as he lay his hand on his gun holster but said nothing. The judge also remained silent as I said a few words and walked out the door with Rod, and we returned directly to the ranch. There was very little conversation on the way back home, but I do remember Rod commenting about the hatred in the eyes of everyone there, including the receptionist. It was a relief to be out of there.

"Nothing further was heard from the Parker camp until I was leaving the barbershop a few days later. As I approached my truck, I was surprised to see Two Gun seated on my tailgate. He stood as I approached. I recall there was a smile on his face, and I noticed that he was not packing his customary two-gun hardware. This was an obvious statement that this was to be a friendly meeting.

"I shook his hand as he stated that he was on a goodwill mission at the direction of Judge Parker. He started with a reminder that we once had been tight friends and had shared some hobbies together. He also retold the story about the time he had bailed Little Red, my best buddy, out of serious trouble. He placed great emphasis on the seriousness of my trouble with Parker princess Lavita Vorhees but said all could be forgiven if I would add a little more detail to the police report I had submitted immediately after the death of Debi Devereaux. He wanted me to say that she had suffered a fall during her climb out of the canyon.

"My response was a question how the Parkers had knowledge of a confidential police report. I also pointed out that he was asking me to commit the crime of perjury, which I would not do. He reminded me again of the Parker power and what they could do to me. I responded that they certainly weren't going to kill me, so what else is there?

"He quipped that at least one member, possibly two, might vote to do just that. I jokingly tossed in that Lavita would not be the guilty one because she felt that she still owned me. He growled that this was no laughing matter, and that I should consider the *deadly* seriousness of my decision, adding that I had very little time to choose. He handed me his business card with his new private phone number and walked away, mumbling something about trying to do me a favor." Showing the card and introducing it into evidence at this particular moment was planned by Mule to create a little drama for the jury and to help authenticate this small part of Tripp's testimony.

"A few messages to call Two Gun followed over the next week, but I answered none of them. Then the series of harassments of my wife by him in his patrol car began. My wife became alarmed immediately. I was not overly alarmed at first. I believed that it was an attempt on his part to persuade me to talk to him. Patricia was convinced that it was an attempt to lead me into a trap to be legally assassinated by law enforcement, so she went to the FBI with her complaint.

"She complied with an agent's instructions to come in and fill out a report according to standard procedures for dealing with law enforcement harassment. But no one ever came around for an interview. The fatal car crash that took the life of my daughter and came close to killing my wife literally ripped my heart out. I went insane. I was certain that it was the work of the Parker family before I had convincing evidence.

"I got ahold of my senses and called the FBI and was promised an investigation. I became impatient and hired a private investigator to ascertain that a second vehicle was involved and to find that vehicle. He was able to examine Two Gun's patrol car but not his personal truck. There was no damage to the car, and to my knowledge, the truck has never been examined.

"When Patricia came out of her coma and positively identified the killer, I could not hold myself back any longer. I decided to take justice into my own hands and to make a citizen's arrest. My plan was to surprise Two Gun, disarm him, secure him in his own handcuffs and drop him at the entrance of local FBI headquarters.

"My first opportunity to catch him alone came almost immediately. It was time for him to have his evening meal in a local bar where he had a habit of dining, so I made an effort to beat him there and ambush him. He was a no show, so I decided to catch him at home where he should be by this time of day, playing gin and drinking whiskey with Judge Parker. I knew from personal experience that this almost daily routine would continue until both would become passing out intoxicated and thus easy to catch.

"I parked my truck out of sight and approached from the rear of the house, intending to enter the door next to the kitchen. House rules had always been that this door would remain unlocked until the personal attendant for Lilia Vorhees tucked her into bed and departed to the servant's quarters behind the main house. To my surprise, the door was locked, which caused me to pause and rethink my strategy. Maybe they had heard that Patricia was awake and talking, prompting them to set a trap in case I showed up for revenge. Or perhaps they were avoiding a visit from the FBI as unlikely as that seemed.

"In any case, I decided to leave and make another attempt to catch Two Gun alone or hoping he would soon be arrested, saving me the trouble. I crept silently alongside the house, taking the short way back to my truck. As I rounded the front corner, I heard a gunshot, stopping me in my tracks. The sound was from inside the house.

"A young man from the scene at the bar and grill was crossing the street towards me. He and a companion came straight to me. He gave me his name and mentioned that he and his brother were my posse and had my back.

261

"At that moment, a woman's loud screams were heard coming from the house. I told the brothers to leave. I broke the stained-glass door window just above the handle and reached through the break to unlock the door. I entered as cautiously as possible and peered around the door to the reception area from the hallway. I found myself staring down the barrel of Two Gun's pistol.

"My hands and saddle gun instinctively went up as a shield in front of my face just as the pistol went off. I felt a sharp pain as the ricocheted round passed through the edge of my flesh below my armpit. My other hand was now grasping the gun hand of a very large and powerful man.

"A second round went off into the floor, but by now both of my hands were holding on to his two hands, with the gun in control by neither of us. Both of us were attempting every damaging move available like knees to the groin, head butts and foot stomping, without meaningful results.

"Lilia was standing near with a gun pointed at us, shouting for us to stop. We each tried to twist the other into a position of a shield. Then, I thought of my teeth as a weapon of last resort. I had to find a way to bite his gun hand. On the next head butt attempt, I managed to bite down on his nose. Blood went everywhere and he bellowed like an animal and brought both hands and the gun up to his face. I was able to bite his thumb and jerk the gun at the same time. The gun came loose and skidded across the wooden floor and disappeared under the couch. He broke my bite on his thumb, but I thrust my thumb into his eye socket. The edge of my thumbnail acted as a blade point. The entry was deep, and I felt the eyeball shift in the socket. He again yelled out with pain. He was obviously blinded in one eye.

"His momentary distraction allowed me to dive first for the gun. I reached under the couch but was unable to find the gun before he was on my back with a two-hand chokehold around my neck. I knew I was in serious trouble immediately and began to try every conceivable move to break his hold. I managed to break it enough several times to catch a short breath, but I knew that I was losing the battle for my life. I managed to cry out for help a time or two, hoping that Lilia might help or that my so-called posse would save me, but I slowly began to fade out. When I came fully awake, I was in the ambulance with handcuffs on my wrists and a uniformed law officer at my side. In the ER I was shackled to my bed and my days in hell were beginning."

With that, Mule Sherman ended the session and turned his witness over to the DA for cross examination.

CHAPTER TWENTY-NINE

Dig a Big Hole DA

Tripp wasn't particularly anxious to be cross examined, but he did feel confident. His mind was in a place where it had been many times just before kickoff in a big football game that follows a good week of practice by the entire team working with a great game plan. Mule Sherman had helped script his testimony, but Will Clarkson was assigned to school him for the cross. These multiple sessions were long and intense, and he was amazed at the amount of cross examination expertise that Will possessed. He brought Tripp a book to read that he had written on the subject and that was being used in some state law schools.

He began their first session by helping shape a confidence-building opening statement. "I believe existing circumstances provide you with a tremendous edge in dealing with the DA, Mr. Warren. He has never before stood face to face before a person of your stature in cross examination. He is going to be very nervous. Throw in the fact that he will be performing on a stage provided by millions of television viewers. We then have a person who will be prone to make serious mistakes in judgment and speech, and you are going to help him do just that by simply keeping the pressure coming from our side.

"He has another weakness that we can exploit. He was a wannabe actor in college and has never lost the fever. He still takes an occasional part in the local theater company that puts on plays around the area. I am sure that you have noticed his tendency to overdramatize his gestures in this trial, especially when he was cross examining our expert witnesses. His facial contortions and body language expressing disbelief to the witness's answers to all his questions is something right out of Shakespeare. I believe that these antics make him a clown to some jurors. I wager that he will ramp up his antics as he deals with you. We have a way to take advantage of that.

Now we have more important things to plan for. He will sort out your perceived testimony weaknesses and go for your juggler on these. Two of the more obvious ones are your claim to enact a citizen's arrest on Mr.

Malham and your extramarital affair with Vita Vorhees."

During a break before cross, Will refreshed Tripp's memory with a few major points and left him with, "You have told the whole true story, now this truth must be upheld and sold to the jury. If you accomplish this, you will win the verdict. One last reminder. You must never show liar's eyes. During your cross, as you start to answer a question, never look away, especially down. Keep your eyes locked on his. Always win the stare-down battle. Maintaining the appearance of being in control is so important."

Everyone now waited for one of the most important segments of the trial. Tripp was not looking forward to the cross examination, but he remained confident.

Court reconvened then Walter Warren made a strange move, something he had never done before at this juncture. He asked Judge Sullivan for a bench meeting. Attorneys for both sides gathered before the bench and the DA began to speak. "Your honor, your reputation for fairness in the pursuit of justice has never been in question. Counselor for the defense brought up the subject of your invisible guidelines and now I raise the same subject. It is my opinion that Mr. Sherman and Mr. Clarkson have been granted unprecedented latitude in biased evidence allowed into this trial. Pretrial propaganda of past bad actions by the deceased victims was cleverly introduced by scandal sheet print media, exposing the entire jury to this bias. Testimony originally banned by you has now been let in. I am reminding you that I, an officer of this court, am entitled to this same wide expansion of standard guidelines. I expect to be able to walk all over your invisible guidelines as did counsel for the defense."

Judge Sullivan cut him short, "You, sir, are getting very close to crossing the line right now with that language. Be very careful how you proceed from here on or I will gobble you up like a duck on a June bug. Now get on with your cross. We are burning valuable daylight."

District Attorney Walter Warren began his cross examination. "Mister Jimmy Jack Joiner, we have attended several functions at the same time, and while we have never been formally introduced, it is clear that we have shown common interests in making our local community a better place in which to live and work. That fact and others make this the most difficult prosecution that I have ever been a part of. I get no pleasure in

265

prosecuting any defendant for murder, because it means that there are deceased victims and grieving families left behind to suffer the sorrow."

Mule Sherman stood as if to protest but the judge motioned for him to sit back down before he had a chance to speak. The DA was clearly testifying and over the line of standard procedure.

"It is even worse to prosecute a person who has become an idol to so many football fans and who is a homegrown hero to thousands of youngsters right here in Ector County. The jury will decide your guilt or innocence based on the facts presented to them. I believe that these facts will show that your long testimony of innocence is full of falsehoods and speculation. It is my job, in the interest of true Texas justice, to correct the record for this jury."

Mule rose again. "Objection! Your honor, Mr. Warren has been talking for weeks and has yet to ask a question."

The judge conceded, "It would be nice, Mr. Warren, if we could hear a question every now and then." Clearly, the DA was getting his requested wide latitude.

With a nod of approval from Judge Sullivan, an aide brought in a life-sized photo cutout of deputy John Malham and stood it in front of the jury box. He then raised a framed photo and asked Tripp Joiner if he recognized the individuals featured.

Tripp answered, "Yes. This is Two Gun Malham being presented an award from Judge Parker for winning a marksmanship contest. This photo hangs in his office. He has shown it to me on more than one occasion along with a gold medal and a copy of the newspaper story."

"How many law enforcement members, if you know, participated in this contest?"

"I have no idea. He told me but I do not remember."

"Was it not more than one hundred people?"

"I'll take your word for it."

266

The DA asked that the picture be placed into evidence and then displayed another framed photograph. "This one also came from his office. Can you explain it?"

"I believe this was taken when the judge was making a political speech when he was running for governor. It shows Two Gun standing beside the judge performing his duty as bodyguard. That is him wearing the dark sunglasses."

"You explained in your deposition that he told you he wore the sunglasses so that he could keep his eyes on any suspicious-looking person without them being aware that he or she was being watched. Is this true?"

"Partially true, Yes and no."

"What do you mean by yes and no? You can't have it both ways."

"I mean that he wore them for other reasons as well. Of course, the most probable was to keep the sun from hurting his eyes, and second, according to him, it allowed him to ogle pretty women."

This brought laughter from the spectator section and even a smile or two from the jury box. The DA moved on quickly. He had intended to ask a few more questions about that particular photo but decided to cut his losses and move on. With the judge's permission, he asked Tripp to take a position next to the life-sized photo of Malham. "If you can, Mr. Joiner, please describe what you see in this picture."

"This is Two Gun enjoying his weightlifting hobby, attired in his favorite shorts with a sheriff's emblem on the side."

"You have stated that you were sometimes invited to share this hobby, as well as others, back in the friendship days. True?"

"That is correct. We lifted weights together many times."

"You had firsthand knowledge of his strength, did you not?" Then exposing his lack of lifting knowledge, the DA asked, "How much weight could he lift, Mr. Joiner?"

Tripp answered, "Squat or snatch or what?" The crowd roared. Even the jurors laughed, and an embarrassed Walter Warren quickly moved on again.

"As we look at this photograph, you would agree would you not, that Mr. Malham was a very large and intimidating person?"

Tripp replied, "He is, or was, this photo is a bit of an exaggeration. He was not quite this big."

"Is that so, Mr. Joiner? Let us look at something. You may return to your chair please." He walked over to his table and returned with a folder marked John Malham Autopsy Report and opened it to a marked page. "Would you read for the court the underlined portion?"

Tripp read, "Height six feet, seven inches; weight 273 pounds; estimated body fat less than five percent."

"And how large are you, sir?"

Tripp answered, "I am about six feet, four inches tall and weigh about 230 pounds. I have no fat that I know of." He replied. "So, Mister Two Gun Malham was considerably larger than you." Tripp did not reply.

"Let me move on. Let's explore some questions about your thoughts and actions leading up to your decision to execute the so-called citizen's arrest. How much time did you use in planning this foolhardy plan? By the way, were you aware that there are laws preventing vigilantes like you from taking the law into their own hands?"

Tripp replied sarcastically, "Which question would you like for me to answer first?"

Walter answered, "Sorry about that. Just answer the first one."

"OK. I probably spent hours of careful planning. I had plenty of time while my wife was in a coma for over a week."

With this, the DA produced a book, asked that it be introduced into evidence and showed it to Tripp. "This title of this book is 'So You Want to Be a Policeman, Do You?' written by Calvin Marlow, a former green beret in Vietnam and a past commander of the Texas Rangers. If you will, open this book and you will find one entire chapter dealing with the training and teaching of safe apprehension techniques and procedures to law enforcement cadets. You will see that it takes weeks of hands-on training for a person to be qualified to make an arrest and apprehension of an armed person. And you believed, did you, Mr. Joiner, that these few hours of planning made you qualified in the arrest and apprehension of an armed man?"

"I did as long as I could get the jump on him."

"I am not going to labor this court with your definition of what 'get the jump on' means, but I will ask this. Given that Deputy Malham was much larger and stronger than you, was an alert bodyguard for more than two decades, paid to be vigilant at all times, a trained and experienced law enforcement officer expecting you to be lured into his trap, do you expect anyone to believe any part of your citizen's arrest testimony? They would be idiots."

"Mr. Warren. I will repeat myself. The answer is yes. I believe that you yourself would obey my order to lie down on your face with your hands behind you and allow me to cuff you if you found yourself looking down the barrel of my 30/30 rifle."

Mule caught Will's eye with a smile. They knew that the DA had just stumbled into a big mistake. He had just called the halo jurors idiots. Walter recognized his mistake and followed up with another question. "Mr. Joiner, our records indicate that you were an honor student in high school and also in college. Would you not agree that this was a positive sign of intelligence? Yes or no?"

"I suppose but I had to work very hard to make those grades."

"Let me rephrase a part of that last question. Given that your wife had repeatedly warned you and finally convinced you that you were being lured into a trap designed to kill you, you were convinced that you could pull off the citizen's arrest?"

"You know my answer. The deputy went through various levels of vigilance every day. Sometimes he was totally vulnerable. Such as when sleeping or showering or falling down drunk almost every night or while

269

getting a shave at the barbershop or even at the shooting range, where he always ended his set with a display of rapid firing, emptying both guns. He never reloaded until he had cleaned both guns. There were other routines."

"Yet, Mr. Joiner, when you came after him, he was not in one of his vulnerable modes. Correct?"

"That is true. I rushed out in a fit of madness, but I testified that I came to my senses in time and withdrew to wait for a safer opportunity. Then I heard the screams."

"But you did not withdraw, did you? You rushed to the attack." Tripp did not respond.

"Let us move on to another subject. Let's switch from violence to love. Let's talk about your one-night stand with Vita Vorhees, may we? Do you and your wife Patricia share the same address, Mr. Joiner?"

"Yes. We both live at the Bar 6," replied Tripp.

"Do you live in the same house at this address?"

"No, as I said earlier, my wife and daughter live in the main house. I stay in a trailer next to the bunkhouse."

"And why is that?"

"Because we are temporarily estranged."

"And why is that?"

"Because of my stupid one-night stand."

"Would you explain for us just what a one-night stand is?"

"I don't understand what you are asking. It is what it says. One time, one night."

"Was it a sexual relationship?"

270

"Yes."

"Mr. Joiner, you have testified that you have had a long relationship with Miss Vorhees going back to your high school days. Right?"

"Yes, but not a sexual relationship."

"You were engaged to Miss Vorhees at least two years. Is that correct?"

"Yes."

"Did you have sexual relations with her during that time?"

Mule Sherman yelled out with an objection at the same time Tripp replied, "That is none of your business!"

The judge responded with a call for a courtroom break and asked the DA to approach the bench for a conference. Walter took advantage of the break to give himself a little pep talk. The hole he dug for this witness in order to prove that his scorned woman theory was a big fat lie was trending towards a grave for himself. He was losing up to now, but he was saving his best shot for last. He had a plan to hang Tripp Joiner with his own rope. The media had paved the way by making this trial a fairytale about a princess and a prince who had been totally in love but were separated by a huge mistake and a series of tragedies but were able to come back together again.

The cross examination resumed with Walter asking Tripp, "During your testimony, you gave a dramatic utterance about a scorned woman who was portrayed as the cause for all the tragic deaths in this case. Did you not?"

Tripp replied, "I did repeat a famous quote, yes."

"Let me also quote a dramatic utterance from the mouth of a former commander of the Texas Rangers. This quote is engraved on a plaque that hangs on the wall of the Rangers Hall Of Fame. It was no doubt meant as a warning to cattle rustlers back in the day, but it still has valuable meaning today. It reads, 'Beware of what you catch lest you end up hanging from the end of your own rope.' Do you grasp meaning Mr. Joiner?"

271

"I am not a total idiot, Mr. Warren, or was that intended to be a joke?"

"Well, Mr. Joiner, let us examine it together and let the jury decide if it was a joke or not. Shall we? I believe that, together, we can prove that there was no scorned woman at all. You have made many motivational speeches to audiences, large and small, since you became a very famous celebrity, have you not, Mr. Joiner?"

"Yes, I have."

"Some of these speeches were made in the interests of various charities, right?'

"Yes."

"Would it surprise you to know that I have been in the audience a time or two?"

"No, I have seen you there."

"I have heard you speak fondly about the history of trick roping performed by your grandfather, who taught you, and your father, who was killed in an accident when you were a baby. Correct?"

"Yes."

"The skilled use of a rope or lasso has remained an important part of your life right up until now. Correct?"

"Yes."

"In fact, throwing loops with your rope at school in the fourth grade was the first time that you came in physical contact with little Lavita Vorhees as she and others were jumping in and out of your spinning ground loops. Am I right, Mr. Joiner?"

"You are."

"Miss Vorhees liked this and similar later experiences enough that she asked you to teach her rope tricks and then persuaded her mother to bring her to your home for more lessons over a period of several months.

Right?"

"Yes."

"Did this extended activity then lead to an invitation to Lavita's residence in the home of Judge Horace Parker?"

"Yes."

"Your friendship and common interests with horses, sports, roping and rodeo activities led to formal dating, did it not?"

"Eventually. Yes."

"This dating led to courtship over many years and that led to the engagement to be married, right?"

"It did."

"Did either of you ever date anyone else during this long period?"

"Not to my knowledge."

"There was a time, was there not, when you were kicked out of this relationship by Lavita's mother?"

"Yes, temporarily." Tripp now knew, for certain, that Lavita had spilled the beans on all the intimate secrets of their relationship. Although Windy was simply repeating details of Tripp's earlier testimony, he felt certain that he was being set up, led into the trap of lying. He was feeling defensive and finding it harder to hold the dominate eye contact and body language that Will Clarkson had schooled him in. He was squirming in his seat and the defense team recognized the dilemma. It was obvious that the DA's long-range goal was to prove that the couple had continued their intimate relationship well past their broken marriage engagement and even past Tripp's marriage to Patricia and to trap him with his own lies. He was trying to hang him with his own rope just he had promised.

"Mr. Joiner, will you explain what you mean by your words 'yes, temporarily?'"

273

I or we, Lavita and I, had to agree to certain rules of future behavior and were then allowed to resume dating."

"What were those rules, Mr. Joiner?"

Mule Sherman objected to this question and was sustained by the judge who then allowed the request for a bench approach by the DA. The DA was hoping to get out the very damaging fact, obtained from Lavita, that her mother had made them both swear an oath on a Bible, to never have an intimate relationship until after their marriage as the condition for resumed dating. Lavita was fearful of breaking the oath and suggested that she and Tripp exchange wedding vows, which she had prepared, and they did just that. The judge refused to allow this bit of evidence to come in and Walter showed his displeasure with another dramatic display of body language meant for the jury. He was hoping that they would read, "The judge has done it to the prosecution again."

He took a deep breath and moved on. "At some point, near the same time, you and Lavita began your professional careers as rodeo performers, right?"

Tripp answered, "No. If you are referring to the earning of prize money by turning pro, she was earning prize money for many months before I was. Every rodeo performance is run against the clock. You must qualify before entry and she began to qualify before I did. She was provided with the fastest barrel racing horses available in all of west Texas by her grandfather, Judge Parker, and she began to win prize money right away."

"Barrel racing obviously requires the use of a horse. Is that also true of your chosen entries?"

"Yes, I entered all the roping events as well as steer wrestling later on after I grew larger."

"What was the preferred means of transporting horses from one event to another by the pros?"

"Most had a two-horse trailer with living quarters built in."

"Did you use this type of quarters?"

"Yes."

"Did Lavita Vorhees do the same?"

"She did. She used one of these for several years before I was able to borrow one and later buy one. She began to qualify for entry before I did."

"Parking spaces were provided for these trailers. Right?"

"Right. All rodeos in every city provided parking areas for entrants with horses. Many shared living quarters with the bull riders and bronc riders who did not travel with their horses."

"Did the two of you park near one another?"

"Yes, we parked side by side for many years until our breakup."

"You say side by side. How close was that?"

"About 10 or 12 feet apart. Just enough room for an awning. Close enough that we could talk to each other when the windows were open."

"Almost like living in the same house. Right?"

"Not exactly. She always had someone staying with her. Always her trainer, and in the early years, her mother and sometimes her friend GiGi. I usually had someone staying with me during my high school years. Later, after I started to college, I stayed alone most of the time."

"You did visit with one another, did you not?"

"Yes of course. We were sweethearts. We spent as much time together as we could, just as we did when were back home."

"After your marriage engagement breakup did you continue your side by side parking arrangement visits?"

"Of course not. We parked on opposite sides of the lot as far apart as we possibly could."

"But did you continue to visit one another?"

"Of course not. We did not even speak in passing."

"That is interesting, Mr. Joiner. Do you know a Randy Wade?"
Tripp felt the trap immediately and it took him a second to answer. "Yes. He was and still is my roping partner in the team roping events."

"Mr. Joiner, do you remember an occasion at a rodeo event in Midland, after the separation, when Lavita Vorhees entered your travel trailer without knocking while Mr. Wade was present? I believe she ordered him out of the trailer saying she needed an hour of private time with you. Do you recall, Mr. Joiner? Yes or no?"

Tripp stuttered a moment and started to speak, "Yes, but that was …"

The DA interrupted, repeating, "Do you?"

Tripp turned to the judge and pleaded, "Your honor. He did not let me answer his question."

Judge Sullivan replied, "I am afraid he did, Mr. Joiner. He asked you a yes or no question and your answer was yes. You are aware, I'm sure, that your attorney will be allowed to follow up with a rebuttal session in which he will be probably will ask you to add to your response. This comes immediately after Mr. Warren finishes your cross examination."

Tripp bit his lip and tried not to allow his feeling of helplessness show in his demeanor. He had fallen in the trap of telling an apparent lie and it was going to hang in the minds of the jurors for a very long time.

The DA knew that he had retaken the high ground. He felt in control again. He was again acting and dancing on the big stage. "Mr. Joiner, I'm sure you recollect your story of the one-night stand at the Hilton, so let me attempt to refresh your memory about another visit from Lavita to your mobile home on your ranch property. Yes or no, please, Mr. Joiner. Did she visit you there?"

"Yes, but she …" Tripp stopped there.

"Will you now admit, Mr. Joiner, that your statement about not having visits with Lavita Vorhees after the breakup was a lie?"

Tripp remained silent as Walter faced the jury with a smile on his face, awaiting the response. He did not need an answer. The damage was done.

"Let me change subjects, Mr. Joiner. Let's talk about sign language. There came a time in your romantic relationship with Lavita when, as sweethearts, you both began to say, 'I love you' to one another. Am I right?"

"Of course."

"She began to blow you a kiss now and then as a way of telling you that from a distance, right?"

"Yeah, I guess."

"After a while, Lavita complained when you were not returning the blown kisses. Right?"

"If you say so," replied Tripp.

A side conversation was going on between Mule and Will. "Her revenge is stronger than her pride," Will whispered. "She has spilled her guts to the DA."

Mule muttered, "Yes, nothing is sacred in her relationship with Tripp."

Walter continued, "You felt that blowing kisses was for a sissy and so you created a secret code sign to replace it. Right?"

Tripp replied, "Yes and No."

"What kind of an answer is that? You can't have it both ways."

"I used an old Indian sign of touching the bridge of my nose, which meant that I was sending her a message. Under different circumstances the meaning of the gesture changes."

Windy Warren, looking perplexed, responded. "Are you saying that you were not returning her 'I love you' with your own 'I love you?' That you were deceiving her?"

"No. I was not attempting to deceive anybody. She knew what it meant."

"So, Mr. Joiner, it did mean, after all, 'I love you?'"

Tripp stuttered, "Errr, yesss."

Both defense counselors, seeing that their client was suddenly being buried alive by the DA gave the prearranged signal to their client to force a break by coughing and then asking for a drink of water. His request was granted, and Mule caught the judge's eye and pointed at his watch, indicating that the time was well past the designated break time. Judge Sullivan was not fooled. He knew full well what was going on, but he granted the break request, nevertheless, over the objections of the DA.

The defense team, knowing that they had a serious problem on their hands, huddled during break, searching for a rescue strategy for their client. Tripp was now clearly upside down in this cross-examination battle. They needed a victory or at least a tie by their prized witness in order to assure acquittal verdicts on all charges.

Will declared that something radical, something outside of normal courtroom procedure, would be required to flip the minds of the jury from the current read of negativity. A plan was developed to create an uproar in the courtroom, one that would surely bring down the wrath of the judge but that had a very good chance of success.

Simple logic told them that Walter Warren was leading his questioning to a climax of "Why"? He would ask the big question after he led Tripp back to his description of the Hilton one-night stand, back to the juice that would hold everyone's attention. The irony of using this particular setting for this question by Walter was that he hated to ask questions pertaining to acts of infidelity because of his own personal experience. His father's womanizing had destroyed his parents' marriage when he was a teenager and had led to intense psychiatric counseling for him. Although he must do so, he knew he would be very uncomfortable as he asked the question, "Why"?

Back in session, the jury and all others in attendance had their eyes on Walter Warren as he asked his first question. "Given the circumstances of the sudden, unexpected break in the midst of a series of questions about your continued relationship of Lavita Vorhees, let me refresh your memory regarding some of your testimony. The record will show that you denied having any contact with her following the termination of your marriage engagement. Yet, you now admit that shortly after the breakup the two of you attended several rodeo events together where she visiting your travel trailer on at least one occasion, and that the two of you share a secret 'I love you' sign with each other. I will continue.

"Will you please tell the court again of the occupation of Mr. Rod Rodriquez?"

"He is our ranch foreman."

"Yes or no. Did he witness the exit of Ms. Vorhees from the front entrance of your current ranch residence"?

Tripp replied, "Well yes but ..."

Again, he was cut off with another question. "Did she or did she not give you the secret 'I love you' sign as she left?"

Tripp gave no answer. His silence provided the response.

"Now!! Let me take you back to the famous one-night stand at the Hilton Hotel."

Mule looked at Will and nodded. "Here comes the big one."

Walter continued, "You claim that you were duped into going to a room expecting to be attending a briefing prior to a regularly scheduled charity group board of directors meeting. You were elected to that board because of your demonstrated ability and willingness to raise money for various charities, many in number. You had fan clubs of seriously ill and maimed children in St. Jude and Shriner hospitals where you often visited. You were a football idol to thousands of adults and children alike. It is reported that your duplicate New York Giants jersey was number three in jersey sales. Most important of all, you had a daughter who you worshiped above all measurable love. Why, why, why then, Mr. Joiner, when you opened that door and saw the nude woman standing there inviting you to commit an act of infidelity that would destroy your whole life, didn't you just turn away? *Why*, Mr. Joiner?"

Tripp carefully began his scripted answer. "I er-I uh-- was expecting you to ask this question and I worked hard to prepare an answer. I was going to answer with a question of my own. I was going to ask you what you would have done if faced with the same situation, but I suddenly realized that you have probably never seen a beautiful nude female body in your entire life."

The courtroom erupted with laughter as Walter Warren stood there with his mouth open on his beet red face. The judge was pounding his gavel and yelling for order when Tommy Dancey jumped to his feet and shouted, "Atta boy, Tripp. Tell him like it is!"

Bull Turpin stood beside him, shouting, "Do it brother!"

Judge Sullivan ordered the seizure of these two by uniformed deputies, the crowd quietened, and order was slowly restored. The judge then dismissed the jury and declared court was adjourned for the day. He directed that a meeting with state and defense council be held in his chambers in 30 minutes with a limit of three members from each side.

Anger was in his voice and fire in his eyes.

CHAPTER THIRTY

The End of Television

The assembled parties had gathered early in the judge's chambers, expecting the worst. There was no friendly chit chat between the opposing sides. The silence was deafening. There were constant glances at the clock as the judge failed to show up on time. He entered like a storm 12 minutes late. The anger was gone from his voice but the fire was still in his eyes.

He began, "Please accept my apology for being late. I got carried away with my lecture of the two jaybirds who stood and shouted in my court. We will not see them again for a few days and, *if* we resume this court, we will see no more television cameras in this courtroom. It is my responsibility to maintain order in this court and I have failed miserably in this case. I allowed live television cameras in a Texas courtroom for the very first time in history with the honest belief that we could demonstrate to the American justice system that Texas justice is the closest thing to true justice being administered anywhere in the world. Instead, I have given them a circus.

"Perhaps I should say that *we* have given them a circus. I believe that we all possess that gene that compels us to seek attention to ourselves. The spontaneous appearance on television, no doubt, brings out the worst in almost everybody, as we witnessed today. Who knows, may heaven forbid, we may see a naked streaker come out from the jury room next.

"Please don't give me that look, Mr. Sherman, you of all people, costumed in your Davy Crocket clothes. And you, Mr. Clarkson, with your one-suit wardrobe, outdated tie and unshined shoes. Or you, Mr. Warren, with your exaggerated face makeup and Shakespearean stage mannerisms. Should we include you, Mr. Hall, a barber posing as a lawyer?

"Now. Let me include myself in the mix of culprits. I allowed the TV makeup artist to attempt to make me look better for the cameras. I also admit that I relished the possibility that presiding over the first televised

281

trial might just put my name in the record books. We are all as guilty as Mr. Dancey and Mr. Turpin, who are now thinking about their actions as they cool their heels in county jail." He halted a second, a bit startled at the puzzled look on their faces. They had expected a venting of his rage but had received, instead, a flushing of his conscience. The real odor of a mistrial was in the air and not a single one of the six wanted that. All were prepared to oppose it.

He continued, "I believe that I have just cause to declare a mistrial at this point, but given the great burden of additional expense that this would bring on both sides, I will delay that decision until I poll the jurors and determine to the best of my opinion whether or not this outburst biased their judgment of guilt or innocence.

"Now, let us move on to deal with Mr. Joiner and his successful attempt to demean Mr. Warren. His strategy was clear to all. He obviously found himself in a very uncomfortable position on the witness stand. He had been skillfully flipped upside down with the appearance of lying to this court and to the public. He knows that his best chances of winning this case ride with his personal testimony, so I can't say that I can blame a desperate man, fighting for his life, resorting to desperate measures, but this type of behavior will not go unforgiven. The prosecution does not have the same rights of appeal as does the defense. It is up to me, the judge, to protect them.

"I am inclined to suspect that Mr. Joiner's behavior might have been planned and rehearsed by the defense team. Mr. Sherman has a notorious past history of dirty tricks outside of legal bounds and has been duly punished for them by other courts. Short of a confession by a member of the defense team, I have little chance of proving my suspicions, but consider yourselves on my watch list. Now for your part in this, Mr. Joiner, I am fining you $500 for your contempt of this court. If you try something like that again, I will revoke your bail and send you back to a jail cell. You are all dismissed." He refused to allow any comment and sent them on their way.

He called the jurors and alternates from the jury room into his chambers one at a time and asked each a single question. "After experiencing this unusual disruption in courtroom decorum, are you still able to judge guilt or innocence based solely on evidence bought before you in this trial? Answer yes or no only." After answering, each was seated in the jury box to await the questioning of others. All answered "Yes," as he had expected, except one who added, "I had already made my decision anyway." The judge promptly dismissed this juror and replaced him with an alternate.

The judge had gone through the motions with this simple, carefully framed question in order to satisfy his own interpretation of proper courtroom procedure, knowing what the result would be. He had already opted against a mistrial. He gave the jury a brief "thank you for your patience" speech and announced that court would resume the next day.

The DA assembled his staff after the confession-like rant by Judge Sullivan. It took several minutes for him to quiet the venting about this strange behavior by a respected judge during a trial and to bring order to his attempt to regain the dominate position in the cross examination. Each senior staff member was asked to give his or her evaluation of the damage experienced, the current status of their case and suggestions for the next moves.

The majority recommended a plea for mistrial. The DA rejected their vote for the mistrial. He was still convinced that his credible eyewitness to the murders would be enough to carry the day. After all, he reminded them, he had never lost a murder case in which he was able to present a reliable eyewitness to the crime. He was also concerned that his witness, who was damaged severely on cross by Will Clarkson, might not be reliable enough in a retrial. He was convinced by now that the case for first degree murder would be lost without her. Also, the Parker family dirt allowed to be brought to light by this incompetent judge went far beyond his expectations. Stack that up against the charitable contributions of the lily-white local football hero who lost his daughter under highly suspicious circumstances, and you lose the conviction for threatening to kill. No, he convinced himself. Our only chance to win is with this trial. We don't stand a chance in a retrial. His decision was made. They reentered the courtroom to await the return of the judge and jury.

Judge Sullivan surprised them again with another request for the key lawyers to join him in his chambers. He wanted to brief them on his meeting with the jurors and his decision regarding contempt of court charges. He shared all the details of the jury meeting and announced that he was delaying any decision regarding possible contempt action against the defense team until more facts, if any, were uncovered. He then followed protocol by asking the prosecution for the first response to his remarks.

Walter Warren hesitated for a moment, searching for the right words to soften the shock that he was about to administer to this famous judge. "Your honor," he began, "I have never doubted your reputation for honesty, and I am certainly not questioning it now, so please do not confuse what I am about to say with a question about honesty. I have practiced trial law for three decades, and I have never before experienced an utterance by a presiding judge like I heard today. I have yet determined how to label it, but whatever it is called, it is far off point of where it should have been directed, which is to correct the deliberate maligning of a court officer in an attempt to usurp fair justice.

"You gave no detailed instructions to the jurors to disregard the incident itself; instead, you gave them the little patty cake speech that is part of your original jury instructions package, knowing what the outcome would be. As far as they knew, there was no punishment issued to the defense. Your only punishment was to charge a small fine to the defendant and threaten to change his living quarters back to his jail cell if it happened again. A jail cell from which he should have never been released from in the first place. Let's be reminded that he was granted this unprecedented privilege because he, an accused cop killer, was allegedly being abused by his guards to the brink of insanity. The proof was provided by the defendant's tale of a giant mouse attacking him in his sleep. Talk about a circus!"

The judge attempted to interrupt at this point, but the determined DA held up his hand as a request for silence and the judge backed off. "I believe that you are a victim of the same subconscious bias that is afforded all our accused superstars by American juries and society in general. This bias has been evident from the beginning. You should have used a gag order to prevent the defense from influencing the potential jury pool with misleading press conferences. A trademark tactic that has proceeded every high-profile trial that this defense attorney has ever been involved in. This defense team has expended tremendous time and money gathering dirt on the two victims, knowing that the results could never be allowed in court testimony. They planned to and were able to illegally taint the jury by using a foreign scandal tabloid to publish it, knowing that the American press would pick it up. And finally, perhaps worst of all, you made no attempt to stop the maligning of this officer of the court by the defendant while seated on the witness stand.

"I believe that I, as an officer of this court, have sufficient grounds to request that you remove yourself as presiding judge of this case and allow for a replacement to be sworn in as provided for by Texas law." Again, he raised his hand and spoke over the judge to finish his remarks. "I am opposed to a mistrial at this point, your honor, and you have made it perfectly clear that you want this trial finished by this court and this jury. Now I am finished, and I relinquish the floor."

Judge Sullivan asked the defense for their remarks. Mule Sherman spoke briefly. "Your honor, I can't say that I agreed with everything that you vented about earlier, but I can say for certain that I disagree with everything Mr. Warren had to say, including his request for you to step down. This is a clear case of the DA playing his odds. Once that he is convinced that he is losing this case, he will ask for a mistrial by a new judge and take his chances on a retrial, where his chances of a win will be weaker than they are now. OK. I am finished for now."

Judge Sullivan had the last word. "Well, I have just experienced another first in my long tenure as a trial judge. I have now been asked by a DA to resign. I have been asked to resign a few times, during trial, by defense attorneys but never by the prosecution. Given that you began your plea with testimony confirming my honesty, I will use that to begin my response. Each juror has sworn, for the second time, to make their decision regarding guilt or innocence on nothing but the evidence presented in this case. The ultimate verdict is their decision alone. Therefore, I will not step down. Let us get on with it."

The DA continued his cross examination of Jimmy Jack Joiner with the reading of the last question asked by the clerk. "Why didn't you just turn and walk away?"

Tripp replied, "I have asked myself that question a zillion times since that day and I have no answer. It was the worst decision I have ever made in my life. It destroyed my life. Saying I'm sorry is not enough. I let everybody down."

With that, the DA turned him over to Will Clarkson for another hour of rehab questions. He was able to complete the answers to questions that seemed to catch him in a lie. Randy Wade was called to the stand as a rebuttal witness in order to explain that when Lavita Vorhees entered the travel trailer and asked him to leave, Tripp asked him to stay and he did not leave the two of them alone, so there was no private meeting between the two. He was then able to continue his explanation that the secret sign of the bull, touching the bridge of the nose, meant, "I am sending you a message; current circumstances tell you what that message is." Careful observance of most of the jury member's facial expressions indicated that the image of a truthful football star was restored. A relieved Will turned his witness back to the judge. With that, the judge dismissed Tripp from the stand. He was figuratively bloody and broken but still alive.

Live television ended in Texas courtrooms that day, but the trial continued, with closing arguments yet to come.

CHAPTER THIRTY-ONE

Mount Up and Ride for Justice

Mule Sherman rose to begin the defense's closing arguments. He hesitated as if he had to gather his thoughts before approaching the jury. This delay was a deliberate tactic to bring all eyes on him as he made his move.

The sound of his boot heels on the wooden floor of the ancient court room, step by slow deliberate step, created a thought from the past for every juror as they wondered where and when they had heard that sound before. For most, it was a foreboding sound of something sinister like the approach of the bearer of bad news or maybe a part of a bad dream or perhaps the approach of the killer in a monster movie. They were now sure the sound was familiar and the tension and apprehension grew with every step.

He stopped in front of the jury and hesitated again. The quiet was deafening. Mule could hear his own heartbeat. He made eye contact with each juror as he moved past the jury box. This was easily done because each juror had eyes locked on his. No one noticed that he had moved silently past. No boot steps were heard.

He began to speak with the steady cadence and tone of a homespun Texas voice that years of experience and training had allowed him to perfect. "Once upon a time, a little rich girl came to know a little orphan boy. She was a 10-year-old true Texas princess and he was a 10-year-old being raised on a modest west Texas ranch by his grandparents. They were drawn together by their mutual love of horses. First as acquaintances, then as friends. This relationship changed to boy likes girl then to puppy love, and after several years, to a torrid and passionate teen romance. College love brought an engagement, and he placed his dead mother's ring on her finger.

"This story covered one entire page in the newspaper because the little Texas princess and the little orphan boy had both become very famous. She was a beauty queen and he was an All-American football player.

287

This could have been, would have been and should have been a true storybook fairytale, but it wasn't. Fairytales all have happy endings. This story did not. In fact, it ended with multiple tragedies. The deaths of four people. The tragedy of all tragedies. I'm not allowed to speak in detail about one of these tragic deaths, but I assure you that you will hear every detail about the other three from me in addition to what you have heard from witness testimony."

The judge had taken away a major defense playing card by disallowing a more detailed testimony about the death of Debi Devereaux. This decision created a heated plea from Mule Sherman. This death was the trigger that initiated all the events and deaths that followed. Judge Sullivan based his ruling on the fact that in his view, this testimony would be prejudicial to both sides. The fact the prosecutor was preparing to pursue murder charges against Tripp through the grand jury, which was somehow leaked to the press, would come out and harm the defense. The confidential police report of Tripp's eyewitness statement and subsequent open court testimony regarding the death at the hands of Lavita Vorhees would prejudice the prosecution by creating a clear picture of the motive for the attempted bribe and the intimidation, which led to the death of little Mary Mae Joiner and the near death of Patricia Joiner at the hands of Deputy Malham, acting on instructions from Judge Parker. Prosecutor Warren understandingly fought against the admission of this testimony because it could weaken his closing arguments to the point of disaster, despite his eyewitness testimony of Lilia Vorhees that Tripp had shot Judge Parker and Two Gun Malham.

Mule's argument that the prejudices carried unequal weight because the negative facts about his client were public knowledge and probably known by the jurors anyway while those about Lavita Vorhees were still secret, was rebutted with, "Prejudice is prejudice. I will do everything in my power to prevent you from finally turning this trial into the trial of Miss Vorhees for her involvement in the death of Miss Devereaux. Ordinarily, I am for letting all evidence come in and let the chips fall where they may but, in this case, the prejudice is just too great."

Mule tried to keep a poker face with this bad news, but he knew that Walter Warren was rejoicing inside his fat head. Mule's strong cards were now left to the testimony of Tripp's wife about the killing of his daughter, the bribery attempt of Tripp, the crime scene blood evidence and Tripp's personal testimony. All of these were, arguably, by biased witnesses and weakened because Patricia's identification of Two Gun was made in the dark of night. However, there was no doubt that this identification was what sent her raging husband to the Parker residence that fateful night. A lesser but still important Parker motive was revenge for the ending of the marriage engagement by Tripp and the ensuing public threats made by Lavita and her mother. "Nobody can dump the granddaughter of Judge Parker and get away with it."

Mule had meticulously and skillfully gone over every detail of his team's mindreading evaluation study of individual juror's reactions to all testimony to date. With years of practice, he was increasingly troubled by juror number two, who was showing all the signs of having been bought. There were more telltale signs than nervousness, smirks and avoiding eye contact. There was perspiration and a look of guilt like that a child who has just been caught stealing candy.

To Mule, he seemed to be in the act of committing a crime and to be very uncomfortable with it. He altered his approach in order to make sure of his feelings by making a statement directed at the profiled character of the man. This man was a band director in a local school, and it was easy to stick a dagger into his conscience. He made a comment about the privilege of working with the outstanding young people in today's society. He detected moisture in the man's eyes as he fixed his stare directly on them. This was, no doubt, a troubled man.

His intention to probe more was delayed as he fought off a rapidly developing physical problem. He had become very hoarse and his voice was beginning to fail. Repeated swigs on a water bottle did not help, and the judge asked if he wanted a break. This was granted, but the remedies tried during recess resulted in only slight improvement. He wanted desperately to finish his closing and carried on for another hour. His voice became a whisper, so the judge dismissed court for the rest of the day and called a chamber meeting.

The defense was given the choice of ending where they were, since in the judge's mind it appeared that all facts had been skillfully argued and defended. Or Mule could allow some other member of the team to take up closing statements in case Mule was unable to continue the next day. Or additions to the closings could be submitted in written form for the jury to read. Mule whispered to the judge and all present that the defense would continue with oral arguments the next day.

The midnight oil was lit by the defense team right after the judge halted the day's activities. It stayed lit until the wee hours of the next morning as Mule developed a plan to finish his closing arguments. His doctor's prognosis was poor. The ability to speak normally would be gone for several days, which meant that Will Clarkson would have to finish the job.

Clarkson read over the summary of Mule's main points and the general theme and announced that he would use his own version or nothing. He still objected to the subtle message of the defense argument, "My client didn't do the killings but if you think he did, they deserved it and he was provoked into it." He had objected to this tactic from the outset and had agreed only to handle expert witness testimony in the courtroom and to work on all other aspects of the case. Mule was now asking him to break their signed agreement and the two bullheaded, egotistical lawyers were at a standoff. Friction had come to the surface.

Mule explained that he had to take this approach in case holdout jurors wanting a guilty verdict for murder might persuade the innocent voters to cave in and trade for a guilty verdict on the breaking and entering and the threatening charges, which would still result in a long prison sentence. He wanted an innocent verdict, or at least, a hung jury.

Clarkson was still somewhat pained by having agreed to serve as co-counsel instead of his customary position as chief counsel. Mule was upset about not being able to finish his closing when he had momentum going his way and was about to make his point about justification. The impasse was not broken.

One other possible option was to prepare a written version of the entire finish and have it read to the jury if he could not get Will to change his position. He asked Will to summarize his version so that option would be clearly understood and be given honest consideration. This was done and carefully evaluated by Mule. It was loaded with more points on crime scene evidence as well as more hammering on the lack of credibility of the prosecution's alleged eyewitness to the murders, Lilia Parker Vorhees. There was a reference to the death of Debi Devereaux, even at the risk of a mistrial. He felt that he had discovered a clever way of slipping it in, then withdrawing his statement.

In Mule's opinion, this was an asinine approach and sealed his decision to keep Will out of it. With Tripp's approval, he decided to ask the court to allow the defense's clerk, Hal Hall, to read the closing finish to the jury. After all, Hal was a law student and self-made case law expert who had been practicing borderline law at his barbershop with his afterhours free legal aid clinic for the poor and mostly illegal immigrants. He had earlier demonstrated his amazing photographic memory, so it should be no problem for him to memorize Mule's finish in a few hours and be able to deliver it with conviction without actually reading it word for word.

The main problem with this option was that Hal Hall had never spoken to a group of more than 10 people in his life, let alone a trial jury and a packed courtroom. On the other hand, he couldn't be frightened to loss of words when he had every word in his hands, so the decision was finalized, and the deal was sealed. The barber would be asked to perform on the stage of the trial of the century. Mule felt that this was his best choice, and if the judge and the prosecution did not agree, he was going to ask for a recess of one week at the risk of alienating the tired jury and possibly losing a few of the fence-sitters.

The defense was granted one more day to prepare a substitute closing plan, and Hal used every bit of it memorizing Mule's notes. Mule spent considerable time preparing him for this monumental task. Speaking in a whisper, he stressed, "We are dealing with a crisis but it is not insurmountable. I believe that given your talents and the toughness, you are perfect for the job. You have never been schooled in the art of jury persuasion, so I am going to give you a few tips.

"It is important that my thoughts be delivered in their entirety because this segment is designed to cover justification for Tripp's actions in response to the news of his daughter's death and to negate the charges of threatening to kill that are important parts of this trial. My notes show you which segments are designed to be directed to specific jurors and must be delivered with direct eye contact with that particular individual. You will be having a direct conversation with that individual, but it will be a one-sided conversation with you totally in control.

"My method of making locked eye contact is to fix my vision on a spot between the eyebrows and not directly in either eye. You are less likely to be distracted by his or her eye movement and changes of facial expression.

291

"Keep totally focused on your next words. If you lose your place in the script, take a breath and glance at my notes. This will enhance the belief by all parties that we are abiding by the judge's permission and the DA's agreement for you to read my words. This is the judge's excuse for allowing a non-licensed lawyer to address the jury.

"I believe that we will beat the murder charges, but the jury might compromise with the other charges that can bring on long prison sentences in themselves. You are allowed to paraphrase a bit but please don't overdo it. Don't fall into my own habit of becoming overly enamored with the sound of your voice such that you talk too long and put the jurors to sleep. I have prepared some words in here meant just for the professor with his Ph.D., because history shows that he is the best bet to be elected jury foreman and become the most forceful talker. There is something in here for the women, who tend to make better jurors for the defense in justification arguments because they tend to be more compassionate, especially considering the one who lost her childhood friend in an auto accident. Also, there is plenty in here for the rancher halos who believe that they are the truest Texas pioneers."

Trial continued the next day with the judge asking if the defense was prepared to proceed. Will Clarkson, now speaking on behalf of the defense was allowed to approach the bench. He asked for a meeting in chambers to make a special request, which was granted, and the plan was presented to the judge and prosecution. The prosecution, seeing an advantage for their side, seemed to be licking their chops, but the judge was hesitant. He suggested instead that copies of the finish be provided by Mule to the jurors to be read simultaneously as he stood in front of the jury box.

Will objected to this and stood firm on his plan. He said, "If the plan cannot be accepted by the court and the prosecution, the defense will ask for a one-week recess, even at the risk of a mistrial."

The judge responded, "I do not understand why you, Mr. Clarkson, one of the best trial attorneys in west Texas cannot finish a few minutes of closing or perhaps even another member of your defense team. Please explain this to me." He looked at both Mule and Will.

Will answered, "It is not part of our original agreement."

"Well for Heaven's sakes, draw up an amendment to your agreement and move on."

Will continued, "I will not use Mr. Sherman's finish and he will not allow me to use mine."

Seeing the dislike for each other in the faces of the two defense lawyers for the first time, the judge replied, "I am tempted to let your closing end where it is and give the case back to the prosecution. What do you say to that, Windy?"

Prosecutor Walter Warren, smelling blood and liking the plan as being to his advantage, answered, "If the defense so chooses, I will approve of any plan that allows the defense clerk to read the finish to the jury, provided that I have a copy in my hand during the reading."

The judge asked, "Does anyone here want a mistrial?"

Hearing the two "No" answers that he expected, he stated that he needed 30 minutes to think about his decision, as this situation was unlike anything that he had seen before. He would announce his decision in the court room.

Promptly at 9:00, he called the court to order and the parties were advised by the judge that the defense could proceed. The defense clerk, Hal Hall, would be allowed to present the finish to closing arguments as prepared by Herman Sherman, chief counsel for the defense. But he denied the prosecution's request for a copy.

With a nudge from Mule, Hal moved toward the jury box. He was now floating on a cloud. He was about to experience his lifelong dream of practicing big time law in the "trial of a century." He told himself that he was ready and confident, but in reality, he was frightened to death. Perspiration was dripping and his hands were quivering. He took a moment to compose himself. He elevated his height to the max then somehow found another inch above his shoe lifts.

Now feeling six feet tall, he attempted to start his memorized spiel but only the sound of a frog's croak came out. His face turned crimson and his red hair prickled. His mind went completely blank. He had forgotten his lines and did not think to look at his notes. His brain took him to his

293

safety net of his childhood when he was confronted by bullies. He cracked a joke. "I am in the position of the door-to-door Bible salesman, who with Bible in hand, rang a doorbell answered by a resident opened the door clad only in her bikini underwear. The shock took away his sales pitch and sent him searching for a Bible verse he could not find, and he fled from the scene. I promise you that I am not going to run away."

This drew a few snickers from the jury and collective groans from the defense team. But it steadied Hal. His next attempt in speaking came out clear and strong.

"Ladies and gentlemen of the jury, my name is Harold Hall. My friends call me Little Red for obvious reasons. I am standing before you because Mr. Sherman has temporarily lost his voice. He has prepared the remainder of his closing remarks for me to deliver to you. This is my first time to stand before a jury and I am a bit intimidated but confident. I am here because I am a part of Tripp Joiner's defense team.

"We first met in the first grade. He was the largest kid in class, and I was the smallest. He quickly became my protector from school bullies who liked to pick on the weakest kids. Now I, in a very small way, have been given a chance to return his favors by helping to defend him. I want to defend him for another reason, the most important reason of all. He is innocent! I believe that the best way for me to do this is to tell you a true story. The Holy Bible says that the truth will set you free, and I want to test that theory."

He was on a roll but off the script. Mule winced in his chair but knew that interrupting him would sink all chances of his planned argument being presented.

"My first job was shining shoes in a barbershop," Hal explained. "I learned Texas society from the bottom up. My job was to shine shoes, keep the shop clean and keep my mouth shut as I listened and served customers. Listen I did, and by doing so, I learned what it means to be a true Texan.

"There were four chairs in that shop and most of the time there were customers in every chair. Thus, there were four conversations going and I tried to tune in to all four. Over the years scores of outsiders, came along amidst the steady stream of Texans. I played a silent game with myself, trying to guess who an outsider was and who was a Texan. It became very easy to get it right. Texans are simply a separate breed of human beings.

"We had very few women customers in our barbershop, but they agreed with all the men, who tended to brag on their female ancestors and tell stories about their boldness, bravery, and most of all, their aggressiveness. Their men were away from home much of the time on cattle drives and such. The women, when left behind, filled the roles of men with great distinction. We still see this aggressiveness in Texas women that we do not see in outsiders.

"Once I became sure that Texans were different. I began to wonder if they administered courtroom justice differently from other parts of the country. I began to read everything published on the subject, and after I earned my barber's license, I questioned the many lawyers who frequent our shop. The answer is yes. We do administer justice in a more fair and equitable manner.

"Back in the days before we had readily available law enforcement, we took justice into our hands. For example, when rustlers stole our cattle, we formed a posse of our peers and rode after them while the trail was hot. Neighbors and strangers alike were asked to mount up and ride for justice. If we caught them with the branded cattle in their possession, we hanged them from the nearest tree. If they were no longer in possession of the cattle, we held them until the circuit riding judge came to town. If we rode after those who killed our children, we were careful not to kill their innocent family members. We established, back then, the practice to make certain that we convicted and punished only the guilty. The result is that our judges tend to let in more evidence and our juries tend to consider more extenuating circumstances.

"Yesterday, Mr. Warren used the word justice 11 times in his closing. By law, he gets to come back before you again after I finish. You will probably hear that word used again, so let's be really clear as to what it really means. Up until now, according to Mr. Warren, it has meant the rendering of a guilty verdict. Please follow me as I explain what it truly means."

Hal was now moving across the box as he searched for and located certain jurors that Mule had created special subtle messages for, the ones that he wanted to make eye contact with. One message was for the person who he expected to be elected jury foreman, the history professor at a local university. One message for the woman who had lost her best girlfriend in a car crash caused by a drunk driver. Another was written for the ranchers and farmers with sunburned faces and white halo foreheads, who understood frontier justice.

Hal continued, "I believe that you each come from a unique breed of people who understand what I mean when I explain that Jimmie Jack Joiner mounted up and rode for justice!" Hal was soaring now and clearly getting positive vibes. He did not know it, but something just happened that probably had not occurred before in the history of Texas jurisprudence. The judge, the prosecutor and the chief counsel had the very same exact thought at the very same exact moment. "What on earth have I done and what do I do next?"

Warren could see that Hal was turning this into a real plus for the defense, and he had missed his chance to prevent it. Judge Sullivan could see that his guidelines had been broken. Sherman, though pleasantly surprised, now knew that he had a loose cannon on his hands and was fearful where Hal might go next. He was explicit about sticking to the script less he caused a mistrial. Fortunately for Hal, none of the three could think of an immediate solution. They did nothing.

"You have the same inherited blood flowing through your veins that flowed through survivors and thrivers who lived under a king before the settlers came, then under a dictator as they fought and won the right to form a free democracy. You have shed that blood in countless wars in the interest of preserving a free democracy and equal justice. You administered justice before you had laws and courts, and I might add, prosecutors, lawyers and judges. You have freed captives, exonerated the innocent, pursued and administered instant justice to rustlers and property thieves. Can you imagine what happened to those killers of children? Can you not also imagine what any man, any person, including you would do if someone killed your eight-year-old daughter? Can you tell me that any one man or woman of you would not confront the person who killed your daughter?"

This raised the prosecutor out of his seat, but he quietly sat back down. "The evidence has shown – no proven – that the only thing Jimmy Jack Joiner is guilty of is seeking out and confronting the man who murdered his daughter. He was met with a bullet to his body that was intended for his head, fired from the gun of John Malham. He fought on gallantly until he was choked into unconsciousness and was again saved from death by the quick action of medics who started his still heart to beating and his still lungs to breathing again.

"Tell me again, as you have been asked over and over in the course of this trial, how an unconscious man could have fired a gun into the chest of John Malham. There was only one conscious person in the room when that shot was fired, and you know exactly who that person was. Mr. Joiner was following his natural instincts that sad day, the instincts that flow in the blood of all Texans.

"Tell me that you do not know the true meaning of justice. Try to tell Jimmy Jack Joiner that there are not two sides to justice. This trial is being watched all over the world because of the famous people involved. You are being watched all over the world because of the magnitude of your decisions. You will become a part of history. You will be asked for interviews and some of you will write a book. Your decisions and the decisions of the judge and all the lawyers in this trial will be analyzed in every conceivable way. Society asks of you, demands of you, that you use your unique sense of justice passed along to you by your Texas ancestors. As a matter of fact, I just happen to have an example of what I am talking about."

He whirled about and walked over to the defense table and removed a large envelope. With it in his hand he returned to face the jury. He attempted to emulate Mule Sherman's walk, making certain that each step sounded on the old wooden floors to keep their focus locked on him. He carefully opened the envelope as if something very valuable was inside. He removed a leather-bound book and held it above his head. Standing directly in front of juror number 10, the history professor, with his eyes fixed between his eyebrows, he began to talk. "This is a book written about a very famous Texas pioneer family. Professor, you have probably read this book. Maybe even quoted from it in your history classes. I would also like to repeat a wee bit of the story here." The professor's eyes lit up and he leaned forward as if to pay more attention.

"In 1825, the government of Coahuila y Tejas bestowed the title of empresario on Stephen Austin and his father, with the assignment to establish colonies of immigrant Americans in the country in what we now call Texas. He enticed a family to come, which included a 17-year-old boy, his parents, a brother, two sisters and an uncle. They were given title to a large tract of land and promptly built a house and outbuildings and began to raise cattle. Some months later, a new company of rangers was formed, and the young man volunteered for a one-year tour of duty.

Action took him more than a hundred miles away. His enlistment period expired, and he returned home. As he topped the final hill and gazed wistfully towards the ranch house, he was shocked beyond imagination by the sight of burned ruins of the log house and all the outbuildings. He forced his tired horse into a full gallop and arrived at the scene to find six fresh graves in the front yard. He suspected immediately what had happened. They had been killed by a rogue band of Cheyenne that had, up until now, been raiding and killing over 200 miles to the north and west. This particular band, led by a chief riding a spotted horse, was taking vengeance on white settlers for the slaughter of the buffalo herds, the Plains Indian tribe's main food source, by white men. Another neighboring family had suffered the same fate. He swore over the graves of his family that he would start what he called a ride for justice, and he attempted to pull a posse together. No ranger company was near enough to be helpful and he knew he must move while the trail was hot. He was unable to get a posse together. Everyone wanted to let the rangers handle it, so he gathered up supplies and set out alone. Fortunately, this brave but foolish act ended when he lost the trail two days later."

The jury seemed to be enjoying Hal's story, but Mule Sherman was not. It was taking Hal too long to make his final point. He wanted the closing argument to end now but he said nothing. Hal sensed the same feeling and searched for a way to cut the story short.

"Not long afterward, Spotted Horse Chief and his band were raiding again. This time, a posse was formed and our hero, still pledged to ride for justice, was chosen to lead the posse. He recruited three members of the Apache enemies of the Cheyenne to serve and trackers to accompany 20 ranchers including to native Mexicans. The killers were tracked, and their village was located in the Palo Duro Canyon in what is now known as the Texas Panhandle. The battle lasted just over two hours. All adult male members of the band were killed. Women and children were spared. The Apache trackers were allowed to take the scalps of the 39 men killed. Arrows, spears, war clubs, hand axes and knives had no chance to stop the slaughter. The posse suffered four dead and six wounded. Our hero suffered some serious cuts that left scars visible all his long life.

"Our hero's name was Solomon Parker, the founding father of the famous Parker dynasty and the great-great-grandfather of Judge Horace Parker."

Then Hal made a point to make eye contact with every juror as he asked again, "Is there any one of you who would raise your hand and say you would not ride to justice and confront the man who was named as the killer of your daughter?" He stared into the eyes of each juror with his own penetrating green eyes. Only two jurors avoided eye contact, but juror number four, a Hispanic man, displayed in his open palm a simple bent penny. A sign to Hal that he was now on his side. He abruptly turned, showing his backside with book held high, and took his seat.

Spectators in the courtroom whispered, and the majority fought back the impulse to give the barber and law student a standing ovation. Even old thick-skinned Judge Abraham Sullivan had to suppress a smile. Mule said to Hal, "Not exactly as written but good job." Hal noticed that he was breathing normally again as he leaned back in his chair.

By law, the prosecution has the last word, the last chance for rebuttal. Walter Warren spent an extraordinary amount of time talking about the sins of vigilante justice and the fact that Jimmy Jack Joiner confronted Malham with a gun in his hands after telling witnesses that he was looking for Malham in order to kill him. He then broke into the Parker residence in order to carry out that threat. It was apparent that he felt that Hal's finish to Mule's closing had scored some points. He then fell back on his strongest asset, the eyewitness testimony of Lilia Vorhees. In fact, this was about all he had left. He had no real answer for the Malham blood on Judge Parker's cane and the forehead wound that was consistent with the cane's wolf head imprint.

Courthouse observers would agree with presiding Judge Sullivan, who later confided to a friend that in the face of the strong closings by the defense lawyers as compared to the prosecution's, Walter Warren was "sucking the hind teat" with what the jury took with it to deliberations.

CHAPTER THIRTY-TWO

Bribery Pure and Simple

The district attorney and his staff had prepared the prosecution's case with great care using the standard blueprint taught in every law school in the country in order to do their sworn duty to render fair justice to the defendant. On the other hand, Mule Sherman, as his reputation suggested, used every scheme imaginable to free his client from all charges. He started with multiple attempts to bias the jury pool, turn the victims into evil devils, intimidate witnesses, disrupt the courtroom with planned demonstrations, offered a trade with the Parker family and even considered blackmail. There was another powerful entity at work behind the scenes, helping the prosecution without their knowledge. This was the Parker family, with their tremendous influence with powerful politicians and unlimited resources. Their motive was understandable. The current queen and princess of the Parker dynasty had committed crimes that must be covered by the conviction of Tripp Joiner.

Tony Bender, chief executive officer of Parker Enterprises and husband of Lavita Vorhees, had seen his workload expand dramatically with the death of Judge Parker. He had always devoted much time and effort shielding himself and the main operating companies from the evil misdeeds, mostly of a political nature, committed by his very active boss. He knew he was hired into the Parker Empire when he married into the family but felt he climbed up the chain of command to the very top because of outstanding performance and nothing else.

Tony reported to a board of directors, and Lilia Parker Vorhees was now chairman. Under this new boss the pressure lessened. He was trusted and respected by his key employees and carried the reputation throughout his business world as a "straight shooter." He had started the process of selling company ownership in quarter horse racing and various properties scattered around the world once used by the judge for his unscrupulous activities. His favorite quip to his friends and colleagues, delivered with the facial expression exposing considerable ambiguity, was, "The *good* news is that I am married to a beautiful movie star. The *bad* news is that I am married to a beautiful movie star. The *good* news is that she is very wealthy. The *bad* news is that she is very wealthy." Now he added to the quip. "My new boss is my mother-in-law. You finish my story."

Now, placed at the top of his list of worries was the protection of his wife's movie career and her possible criminal indictment in the death of Debi Devereaux. No conversation between his wife and his mother-in-law was devoid of that subject. They were not satisfied that a guilty verdict rendered to Tripp Joiner in the murder trial would completely derail his accusations and testimony before a grand jury.

Prior to her testimony, Lilia Vorhees had become a complete basket case. On the one hand, she was accidentally given the opportunity to live out her lifetime dream of performing on stage to a live national television audience. On the other hand, she suffered from severe stage fright and the testimony rehearsals with the DA's office. She had broken down under practice cross examination and showed a slight tug of a conscience when she allowed the guilt of lying under oath to destroy the life of Tripp Joiner to creep into her mind.

Even worse was when she took the stand for real. Will Clarkson completely had his way with her and made the Parker family seem like a bunch of crooks. She also lost her cool which opened the door for the defense to bring testimony regarding Debi's death and cussed the defense attorney. She, as did Lavita, wanted additional insurance. It was at that time that they decided to make a "Parker" move.

One asked, "I wonder what Judge would do in a situation like this?"

The two turned to one another and simultaneously blurted out, "He would turn to bribery, pure and simple, as he has done so many times before."

So, they called Tony in and instructed him to do just that. This instruction stunned Tony, so Lilia repeated the command. "You must fix the jury. We must know that we have the assurance that the jury cannot free Tripp Joiner in this trial."

Tony replied, "You know that you are asking me to commit a crime. There must be some other way."

"Yes, there is another way," replied Lilia. "You could take the same action as Judge and Two Gun attempted to do."

With this, Tony left the room. Everyone knew what she meant. She was implying the unspeakable that Tripp Joiner had been lured into a trap so that he could be legally killed by Two Gun, ostensibly in the defense of the judge. This ended the conversation for the moment, but Tony knew the subject was not dead and he could not erase the stench from his nostrils. The judge was dead and buried but still able to suck him down the Parker sewer and Tony had no doubt about what his decision would be. He had no choice.

Tony made a move in the right direction by calling in political favors all the way up to the governor's office, asking for pressure on the DA for a premature indictment of Tripp Joiner in the Devereaux death. Or at the very least, he suggested a leak to press confirming that given that Joiner was the only person admitting to be present at the death scene and his having been in possession of her dead body, he was going to be charged. This bought him time to plan how to go about buying a juror.

He was now mired in the Parker sewer, a real devil's workshop. He started by obtaining an updated copy of the jurors' profile dossier used in juror selection. Searching for a target, he found three likely prospects and started with priority number one.

Ross Pope, the 39-year-old junior high school band director, now married to his second wife, a physical education teacher at the same school. He was deep in debt with a new home, a new car, a toddler son and child support for three children by his first wife. "Perfect." He looked no further for now.

He began working on a plan that was his own, but it could have been one right out of the judge's playbook. Logic told him that if he could find a way to buy the juror without his knowing that it was, in fact, a bribe, then the juror could not ever admit to it being a bribe, not even to himself. The logic was indeed simple, but the execution would be tricky and very expensive.

First, implementation must begin while the trial was underway. The deal must be sealed with reasonable expectation before the trial ended. There was always the possibility that targets could have a change of heart, but some risks had to be taken. He was reminded of the many times that

Judge Parker had bragged about using other people to do his dirty work for him, often without their knowledge. He would say, "If you are going to use someone without his or her knowledge, you must grease the skids sufficiently so that when and if they discover that they have been used, the price and suffering will be too great to complain."

Tony needed three days to complete his plan except for a few details that were left open for flexibility. He added the description of his role players to his three prioritized targets. These were the people he would "use" for the project, but only he would ever know the entire plan and its actual goal.

He started with the outside public relations firm already at work as damage control to support rebuilding of the Parker empire image and to soften the impact on Lavita Vorhees' career that the leaked rumors of the Devereaux death would bring. He was now speaking to the managing partner in charge of the project, Brock Wormington.

Tony asked for an update and was told that two photo ops were coming up soon, and he was also working on a planned appearance by Lavita in the next world championship rodeo. This was one that she had always entered in the past and the promoter was wanting an answer. Plans for extra special display of her beauty and talents were under way. There was no way that Tripp Joiner could make his customary entry in the roping events and he was searching for a way to spin that fact into something useful.

Tony told him to keep up the good work and then got to the reason for his call. "Brock, I need for us to expand the scope of our project. This dirt that the defense has been able to leak to the public due to Judge Sullivan doing done a poor job of stopping it has done considerably more damage than expected. Most all of our companies have been hurt and our charities, in particular, have been hard hit to the point that I am deeply concerned.

"Conditions will worsen after Lilia gives her testimony at trial. The only way that the defense can discredit her testimony will be to attack her personally. She has enough character flaws to give them ample fuel.

"We need to do a large charity donation to a hospital for crippled children with all the publicity that you can drum up, using Lilia in each

303

of the photos, of course. Milk it for all it's worth. We get a secondary benefit from this in that it will boost her morale and take her mind off the trial for a bit.

"Now. Let me lay a new project on you at the risk of making you too rich for your own good. I have a fresh idea that is a bit frightening because it is going to be so very expensive without an absolute guarantee of total success. Some of our moves will be risky, but if we pull it off, I can see two major benefits. We dramatically improve our protection of my wife's career and make a nice profit at the same time.

"I want to produce a documentary featuring the trial jurors after the trial. This has been done successfully before in very high-profile cases and ours is as big of a trial as it ever gets. It would be a one-hour program with two features. The first part will have the same setting typical in this sort of thing – participating jurors sitting in a group answering scripted questions from our moderator. The second feature is the home run. We are going to turn a selected juror into a hero and introduce him or her to the world on national television. He or she is going to be the brave one who was strong enough to bring justice in spite of our hero worship culture that does not like to kill our sports heroes. Filming would be started immediately after the trial. Our profit would come by giving the general public an up close and personal view of the people who toiled and rendered a difficult verdict in the "trial of the century" and selling it to a major network at a very hefty price. What do you think of my idea?"

Brock replied, "I like the idea of the documentary, but I see two immediate problems. Our juror must be one who has voted guilty, right? And because of jury sequestration, we have no way of communicating with the chosen one while the trial is under way."

"I will answer your first question this way. The DA told me he has never lost a murder case of this magnitude when he had an eyewitness with the credibility of this one. He expects a unanimous verdict of guilty. Odds are against having a split verdict. If we lose our first choice, we'll move on to our second choice and so on.

"Now for the second question. My plan doesn't call for communications prior to trial ending but if it did, let me explain sequestration as usually practiced in Texas trials that last weeks and even months. Jurors are housed in the same hotel but in separate rooms. Spousal visits are

304

allowed. Remember, both sides want to keep their jurors happy. This discussion about early juror communications makes me uneasy so let us dispense with that by moving on to a very important part of the plan.

"It is vital that the proper moderator be hired for this documentary. You will do the search and hiring but I will have final approval of your selection. The perfect choice would have as many of the following characteristics as possible. He or she – although I would prefer that it be she – must be high profile enough to add to the star power of our piece and be recognizable at her introduction to her first contact, the target's spouse. She must be an independent journalist with no contractual ties to a major news organization. She must have a reputation for boldness, even brazenness. She will be expensive. Do not quibble about her fee, but it must be tied to certain incentives such as the selling price and our estimated profits. Give her the title of co-producer as well as moderator. You will be her boss and my name must never be mentioned. She will be the only immediate contact with the juror's spouse. She must be thoroughly schooled on all details, and for her own protection, she must avoid any conversation with the spouse about bringing up this proposal during trial. I will follow up with more details as need be as you keep me up to speed on your progress. You can bill me for your time and expenses at your current rate. Now, let me know what questions are on your mind."

Brock agreed to think on this a bit and get back with questions, but in fact, he immediately got to work.

The project shifted into high gear with the hiring of Lib Lester, veteran correspondent for several magazines and a regular on television. She fit most of Tony Bender's wish list and did, indeed, drive a hard bargain on her compensation fee. She was delighted with the quality of her information packet and made quick work of cram time, starting the leg work on her third day in town.

She found her prey in a grocery store on Saturday morning. "Hello, Ms. Pope. How are you today? My name is Lib Lester. I am a TV correspondent." She held her business card in her hand. "You have probably seen this smiling face on television."

This brought a quizzical smile to Ms. Pope's face. "How do you know my name? And how may I help you?"

Lib answered, "All things, perhaps too many, are known to news gathering snoops about the jurors and their families in the Tripp Joiner trial. You will all become very famous soon, and let me add, with fame comes fortune in most cases."

Now looking at the card, Ms. Pope responded, "I do recognize your face now but pardon me for being a bit taken aback by the suddenness of this. I am not understanding what is happening here. Is this a chance encounter or did you deliberately seek me out?"

"Oh, I did seek you out because I have something exciting to talk to you and the other jury families about. I have been hired to produce and moderate a documentary about the jurors, focusing on one, carefully selected family. This is not a good place for us to have a private discussion. May I wait for you to finish your shopping so that we might go someplace else, perhaps your home? I just want to be the first to talk to you, to get my foot in the door ahead of the other reporters."

"Oh, not my house right now. It stays in a terrible mess with my three-year-old running loose. My parents are sitting him now and plan to stay for supper. I am working tomorrow at the school. Let me figure something out and I will give you a call. Can I call you?"

"My answering service number is on the card, and I will check in with them later tonight and tomorrow. Just leave a message with them and I will call you back. By the way, I have your husband as Ross Pope and your name as Rose. Does that not confuse things sometimes?"

"No, I go by Rosie, so please call me that. You know, like Rosie the Riveter, ha?"

"OK. I'm gone 'til I get your call. Please make it real soon and please do not mention this conversation with anyone tonight. I have prepared a packet with the basic outline of the planned documentary, which I will leave with you. This will answer some of your immediate questions, and I'm sure, trigger more questions, which I will answer at our meeting."

They exchanged "nice meeting you" pleasantries and parted.

Lib hailed a cab, and with time to kill, asked the driver to take her to the largest sports bar in town. She was looking for the hangout for TV media in town for the trial. The cabbie made a suggestion and off they went. The cabbie was well informed. She struck pay dirt at the first stop.

She was looking for a familiar face when a shout behind her came from a voice out of her past. It was Dan Lawler from CBS, with whom she had worked years before.

"Hey Lib! Lib Lester. Come join us." Dan beckoned and asked, "In town for the trial?"

"Yeah. You?"

"Yep. Have a seat and let me introduce my broadcast crew."

Lib began what would become a lengthy but informative conversation about the trial. "Guilty or not guilty? What's the scoop? I have been working overseas for nearly a year."

Dan replied, "Oh, the dude is guilty of something, for sure. Too many eyewitnesses. One at the shooting and several where he made his threats to kill. Given what history shows us, guilty verdicts don't always follow guilty acts when celebrities and sports heroes are on trial. Can you remember the last time one was convicted? I can't, nor can any of these guys sitting here. This case has more subterranean plots than a children's fairytale.

"A new rumor is that the secret police report on the tragic death of the girl who is a sister to Tripp Joiner's football teammate places Lavita Vorhees and Tripp Joiner at the scene at the same time. What we have here is a never-ending saga that may continue for years to come and will most certainly end the career of one of the greatest NFL quarterbacks who ever played the game. This is as big as it gets, baby!"

Lib replied, "I guess that's why I am here. Maybe I should write a book."

Each member of the group voiced his opinion about guilt or innocence, without a single one voting not guilty. The jury at this table had cooked Mr. Joiner's goose. Yet it had opened Lib's mind to a lingering question that she could not share with anyone else. Trial chatter continued, but Lib could not take her mind off the serious question.

Considerable time had passed by now, more than Dan Lawler realized, and he looked around saying, "My crew is going somewhere else for dinner but I am eating here. Lib, I find myself in a generous mood tonight and I would like for you to join me."

Lib noticed by the surprised looks on the faces around the table that this was a command for him to be left alone with her. She was not sure if this was meant to be a romantic move, so she took no chances and threw out jokingly, "No thanks, Dan. I have not washed behind my ears tonight so I will take a rain check."

Dan ended it by replying, "There will be no rain check tonight. I leave town at first light tomorrow. I must get back to my desk job."

They stood to exchange goodbyes with puckered lips and a brush of cheeks, and Lib left rapidly without looking back. Her ego wanted her to think that the famous Dan Lawler was staring at her backside, so she shifted into her sexiest stride and left the building to look for a cab. One was at the curb. The cabbie was holding the rear door for two entering passengers. Lib, displaying her propensity for boldness, hopped into the front seat. The driver entered to find her sitting with two 20-dollar bills displayed in her extended hand. "I have an emergency to attend to. Please drop me off at my hotel first."

The cabbie, hearing no objection from the rear seat, took the money, started the engine, asked her destination and drove off. Lib's problem was not a real emergency at all; it was the lack of patience. She simply did not want to wait for another cab. She needed to touch base with her answering service then think about how to find an answer to her question.

If leaked to the public, the rumor about Lavita Vorhees and her possible involvement in yet another death scandal could have major, even devastating, effects on the documentary. She was expected to make a cameo appearance in the show in order to expand the potential viewing audience and raise the marketing value. The chance to meet and work with her was also a lure to entice the targeted family to take the bait.

Lib's first inclination was to call Brock Wormington, but she could see danger in this. He must surely have a backup moderator in his pocket just as he had other juror backups. Her mind was in turmoil. She was

308

beginning to let paranoia creep in. What if this whole thing was a plot by the Hollywood movie studio that would be signing her paycheck? A plot to protect the career of their hot new movie star. Paranoia would indeed be raging in Lib's mind if she knew that the hidden ownership of the production company was in a branch of another Parker company. Judge Parker had purposely organized it this way in order to bankroll Lavita's early movies in secrecy.

She began to wonder again if this was an attempt to bribe a juror in order to keep Tripp labeled as a cop killer as long as need be, but she kept coming back to the fact that this was a sequestered jury and no juror could be reached by a bribery attempt. That, after all, was what sequestration rules were for.

She began to connect the dots. Everything pointed to Lavita. She began to talk aloud to herself, a product of living alone for most of her adult life. "I can't believe that this dumb blond, bambino actress would be intelligent enough to create an ingenious bribery attempt, if this could, in fact, be a bribe." She chuckled a bit as she was reminded that she had serious aspirations as a teenager to be a blond, bambino actress just like Marilyn Monroe. Then the real Lib Lester regained control of her conscience.

"Who cares if this is bribery or anything else they want to call it. I am in too deep now to turn back. My financial rewards are too great for me to care. As long as I protect myself, no one can touch me. I can't turn back now. It has always been part of the plan to never suggest involvement of the target prior to the end of the trial. I will record all my conversations with Rosie on this little tape recorder that I carry in my purse and have used many times in interviews. I can, I must, make this happen – and soon."

Two days later, Rosie Pope arranged to meet with Lib in her hotel room to be schooled in the details of the after-trial documentary. Lib was ready to record the conversation.

Rosie had prepared a long list of questions and it was obvious that her main interests centered on monetary reward. "What is the most money we can make and the least?"

Lib danced around this a bit. "I think that you are looking at more than a quarter million dollars for your part. It depends on how many reruns can be sold and how many members of your family participate. We plan to use you a lot because you are so photogenic. The use of your young son would enhance the human interest story and so would your teenage stepdaughters.

"The amount of time that Lavita Vorhees gives us will determine, to a great extent, the market price and the rerun value, but no doubt, your take will be enormous. If I told you what they are paying me for my role, it would blow your mind. It proves that they are certain of a big success."

Rosie was stunned. "Wow! But aren't they being a bit presumptuous? I mean, how can they be sure that my husband will agree? He is a very shy person and will not like appearing on television."

"Don't worry. The broadcast will be taped, not live. His dialog and ours will be corrected of all flub-ups. We will all look and sound like experienced professionals. But you are right. They can't be absolutely sure. That is why they have others lined up as backups. They are confident of a unanimous verdict, but if not, we use the next qualified juror on our list who has voted guilty. They will probably be paid less than you because they will have less appeal to the networks. What has more appearance of bravery to an audience than a shy band director with a beautiful schoolteacher wife and several children? All you can do personally is to hold your position of the moment, which appears to be positive. Am I right?"

"Yes, absolutely!" replied Rosie. The nervousness had left Rosie, but she seemed to remain a little tense. It was time for Lib to insert her recorded safety quip into the conversation and send her on her way. "Remember, do not share this good news with your children or your parents or anyone else who might accidentally let it leak. Ross will be surprised and delighted with this big payday after the trial." She then took an envelope from her purse and placed it in Rosie's hand. I am being reimbursed weekly for my expenses, so I thought it only fair that I share a small bit to cover yours. You have missed work and will miss more when we meet again. There must be childcare expenses, cab fares, meals and so on. I consider you as being on my payroll now and this will keep the other news bleeps from hiring you first."

Rosie peeped inside the envelope and saw a $100 bill on top. She would shortly thereafter, count nine more. Her enthusiasm ticked up a few notches as she continued home.

The two renewed their conversation a few days later and Rosie was clearly more upbeat. She wanted to meet again soon. She had questions about how the family should dress for the big event and she wanted to exchange ideas about the content, particularly her own speaking part.

"Don't worry about the clothing. The studio wardrobe department will dress you all. I also have some ideas that I want to bounce off you. Maybe we can use some shots of Ross directing his band." Her real and only reason for the meeting was to keep Rosie on the hook.

Meanwhile, Ross was realizing that serving as a juror in a trial of this nature was more challenging than he expected. The burden of having been given life or death powers to be used on a superhero was heavier than he was prepared to handle.

He had begun to feel the pressure amidst the members of the jury pool of his first day in court, even before he was selected as a juror. It was obvious that a very large percentage did not want to be there at all, much less participate in a murder decision. It would be simple to get himself dismissed by admitting his bias, and he truly had one. He had no doubts, but that Tripp Joiner was guilty. The media had said as much. Most everyone that he knew thought so with the exception of the football coaches at his school. His wife and his parents believed so. He had to give himself a pep talk. In spite of his shyness, he would enjoy the special recognition. His kids in the band would show him more respect and that would apply to his domineering wife as well. It might enhance his chances of being promoted to high school band director when the position came open. This would mean more income to help cover his mounting debt.

He was jolted from his thoughts by a fellow stranger seeking conversation. "I imagine that we will be seeing the Parker family movie star, Lavita Vorhees, in court every day. I have seen all her movies, but I have never seen her in person. Have you?"

"Well actually, yes. She attended the junior high school where I teach." Ross was dragged into the conversation.

Hearing this, others joined in. "Oh, I thought, given her family's wealth, she surely attended private school."

Someone else added, "Judge Parker is the one who had all the money. Just how wealthy is he? Or I should ask, how wealthy *was* he? I'll bet the deputy sheriff standing here could tell us a lot about all this. Couldn't you, deputy?"

"You bet I could, but I won't. First, don't joke about the judge. He had his enemies but was well liked by the sheriff and all the deputies. I served under him during his entire term as county judge and knew him well. All his bodyguards were selected from our ranks from the beginning until his death. One of them was as personal friend of mine." He was talking after saying that he wouldn't. "Lavita Vorhees is his only grandchild and he worshiped the ground she walked on. As a child, she was always hanging around his office or riding in his car. He would do and give her everything she asked for. She wanted to be a movie star and he gave her that. His unlimited oil production made him one of the richest men in Texas and she will eventually inherit all he had."

More listeners had gathered, and the deputy seemed to be enjoying center stage. "Few people know that he bankrolled all her early movies, enabling her to be placed in a starring role from the git-go. After a few movies, he bought the studio without her knowledge."

With that, the guard was summoned by his superior officer. Another deputy joined the conversation. The woman sounded convincing when she confirmed the guard's statement. "That is all true, but let me tell you what is truly sad about this whole situation. The media, and I mean all the media, TV and newspapers, seemed to have forgotten about the tragic side of things, the deaths of so many people. They have turned this tragedy into a fairytale about the romantic relationship between Tripp and Lavita."

"Yeah. Like the hero and the princess," another spoke. At that moment, Ross Pope's name was called. Finally, it was his turn for the jury selection interview.

Tripp paid close attention to the jury selection process as well as all the public comments coming from lawyers on both sides as they were constantly hounded by the army of reporters looking for a scoop. He was struck by one statement being made about the preference of the type of juror being sought. Both the defense and state lawyers were singing from the same song book and they could have been singing in unison.

"Our side is looking for jurors who will make their decisions based wholly on the evidence presented at trial." While at the same time, they were putting all their resources to work seeking a bias in their favor or at least discovering a weakness that could be coaxed into a bias. To Tripp, the hypocrisy seemed to be with their public statements. He was learning a lot about the imperfect dispensation of justice with trial by jury. His spirits had been lifted by the pep talk from Mule Sherman with the promise of almost certain victory because of Tripp's superstar image and Mule's record of having never lost a murder case with a superstar client, but now his confidence was slipping. All media sources seem to have declared him guilty before jury selection was completed. Phrases like "uphill battle, mountain to climb, too many eyewitnesses, plenty of motive" were constantly used.

Instinct told him that that the media's pronouncement of guilt had created a jury pool predisposed for a guilty verdict. He was also troubled by the overwhelming amount of verbiage and print devoted to his past romantic relationship with Lavita Vorhees. The word fairytale was used in most every piece.

This uneasiness led him to ask his childhood friend, now defense team assistant, Hal Hall to research Mule's case history. It was true that he had technically never lost a murder trial, but he had experienced two hung juries that had later been plea bargained down to no jail time. He had a rape case involving a famous actor that resulted in a hung jury that was never retried when charges were finally dropped. Hal also investigated the DA's claim that he had never lost a murder case in which he had a credible eyewitness, but he was unable to do a complete job. All of this did nothing to improve Tripp's mental health as he slowly drifted towards insanity.

When the trial first got underway, it immediately became clear what the main crowd attraction was. Everyone was watching and talking about the two superstars. This included the jurors. Even Judge Sullivan found himself seeking out the location of the movie star at the start of proceedings. Whispered buzz around the courtroom most always included her wardrobe or hairstyle selection. Much fuel was added to the

313

fire on the day of Lavita's dramatic, tearful exit from the courtroom. No doubt, the fairytale image and atmosphere never waned during the entire trial.

Jury sequestration was hard on all the jurors, some considerably more than others and it was being discussed more often during breaks. One brought up the subject in the presence of Ross and two others. "I would pay a thousand bucks for one night's rest in my own bed."

"Me too," said Ross. I could use some up close and personal time with my wife. Know what I mean?"

Another added while looking around to make certain that no one else could hear, "That would be possible, you know. I have been scouting around some at night after the bed check and I have seen no sign of our escorts. I believe that our guards go home about then. That stuff about 24-hour vigilance is a bunch of baloney. I went down to the bar, had a beer and spotted a phone booth in the back. The main entrance to the bar is on the street. A person could make a phone call and slip out and back in at any time before the 2 a.m. closing time. As far as spending the night at home, it would mean returning at daylight through the hotel lobby. A bit more dangerous."

"I was joking of course," replied Ross. "I live on the other side of the county. Not enough time. What would they do, you think, if a juror got caught?"

"Oh, he would be dismissed and one of the alternates would take his place."

Ross said nothing but the wheels were turning in his head. A simple phone call would be nice but a visit would be much better. It would be safer for a wife to slip in through the bar and up the stairs, spend an hour and then slip back out the same way. No guard, if present, would recognize her. This thought stayed locked in his brain for daydreaming purposes if nothing else. Rosie and the kids had been subjects of his real dreams on several occasions recently.

The prosecution's case had strengthened Pope's belief that the defendant was guilty on all charges. He believed the eyewitnesses testimonies, and the expert witnesses balanced themselves out. But Ross began to waver considerably on the murder counts as Tripp Joiner took the stand and told his complete story. The description of the death of his daughter and injury to his wife had a profound effect on this father of three girls. It also nudged him closer to his burning desire to sneak a phone call to check on his family's welfare. He fought his temptation until close to the end of testimony, when he caved.

His first move was to slip down the stairs and into the bar, making certain that he saw no recognizable face along the way. He ordered a draft beer and found a seat in a corner near the phone booth. About halfway through the beer and making sure that no one was looking his way, he slipped into the booth and called home.

This 11:30 ring startled his sleeping wife. It took her a second to get her bearings and a few more to get over the shock. He wasn't sure what the reception might be, so he was pleasantly surprised by her reaction.

"Man, you do not know how happy you just made me. Your timing is perfect. Tell me later how you pulled this off, but first, let me give you some really great news. We have just stumbled into a fortune." With that, she began to describe all the details. "We are going to be rich and you are being turned into a brave hero. All of this on national TV. We will share time with a movie star."

Ross was momentarily speechless as his brain processed this too-good-to-be-true bombshell. Given the fact that this trial had turned into a fairytale about a princess, this proposed production must certainly have something to do with her. It did not take him long to connect the dots. This was a bribery attempt by someone to make certain that Tripp Joiner would come out of this trial with a guilty verdict. The state does not bribe jurors, so it must be the Parker family, probably Lavita Vorhees, who wanted to bury Tripp Joiner once and for all. Someone had to be very ingenious to come up with a clever scheme like this. Who would ever believe that a dumb blonde Marilyn Monroe lookalike could make this happen, but she had the most to lose in Tripp running free.

Rosie continued her gleeful news. "All you have to do is to not let them change your mind about his guilt. Everybody knows that he's guilty."

Ross was not about to admit that he was on the fence and leaning towards innocence on the murder charges. He was now bought and paid for. He had been an honest man his entire life but maybe the old adage was true after all, "Every man has his price." Nor was he about to face the wrath of Rosie.

Ross endured the remainder of the trial by tuning out the strong defense case, mostly during closing arguments. One way was to drift into daydreaming. He placed himself in a new convertible. He toured the town with his daughters waving to friends. He drove it school for his band students to sit in and his peers to oh and ah. He walked into the Caravelle boat dealership and purchased the fiberglass fishing boat that he had been dreaming about. He would no longer need to borrow his father's beat up old aluminum jonboat. He and Rosie could pay off the home mortgage and he could catch up on his past due child support payments. With program reruns, maybe he could do it all. His plan to entice Rosie to a late-night meeting in his room had failed because she convinced him that no more contact should be made between them for fear that he would be dismissed from the jury if caught.

His strange body movements and facial expressions in the jury box had not gone unnoticed by the defense team, particularly Mule. It was obvious that Ross was lost to the guilty side. Their skills were severely tested as they attempted to record his contortions and facial expressions. The prosecution team was not blind to his actions either. He appeared to be a man in mental agony, and he was. Maybe it was extreme fatigue like that being seen in many of the jurors, especially those who had already decided their verdict. They were bored and ready to vote. But it appeared much deeper than that.

In the days after his decision to accept the bribe, he developed the paranoia of eyes glaring at him by people who knew of his action. He was certain that the princess and her group knew so he avoided all eye contact in her direction. Then he began to think that the defense team knew and even the DA and the judge. He was surely headed for prison, but he couldn't shake his decision.

Ross Pope, now in a high stakes, life-or-death poker game being played in the devil's own sewer, had just made his move. He was gambling with another man's life and all his chips were in. The real irony was that both men had been, up until this trial, honest law-abiding citizens.

316

CHAPTER THIRTY-THREE

The Virdict

The last closing argument had been made. All evidence was in. The long trial was nearly over.

There was a brief feeling of relief by the teams on both sides, but a new tension began to build in the minds of all involved. It was time for Judge Sullivan to dismiss the alternate jurors and to give the formal instructions to the seated jury. As he approached them, it was easy to determine the alternates from the rest. They were the ones with the happy faces. They were free at last to return to their normal lives. The remainder clearly displayed evidence of the buildup of tension on their faces and in their body language.

The judge gave them his usual "thank you for your service" speech. This was a departure from the one he had scripted to fit this very unusual and high-profile trial, but he was feeling a sudden surge of weariness and anxiousness to get his duties with the alternates over with and to prepare the jury for deliberations. One of the alternates raised her hand, a clear indication that she wanted to speak. He granted her wish with a thought, "now what could she possibly want at a time like this?"

She requested permission to sit as an observer to the deliberations. He replied with a terse "No, you may not," with no explanation. "What next," he thought. "Another first. Will they ever end? We had a licensed barber giving closing defense arguments. We had the television disaster. We had the planned demeaning of the DA by the defense. We had the spectator disruption, which may also have been planned. We had my own ill-advised stupid apology. Dear Lord, please bring on my retirement."

Each juror was handed a standard sheet of instructions as how to start deliberation proceedings by electing a foreperson and so forth. The judge, attempting to appear as near to Oliver Wendell Holmes as he remembered, lowered his voice and began his instructions.

"Ladies and gentlemen of the jury, I speak with all the truth and sincerity that I could ever conceive of when I say to you that you are being asked to make the most important decision of your lifetimes. You are being asked to determine life or death of a human being. This particular defendant is a man who is worshiped as a hero by millions of people. The funds that he has raised for charity, particularly for children with the need for lifesaving research and treatment, has undoubtedly saved many lives. He is a father who has lost a daughter to causes indirectly related to this trial. All of these facts must be removed from your mind as you determine his guilt or innocence on all three charges against him.

"You must make your decisions based only on the evidence presented in this trial. You have sworn an oath to do just that. You violate this oath, and you will live a lie for the rest of your life.

"You must judge him just as you would a common unknown citizen from anywhere in the world. This trial is now in your hands but the option to review evidence is still yours. You may ask for any segment of recorded testimony at any time by making this known to your jury foreperson in writing. You may ask questions of any fellow juror about his or her interpretation of the evidence. A unanimous vote of guilt or innocence on each count is needed in order to render a verdict in that particular count. Go now. Take a break and then begin your deliberations."

After the break, each juror took his or her numbered seat. Following instructions, those desiring to serve as foreperson stood up. Four candidates stood. Two halos, a woman, and as expected, the college professor. One of the ranchers deferred to the other rancher standing, by nodding his head to the other and sitting back down.

Per instructions, a secret ballot was taken, and the results were displayed on the table. The woman received two votes, the professor had four and the rancher had five. The runoff gave the election to the rancher by six to five. He took charge of the proceedings with a brief statement.

"Let us begin by agreeing that we have all come to know each other well enough by now to address others by our first names or by our assigned numbers. My name is Coleman. Starting with number one, then in numerical order, go around the table and state your name."

Everyone followed instructions exactly except for the college professor, who said, "I am Professor Leander. I will begin by asking for a written verdict vote on each count in order for all to know exactly where things currently stand." The foreman granted the request.

One juror voted guilty on all counts. One voted guilty in the murder of Deputy John Malham, guilty in threatening to kill and innocent in the murder of Judge Horace Parker. Two voted not guilty to the two murders and guilty to the counts of threatening to kill. The remainder voted not guilty on all counts. The foreperson announced the totals, and beginning with juror number one, went in numerical order around the table, asking each to announce his vote and reasons supporting it.

Most of the media continued the habit of gathering at the same favored watering hole to wager, this time on the length of jury deliberations. Only one wager was for less than one week. There were several conversations about going back to home base for a few days' respite and return for the verdict. They were underestimating the persuasive determination of jury foreman Coleman Mathews.

"Let's get this cow branded and go home for some tender love and home cooking." He pushed through vote after vote and cut short the lengthy arguments with interruptions like, "Let's get on with it" and "You are repeating yourself."

By the end of the second day the not guilty arguments and repeated calls for testimony transcripts had changed all votes, except one, to innocent on all counts. Ross Pope held his position of guilty on all counts.

Hours of attempted persuasion by several fellow jurors failed to convince him to change his vote. He folded his arms, bowed his head, closed his eyes and stopped all responses to their badgering. Word was sent to the judge that there existed a hung jury situation. They were called back to the jury box only to hear the judge say, "Go back and give it another try." They toughed it out it with renewed effort for four more hours and retired for the day.

A fresh idea occurred to Ross. The anger being directed at him was causing him to hate the world and he wanted to fight back at the people responsible. People in the Parker family were the obvious cause. He was now convinced that they were prepared to spend a vast amount of money to keep the cop killer label pasted to the forehead of Tripp Joiner. He now saw a chance to vent his anger and get filthy rich at the same time.

Money was like peanuts to the Parkers and he could see a way to raise the offer now on the table. That night after bed check, he slipped into the bar once again and called his wife with new instructions. "Call your contact immediately and tell her that my price has gone up to one million dollars, tax free and paid under the table in addition to the TV interview money. I am the only guilty vote left and they have no other to switch to. I will call you back in three hours. Do you understand me?"

"Yes," she answered, and he hung up the phone.

When he called her back, he was told that there was no answer yet. He reminded her, "The bar closes in 45 minutes. I will call for my answer in 30. It is their last chance." He got the answer that he expected. He was now a millionaire.

Pope survived the terrible pressure of one more day by thinking about how his promised wealth would buy him his new, longer list of dream toys. He went down his list one by one, starting with a Caravelle boat.

Finally, the verdict was presented to the judge. A mistrial was declared. Judge Sullivan gave his final speech and the jury was sent home. Mule was packing up his gear as he turned to Will and said, "I truly expected a better verdict. We should have won this one clean and clear. Our victory is not complete. I am wondering if we have just experienced a first in my career. I have never known of a juror being paid for a guilty vote. I sense the odor of bribery here. Do you?"

"No, and I don't believe that is what happened to us here, but nothing would surprise me now that I have seen what you would do to win."

"The greatest battle victory ever won was by using the Atomic bomb in World War II. No one remembers and few care that untold thousands of innocents were killed. Only victory counts. I will take and use the bomb every time."

CHAPTER THIRTY-FOUR

Numbers 32

The hung jury verdict was considered a partial victory by the Parker Family. The trial resulted in continued restraints placed on Tripp Joiner and the possibility of a new trial leading to prison time and the destruction of his football career. Their immediate worry was about their crime of bribery, which had to be completed with delivery of the agreed sum to the bribed juror. Even the first portion, which had a legal look to it via the planned TV show, needed to be altered.

Since no other guilty vote on any charge had been rendered other than by Ross Pope, the appearance of several innocent voters against one guilty voter would make the interviews appear too out of balanced, so it was decided to limit the interviews to two jurors. One for guilty and one for innocent. They would be interviewed separately. These would be taped and edited, not live as originally planned.

Pope, the key interview, was heavily schooled. He said he based his reasoning mostly on the eyewitness testimony of Lilia Vorhees. The show was quickly aired before an audience of millions of viewers. In spite of the potential market size, many promised advertising sponsors had dropped out, so the show lost money. The college professor, who had voted for acquittal on all counts, quickly agreed to participate and was paid a sum equal to Ross Pope.

The most formidable issues now were the retrial of Joiner and keeping Debi Devereaux's death away from a grand jury. A large number of people, politicians and wealthy supporters of political campaigns and friends of the murder victims were urged to pressure the DA to retry Tripp Joiner immediately. This effort was spearheaded by Lilia Parker Vorhees herself. The stress of it drove her to consume more and more booze.

She came up with the idea of a letter campaign by the many charity organizations helped by the Parker Charity Foundation. This meant creating a list of letter writers. Her staff pulled together every news release, photos and personal recognition awards with names attached.

This huge stack of paper landed on her bedroom desk, where she worked for a while. She ended up where she always did eventually – in her bed with the television on, a lit cigarette and an open bottle of Jose Cuervo. The stack of papers spread all around her. This was a perfect formula for disaster. A drunk woman, a chain smoker, in the middle of a pile of paper, juggling an open bottle of inflammable liquid.

It took only two days for the disaster to happen. The flame quickly engulfed the paper, clothing and bedding. She screamed as she slapped at the flames around her face, falling on the floor beside the bed. She looked towards the alarm button connected to the servant's quarters. She was all alone and panicking. The wall behind the bed was now afire and the smoke was blinding. She managed to crawl to the stairs and started down, falling as she went, all the way to the bottom.

Her driver and the yard man were playing cards in the quarters and were the first to see the fire. One dialed 911 as the other broke in the back door. The two of them raced inside with a fire extinguisher and doused her smoldering clothing as she was pulled outside the building. Firefighters arrived just before law enforcement and ambulance. Word spread fast and an excessive number of police and sheriff's office personnel followed. "Judge Parker's house is on fire." They were still arriving as the ambulance departed for the nearest ER.

Close family members arrived quickly. Lilia was stabilized and the decision was made to transfer her to the Military Burn Center in San Antonio via medical helicopter. Family members took the family plane and arrived before the helicopter. An extensive examination showed third degree burns over 50 percent of her skin and a broken hip. She was described as "critical." Skin grafting was started by some of the most highly skilled burn treatment personnel in the world employed at the center.

Lilia rallied on the fourth day and regained consciousness. She recognized her family members and ask for a priest. The rotating chaplain on duty was military and not catholic. The family asked for a catholic priest and one was found quickly.

"My name is Father Phillip McDougal and I am at your service.

322

Reverend Wilkens briefed me before I came in so let us get down to business." He walked bedside and took Leila's bandaged hand.

"Pray to Christ for me father," she said. It sounded more like a Parker command than a plea.

He replied, "Yes, of course, my child. Let us have the sacrament of confession." He looked at the family members, a signal for them to leave the room.

Lilia closed her eyes and began, "I confess to almighty God and to you, Father, that I have sinned. My last confession was months ago. I have committed mortal sins. I killed my father's murderer and blamed it on another. I also lied in court under an oath to God. I am sorry for my sins and ask for forgiveness." She crossed herself. "God the Father, Son and Holy Ghost."

The priest was stunned into total silence. His brain connected all the dots immediately. He understood the immenseness of what he had just heard. He was a football junkie and thus had devoured every word of media blab about the trial. He was up to speed with the mistrial declaration and the probability of a new trial being set soon. Now only he, God and Lilia knew the whole truth.

His training and experience had not prepared him for this. He managed to stumble through a few words and called the family back into the room. Fortunately for him, a doctor came in with some test results and wanted to discuss options with the family. He mentioned that he would be available in the hospital chapel if the family wished and left.

Father McDougal went directly to the chapel, fell on his knees and began to pray for guidance. He managed to tough it out for an hour then went home. From there he called his bishop and asked for advice.

Bishop Foley asked for time to meditate and promised to get back to him quickly. The bishop had also never faced a situation like this, but it took less than 40 minutes to call Phillip back. "Pack your bag. We are going to see the DA. I will drive and pick you up in a short while."

They drove through the night in order to arrive at Walter Warren's office before he got to work. He had been given ample notice but no details.

Only, "We've been to visit Mrs. Vorhees at the Burn Center and must have a private meeting with you."

The drive was long but not boring. Phillip was driving and was surprised to see the bishop take a flashlight from the glovebox, open his bible and begin searching the scriptures. After many minutes, he had to ask what the search was about.

"I have been reading what the Bible says about confession of sins. I have often preached that your sins will find you out. It's found in Numbers 32:23."

"How true, how true!" Philip responded.

Walter was surprised to see them arrive so early. His curiosity drove him to say, "Let's get down to serious business."

Bishop Foley spoke first. "What we are about to tell you is strictly between us. Our conversation cannot be recorded. If you are a catholic, you know why."

"I am aware of your rules about sacred confessions, so continue please."

The bishop nodded to Father McDougal, who told the complete story. The DA asked him to repeat the exact words of the confession as he took notes then replied, "You understand that if facts are as you stated, your true mission is to save an innocent man. You will have to testify in the proper venue."

"We cannot and will not do that." Bishop Foley stood up, preparing to leave. "I am sure you have used your authority to dismiss charges in the past, based on new evidence that comes into your possession, have you not? Thank you very much for granting us this time today. Our prayers will be that God will guide you with your decision."

The DA wanted to say more but only offered, "Thank you for coming and sharing this with me. Have a safe trip home." His headache was intense and growing by the minute. He had to get this confession from the killer.

Windy immediately called the Burn Center to check on the condition of the only one who could put a lid on this case. The news was not good. Her condition was classified as grave. Now the senior staff members were gathering outside his office, awaiting the expected briefing. If Tom Edison had graced society with a curiosity meter, one in the DA's office would have exploded about now. Still, Windy did not open his door, and the crowd knew better than to knock. He made a monumental decision without a consultation meeting. Unheard of in his tenure. He was buying time to choose the right words to break the news.

At last he opened the door. "New evidence has come to me regarding the Parker murder case, compelling enough for us to drop the remaining charges against defendant Joiner. I am not at liberty to share that evidence for now. I know this action may be unprecedented, and I apologize for my actions. I will meet with the defense and the judge today and advise them of my decision. I know that I need not warn any of you of the consequences if you leak this. Have a good day and keep your mouths shut!"

Because Mule Sherman had left town, Windy set a time with Judge Sullivan and Will Clarkson in the judge's office. "I am filling papers, as we speak, to drop all charges against Mr. Joiner," he told them. "I received compelling evidence today of his innocence. I am unable to share this evidence until a certain witness is willing to go public."

Judge Sullivan was the first to respond. "This is preposterous. You are telling me, the presiding judge, that you have enough proof of innocence to dismiss charges but can't share it with me? I have never seen or heard of anything like this. You have just made your life miserable for a very long time."

Will asked, "Do we have a dismissal or not?"

"Hold on," said the judge. "Don't you go running out of here with your good news just yet."

Windy finally answered, "My witness is Lilia Vorhees."

A knock on the door stopped the conversation. There was a call from the Burn Center. Lilia Vorhees had died more than two hours ago.

"Wow," said the judge. "You are in a real pickle now. You have no one to

325

corroborate the evidence."

"I am man enough to handle it," said Windy. "The dismissal directive still stands, so, Will, take it from here. I can imagine that New York Giants football fans will be happy fans today."

Will responded, "I would think that the Joiner family will be the happiest of all."

The Parker family went strangely silent. Did Lilia confess to them also?

Headlines exploded worldwide. Members of the media who were prone to describe this saga as a fairytale got their happy ending after all. Barbershop scuttlebutt was "Shoeshine boy helps Mule Sherman remain undefeated." Walter Warren, famous district attorney, never tried to count the number of times he was asked, "What was the evidence?" He was forced out of political office and into the back office of an obscure law firm doing mundane paperwork, never again appearing in a courtroom.

That same question endures today in most gatherings of people inclined to chit chat, especially football fans and lawyers in New York City and the vast plains and mountains of west Texas. What was the evidence that closed the lid? Only two priests and Walter Warren will ever know.

Vita Vorhees was propelled to super movie star status by the notoriety of the murder trial and became the top invitee to parties of the rich and famous, still hating the man who dumped her and blaming him for the death of her grandfather and mother. She was overhead, time and again, saying, "The great Tripp Joiner was saved by a redheaded orphaned shoeshine boy who came to town in a box."

Hal Hall ultimately graduated with honors from the University Of Texas School Of Law. He joined Mule Sherman in his firm as junior partner. The lure of an established practice that defended only the rich and famous was enough to pull him away from his barbershop and out of his inferiority complex. Suddenly he discovered that finding women to date was easy.

His paycheck from the Joiner case exceeded one year's barbershop income. Close examination of costs billed to his friend Tripp astounded him, particularly those incurred only for the search for dirt on Judge

Parker. Only the very wealthy could afford these types of expenses, tipping the scales towards acquittal verdicts.

He was now more convinced than ever before that justice for the rich or poor is unequal. He pledged his heart towards fighting to correct that inequity. He continued to support immigrant groups in their ongoing battle against the drug cartels. The irony that he was taking the path of defending the rich while seeking ways to elevate justice for the ordinary defendant was missed entirely.

Tripp Joiner returned to full NFL quarterback form in less time than his coaches expected. He played four more years with the Giants, leading them to one more league championship. His mind was able to block out all the effects of his terrible tragedy during games, although his wariness of having to watch his blind side for a tackle by a defensive lineman was intensified. This feeling was now present in everyday life, with a scorned woman still living in his same world. Her pictures seemed to pop up everywhere as she continued her stardom in movies and television.

Tripp eventually retired to running his ranch with Patricia. They gave birth to a son with his father's oversized quarterback hands, and Patricia promised a daughter would soon follow. He would again have a daughter to sit on his lap, who he could sing lullabies to and help skip rope in her red tap shoes.

A grand jury was never called by the district attorney to examine the facts regarding the death of Debi Deveraux. Law-abiding citizens in her hometown of New Orleans continued to ask, "Why?"

The two orphans, now close as brothers, Tripp and Hal, huddled with Zip Devereaux and swore to seek help to someday bring Vita Vorhees to justice. But they found no perfect justice, because "big money still talks and murder still walks."

In Texas, coyotes still howl, whippoorwills and katydids still sing and football is king.

Little girls still jump rope with TAP-TAP-TAPADEE-TAP.

The truth about the society we live in is painful but still true.

ABOUT THE AUTHOR

In a story that has mulled over in his head for over twenty years, this is Ernest Avra's first attempt at a novel. It draws from his many years of relationships and experiences as a business owner, elected official, and community leader. Now at the age of 89, he has realized a longtime goal of becoming a published author.

A father of four, his most accomplished title, that of being 'Poppy', is shared by his thirteen grandchildren, their spouses, and his nine great-grandchildren. Avra resides in Conway, Arkansas, with his wife of 70 years, Jo.